Fly Girl

Regards,
Kurt Willinger

Kurt Willinger

THE P PRESS

Fly Girl

Copyright © 2010 Kurt Willinger

This is a work of fiction.

Cover image: Time & Life Pictures/Getty Images.

Manufactured in the United States of America.

For information please contact:

The P3 Press
16200 North Dallas Parkway, Suite 170
Dallas, Texas 75248
www.thep3press.com
972-248-9500

A New Era in Publishing™

Hardbound ISBN-13: 978-1-933651-75-0
Hardbound ISBN-10: 1-933651-75-X
Paperback ISBN-13: 978-1-933651-74-3
Paperback ISBN-10: 1-933651-74-1

LCCN: 2010903309
1 2 3 4 5 6 7 8 9 10

Author contact information:
flygirlnovel@yahoo.com.

For Doris,
my partner

PROLOGUE

The deputy gingerly sidestepped down the sodden embankment to the muddy streambed where the car lay on its side.

"Criminy!" he muttered through clenched teeth as the loamy ooze curled over the soles of his shoes. *Just polished those brogans.* Sheriff's Deputy Edmund Maloney prided himself on his appearance. *I hope those night shift mugs didn't filch the shoeshine box.*

"He's over here, Eddie," waved the truck driver who had called in the accident and was now standing several yards from the overturned car. He was tall and slender with thinning red hair and a prominent Adam's apple, clutching his sweat-stained fedora reverentially before him, loosely fitting gray coveralls spattered with the mud of the waterlogged gully.

"Listen, I'm a good hour and a half overdue. My skinflint boss is gonna be awful chafed. You'll bail me out here, wontcha?"

"Sure, Patsy. You have him call me."

Some twenty feet from the overturned Model T lay the body of a well-dressed man, head cocked sideways at an unnatural angle, a bemused expression engaging the face. His eyes were barely open as if about to express chagrin at being victimized by a carelessly tossed banana peel. There were no visible marks or bruises.

A two-fingered touch at the throat. "Dead, awright. The kid okay?"

"Got 'er in the truck. She's real quiet. Lotta mud on her but I don't think she's hurt any."

"Awright, Patsy, thanks. Be a guy and wait with the kid 'til the ambulance comes. I've gotta once over this gully. Gonna have to write it up. Nice lookin' fella."

"Sure is . . . was," said truck driver and former corporal of the Great War, Patrick Cahill, as he clambered back up to the road. "Poor 'lil tyke. She don't know. I ain't gonna be the one who tells her," Cahill declaimed over his left shoulder. "Hear! It ain't gonna be me."

"Not you, Patsy. Somebody'll tell her. Prob'ly me," Maloney sighed as he solemnly drew the notepad from his hip pocket and began to scribble the particulars of today's tragic mishap. The deputy stood, both shoes submerged to the laces, pant's bottoms sipping at the dark, fetid muck. He no longer seemed to care.

Up at the top of the embankment, eight-year-old Margaret Cohan sat shaking in the passenger seat of the panel truck parked at the side of the road. She took no notice of the cars, which slowed as they drove past to view the scene of a truck and a police cruiser on the shoulder.

She was frightened. Something terrible had just occurred. The car had veered off the road and rolled down the embankment. It all seemed to happen very slowly. At the bottom, the girl wriggled out of the car's side window to find her father lying on his back in the wet grass. She tried to rouse him but he wouldn't wake. "Daddy! Daddy! Open your eyes!" That's when the man appeared and carried her up the hill, away from her dad, and put her in the truck.

Daddy, I'm scared. Where are you? Come up. I'm really scared. She wanted to shout but kept still.

When the policeman drove up she thought he was there to arrest her, but he merely looked in at her and disappeared down the hill.

We were having such a fun time driving on the road together, Peggy thought. *He called me Principessa. He always calls me Principessa. I love when he calls me that. It's the most wonderful thing to be. Where are you, Daddy? I'm so scared.*

Maloney's accident report read as follows:

July 1, 1929. A motorist suffered a fatal neck injury on the Boston Post Road between Stamford and Greenwich, Connecticut, at approximately 4:40 p.m. today. His Ford automobile ran off the road into a culvert. Tire tracks indicate that the driver veered onto the soft shoulder and subsequently toppled down the embankment, where the vehicle was found overturned. The tires were intact, and so tire failure may be ruled out as a contributing factor.

The accident site was approximately sixty yards north of the Hansen Street turnoff. The vehicle was heading south. Papers on the body identified the deceased as Martin Cohan, a lawyer who resided in Flushing, Queens, New York. The lone passenger in the vehicle, Margaret Cohan, age eight years, daughter of the deceased, was unhurt. The Round Hill office is in the process of notifying the wife, Stella Cohan, who, according to the little girl, also resides in Flushing, New York. The child will be taken to her mother's home in a Round Hill office car.

Edmund Maloney, Deputy Sheriff
Round Hill District Office
Stamford, Connecticut

PART 1

Three Years Later

The modest, three-bedroom clapboard house of Martin and Stella Cohan stood at the corner of Chestnut and Main on a small lot in Flushing, New York. The front yard was overgrown and the structure cried out for a new coat of paint, but with the passing of Mr. Cohan it was unlikely that these refurbishments would be forthcoming. Hard times had fallen upon the residents of this home and despite a small insurance settlement, the family was struggling. It was not only money that was in short supply; the joy that once resonated throughout the modest dwelling was noticeably absent.

The death of Martin Cohan had imposed a strain on the relationship between Stella and her daughter. Their three-year-old wounds remained raw and open. On this weekday morning mother and daughter were in the kitchen, preparing for school and work, respectively.

"Mommy?" Eleven-year-old Peggy hesitantly approached as her mother was removing the tray of water from the icebox.

"Yeah?"

"Mommy, last night . . ."

"Yeah, what? Oh, dammit!" Stella Cohan grimaced as the overly full pan sloshed sideways and spilled on the tan linoleum floor. "Wipe that up, Peg," muttered Stella Cohan past the cigarette dangling from the corner of her mouth.

Peggy hurried to wipe up the spill with a dish towel as her mother replaced the pan.

"Mommy?"

"Not the dish towel, dummy, a rag. Under the sink."

The girl found a rag and hurried to wipe up the remaining water.

"Mommy."

"Whaaat?"

"Last night, Uncle Edgar came into my room."

"Yeah, so?"

"I was sleeping."

"And?"

"He sat down on the bed."

"So?"

"He touched me."

"Touched you?"

"He moved his hand up my leg."

"Oh, c'mon . . ."

"I didn't move. I made like I was still asleep."

"So, what's the big . . . ?"

"Then he put his hands under the cover."

"What are you saying?"

"He touched me. Between my legs, Mommy. He kept doing it."

Stella Cohan hauled back and slapped her eleven-year-old daughter so hard she was propelled across the kitchen and into the ice box door. The mother's eruption of unbridled anger wounded the child far more than the blow or the impact of the fall.

"You little slut. You wanna ruin this for me, don't you? You're really out to get me, aren't you?" She bent to place her face within inches of her daughter's. Peggy had slumped to the kitchen floor, hurt, confused but refusing to cry. "You killed my husband, leaving me with nothing. Now you want to screw this up for me. My chance to be happy."

"I didn't kill him. I didn't kill Daddy."

"Weren't you driving? You told me you were on his lap driving."

"Daddy let me steer the car."

"So, what happened? You crashed the car. And you lived and he's dead. You killed my husband. Why couldn't you be dead, you horrible little witch."

The little girl recoiled at this outpouring. It was difficult for her to breathe. She wanted to cry but no tears would come. The hate directed at her by her own mother was incomprehensible. Their relationship had never been easy, but until this moment she had no sense of the depth of her mother's resentment. *Did I kill my father? Am I a terrible person? I am. No wonder my mother hates me.*

Eyes wild and teeth gritted, Stella Cohan once again thrust her face toward her cringing daughter.

"You evil little witch, you make up this lie about Edgar. He's got a good job. He likes me. He'd marry me if it wasn't for you. No man wants some stupid brat hanging around. I'm still a young woman. My life could be peachy if it wasn't for you. No! No more lies about Edgar. Hear me?" She drew her arm back, threatening another blow. "I'll put you in the orphanage, I swear."

Peggy's mind struggled to comprehend her mother's venomous tirade. *She hates me. Really hates me. She wishes I was dead. She doesn't want to be my mother anymore.* The girl appeared stricken. She stood as if in a trance, no longer hearing her mother's invective. Her mind focused inward, disconnected from the reality around her. The strange remoteness that suddenly came over Peggy unnerved Stella and caused her to abruptly halt her verbal assault.

"Hey, maybe I got a bit too excited," Stella said, lamely attempting to soften the encounter. "Edgar was probably just trying to be nice. He's really a swell guy. You just misunderstood. Okay? What d'yuh say we forget it?"

As her focus returned to the present, Peggy eyed her mother coldly and thought, *Forget it? No. Never.*

The next night, "Uncle" Edgar paid another visit to Peggy's room. Once again he put his hand beneath her covers and slowly moved up her leg to her thighs. This time Peggy did not feign sleep but pushed his hand away.

"I don't like that," she told him, looking him squarely in the eye. "I want you to go out of my room."

"I'm just here to tuck you in," he replied. "A little girl ought to be tucked in."

"Don't want to be tucked in," was the girl's response.

"All girls like to be tucked in. What's wrong with you?"

"Don't want to be," repeated Peggy.

Peggy knew it was useless to call out or do something that would "ruin it" for her mother. *Where is my daddy?* she thought, as she continued pushing Edgar's hands away. *Make him stop. Please, someone.* When Edgar tried to kiss her she turned her head away. *I'm alone in the world,* she realized. *All alone.* And the tears began to flow.

Uncle Edgar, in an attempt to quiet the girl, offered her a quarter. Peggy accepted the quarter and with the coin clutched in her hand, grimly endured the violation. The routine of abuse continued almost nightly and Peggy could see no other recourse but to submit. But each time, she insisted on her quarter. It was her only consolation. As the abuse persisted she sometimes demanded more change. Thirty-five, forty cents. She exacted movie magazines, dime novels, even costume jewelry from Uncle Edgar. And each time she became more adept at spiriting her mind and feelings off to some distant place. A place where dads and daughters laugh together and there are no orphanages or visiting uncles.

Peggy, now in growing awareness of her power, began to negotiate with her abuser, eventually coming to manipulate the man. The sexually immature "Uncle" Edgar was sent out by Peggy to fetch ice cream, hair barrettes, candy bars, comic books. In Stella's view, Peggy and her man were getting along so nicely.

Peggy, who had learned to cope with her situation by stifling her emotions and exacting compensation, wondered to herself, *Are all men this easy?*

An icy truce prevailed in the Cohan home during the next two years. "Uncle" Edgar eventually gave way to Uncle Mike, then Uncle Norton, and then Uncle Rocco. The grass was cut by a sympathetic neighbor with Peggy pitching in to do the raking. Stella found a more permanent office job and Peggy, grown tall and strikingly pretty, entered her first year of high school.

Outside the auditorium, Peggy Cohan stopped to read the notice on the bulletin board announcing auditions for the school play. A short, red-headed girl walked up beside Peggy to also inspect the notice.

"You thinking of trying out?" Peggy asked.

"Naw, they rehearse after school. I need to get home."

I don't, Peggy realized.

The production was loosely based on HMS Pinafore. Mr. Maxwell, the English teacher, with Hortense Fenner and Willard Blake from his after-school creative writing class, altered the libretto to reflect conditions at Flushing High in 1934 instead of a British warship in 1877 Portsmouth. It was re-titled FHS Pinafore. The part of the young love interest, Josephine, was given to Margaret Cohan, a pretty blonde freshman. Buttercup would be played by Cecelia Castelagno, also a freshman and a girl possessed of a very lovely voice.

And so, the classic tale of frustrated love and social rigidity was crudely adapted for the auditorium stage of Flushing High. Gilbert and Sullivan must have been bumping their heads on the lids of their coffins as the show went into rehearsal.

As expected, confusion reigned during the initial run throughs. Then, slowly, the youngsters learned their parts and songs and soon began to feel comfortable in their roles. When the players felt secure enough to listen to each other, they began to have fun.

It was all coming together nicely until a complication arrived from outside the company. Carl Helmer's sophomore girlfriend, Muriel Farmer, cocaptain of the cheerleaders, dropped in on one of the rehearsals. She took umbrage at the degree of enthusiasm her boyfriend and that little floozie freshman girl showed during their love duet. She chose to express that umbrage in the presence of the entire company.

"You're draped all over him like some brazen Jezebel. You'd best keep your distance if you know what's good for you, miss. He's mine! Got it? Or I'll fix your little red wagon," Muriel Farmer declared ominously. She then turned and flounced out of the auditorium with her two pep squad companions, the skirts of their cheerleader outfits twirling as they exited.

The cast found it difficult to concentrate on rehearsal after Muriel's excoriation. Everyone was a bit shaken until someone suggested that they rehearse the janitor's chorus number to lighten the mood.

Cecelia sidled over to Peggy. "You okay, hon?"

"I'm fine," said Peggy.

"Try not to let her bother you," said Cecelia. "She just thinks who she is."

"Yeah, I guess . . . but thanks, Cecelia," said Peggy, grateful for the consoling words.

"Call me Cece," said Cece.

"I will," said Peggy, "and you can call me Jezebel."

The two girls chuckled and the cast members who observed them were relieved that the unpleasantness was on its way to being forgotten. But Peggy Cohan was determined that it would not be forgotten. Not until the war was over. A war that had only just begun.

"I don't know what to say," said Carl, as he tentatively approached Peggy. "How does she get that way? She's usually . . . kinda . . . nice."

Peggy looked into her costar's eyes, flipped her honey blonde hair just slightly, and smiled. "To tell the truth, I can't really blame her. If I had a great beau like you, I'd be a little jealous myself." Peggy now smiled a little embarrassed smile, blushed, and locked her eyes onto his. The smile transformed into a little pout. The poor boy was a goner though he didn't know it yet. In subsequent rehearsals, Carl and Peggy became very close. By the last week of dress rehearsal he had asked Peggy to the prom.

It fell to Cece, who had an appreciation for vendettas, to deliver the *coup de grace*. Strolling over to the gaggle of cheerleaders out on the sidelines of the athletic field, she posed a question to Muriel within earshot of the rest of the squad.

"So, Muriel, you going to the prom? I was just wondering because Carl has asked Peggy Cohan."

Cece waited for the reactions of the girls, then turned casually on her heels to report back to Peggy in the auditorium.

"She turned green! Positively green!" Cece recounted. "And the rest of the squad, they pitied her. You should have seen. It was the tops."

"After the prom, she can have him back," said Peggy, matter-of-factly.

Cold, thought Cece, *but kind of neat. I like this girl.*

The play performed to a full house. The songs played well and the audience laughed in all the right places. It was a hit. After the triumph, the cast enjoyed celebrity status for several weeks in the school hallways. But the most lasting effect was on the two cast members, Peggy Cohan and Cece Castelagno. The performing bug had bitten. The girls had decided. They were going to be stars.

Three years later on Union Street in front of Flushing High, a slender young man wearing a pork pie hat with the brim turned up, saddle shoes, an argyle sweater, and a polka dotted bowtie, hurried to catch up to two girls walking along in deep conversation.

"There they are, always together like two bugs in a rug. Whadya say ladies, I can buy you a soda if you're willing to share." The self-styled lothario waggled his eyebrows á la Groucho.

"Why don't you go water your animals, Ricky Rudolph Vaselino Jameson?"

Rick Jameson was the water boy of the high school's football team and the remark of the pretty brunette wiped the leer off his face.

The blonde bestowed an approving glance at her friend, as if to compliment an especially deft tennis stroke. Jameson muttered some inaudible retort and veered off, allowing the two girls to resume their walk and conversation in peace.

Margaret Cohan and Cecelia Castelagno had become best friends. Their association was based on a shared dream. Two dreams, actually. Peggy's, to be a great actress and a Hollywood movie star. Cece's, to be a singing sensation on the radio. Each girl treated her friend's dream as reverentially as her own. It was a friendship nourished by the possibility of dreams and the absolute conviction that the other would achieve hers. Each was the other's first and most devoted fan.

In the spring of 1937 most people worked hard, if they had a job, and kept fripperies, like dreams, to themselves. But Cece and Peggy, at age sixteen, could still afford the luxury.

Cecelia's Uncle Carmine was big in the Musician's Union, close to J. Caesar Petrillo himself. All it took was two phone calls and his favorite niece and her friend were in show business. Usherettes on Broadway. The show *Anything Goes,* starring Ethel Merman, was sold out every night. Cece and Peggy worked the Alvin Theater Wednesday matinee, Thursday, Friday, and Saturday evenings.

In their prim little black dresses with white lace collars, armed with flashlights and stacks of playbills, they adroitly seated patrons and charmingly bid them an enjoyable evening.

The women took little notice of the usherettes. Most of the men, however, noticed, invariably stealing a furtive second glance. After all, the girls were knockouts. Some of the men, when safely out of earshot and scowling range of wives or dates, attempted to flirt with the girls. "Hey, sweetheart, you should be up there, y'know?" and "So, what do you do when you're not ushering?"

Peggy and Cece would respond with a smile and offer as little information as possible. Keep it cordial, but impersonal, was their rule. They were both underage and didn't welcome the extra attention. This, after all, was the first step of their dream. If not the first step, it was at least the step preceding the first step.

The girls soon devised strategies to keep the wolves at bay. "If I flick my light, come and get me." When the light flashed the other would respond with, "C'mon, c'mon, the manager wants us right away." Or, "There's a lady lost her shoe down in center orchestra."

One night during the first intermission, a short, stocky, shiny-pated, middle-aged man wearing a double-breasted suit and two pinky rings attempted to engage Peggy in conversation.

"So, you like this ushering job?"

Peggy's light flashed up at the rococo balcony.

"Yes, very much."

"You live in town?"

The beam flickered more urgently at the gilded cherubs and curlicues festooning the ceiling.

"No, but fairly close to the city. Now, I must go to help . . ."

Peggy edged away trying to remain cordial despite the interrogation, her light flashing an even more urgent SOS.

"I got maybe a proposition for you."

Here it comes, she thought.

"No, I don't think I'd be interested. Thanks, anyway."

Then Cece arrived.

"Peg, c'mon, the manager wants us. Right away!"

"Sorry, gotta go." Her smile was pure relief.

"Hey, here, take my card. You'd be perfect to model my spring line." He shouted, "Satin shifts like the one you're wearing, only in daytime colors. Here, take the card." He leaned to extend the slightly wilted card toward the retreating girl like the baton in a relay race. "You should call."

Peggy took the card as she made good her escape. *Pinkus Garfinkel. Summertime frocks and first class cruise wear. 239 Seventh Avenue.*

When the curtain went up, Peggy and Cece inspected the card.

"You think he's for real?"

"Might be."

What the heck. They called at ten the next day. Cece dialed. Peggy spoke. That afternoon the girls located the garment center's address. A 35th Street loft. Mr. Garfinkel was there in short sleeves amidst clattering sewing machines and the hiss of steam. He appeared flushed and harried, a disconcerted Jewish white rabbit out of Wonderland, darting about the cluttered facility.

"Sadie, still on the same piece? C'mon already!"

Sadie looked up from her humming Gritzner and parried his remark with a long-suffering eye roll.

"Girls, I promised one o'clock," he said, now directing his comments to the women at the pressing apparatus. They continued working, seemingly oblivious to his exhortations.

He walked through the area where two lean men, both wearing waistcoats and white shirts open at the collar, stood at wide tables with scissors cutting cloth. Garfinkel simply nodded and uttered an approving "um-hmm."

It seemed the cutters occupied a higher stratum than the women in the shop. That, or they simply couldn't be hurried.

"Can I help you girls?" said the plump lady in the floral dress. She wore two pair of eyeglasses, one on her nose, the other suspended from a piece of knotted piping around her neck. She was sitting behind a paper-strewn desk which served as the reception and office area of the little business.

Peggy produced the card. "Mr. Garfinkel asked me to come over. I called this morning."

The office lady's suspicious squint relaxed and turned warm brown in recognition.

"Oh, yeah, sure," she said as she appraised Peggy. "Pinky! Uh, Mr. Garfinkel!"

Garfinkel chugged through the shop toward them.

"Good, you came. Whadaya think, Selma?"

She gestured to Peggy with her index finger, pointing downward, making a little spiral in the air. "Could you turn around, please, for me?"

Peggy complied, making her twirl as graceful as her slight embarrassment would let her.

"A four. A healthy four. Whadaya think, Sel?"

"Yeah, I see it. Yeah," said Selma, nodding delightedly.

Pinky was pleased with himself. "You see it? Even in that dark theater I could see it."

Selma turned to Cece. "I'm sorry dear, but we don't have anything for you right now. But if you leave us your . . ."

"Oh, I'm not here for . . . I'm just here with my girlfriend. She's the one that's interested . . . I'm not . . ."

Selma smiled, a bit relieved that the dark-haired girl would not be disappointed. "Would you like a glass of tea? Sit. We could talk about the show."

Peggy was excited. Modeling wasn't quite show business, but it was a step up from herding cattle. *At least people are there to look at me.*

4

Cece's break would have to wait until the wedding of her favorite cousin.

The family was amazed one day when Freddie showed up with a girl. He was so quiet and sensitive. Always with his nose in a book. He actually liked to read poetry. And not always the kind that rhymed. Unlike the other roughneck cousins in the family, Federico didn't seem to be interested in girls.

The couple met at night school in the city. Alice, a secretary for a group of lawyers, was taking legal courses for no credit. Freddie was taking English Lit. Someday he hoped to teach. They made it a habit of meeting for coffee after class. After a while, they realized it wasn't the coffee they craved.

A few weeks later, in an act of consummate bravery, Federico confronted Alice's father and asked for and received his blessing. The girl had cleverly presold her dad several days before. On the other hand, Federico's possessive mother thought it was the worst idea she had ever heard. Mamma grumbled, she sulked, she took to her bed, but the marriage seemed to be unstoppable.

"Lookit how happy they are. C'mon, Ma," urged the family.

With the banns posted and the date set, Mamma still refused to accept the girl. She was Catholic, but not Italian. She was old. Two full years older than twenty-year-old Federico. "And certainly no beauty,"

Mamma pointed out repeatedly. "What is she? Irish or something? Look how pale she is. And so thin. Her eyes are too far apart. She has no bosoms. She will produce sickly babies."

Marie kept this up for weeks, regaling anyone who would listen. After a time, Freddie's father, a taciturn stonemason who had immigrated from Calabria to build American reservoirs and public buildings, pronounced the issue settled.

"Shaddupa, Marie."

Marie, wide-eyed, was shocked into silence.

"At leas hesa no sissy boy," the future groom's dad muttered into his *Il Progresso.*

"I want you to come," Cece told Peggy.

"Aw, Cece, it's a family thing."

"You're coming!"

"I won't know anybody."

"You know me. You're coming!"

"C'mon, Cece. I don't have a date."

"Neither do I. You'll be my date."

"Oh, great, we'll dance together."

"There'll be plenty of cousins to dance with."

"C'mon, Cece."

"You're coming! Saturday, St. Timothy's."

Peggy's shoulders slumped as she exhaled in defeat. "Saturday," Peggy nodded.

After an eleven o'clock ceremony in an overflowing church, the reception and dinner was held at the Waldorf Astoria on Park Avenue. The O'Connors, it seemed, had money.

As the guests filed into a large, opulent reception room, two separate bars doled out the libations. A piano tinkled pop tunes and light classical as the couple's family and friends recovered from their respective odysseys from "the Island" and the wilds of Westchester into the city.

When Peggy and Cece made their entrance, most male heads turned at the sight of the attractive girls. Few wives, mothers, or sisters paid any attention at all. At weddings, women feel involved and necessary. Men, on the other hand, are well aware that they, with the exception of the lamb at the altar, are superfluous.

Cece wore a firecracker-red dress with a black sash and platform shoes. Her dark hair was swept up, revealing dangling, glittering earrings. Peggy wore a low-backed, white sheath dress. Her hair was also up in a sophisticated swirl, with a single pearl adorning each ear.

"Hey, who's that with Cece?" said Vinny LaScalza out loud to no one in particular.

On the opposite side of the hall, Vincent Repaci silently voiced the identical thought.

Separately they charged through the broken field of wedding guests to present themselves to their dear cousin.

"Cece, you look real nice. How 'bout you introduce me to your friend here." The first move went to Vinny L.

Determined not to have lost the initiative, Vinny R. said, "Cece, I don't believe I am acquainted with your friend."

"Peggy," Cece said resignedly, gesturing to her cousins. "I'd like you to meet Vinny and . . . Vinny."

"Ha ya doin?"

"Wha'd'ya say?"

"This is my girlfriend, Peggy Cohan."

"So nice to meet you," Peggy said graciously. "Two Vinnys, no waiting, how convenient." She extended her hand to the puzzled pair.

Vinny reached past his cousin, grasped Peggy's hand and shook it vigorously. Without letting go, he said, "I thought this was goin' to be a boring party, but not anymore."

Retrieving her hand, Peggy said, "I'm so glad." She then turned to the other Vinny and said, "I'd love a cocktail, Vinny. Would you mind?"

When Vinny R. gallantly scooted off to the crowded bar, Peggy, making conversation, asked the remaining cousin, "So, Vinny, what do you do? You a student?"

"Nah, I'm in ice."

"Ice? Like an ice company?" asked Peggy.

"Yeah, I deliver ice."

"Oh, you're an ice man. How interesting."

Vinny L. nodded, pleased that the pretty blonde found something about him interesting.

Vinny R. returned carrying a glass of wine and a mixed drink. "Here, Peggy, I got you a Manhattan. On accounta we're in Manhattan. Get it?"

"That's perfect. Thank you, Vinny," said Peggy.

It was then that the sliding doors parted revealing a much larger and, if possible, more opulent room set with tables. As the guests streamed into the main ballroom, Cece beckoned to Peggy.

"C'mon, Peg, I fixed it for us to sit at the kid's table. Believe me, it's much less complicated." She turned to her two boy cousins. "Nice seeing you, Vin, Vinny."

"Nice meeting you," Peggy said as she was whisked away by Cece.

The band played a short fanfare as Cece and Peggy seated themselves at a large table already occupied by preadolescent kids. The trumpet player stepped to the mike and introduced Phil Stanton and his Newport Nine, featuring the vocal stylings of Miss Francie Witherspoon. Francie, a slim blonde with a spit-curled bob and a nice caboose, smiled and slowly crossed her legs.

Phil greeted the guests with a "High-ho everybody!" He started things off with the Charleston, which managed to get some toes tapping but did little to bring the two alien clans together. Then Francie sang "Blue Moon" and "Keepin' Out of Mischief."

During Miss Witherspoon's very torchy rendition of "Body and Soul," the Vinnys appeared and directed the children on either side of Peggy to leave.

"Get lost, kid."

"You! Take a hike."

They seated themselves in the hastily vacated chairs.

"Hey, can you play 'Che la Luna Mezza O'Marre?'" someone

shouted to the band leader. Stanton either didn't hear or was trying to ignore the request, but the gauche side of the hall persisted.

Finally, Stanton had to concede. "Sorry, don't know it."

The minority now had a cause. "Play 'Che la Luna.'"

"Yeah, play it!"

"Celia, you sing it."

"Yeah, Celia, sing."

Cece shook her head, no. But the Mediterranean crowd was adamant. Their honor was at stake. Peggy encouraged her friend and gestured with a grin and cock of her head for Cece to stand up and answer the call. Cece solemnly handed the toddler she had been dandling back to its mother and nodded in assent.

When she began to sing beside the table everyone shouted for her to move up to the bandstand. She resignedly strode to the stage where two saxophone players gave her a hand up. Peggy, along with most of the crowd, applauded delightedly as Cece took the stage.

Cece turned to the dinner-jacketed bandleader and asked, "Do you know 'Che la Luna?'" He shook his head no, but said, "Go ahead, we'll try to follow."

From her chair on the bandstand Francie Witherspoon uncrossed her legs, leaning forward and smirked sadistically. This was gonna be good.

Cece started a bit tentatively but gained confidence with the second verse. When the band joined the simple tune, Cece's inhibitions melted away. The enthusiastic audience clapped in time and by the fourth verse, the one in which lazy Mary is advised to marry a fireman because she smokes in bed, the hall was rocking. Even the Micks joined in. At the end, the applause was deafening from both sides of the chamber. Cece was a hit. The approval, the joy, the love was palpable. Cece was hooked for life. Wanting to be a singer became *wanting to be a singer*. The only person not happy at the end of Cece's performance (not counting the groom's mother) was Miss Francie Witherspoon. She was livid and informed Mr. Stanton of the fact in a few terse words. He was sleeping alone tonight if he didn't get her off.

When the two Vinnys flanked Peggy, she leaned close to the one on her right and squeezed his hand, "Such a shame that Vinny is here with us. If he wasn't, you could be my date for the evening." Vinny R.'s eyes widened. Shortly thereafter, she leaned toward the other Vinny and, amidst the shouts of "Encore!," whispered, "Get rid of your cousin and we've got the evening to ourselves." Vinny L. responded with a nod and a resolute, "Yeah!"

The audience, meanwhile, persisted in its hectoring.

"Another song!"

"Yeah, one more."

"Encore!"

"C'mon, Cece!"

"Sorry," the bandleader apologized. "She can't. It's a union thing. We can't allow . . . she's not in the union. S'out of my hands." He shrugged sheepishly.

"Who says?" a gravelly voice bellowed from the audience.

"Pardon?" Dapper Phil didn't quite hear the remark.

"Who says she ain't in the union?" Uncle Carmine's voice boomed amidst the hushing audience.

"Well, clearly, she's not . . ." the bandleader stammered.

"I'm Carmine Affrunte, chairman of the executive committee of Local 802, an I say she's in the union. An if you don watch yer ass, you ain't gonna be in the union. *Capisce?*"

While Cece was allowing herself to be cajoled back to the stage, the two Vinnys at the kid's table stood up, glowered at each other, and stalked out of the ballroom towards the hotel corridor.

Up on stage, Cece sang two more songs: "On the Sunny Side of the Street" and "I've Got Rhythm." Both were received with exuberant applause. Just outside the ballroom, the muffled sound of a disturbance could be heard. Peggy watched as the newlyweds' dads hurried out to deal with the problem. She smiled a satisfied smile, then refocused her attention to the stage and the performance of her friend. Cece bowed graciously at the applause and elected to finish up with another ethnic number. Even as a beginner, Cece possessed uncanny instincts as a performer.

"This is a song about my girlfriend, Josephina. She lives in an apartment building in Brooklyn. It goes like this . . ."

She started the Louis Prima song slowly as if it was a ballad.

"Josephina, please no leana on the bell
When you moosha, please no poosha on the bell
I hear Mrs. Calucci tella Mrs. O'Flynn
Somebody keeps ringin' but nobody comes in . . .

The O'Connors exchanged a glance and then grinned. They hadn't always lived in Westchester.

. . . You can squeeze alla you please, that's all right,
But don't keep us from sleep every night . . ."

Big finish. All the musicians were now into it.

". . . When you moosh in the hall
Stay away from the wall
Josephina please no leana on the bell."

The second time around, the entire audience joined in.

"When you moosh in the hall
Stay away from the wall!
Josephina, please no leana on the bell."

Even the bride and groom, who up until now had the demeanor of a pair of nabbed horse thieves contemplating the gallows steps, smiled and applauded.

When the two dads returned from the outer hallway and rejoined the festivities, they had bonded over having together dispatched the pair of troublemakers. Italy and Ireland came together that night. Old

World and New found common ground in their humanity. The match might have a chance after all.

Sealed envelopes were hastily pried open and additional "presidents" inserted. The mothers of the bride and groom were actually civil to each other. Only Phil Stanton did not leave the hall happy that evening, knowing no way was he going to get laid tonight.

"Whatever happened to the two Vins?" Cece asked Peggy as they headed home on the subway.

"They probably got bored and left," Peggy offered. "They didn't strike me as music lovers."

Cece received her probationary union card in the mail the very next week. Was it actually happening?

When the saxophone player switched bands a few weeks later, his new boss was grumbling about losing his girl singer.

"Ran off with the bass player. He was a great bass player." It was an old joke.

"Y'know, there was a terrific kid I heard at a wedding. You might wanna take a listen."

He did.

The two fledgling career girls rented a small apartment over on East 54th Street. It consisted of one bedroom and a front room converted into a second bedroom. Cheap. Four flights of stairs to climb. A chipped old claw-footed tub in the Lilliputian bathroom. Clothes rods lining all the clear wall spaces. It was cramped, but pure heaven. The stage-struck girls had a place of their own. Cece was right. It was indeed happening.

5

When it came to modeling, Peggy Cohan was a natural. The slim, leggy girl quickly mastered the standard pose; hips pushed out, face bearing an expression of vapid ennui. On her earliest jobs, she couldn't decide what expression to make, so she thought of nothing. "Nothing" registering on Peggy's fresh and pretty face seemed to be just what the trade wanted. She quickly moved from robes and dresses on Seventh Avenue to the Conover Agency uptown, which was doing fashion newspaper and magazine work. Peggy the model was soon in demand. The pay was four dollars an hour; good money for 1938. Extraordinary money for a teenager. The slim girl with the large, wide-set hazel eyes served her apprenticeship in the rough and tumble of the garment center, often employing her wit and sense of humor to fend off buyers who wanted to "feel the merchandise."

"Sure, Sol, I'll be happy to have dinner with you tonight at your hotel, but I'm going to have to call your wife in New Jersey to make sure it's okay" or "My boyfriend is a fullback on the football Dodgers. I know he'd love to meet you."

Peggy never forgot that modeling was merely a stepping stone to her dream of becoming a great actress like her idols Bette Davis and Katharine Hepburn. If along the way she happened to become a movie star, that would be okay too. In the meantime, before her inevitable appearance on the thirty-foot screen of the Loew's Keith's, modeling would pay for her apartment, clothing, and acting and flying lessons.

Once a photographer flew Peggy to a location in Maine in his own private plane. He let her take the controls of the four-place Stinson and Peggy loved it. She was good at it, too. A natural at flying, Peggy loved the company of clouds. After a few lessons, the photographer suggested a highly personal payment plan for her continued instruction. Peggy continued her lessons. The photographer requested Peggy for many of his location assignments and the pair trysted whenever the opportunity presented itself, including frequent "payment" sessions in the confined space of that small cockpit. The plane had no autopilot, which meant that someone had to have their hand on the yoke at all times. *Men are so easy,* Peggy mused. *Just eager lil gherkins hoping to become cucumbers.* Between location shoots she continued her flying lessons on the weekends at Flushing airport near her mother's home. The flying bug had bitten. Peggy not only soloed in minimal hours, but was well on her way to her private license.

Could anyone have a more glamorous life? Modeling beautiful clothes, earning good money so she could buy beautiful clothes, attending Broadway shows, operas, the symphony, and hitting the classiest night spots with men who were willing to wine and dine a girl for the privilege of wearing her on their lapels.

On one occasion, a friend of Peggy's at the Conover Agency arranged a blind date for Peggy and a friend. Two banking executives were spending the night in town, looking for some fun. Peggy called Cece and arranged the date. It would have to be late because Peggy had a job.

The shots were for a spread entitled, "Beauty and the Beast." The idea was to pose three models in five different evening gowns with their "dates," who would be personified by exotic zoo animals.

"You and your friend meet us at the Central Park Zoo. Tell 'em you're with Conover and they'll let you in," Peggy told the "big" spender on the other end of the phone line. "We should be done by nine. My girlfriend will meet us there and we'll paint the town, okay?"

"C'mon, Peggy, get off the phone. We've got to finish makeup. You're up next after the seal shot," announced the production assistant.

Wild animals and gorgeous models in evening dress. The magazine editor thought it was a boffo idea. Fifteen fashion shots: ten for the book, five for back-up or a future mailing piece or insert. Only one problem: the animals didn't choose to cooperate. They refused to work for scale (get it), they didn't want to work for peanuts—or so the jokes went.

When the photographer's bright lights were switched on, the animals instantly became camera-phobic and scooted back to the depths of their cages. All the baby elephant wanted to do was hide behind its momma. The lion, tiger, leopard, and black panther wanted no part of the fashion game, no matter how beautifully the model was dressed or how hard the keepers poked them with their pointy little prodders.

By seven p.m., things were looking grim. The girls were dressed and ready but the animals were refusing to play ball.

The initial shot was to be on the deck of the seal pool but the elusive little critters stayed underwater, out of camera view. The model, a lovely brunette wearing a sleek off-the-shoulder in gray (to match her seal date), stood waiting on the concrete decking. Meanwhile, the seal wrangler paced behind her waving an aromatic herring at the pool of water. The seal never came out and the model fought the nausea caused by the aroma of chum bucket.

They had booked the zoo until nine with an hour option. So far, no photographs had been taken and more than half the time had elapsed. The magazine's art director, whose idea this had been, was considering *seppuku*. He was waving his arms and repeating the word "fiasco" to the birds over at the aviary while declaring his career over. It was back to designing hats for him.

When Cece arrived, Peggy was posing in front of the mandrill's cage. The splash of purple fabric on her gown matched perfectly with the lurid color of his muzzle. Of all the creatures, the mandrill was the only animal unaffected by the lights and bustle. He simply stared out between the bars, contemptuous of all the spectators.

"Kinda like my Uncle Carmine," observed Cece.

In the end, they managed to get five good shots. A girl in a red strapless with the baby elephant; the photographer felt that its momma's legs could be retouched out. A redhead in a green gown with a peacock who somehow was induced at the last moment to fan out his marvelous tail. Peggy, in a black satin gown with a panther caught in mid-leap behind her. Peggy, again, with her belligerent mandrill. The redhead, once more, with a rather dazed-looking wolf that some brave soul had dressed in a black satin bow tie.

When the shoot had wrapped and the art director was being calmed by his assistants and assured that the evening had been a success and his career was still intact, Peggy and Cece's dates arrived.

"Sorry fellas, we could have used you," said the photographer's assistant to the two men dressed in evening wear, "but the shoot's over."

"I say, we're not . . ." Trip Barton began to explain to the young man when he was interrupted by his friend, Tyler Hughes.

"They think we're models, Tripper. That's jolly rich, isn't it, Peggy?"

"Certainly is," Peggy answered. "Now, where are we going? I'm starved."

"Shouldn't we first decide who is to be whose date?" Tyler remarked.

"That might depend on where we're going," said Peggy, a sly expression on her face. "So, give me a hint. I need to know how to dress." Peggy was wearing the white satin gown with the purple slash of fabric across one shoulder.

Cece rolled her eyes at her friend's crassness.

"I was thinking 21 for starters," Trip Barton offered.

Peggy then turned to Tyler and pointed to his chest. The gesture mimicked that of an auctioneer asking if a higher bid was in the offing.

Tyler Hughes responded with, "Stork Club?"

Peggy smiled and slipped her arm under his. "Where we parked?" she asked Tyler as they walked out towards the zoo's entrance.

Cece then took Trip's arm and said, "I guess you wound up with me," as they headed for the gate. Trip smiled, not at all disappointed.

"Miss Cohan!" the wardrobe assistant shouted, as the couples departed. "The dress!"

6

One day Peggy's good luck turned even better. *LIFE* magazine was doing a feature article on the Red Cross and the humanitarian aid they were providing to European refugees. It was a five-page feature with a color spread. Real nurses, real hospitals. For the color portion, *LIFE* elected to use models. The session was shot at a local hospital. Peggy was posed in a Red Cross volunteer's uniform, sitting in a chair, presumably reading a bedtime story to a little refugee boy. The lad, who was actually recovering from a tonsillectomy, was being miserable and uncooperative. After all, his throat did hurt. He scowled and fidgeted continuously, despite pleas from his mother, the photographer, and the real hospital nurse.

The session was running long and the photographer had just about abandoned all hope of getting the shot.

In exasperation, Peggy leaned toward the boy and whispered, "Stop your damn squirming, you little shit, or I'll pull down your 'jamas and swat your backside."

The shocked child quieted instantly, then turned to Peggy with a wide-eyed look of hurt which caused her a momentary pang of regret at having spoken so harshly to the boy. At that instant the shutter clicked. The resultant photograph evidenced the loving concern of a dedicated and beautiful Red Cross volunteer for a frightened little refugee boy. When it ran, the magazine was besieged with letters inquiring about the identity of the lovely young nurse. The Red Cross adapted the photo for a poster which was widely used in fundraising. Remarkably, donations more than doubled. Everyone wanted to know, who is that girl in the Red Cross uniform with the honey-blond hair and the compassionate eyes?

When the magazine hit the stands on the west coast, three movie studios asked the same question. Paramount and MGM each sent a middle level recruiter to the Flushing residence of Miss Cohan with an offer of a screen test and a preliminary contract. International Pictures sent Arnie Zimmerman himself. When he saw the picture in *LIFE,* he decided that this young peach would be his.

He arranged to meet Peggy at her mother's house in Flushing and appeared with flowers and a five-pound box of candy. Since the girl was underage he would need permission from the mother. Peggy, who had not lived at home for nearly a year, went along with the charade. She warned her mother not to "screw this up." Arnie was charming and witty, complimenting Stella Cohan with the suggestion that if she had come to Hollywood when she was Peggy's age, she herself might well have made it in the movies. But Arnie could tell Stella Cohan was buying none of it. *Nice long legs on the kid, and the eyes, what are they? Hazel? Set wide apart. Kind of look right through you.* It was during the small talk that Arnie noticed a menorah on a corner bookshelf. *A menorah in a Cohan's home? Cohan's an Irish name, isn't it?* Peggy's mother explained that her deceased husband had been a lawyer and, for "business purposes," legally changed their name. By altering one letter of his family name, the Jewish Cohen became the Christian Cohan. Unfortunately, poor Martin Cohan didn't live long enough to benefit from this subterfuge. His life was cut short, she explained, in a motor accident on a rain-swept road in Connecticut.

"Taken in the prime of life," she emphasized, eying Peggy pointedly.

Arnie Zimmerman saw the opening, paused solemnly for a few seconds, then went for it. With consummate charm, he declared that only a nice Jewish family man like himself could be trusted to watch over a nice Jewish girl like Peggy, and that her late father would no doubt have given his approval. Stella Cohan glanced at Peggy, who was acting out the character of loving daughter because she needed her mother's approval. She hadn't said a word during Arnie's pitch, but the girl's eyes revealed how desperately she wanted to go. Stella Cohan was enjoying her newfound power and was determined to string this out. She explained that her job precluded her accompanying her daughter and that the girl was simply too young to go off to California by herself. Three thousand miles away—it was just too far. But Arnie's salesman's sense told him that the woman was negotiating. He then promised solemnly that he, Arnold Zimmerman, personally would escort Peggy to Hollywood and look after her while her dreams took form.

"Sort of like a fairy godfather, if you'll pardon the expression."

Stella Cohan eventually agreed to let her daughter make the trip . . . for the consideration of five hundred dollars. *Ouch, that stung,* thought Arnie. She even magnanimously offered to call the other studio representatives and inform them that her Peggy had chosen International. "Then it's done," Arnie said, clasping Stella's hand. When the two women's eyes met, Stella's face registered the contempt a victor might have for the despised vanquished. Peggy's radiated a flash of disdain. Arnie caught the exchange and noted that his starlet's hazel eyes suddenly flashed a violent green. He wondered if the new Technicolor film could catch that.

7

The postcard arrived in the afternoon mail. On the front, a tinted photograph of a hillside crowned by fifty-foot-tall letters proclaiming "Hollywoodland." Cece turned the card over.

Dear Cece,

After four days on the train we finally arrived. It's sunny and wonderful! Been shopping for the most gorgeous clothes ever. Had my screen test yesterday and am meeting lots of interesting people. I've got my very own little house on the hotel grounds. Fresh flowers every day. Everyone's so nice. I love it here. Next week, they're throwing a party in my honor. Oh, Cece, it's everything I imagined it to be.

Love and kisses, friends to the end,
Peggy.

Peggy Cohan, wearing a blue-flowered party dress, stepped lightly through the French doors of her bungalow into the hotel garden and the balmy evening. This was the night of the press party. She tilted her chin upward slightly. "Mmm," she murmured. "What is that fragrance?"

She found herself amidst a grove of small trees, crowded with delicate white blossoms, huddled between the main building and the cottages. Arnold Zimmerman appeared and strode to the girl's side.

"Mr. Zimmerman, what's that smell? Can you tell?" the girl asked.

"I dunno . . . flowers. Maybe Flit," he answered vaguely. "C'mon."

As the pair strolled the path through the scented grove, she considered the fragrance; pleasant, but slightly overwhelming, yet somehow familiar. *But what? Dime store perfume—or Creamsicles! Yes!* The aroma reminded the girl from New York of the delicious taste of Creamsicles. Creamsicles, a much more familiar scent to young, aspiring movie star Peggy Cohan than orange blossoms.

They reached the open door of the reception room. Arnie gallantly gestured for Peggy to enter.

"Here we go, kid."

They entered arm in arm. Peggy, like a blushing bride full of excitement and anticipation. Arnie, with the expression of a proud father who knew that, instead of giving the bride away, he was going to get to keep her.

Peggy looked fresh and radiant in her simple blue dress, minimal makeup, and two small tortoiseshell barrettes in her honey-colored hair. Arnie looked every bit the shtarker in his custom-tailored mohair suit. With his white brocade tie and star sapphire pinky ring, Peggy thought he very much resembled Mr. Garfinkle, her first boss.

Peggy chatted with the press, calling them ma'am and sir. Since she didn't know which ones were the most important and could do the most for her, she was equally cordial to all of them. As she mixed with the crowd, she reminded herself; hopeful, aspiring newcomer. Acting. She knew the part. In the midst of their questions, she asked them about themselves, about their jobs and families, and where they lived. She found them all so . . . interesting.

Peggy didn't take a drink or eat, which was duly noted, and as the evening wore on she asked Louella for the time. When the reply was, "Ten forty-five, why dear?"

She answered, "I promised my mom I'd be in bed by eleven, so, I'm sorry, but I have to go."

Peggy then attempted to say goodnight and shake hands with

everyone she met that night. It seemed as if she was actually pleased to meet them.

Many were surprised to see her exiting with Arnold so early. These things usually drag on so as to wring the last drop of positive juice from a studio coming-out party. It was appreciated by many that they would get home at a reasonable hour tonight.

Arnie chattered expansively at her side as they strode the curving path towards Peggy's bungalow.

"What a night! They loved you! Ate yuh up. Hedda practically adopted you. I knew this would work. And you did great, kid. And where did you get that 'your job is interesting' stuff. They sure went for it."

The press party was Arnie Zimmerman's idea. *Let 'em all meet the young model, just a kid really, alone in a strange city, beautiful, smart, and hoping for her big break in pictures.*

"Instead of trying to sell you to that pack of wild dogs, we're gonna enlist the bastards as aunties and uncles. They're gonna be pulling for you, kid. Like Cinderella before you even make a picture."

And that's the way it happened. Arnie's strategy had worked to perfection. Maybe it was because cynics really want to believe in fairytales or because the seventeen-year-old girl's special kind of freshness was as rare around Hollywood as snow tires or integrity.

"You did it, kid. You did good," said Arnie.

Peggy smiled weakly, feeling slightly undeserving of her triumph.

As they reached the door to Peggy's cottage, Arnie took both her hands in his and said, "Hey, arentcha happy?"

She nodded and leaned over to give her balding mentor, who was nearly a head shorter, a kiss on the cheek. Arnie turned his head to squarely meet her lips and embraced her with surprising strength, pulling her body close to his. The kiss was anything but paternal and the girl found it difficult not to recoil. *'Til now,* thought Peggy, *Mr. Zimmerman has been such a gentleman. Here we go.*

"I'll be back soon, baby. I've got to schmooze them flacks back there. Nice idea, that business of your eleven o'clock bedtime. They ate it up. Keep a candle burning for me. We're gonna celebrate, baby, just you and me."

"Baby?" *Now he's calling me baby?*

When she first met Mr. Zimmerman back in New York he was so fatherly. *I should've known. Arnie Zimmerman is just another man. Another gherkin.*

Now, sitting alone in her fancy cottage, Peggy was experiencing an uncomfortable ambivalence. Weren't all her youthful fantasies about to become reality? Wasn't she about to take her place in the firmament of movie stars? Katherine, Bette, and now, Peggy. Or should she be Margaret? It did sound more grown up. It all seemed so inevitable. Even as a child, Peggy was able to employ her looks to get her way. She came to believe that no man could resist her. It wasn't so much that she was vain—she simply accepted her looks as a fact. Just as someone might have a pleasant singing voice or the ability to juggle. *Some people are okay looking, some are homely, and some are pretty. I guess I'm pretty. Is it my fault that people seem to fall over themselves to be in the presence of pretty? Especially the boys. All ages of boys. Sometimes being pretty can be a problem, but more often than not it makes everything so much easier.*

It's just that Mr. Zimmerman was so, well, uncle-like. It was kind of comforting. So, is tonight being pretty going to be one of those "problem" times? No. Nothing has changed, really. Arnie Zimmerman is no different from any other man. Men with shiny new cars who'd pay for a show and a nice dinner and expect a girl to come across. Heck, I'm an old hand at that. This one's no different. Maybe a little older and a lot more used to getting his way. Plus, he's got the leverage. Arnie Zimmerman holds the key to everything I've ever wished for. He can make it all come true. Or not. So what does a little shtupp mean in the face of a movie career? Peggy spoke the comical Yiddish word, "shtupp" out loud, hoping it might trivialize the situation she was facing. Her ploy was ineffective. Why was she suddenly becoming so virtuous? Death before dishonor? *Come on. What's the big deal?*

The studio mogul returned to the cocktail party grinning like the cat who was expecting canary for supper. With calculated exuberance he plunged into the nattering groups of agents and journalists, pumping their hands and good-naturedly accepted their plaudits and assurances of success. Arnie knew full well that one must never trust such crap. When the hors d'oeuvres are first class and plentiful and the aged scotch flows freely, discouraging words are seldom heard. But Arnold Zimmerman also had a sense for the emmiss, the unvarnished truth of the matter. They might well hate the kid and say so tomorrow in the columns, but every instinct told him that this was not the case. They had latched on to the kid. Embraced the game rookie actress. It made sense for the studio, too, with so many young men being drafted for the inevitable war. Some of the older established stars might come off a bit matronly to the boys. Peggy was a kid just like them. And tested even younger. *Yeah, I got a winner on my hands, I can feel it.*

"Oh, yes, she had to go to bed. No, Moira, she hasn't got a screen test tomorrow. We've already done one. Camera loves her. Yeah, Billy, she promised her mother she'd be in bed by eleven. Really! They're very close. Fine woman. Works for an insurance company."

In a far corner of the room, two of Hollywood's junior remoras were observing Zimmy as he worked the cluster of important columnists.

"Helluva salesman, isn't he?"

"None better! I wonder if he's put the clamps to his latest little protégé yet?"

"Well, if he hasn't, it's only a matter of time."

The two men raised their drinks and chuckled lewdly at each other.

"It won't be long."

"Damn right, it's probably pretty short."

The pair of flacks chortled as they drained their glasses of twelve-year-old scotch.

Arnie Zimmerman felt like skipping as he hurried along the path toward bungalow six. He didn't skip, though. As a short, overweight child, he never learned. The other children would point and laugh as he tried, only managing something with a jump and half run. *To hell with them. I don't need to know how to skip.* The memory returned after all these years. *Well, today they skip when I tell 'em to.*

He switched the champagne bottle to the hand clutching the two glasses and knocked on the bungalow door. When there was no answer he knocked again, a tad harder. *Maybe she's asleep?* Arnie reached into his jacket, pulled out the extra key and unlocked the door.

"Hey, Peggy, you awake?" whispered Arnie as he entered the room.

He kicked off his alligator shoes and, bearing the champagne and glasses, tiptoed toward the bedroom. He took off his jacket and hung it neatly in the closet.

"You sleepin'?" Arnie said as he approached Peggy who was sitting up against two pillows.

"No, Arnie. I'm up." Peggy finally spoke.

"I think we're in," said Arnie as he put down the wine. "No negs at all, kiddo. I got a sense about this stuff." He sat on the edge of the bed and began removing his pants. He rose and laid the trousers over a chair, neatly, so as to preserve the crease. Then he removed his tie. He didn't untie it but simply opened the loop and pulled it over his head. Then he removed his shirt. He stood, a glass of champagne in each hand, in striped shorts, garters, black socks, and an undershirt revealing sloped, hairy shoulders.

What a dreamboat, thought Peggy, as he sat down on the bed, proffered the glass of champagne, and grinned what she supposed was his victory grin.

"To success!" Arnie declared as he clinked her glass with his.

Peggy drained her glass and immediately offered it for a refill.

It's going to take a lot more than one glass, was Peggy's immediate thought.

"You know any cheers?" Arnie asked as he poured.

"Cheers?"

"Yeah, like a cheerleader."

"No, I don't."

"S'okay," Arnie replied. "Drink up."

As she chugged her second glass and gestured for a third, she found

Arnie nuzzling her shoulder.

"You're so smooth and tight. I bet you're really tight."

At approximately 2:15 a.m., Hertha Zimmerman pulled up to the front portico of the Beverly Hills Hotel and instructed the boy not to bury her white Cord convertible; she'd only be a few minutes. The studio chief's wife was dressed in a blue chenille robe over pale green flannel pajamas with a black flowered kerchief covering her dyed black hair. On her feet were backless, purple fuzzy house slippers. But even odder than her dress was the dull, disconnected expression on her face. Her right hand was thrust into the pocket of her robe where it gripped a short barreled .38 caliber Smith and Wesson revolver. Mrs. Zimmerman, wife to Arnie Zimmerman for the past twenty-eight years, walked mechanically through the lobby of the hotel and headed for the door to the gardens. Her timing was extraordinary. Arnold Zimmerman was just leaving bungalow six, his jacket over his arm and his shirt and tie undone. He walked jauntily down the path with the demeanor of a man who had won the Academy Award, the Nobel Prize, and just passed "Go."

This pissed off Hertha Zimmerman. As if it was possible for Hertha Zimmerman to be any more pissed off.

"Arnold!"

Arnold stopped in his tracks.

"Hertha? Is that you?"

"Arnold, you bastard!"

Arnold walked guiltily toward his wife. "What are you doing here?"

"What are *you* doing here?" she replied.

"Herthie, honey. Business!"

Herthie drew the revolver from the pocket of her robe, cocked the hammer, and calmly aimed. The firearm discharged, shattering the quiet of the night with a frightful, echoing report. An orange hanging from a limb three feet above Arnie exploded, showering the stunned man with juice and pieces of pulp. She immediately squeezed off a second shot as Arnie tried to flee, backpedaling frantically. He stumbled and fell. The bullet went wild, as did the next shot. The fourth struck Arnie in the hand as he crouched on the ground, scrabbling to avoid her. He had raised his jacket before him in a desperate and ridiculous effort to ward off the bullets. The slug, deflected by the small bones of his hand, struck the flagstone walk, gouging a small groove in the stone. The fifth bullet struck Arnie in the chest, tearing into the lower left chamber of his heart, which after a series of wrenching spasms brought the life-sustaining organ to a shuddering halt. But Hertha Zimmerman continued firing. She calmly fired a sixth shot that lodged in the shoulder of her dying husband. She was not close enough to hear his faint, final words.

"Aw, Herthie, honey, I only loved you."

In her unhinged state, she was not even aware of the impotent clicks of the hammer as she mindlessly continued pulling the trigger on the spent cylinders of the gun. It mattered little to her that he was already dead. She needed to continue killing him.

Peggy was in her cottage contemplating her situation. *What's the big deal?* she argued. Some other self argued back. *So why do you feel like a piece of crap?*

Her thoughts were disrupted by some loud noises. They sounded like gunshots. Right outside. Peggy cracked open the door and peeked out. On the path two bungalows down, a crowd was gathering. There were screams and shouts and a woman was crying. Peggy could make out someone lying on the ground. *My God*, thought Peggy, *someone's been shot. Poor bastard.*

Peggy closed the door on the tragedy outside. *I should feel great. Everything I ever wanted. So, why am I feeling like this? Get over it, stupid!* She remained fretfully awake for another two hours, eventually falling asleep in the chair.

She was awakened in the morning by a series of rude knocks at her door. Peggy arose, her neck slightly kinked, and walked to the door, opening it slightly.

"Yes?"

"Good morning, Miss Cohan, I am Detective Inspector Santos." He offered a brief glimpse of a gold badge and asked, "May I come in? I'd like to ask a few questions."

Peggy stepped aside and let him enter, offering him the very chair in which she had spent the night. She sat facing him, on the edge of the rumpled bed.

The detective was in his early forties, dark complexion with his hair short in an almost military cut. His dark brown eyes darted about the room scrutinizing every detail, which included the spent champagne bottle and pair of empty glasses. His face bore a faint expression of disgust which bothered Peggy because she sensed it was directed at her. She noticed that the dark gray suit he wore was slightly shiny at the knees and elbows. It had the look of a uniform worn every day. *Oh, right. The trouble last night. He's probably here to ask if I saw or heard anything that might be helpful.*

Geez, she's young, thought Santos. *Still in her teens, I'll bet. Real looker, though. What's wrong with these girls? Don't they have any upbringing? Selling themselves to the highest bidder. A day in this room must cost a week's pay at least.*

Emiliano Santos was a very moral man. A man who had worked his way up. Night school, law courses, self-discipline. He had made something of himself. He had earned respect. The excesses and depravity which he encountered every day in Hollywood sickened him. These godless people, who with the help of uncanny luck or peculiar talents, accumulated the wealth of kings, then lived their privileged lives like barnyard animals. And here before him in this opulent setting, he found himself face to face with one more of them.

He did not spare Peggy's feelings when he told her that Arnold Zimmerman had been shot to death outside her door last night. The words stunned the girl. Santos noted that her surprise seemed genuine. *Okay, maybe she didn't know.* He had been informed that Peggy was the most recent project of the dead man's studio. And that Zimmerman was personally guiding her career.

"Is that true?"

Peggy nodded vaguely.

He had also learned of Zimmerman's reputation. A man who liked to be "intimately" involved in the careers of his new female prospects. Last night's party guests were all too happy to spew the gossip on Zimmy. Santos informed Peggy that the murdered man's wife had done the shooting in an apparent jealous rage at the infidelities of her husband. He asked if Peggy had seen Mr. Zimmerman or had spoken to him after witnesses had reported that he escorted her to her room.

The stunned girl couldn't answer. *This can't be real,* she thought. *I must be dreaming.* She could only murmur, "Oh, my God. Oh, my God," over and over.

Santos paused, and then repeated his question.

Peggy nodded dumbly. Yes, she had seen Arnold Zimmerman again that evening. "He came back for a drink," she said, gesturing to the wine and glasses on the dresser. Yes, she had heard the noise; the shots. No, she had no idea who it was on the ground at the time.

"Thank you, Miss Cohan," said Detective Santos, closing his notebook. "I have no more questions. Your account of last evening is consistent with my information." He stood and moved toward the door. "Good morning." He stopped at the open door and turned abruptly. Looking at Peggy he shook his head. "Looks to me like she killed him because he was with you in your bungalow. She pulled the trigger, but if he wasn't with you he wouldn't be dead. How's that make you feel?"

Peggy gasped. "I'm . . ." Tears welled up in her eyes. She covered her mouth with her hand. She couldn't breathe.

Santos knew he had gone too far. As he closed the door of the bungalow behind him, Santos heard the girl making faint gasping noises. *Should have kept my mouth shut,* he thought as he stepped into the bright morning. *Maybe I was a little rough on her, being so young and all.* He held that thought for a few short moments. Then, *Nah! These doxies are tough as nails.*

8

Peggy remained in the bungalow that morning. She neither ate nor dressed. She spent the time attempting to comprehend what had happened. *Is there something wrong with me? Am I poisonous? Why do I make people die? I don't mean to. Am I evil? I don't want to be. But I can't help it. I'm a horrible person. And that poor man. He was a pig. But still . . . he's dead. And his poor wife. And what's going to happen to me?* At this thought Peggy felt even more guilty worrying about herself after the death of Arnold Zimmerman. She considered calling Cece but as she reached for the phone, it rang. Marge Cummings, Mr. Zimmerman's secretary, was calling to inquire about how Peggy was doing.

"Fine, I suppose. It's . . . quite a shock."

After some minutes of small talk, Marge asked if Mr. Zimmerman was in the bungalow when he was shot.

"No. He was outside in the gardens on the walk."

This information seemed to provide Mrs. Cummings considerable relief. She then told Peggy to sit tight and a car would be sent for her tomorrow or the next day so she could come to the studio and meet the new head of production, Mr. Nathan Zuckerbrod.

Peggy spent two more fretful days in the bungalow. Her only contact with the outside world came from the room service waiter and newspapers left at her door, in which she read and reread the reports of the death of Mr. Zimmerman. On the morning of the third day, when Peggy had resolved to leave the city, a call came to tell her that a car would pick her up within the hour.

The distinctive two-tone Packard Phaeton barely slowed as it charged through the International Pictures's main gate. It was Mr. Zimmerman's car so it commanded an instant wave-in. It mattered little to the guard, retired army master sergeant, Alden Quinn, that Arnie Zimmerman was no longer among the living.

The limo turned right at the sound stages, then homed into a solitary parking space beside the executive offices. Its sudden arrival startled a painter in white coveralls who was lettering a plaque proclaiming the new possessor of the spot. As Peggy exited the car, nodding to the driver who held the door for her, she read the unfinished sign. *Nathan Zuck. They must be at the end of the alphabet,* Peggy noted cynically to herself. An attractive, well-dressed woman emerged from the building, smiled warmly and extended her hand.

"Hello, Peggy, I'm Marge Cummings. We spoke on the phone."

"Yes. So nice to see you again," Peggy responded weakly.

"It's been very hectic, as you can imagine. Come in," beckoned Marge. "Make yourself comfortable. I'll let Mr. Zuckerbrod know that you're here." Marge disappeared into her office.

The outer offices were done in dark mahogany with lots of polished brass trim. Something the set designers had concocted from the film Wellington, recreating the ambience of the offices of the British Admiralty. It looked remarkably authentic. Peggy sat on the edge of a huge leather chair while six women noisily plied their typewriters. While giving the impression of being totally attentive to their work, each managed to steal a glance at the young woman, who offered a weak smile and nod when eye contact occurred. Above Peggy's chair hung a cork bulletin board where several notices were tacked. Peggy read the most recent, signed with the initials "NZ." It announced that a half day would be allowed for employees to attend Arnie Zimmerman's funeral. If anyone chose to attend, four hours would be deducted from their paycheck. None of the secretaries had taken time off to attend.

The closest typist addressed Peggy. "Can I get you anything, hon?"

"No, thank you."

"Coffee?"

"No, thanks."

"Tea?"

"Uh, no, really. I'm fine."

The last time Peggy entered this office, Mr. Zimmerman's paternal arm had been around her shoulder.

"Hi, girls," he had shouted. "Meet Miss Peggy Cohan, our newest, gonna-be-big star."

Everyone had been smiling. Everyone had been so nice. She had held the keys to the city. Today she felt like the Fuller Brush man. She, needing to sell brushes, the world, bald as a cue ball. But she did have a contract.

Peggy sat quietly, hands in her lap, for what seemed to be an eternity. Forty minutes later, Mr. Zuckerbrod summoned her. Marge led Peggy into Mr. Zuckerbrod's office, formerly Mr. Zimmerman's.

"Come in, come in!" Zuckerbrod waved from behind an ornately carved desk. The desk stood on a platform, at least a foot high, giving the new head of IP the advantage of looking down on anyone who entered. He waved Marge away with a flick of his wrist.

"Sit! Be comfortable," said Zuckerbrod, working at being amiable. Behind him the flames of a huge gas fireplace writhed behind the protective glass.

Peggy sat in the chair indicated. It seemed lower than a normal chair. Almost like a piece of children's furniture. It probably was her imagination.

"So?" said Zuckerbrod as he looked Peggy up and down, taking her measure.

"So?" Peggy shrugged self-consciously.

"So, you were Arnie's project."

"I guess . . ."

"I've got your contract right here." Zuckerbrod waved the document.

"Standard seven-year deal. Stand up. Lemme see you."

Peggy stood. Made a little turn in an attempt to lighten the situation.

"Uh-huh, come around here. Closer."

Peggy walked around to the side of the platform behind the large desk. Zuckerbrod swiveled his chair to face her.

"I'm going to look at your test soon as I can. You could be a big star, y'know? Depends on you."

"Well, I hope so, Mr. Zuckerbrod. It's been my dream . . ." Peggy sensed the studio head's demeanor change. His eyes turned predatory. He licked his lips.

"It all depends on you. Know what I mean?" He touched himself.

I can't believe it. Peggy fought to hide her revulsion. She focused her eyes on his face.

"Y'know, you may have a contract and we have to pay you but you don't have to work."

"I don't under . . ."

"Simple. You don't get to make any movies unless I say so. Get it?"

"But why wouldn't . . . ?"

Zuckerbrod zipped down his fly and exposed himself to Peggy. He looked down, then met Peggy's eyes and grinned. "If you wanna make movies, you're gonna have to polish the old apple. Got me? Just wanna make sure you know who is boss."

Peggy recoiled in disgust. *I can't believe this is happening. Are all these people crazy degenerates? What kind of place is this?*

"No!" said Peggy.

"No?" Zuckerbrod smiled, sensing a negotiation. Negotiation was Zuck's second favorite thing. "Your daddy's dead, Miss Cohan."

"What do you know about it?" Peggy spat back.

"You need a new daddy. I'm offering." He fondled himself.

"You go to hell," said Peggy as she strode to the front of his desk where it obscured Zuckerbrod from the waist down.

"Hey, no ticky, no washy."

"What if I screamed?"

"Scream? Scream all you want. Those skirts out there need their jobs. You think they're gonna risk it for you? C'mahn."

Peggy now began backing up to the door.

"You're a pig, you know that?"

"This lil piggy is gettin' soft. You better get on the job or you'll lose your chance."

"Screw you!"

"Oh, now you're trying to make up?"

Peggy snatched open the door, turned and said, "You're a disgusting son of a bitch." She then slammed the door and ran. Zuckerbrod laughed at the closed door. "It's true, I am." His acknowledgement caused him to laugh even harder.

Peggy ran through Marge Cumming's office, past the clerical pool, and into the street along the sound stages.

Marge Cummings knocked at her boss's door.

"Come in," he shouted, his eyes wet from laughing.

"What happened?" Marge asked.

Zuckerbrod was standing beside his fireplace, the Peggy Cohan contract in his hand. He was still chuckling.

"What happened?" Marge asked again.

Mr. Zuckerbrod giggled as he tore the contract in half, parted the glass, and tossed it into the flames.

"Lawyers, who needs 'em?"

As the fire consumed the document, he broke into uncontrolled laughter at the puzzled look on Marge Cummings's face.

When former Army sergeant Quinn stepped out of his guard shack to see who had just run past in such a hurry, he saw a leggy, blonde girl on the street outside the gate. She was still running.

9

Cece, this is Peggy. I'm coming home. It's been awful. A terrible mess. Can I stay with you? I don't know where else to go."

"Of course, Peg. Your bed's still here. I've been using it to lay out my sweaters. I may be out of town next week, but, sure . . . come on, it's your place, too. How are you? I mean, you okay?"

"Oh, Cece, it's been so . . . I can't even explain . . ."

"I read about it in the paper, Peggy. Mr. Zimmerman got killed?"

"I still can't believe it. I just need to get out of here. I'll be on a train this evening. This is a terrible place, Cece."

"You come on home, Peg. I'll be here. Everything's going to be all right. You'll see."

"Cece, I can't see how anything's ever going to be all right again. I'll call you in a couple of days. G'bye, Cece . . . Cece?"

"Yes?"

"Thanks."

10

The air horn blared twice and the Super Chief eased out of Union Station and perpetual springtime to begin its acceleration toward the opposite coast. A 3500hp diesel hurled the glistening snake past the city limits and out into the wide expanses of fields and farms that made up the Los Angeles basin. Lush green gave way to mountain vistas as the city and its sins were left behind.

Peggy sat listlessly in the window seat, focused on the inside of the glass inches from her face. San Bernadino, Barstow, Flagstaff, country miles and state borders flashed by. For Peggy, it was all reduced to a glaucous blur.

The unnerved girl replayed the events of the week in her mind. Tragic. Degrading. And mean. Events that triggered a flight response in the once aspiring movie star. Even in the anonymity of the gently swaying parlor car, Peggy felt tense, coiled, ready to bolt. She knew her decision to leave had been right. *I may not be Princess Virtue or nearly as tough as I thought I was, but that's a bad place. A place I don't want to be.*

An elderly woman in the seat behind prodded Peggy, startling her. She was offering some fruit. "A nice, ripe pear or an apple, dear?" Peggy began to shake her head but the woman's persistent smile and kind eyes prompted her to accept; mouthing a weak thanks for the pear, Peggy tasted the fruit and realized how hungry she was. She hadn't eaten much in the past few days.

A tall boy with a crew cut in a khaki uniform stopped in the aisle beside her seat and asked, "How far you goin'? I'm to Chicago."

Peggy looked him square in the face. Her eyes narrowed; then she coldly turned away to resume her inspection of the window glass. The soldier turned, walked back to his seat, and shrugged defeat to his grinning cronies.

In St. Louis, Peggy called Cece and gave her an estimated arrival time. "I'm changing to the 20th Century Limited in Chicago. I'll be at Grand Central at eight Thursday morning. If you're not going to be home, would you leave the key somewhere?"

Cece said she'd come pick her up.

"You don't have to, really," said Peggy, who was relieved that her friend would be waiting.

Through a frigid New Jersey drizzle the Limited dove beneath the Hudson and surfaced a few minutes later in Grand Central Terminal. Bags and belongings were gathered up as the passengers disembarked. Peggy handed her claim checks to the Red Cap. At the gate, Cece was waiting. Peggy hurried to her friend and the two girls embraced. As the passengers flowed around them, Peggy clung to Cece. They remained in that position for a long time. Cece had never seen her friend so defeated. After several minutes and a few deep breaths, they retrieved Peggy's bags from the Red Cap's cart. Just two old suitcases. Two new larger trunks packed with the most beautiful clothes ever purchased were left in Beverly Hills in the hotel bungalow.

"Let's go home," Cece said.

Peggy nodded.

It wasn't until they were on the subway uptown that Cece broke the silence.

"So what happened? What about Hollywood?"

"Cece, I'd rather not, please? This is our stop, isn't it?"

For several days Cece observed her friend's listless behavior and uncharacteristically chose not to question her. Instead she put on a display of cheerful normalcy. Peggy did not respond. Certainly the horrible death of Mr. Zimmerman must have upset the girl, but Cece sensed there was more to it than that. More than the mourning of an acquaintance's passing.

There were other signs. Peggy seemed especially lax in her appearance. For someone once almost obsessive about her looks, Peggy now seemed not to care. On the rare occasions she changed out of her pajamas and robe, she wore an old shirt and slacks. She owned several pair of slacks in imitative tribute to her idol, Katharine Hepburn, but she had always loved to wear her dresses. Now a baggy shirt and slacks became her uniform.

Peggy's listlessness worried Cece, especially when she left for a few days to sing out of town. Peggy would remain in the apartment in her pajamas listening to the radio, often not even bothering to get out of bed. The vivacious young woman who left to conquer Hollywood a few weeks ago had disappeared.

"You should go home, Peg."

"What do you mean? I am home."

"I mean to your mom's house in Flushing."

"Oh, no! I wouldn't want to go there. She wouldn't want me."

"I spoke to her. She'd like to see you."

"You spoke to her?" said Peggy, eyeing her traitorous friend.

"I don't like you being alone when I'm on the road," Cece tried to explain. "We're playing Philadelphia next week, two weekends. I'd rather you weren't alone. Go visit. It would get you out of this little apartment."

"I'm not sure that would be a good idea," Peggy replied. "My mother and I . . . well, we . . ."

"Your mother wants you to come," said Cece. "She said she needs to see you."

"Needs to see me?" Peggy parroted the words angrily.

Mother and daughter faced each other in the doorway of the Flushing house.

"Hello, Stella."

"It's good to see you, Peggy. Let me take your bag."

"No, don't trouble, I can carry it." They entered the house.

"I took a day off from work."

"You didn't have to do that."

"I wanted to. Come, I fixed up your room."

Mother and daughter treaded softly around each other during the next few days. A shaky truce was in effect. The girl, subdued and vulnerable, the mother sensing that a hands-off approach was appropriate.

Stella Cohan was never much of a cook, but she made breakfast for her daughter before going to work. The waffles were mealy, the bacon flaccid, and the coffee much too strong.

"Enjoy!" chimed Stella as she left the house.

It's a bit late, thought Peggy, *for her to try to be a mom.*

On Saturday morning, Stella attempted to engage her daughter. "So, tell me. What happened?"

"Mom!"

"You screwed it up, didn't you? I know you did." The mother eyed her daughter, nodding sagely.

"Cut it out, Stella," said Peggy, pleading.

"Y'know, I'm not gonna give the money back," Stella announced emphatically. "You think they want the money back?" Stella continued.

Peggy turned, exasperated, and walked out of the kitchen, shaking her head.

"Uh-uh, I'm not giving it back," declared Stella, following her daughter. "You think I should give it back? You probably do."

"Quit it, ma."

"C'mon, fight with me," Stella demanded. "Aren't you gonna argue? C'mon."

"No," Peggy replied dejectedly.

"You've got to talk to me, Peggy, I'm your mother."

"Stop, Stella," Peggy replied. "I don't want to argue, talk, nothing! Can't you understand?"

"But maybe I can help."

"You can't," Peggy snapped, "you're the last person in the world I'd want to . . . Get off it, Stella, or I'm going back to the apartment."

"Okay, okay, take it easy," Stella said, now attempting to calm her agitated daughter.

Later that morning, Stella suggested that Peggy go over to the airfield and visit with that nice Timmy Farrell.

"Mom, since when do you think Timmy is nice? You called him a stupid grease monkey."

"Oh, well, perhaps I was a little tough on the boy. Go ahead. Maybe he'll give you a ride in a plane."

"Mom, I'm a licensed pilot. I can fly by myself."

Timmy Farrell ran a small aircraft parts delivery business out of Flushing Airport. He was a master mechanic, trained on the job. He had worked for his dad, who ran a maintenance shop in the main hangar out at the field. He was also a top-notch flying instructor.

Peggy and Timmy attended high school together. He was a senior when she was an entering freshman. They hadn't been friends, but what teenage boy would have failed to notice the prettiest girl in school? When Peggy approached him at Flushing Airport for flying lessons a few years later, he was inclined to help, giving Peggy lots of airtime in the high-winged Piper Cub and discounting the usual fees. He permitted Peggy to solo in the FAA minimum. It wasn't a special favor. Timmy could see that Peggy was a natural in the air, never horsing the aircraft around, but rather coaxing the controls to obey. Peggy had a light touch.

When Peggy dropped by the field and asked to borrow a plane for a joyride, Timmy found it difficult to refuse his former student.

"Have fun, Pegger, but don't be too long. Fuel's gettin' tight, with all the war talk 'n all."

"Won't be up long. Thanks," was Peggy's reply.

As Peggy preflighted the exterior of the bright yellow Cub, she examined every control surface, every panel, every bolt with meticulous care. It was like being reunited with a dear and nearly forgotten old friend. A friend not of flesh and bone but of non-judgmental aluminum and fabric. She tossed the two sets of chocks aside and climbed into the cockpit for her interior check. Soon Peggy was rolling down the taxi strip. Clearance from the tower came in the form of a green light aimed at her as she lined up on the runway. She began her takeoff roll and at sixty knots, deftly lifted the Cub from the concrete and began a series of slow climbing turns to altitude. At three thousand feet, Peggy leveled off and for the first time in so very long allowed herself to relax. The wind against the windshield seemed to whisper a sibilant, "Say, Peggy, long time no see." There were hardly any clouds on this crisp December day. Over to the northwest were some high cirrus.

"Why so serious?" Peggy punned to the clouds. And then she realized that she was not only smiling but that she had made a joke.

Down below she could make out the south shore of Long Island, Jones Beach, Fire Island, the Hamptons, and then, Land's End at Montauk. There were moving cars and people down there. Kids sledding in the remnants of an early snowfall and stalwart sun worshipers at the beach. Unburdened at last, she made a series of slow banking turns and immersed herself in the exhilaration she feared she might have lost forever. Up here the sky was clean and accepting. Here she had forgiveness. As long as the fuel held out. *Shouldn't waste fuel,* Peggy reminded herself. She reluctantly turned back, following Long Island Sound to Flushing Airport, and landed, the tank more than half full. When she rolled to a stop, cut the engine, and hopped out to set the chocks, much of the aching gloom returned. But not all.

Timmy came out to help Peggy tether the wings and secure the plane.

"How was it?"

"Oh, great. Thanks Timmy. I really appreciate . . ."

"Yeah, yeah, just part of the service, ma'am."

On the next Sunday, the Japanese attacked Pearl Harbor. President Roosevelt announced on the radio that the country was at war with the Japanese Empire. A few days later, Germany declared war on the

United States. America was finally in it despite all its efforts to remain on the sidelines.

At first the country was stunned, but Americans quickly responded to the two-pronged threat. Young men lined up in droves to enlist. Everyone, men and women, and even the kids, resolved to contribute to the war effort.

In the face of all the patriotic fervor, Peggy Cohan remained detached. She was still focused inward. And she viewed herself with contempt. While the life of virtually every adult in America had been altered by the onset of the war, Peggy remained oblivious to it all.

Until the telegram arrived.

"This came for you, Peggy. Looks important," said Stella as she studied both sides of the envelope in the hope that she might divine its origin.

"Who's it from?" Peggy asked, refusing to look at the letter.

"Don't know."

"Is it from California?"

"Can't tell. You've got to open it."

Peggy felt a chill. Could it be a message from the studio or some unpleasantness relating to the death of Mr. Zimmerman? Or some other studio?

"It's your telegram, Peg."

Peggy shrugged. "You open it. If it's from International, throw it away."

It was not from Hollywood. It was from Washington, DC, and Jacqueline Cochoran, the famous aviatrix.

It read:

FAA records indicate you hold a current pilot's license. If interested in joining the All Women's Flying Auxiliary Corps, contact Jacqueline Cochoran, Washington, DC, for interview, physical exam, military flight checkout.

JH Cochoran
Chief of Operations, (WFTD)

"That's the craziest thing I ever heard of," said Stella Cohan, shaking her head derisively. "She wants to send girls off to war, flying airplanes? Being shot at?! Crazy! The woman must be completely bugs."

Not so crazy, thought Peggy. *A really interesting idea, in fact.*

The next day, Peggy found Timmy doping a patch on the aileron of a plane in the hangar. "Hey, Pegger. Wha'dyuh know, wha'dyuh say?"

"Hi, Tim."

"You hear the latest? Japs got the Philippines, the rats."

"Uh, yes. I heard. On the radio . . . Timmy, look. I got this telegram."

Peggy handed Tim the message from Jacqueline Cochoran.

Tim was impressed. "Wow. That's nifty. You gonna go? You ought to go."

"Well, I was thinking, maybe . . ."

"Hey, Peg, that's swell. I went down. They wouldn't take me. The ankle, y'know."

Years ago, Timmy Farrell had broken his ankle when he slipped from the high bar during a gymnastic exercise. He was showing off. When it healed, he was left with a limp.

"But I'm trying the Navy next. They need flyers, too, you know."

"I guess they do. Tim, it says there'll be a checkout flight."

"Yeah," Timmy replied. "Prob'ly basic handling, competence. They just wanna make sure you're not a ka-bibble."

"I have to pass that checkout ride. Timmy, it's important. Could you show me? Give me a real military-type checkout."

"You shouldn't have any trouble."

"I want to make sure."

"Peg, fuel's scarce. It's sure there's gonna be rationing. We've been told, forgo recreational flying."

"Timmy, it's really important. Please? Timmy?" She tossed her hair as her lips formed the patented pout that few men could resist. Timmy Farrell was no exception.

"I'd have to suck some gas from a coupla planes. Okay. Some pals in the Civil Air Patrol showed me a few things. Might help. How 'bout

Thursday, say noon?"

"Thanks, Timmy. You're the best." Peggy leaned over and planted an exuberant kiss on the young man's cheek. His face reddened while a grin spread nearly to his ears.

"See ya Thursday, 'bout noon."

Peggy walked off, quietly pleased. *At least some things still work.*

Early that Thursday Timmy took Peggy up for her "military lesson." He showed her some maneuvers that Army instructors might ask her to perform. There were power-on stalls, power-off stalls, all of which Peggy recovered from deftly. He showed her a loop with an Immelmann roll at the top, lazy eights, and slow rolls. He then had Peggy execute a Chandelle maneuver; a climb and a natural drop to a recovery. Basic "stalls and falls," he called them. Peggy grasped the new techniques quickly.

They then performed some wingovers around a church steeple and a local radio station antenna. Peggy learned how to correct as the nose dropped in such a tight turn. Timmy then directed Peggy to return to the field.

A bit soon, Peggy thought, but she complied. When they taxied to the parking ramp, there was an old biplane sitting next to Timmy's spot. When the Cub was parked and chocked, they walked over to the old ship.

"Peggy Cohan, I want you to meet a real war hero. Abner Morgan. Abner, this is Peggy Cohan, a damn good pilot."

"Pleasure to meet you, young lady," said the burly mustachioed barnstormer, as he bowed gallantly. He was laying on the codger bit rather heavily, dressed in railroad overalls with a well-worn olive, drab military shirt underneath. He dashingly sported a long white silk scarf, which lent a certain panache to his persona. To the uninitiated, the scarf might appear an affectation, excessive for the purposes of protecting the pilot's throat in the air. In reality, it served a more functional purpose. Vintage engines habitually gushed oil and the scarf was necessary to keep windshields and flying goggles clean and visibility clear. Accenting his outfit were silver-bullion embroidered wings along with several ribbons sewn onto the bib of his overalls. Together, with his worn leather flying helmet, he looked as ancient as his aircraft, a WWI Curtis JN-4 *Jenny*. Abner Morgan was only forty-six years old, but his outfit made him look like a long lost Wright brother.

Peggy was trying to understand the purpose of the introduction when Timmy explained.

"Abner's going to take you up in the *Jenny*. Let you handle the controls. Give you a brand new experience."

"Real flying, I call it," grinned Abner as he handed her a pair of goggles. "C'mon, hop in," he said, indicating the front seat.

As the old biplane started down the runway, Abner shouted to Peggy, "Go ahead, lift her off."

At this airspeed? Peggy thought, pushing at the already maxed throttle. But she hauled back on the control stick and the game old biplane literally hopped into the sky. Twice the wing surface, twice the lift. The exhilaration was greater than she had ever experienced in a closed cockpit. The air rushed past in a breathtaking flow like the caressing race of a waterfall. If any of her friends, the clouds, should appear, she realized she could easily reach out and touch them. Turning and diving and looping, *Jenny* made her heart soar in unison with the aircraft. It was a newfound happiness that lifted Peggy. A happiness that she worried might be undeserved.

Abner leaned forward and tapped Peggy on the shoulder. "It wasn't all tea and cakes at Verdun, y'know. The bloody Hun was trying his darndest to kill us. See that barge in the sound?"

Peggy nodded.

"Dive on him. Mind your altitude. Now keep that ole boat in the middle of the windscreen. Fill the windscreen with the target. Don't drift. Dead center. Now give him a long burst with your twin Vickers. Ah-ah-ah-ah-ah-ah-ah. Got him. Pull out now. Don't get yourself hypnotized. Seen a few lads buy it that way. Let's go 'round and do it again."

Peggy pulled up the *Jenny*. and made a banking turn and from one thousand yards out lined up once more on the slow-moving vessel.

"Keep him in the exact center. Stay with him. Fill the windscreen. Ah-ah-ah-ah-ah-ah-ah-ah. No doubt about it. You got that Heinie. Some fun, huh?"

Abner then had Peggy make a few gun passes at a nearby radio tower, where she emptied her imaginary machine guns at the imaginary Heinie lurking at the top behind the red light.

"Good job! Good flying," Abner told her. "Now, let's do some landings."

After several touch-and-goes by the veteran pilot, with Peggy holding her front stick lightly to follow his motion and timing, she made her own landing; a fairly smooth two-pointer, keeping the tail wheel up a tad longer than necessary.

Later, on the ground, Abner told Timmy, "She'll do. Right quick to learn."

Peggy and Timmy were still smiling from the compliment as the obsolete pair of sky creatures taxied out to the runway and took off. Timmy turned to Peggy and said, "How was that?"

Peggy's face broke into a wide, contented grin.

"Thought you'd like it."

Together they watched Abner and his *Jenny* vault into the air, make a climbing turn and then wave adieu with a slow transverse of the field.

11

While Peggy Cohan was immersed in a flying lesson at Flushing Airport, the President of the United States, Franklin Roosevelt, sat in the Oval Office reading the latest report from Wake Island. He sighed, dejectedly tossed the folder onto his desk, removed the pince-nez reading glasses from his nose, and rubbed his eyes.

"Pa, we are sorely in need of some good news. A show of retaliation. A victory. Something. When, for heaven's sake, are we going to do something?"

Retired Major General Edwin M. "Pa" Watson, the commander in chief's military secretary, nodded solemnly in agreement.

The idea came from a submarine commander, who related it to his admiral. Consider the possibility of a fully loaded, medium-sized twin-engine bomber taking off from an aircraft carrier to bomb the Japanese home islands. In order to accomplish this feat, a unique commander must be chosen and the aircrews would require special and extremely unorthodox training.

Eglin Field, Florida
US Army Air Corps
March 4, 1942

With the engines coming up to take-off power, the navigator

tapped the cigarette pack taped to the bulkhead of his work station two times for luck. Behind the cellophane, a color photo of a pretty young nurse shone out at him.

"Here goes nothin'," announced Capt. Bed Crandall as he and his copilot released the Mitchell's brakes and began their take off roll.

After an abbreviated run, Lieutenant Sam Caloon declared, "This is the craziest outfit I ever heard of," as he hauled back on the yoke of the *Boogie Woogie Baby* in unison with his pilot. The airspeed indicator had barely reached fifty knots.

The aircraft nosed up smartly, but both pilots worried that the radical angle wouldn't provide sufficient lift to coax the twin-engined B-25 bomber into the air. The entire aircraft reverberated as the tail skid encountered the concrete runway with a grinding clang.

"Oops," said Crandall. "We mighta overdid it."

But they were airborne. Lieutenant Caloon had already lifted the gear handle to "up" and set the flaps to "normal."

"Well, we're flyin'," said the copilot with a certain degree of diminishing skepticism.

From the navigator position, Lieutenant Nick Tolkin shouted toward the two front seats. "Head out to the water, continue due south for fifteen minutes, then return to Eglin and make a normal landing to the west."

"Gotcha! S'what they want, s'what we give 'em," said Capt. Crandall as he throttled back to the cruise setting.

Radio man/gunner Tech. Sgt. George Pua stuck his head into the flight deck area. "Hey, c'mon Skip. We guys tryin' to sleep back here."

The two pilots exchanged a smirk and an eye roll.

"You're makin' jokes?" said crew chief Tech. Sgt. Roscoe McCabe to the easygoing Hawaiian. "If that skid is crunched, ole buddy, you're gonna be helpin' me replace it."

"Screw you, McCabe."

"Hey, guys, simmer down," Nick Tolkin reminded his crewmates.

"Yes, sir, lieutenant, sir," said McCabe as he rendered a gimpy salute to the navigator.

Tolkin responded by thumbing his nose and wiggling his fingers at McCabe, a gesture which elicited grins from all five members of this closely knit aircrew.

"You think we tore up the skid any?" asked right-seater Caloon.

"We'll know when we land," answered Crandall.

In the Eglin tower, Lt. Col. Jimmy Doolittle and his Navy advisor on carrier flight procedures, Lt. Henry Miller, were observing the take offs of the new squadron's planes. A Mitchell was on its take off roll; using too much runway, taking too much time.

"'Too hard! Over seven hundred feet, Jimmy," announced Lt. Miller as the aircraft became airborne.

"Jacobson's crew, isn't it?" Col. Doolittle asked.

"Yes sir, one of our most experienced pilots."

"Maybe the older they are, the more reluctant to change their habits. Old dog, new tricks y'know."

"Maybe. *Boogie Woogie Baby*—that's Crandall's crew—made it in 455 feet, but might've scraped their tail a bit."

"Well, short of damaging the aircraft, that's exactly what we want," declared Doolittle. "A commitment to doing something entirely different."

The *Boogie Woogie Baby* made a routine landing, taxied to its former parking place, shut down its engines and was chocked by the ground crew. Caloon and McCabe exited hurriedly to check the tail skid.

When the ground crew chief sidled over out of curiosity, Caloon asked him, "What d'yuh think?"

The mechanic cocked his head, pursed his lips and said, "I seen worse."

"A little scraped, hardly dented," observed the relieved McCabe. "A coupla dabs of paint, no one's the wiser."

Sgt. Pua came over, leaned in toward the skid. Smiling, he said, "We got a way with one, brudda."

As the aircrew gathered to view the tail skid one could observe nothing particularly distinctive about these Americans. They were young men, of medium height and build, with the redheaded McCabe slightly taller than the others and Pua, the Hawaiian, slightly stockier. Crandall, the captain, had blond hair, his copilot, Caloon, brown hair. The round-faced Polynesian's hair was stick-straight and black. Nick Tolkin, the navigator, had a dark complexion with dark, curly hair, plus the disarming incongruity of piercing blue eyes. But in terms of a desire to get into the fight and a determination to "win through", the men of this aircrew were no different from the many thousands of young Americans who had come forward to serve their country. Ready to do whatever it was that their country asked of them. At this moment their country was asking them to execute a take off with a medium bomber from a 400 foot strip of land.

Just then a jeep careened toward the crew and skidded to a halt beside the plane.

"Sirs," declared the jovial driver, a private with a crew cut who had his cap stuffed in the back pocket of his fatigue pants. "You'se is supposed to report to Ops. C'mon, I'll take you. No charge." His manner conveyed all the insouciance of a New York cabbie.

Capt. Crandall took the seat next to the driver and the rest of the crew began to drape themselves over the remaining seats and flat surfaces of the jeep. Inexplicably, Nick Tolkin hopped off and sprinted back to the aircraft.

"Hey, where you going?" Caloon shouted after Nick. "Forget somethin'?"

"Yeah," said Nick over his shoulder, "my cigarettes."

Back in the plane, the navigator removed a flattened pack of Luckies from the bulkhead above his workstation. Beneath the cellophane was the photograph he had torn from a magazine; a pretty blonde nurse holding a book. The girl's attention seemed to be directed to someone or something beside her but that portion of the picture had been folded under.

Tolkin carefully stowed the pack and photograph in the breast pocket of his flight suit, buttoned it up, and hurried to join his mates in the jeep.

They sped off to the operations building where they would receive the comments and criticism of Col. Doolittle.

The training lasted three weeks, at which time most of the crews had mastered the short take off technique. The order to Doolittle to "get on your horse," which came from Washington, meant that ready or not, the B-25s would proceed to McClellan Air Field near Sacramento to receive the designated modifications for the mission. There, auxiliary fuel tanks were installed, along with new high-efficiency propellers and specially adjusted new carburetors, all of which would increase the range of the aircraft by another five hundred miles.

Once modified, the special squadron of B-25s flew to Alameda Air Station in San Francisco. There, the planes were drained of fuel, hooked up to a Navy "donkey," and towed to the docks to be hoisted onto the flight deck of the USS Hornet, America's newest carrier.

The crew of *Boogie Woogie Baby* assembled on the dock as the crane lifted their plane. The five airmen observed the process the way a father watches his little girl pedaling off on a two-wheeler for the first time. As the empty crane swung back towards the dock to hook up the next B-25, the *Baby's* relieved crew boarded the carrier. They saluted the flag, then the officer of the deck, stating name and rank and announcing, "Reporting aboard for duty, sir." Lt. Miller looked down from his vantage point on the flight deck, pleased that the flyers had remembered the Navy protocol he had taught them.

When sixteen aircraft had been loaded, Col. Doolittle announced, "That's it. These are the planes that will go." Five B-25s would be left behind, but their crews were ordered aboard to serve as back-ups for the mission.

On April 2, 1942, under cover of a dense fog, the first component of Task Force 16 weighed anchor and steamed out under the span of the Golden Gate Bridge and headed out to sea. The Yorktown class carrier, Hornet, was accompanied by the cruisers *Nashville* and *Vincennes*. Destroyers *Gwin, Meredith,* and *Grayson* and the oiler, *Cimarron,* would rendezvous in the middle of the Pacific with the carrier, *Enterprise*, Admiral Halsey's flagship, and its complement of escorts. Their goal: to put Special Aviation Project Number 1 in position to accomplish its mission. Ordinarily a task force of this type included a battleship or two, but because of the action at Pearl Harbor, no battleships were available.

Two days out at sea, Col. Doolittle called his crews together for the long awaited announcement of the target of their mission. "In a few short days, we will be striking at the very heart of the Japanese empire. Our target is Tokyo." The briefing room erupted with cheers and enthusiastic shouts.

"We're gonna hit 'em where it hurts!" someone exclaimed. "Right in the breadbasket!"

The army top brass understood that an attack on Tokyo by a small contingent of medium bombers would cause insignificant damage and have negligible military value, but they fully appreciated the enormous psychological effect of such a venture. The war in the Pacific was not going well. The Japanese were expanding their territorial sphere almost at will. Since Pearl Harbor, the Philippines and Bataan had fallen and MacArthur was forced to evacuate Corregidor because of its imminent capitulation. President Roosevelt implored his generals to find a way to take the war to the enemy as quickly as possible. This mission was the answer to the commander in chief's request.

Victory had come so easily for the Japanese that they began to see themselves as invincible. Their propaganda confidently assured the people of the home islands that the war would never touch their own sacred soil. This daring raid would hopefully cast the first shadows of doubt on the invulnerability of the Empire.

As the Hornet and its escort of destroyers, cruisers, and tenders steamed westward, the B-25 crews received their briefings. Enlargements of photos taken by many different agents showing various views of the Tokyo area were displayed and discussed. And then a remarkable 16mm film of the Tokyo skyline was shown. It was taken by Moe Berg, catcher for the Boston Red Sox some eight years past. Berg, while visiting Japan on a baseball exhibition tour, filmed the city from a tall building. He captured Tokyo and the outlying areas in marvelous clarity.

Areas of Kobe, Osaka, Nagoya, Yokohama, and Tokyo were designated as targets. Each crew was permitted to select its own specific target and escape route to China. Colonel Doolittle stressed that concrete structures were to be avoided because minimal damage could be inflicted. He also declared residential areas off limits, then added the admonition that no hotshot should attempt to drop an egg on the Imperial Palace. "Put a shipyard or factory out of action and you will help our cause far more than an insult to their 'divine' emperor."

"There will be airfields in China alerted to your coming. Fires will be lit to outline the strips where you will be able to refuel and continue on to Nationalist-held Chun King. Be prepared for some last minute changes on the location of the fields since there's been a considerable increase in Japanese incursions on the Chinese mainland."

"Question," said navigator/bombardier Tolkin as he raised his hand.

"Go ahead," said Lt. Commander Jurika, the Hornet's intelligence officer.

"Why not land in Russia? It's just as close and they are our allies, aren't they? Plus, they haven't been invaded by the Japanese."

Jurika and Doolittle exchanged a glance and Jurika waited for Doolittle to answer.

"It gets a bit complicated, Nick. I can understand you wanting to visit your hometown and all."

Doolittle waited as the crews chuckled at his little quip.

"But it seems that option is closed to us. Politics. Something about the Russians not being officially at war with Japan even though they are our allies. With all the trouble they've got with the Heinies, I don't think they want to provoke the Japanese on their southeastern border. Suffice it to say, we will hightail it to China after hitting our Japanese targets. That's not a straight answer but it's the best I can offer."

"Yes, sir. Thank you, sir," said Tolkin as he took his seat.

As the convoy plowed forward into the turbulent April weather of the Pacific, the mechanics worked round the clock to ready the B-25s for the mission. Fuel leaks, electrical problems, and jammed gun turrets plagued the stressed maintenance crews as the distance to the Empire of the Rising Sun grew shorter.

Thousands of miles to the east in a federal office in Washington, DC, two stylishly dressed women shuffled through stacks of paperwork.

"Here's a strange one," said Jane Medford, special assistant to Jacqueline Cochoran, as she sifted through the morning's pile of responses to her telegrams.

"Why strange?" asked Jackie.

"Well, she's so young. Barely eighteen. Got the hours but no college . . ." answered Marge.

"Well, if she's too . . ." Jacqueline began to say.

But Jane continued, "Her name is Peggy Cohan. Fashion model. Name ring a bell?"

Peggy Cohan? Jacqueline repeated the name silently to herself. "Yes, of course! She's a top girl. Conover girl. You say her hours are good?"

"Over a hundred," Jane read from her letter.

"Let's send her an invitation. We could use a little style in this outfit. Plus, if she can fly worth a lick there might be some juicy publicity opportunities for our cause."

"And the college?"

"Heck," said Jacqueline, exaggerating her drawl. "I ain't never went to no college and it ain't done me no harm."

"Okay, Jackie, she gets her invitation."

"Fine," said Jacqueline Cochoran, "what else?"

"Lunch today with Mrs. Roosevelt."

"Yes, of course, thank you Jane. There'll be photographers. I ought to buy a hat."

12

Insterberg, East Prussia
A Luftwaffe Airbase
April 17, 1942

It was long past sunset when the strange aircraft overflew the base. The few who noticed its presence in the fading light were struck by the unusual sound; more like the strident rasp of a rocket than the familiar growl of piston engines. The craft circled slowly in the final shimmering light of dusk, lowered its landing gear, and set down gently on the long concrete runway just as night enfolded the base. Only an odd guttural roar bracketed by red navigation lights evidenced its presence. Earlier that afternoon the order had been given for all operations to be suspended. Returning missions were recovered, serviced, and buttoned up for the night. The normally hyperactive Luftwaffe installation was experiencing an impromptu stand down, as if in anticipation of something extraordinary.

During the night, security vehicles were observed charging noisily back and forth around the base. Extra details had been turned out to patrol the perimeter, roadways, entrances. In the morning, all maintenance was suspended, civilian access to the base was curtailed, and the labor gangs who cut grass and performed runway maintenance were directed to remain in their huts for an unprecedented day off.

The concrete ramp in front of the main maintenance hangars, normally crowded with aircraft, had been cleared. Today the space was filled with more shiny staff cars than anyone had ever seen in one place. At approximately ten a.m., a long, six-wheeled, tan and black Mercedes approached the main gate. The staff car did not slow nor did the guards impede it. The large car drove directly to the ramp and stopped in front of the other vehicles. A young major bounded from the front passenger seat and hurried around to open the rear door. Adolph Hitler, the Führer of the German state and master of Europe, stepped out. He wore an open trench coat over the simple gray uniform of a Wehrmacht officer. There was no rank at the collar or on the visor of his cap. Only the Iron Cross, first class, adorned the breast of his jacket.

He was immediately greeted by Field Marshal Hugo Sperrle, the commandant of Luftflotte II. This base at Insterberg, East Prussia, was the headquarters of his command. The Führer acknowledged the man with a perfunctory nod and strode briskly past him toward a group of officers standing at attention in what seemed to be a prepared viewing area.

The Führer waved the group at ease and after shaking the hands of the most prominent of them—Hermann Goering, Ehrhard Milch, and Inspector General of Fighters, Dolph Galland—he turned and addressed the lone civilian in the group. "Well, Professor Messerschmitt, what sort of wizardry do you have for me today?" The Führer had been briefed that there would be a presentation of a new type of aircraft but he playfully chose to feign ignorance.

"I would prefer to present it in a little demonstration, mein Führer, if that is acceptable."

The Führer made a slight nod and waved his hand, giving his assent to proceed.

"If you would then direct your attention to the east end of the runway, mein Führer," Messerschmitt said, and pointed.

As the group turned to the indicated direction, the aircraft designer made eye contact with Goering and Dolph Galland, both of whom had barely suppressed smirks like mischievous boys.

Their reactions, although subtle, were observed through a pair of compact yet powerful binoculars held by a raggedly dressed man crouching behind a low storage shed some two hundred meters distant. The man was part of the labor gang that performed runway maintenance; a crew made up of petty criminals, drunkards, and misfits harvested from local jails. He wore a green inverted triangle on the left breast of his coat, the designation for "habitual criminal." In the Reich, everyone was put to use. This particular misfit, however, happened to be a British agent. The spy, nearly unnerved by the appearance of Adolph Hitler himself, shakily turned his glasses to the direction Dr. Messerschmitt was pointing.

It was then that the spectators heard the sound. Low, eerie, mournful, like a large animal in distress. Everyone, the Führer, his generals, the soldiers, and the spy focused on the intense, unearthly moan. The sound grew louder and more urgent as it approached. Then, at the far end of the field, it appeared. A sleek, shark-like, twin-engined aircraft taxiing onto the main runway. Aside from its rakishly elegant appearance, there was something odd about it. But what? Its motors. There were no propellers. As it drew closer, revealing sooty smoke trailing from its engines, the observation was confirmed. No visible propellers. How does this thing fly? What is the technology behind it? Could it be a rocket? These questions and more flashed through the minds of both the official spectators and the hidden observer. They also shared the conclusion that the strange new aircraft wasn't moving very quickly. In fact, it was still rolling, making a frightful din, when most aircraft should have been airborne. To the relief of all, including the British agent, the aircraft's nose lifted and the propeller-less craft rose laboriously from the concrete. As it did, the howl segued to a crackling, earsplitting shriek. The craft seemed to shudder as it struggled to gain altitude. Not a very impressive rate of climb, concluded the observers, both official and unofficial. A telescope mounted on a tripod stood in the viewing area. Messerschmitt stooped to view his invention through the eyepiece for a moment, then bade his Führer look. Hitler peered through the scope and tracked the aircraft's laborious ascent until it was out of sight.

Judging from the expressions on the face of the Führer and most of the other spectators, the demonstration had left them decidedly unimpressed. Goering, Messerschmitt, and Galland, however, were smiling. They seemed unconcerned with what could only be considered a less than stellar initial impression. Professor Messerschmitt turned to his unimpressed Führer, offered a slight smile and held up his finger as if to say, "Bear with us for a few moments, sir!" The Führer responded with a curt nod but his face revealed his undisguised disappointment. Undaunted, Messerschmitt confidently gestured to the westerly sky, the direction the propeller-less aircraft had taken. The Führer indulgently turned his attention to the direction indicated. The others followed suit.

With virtually no warning it was upon them. Diving out of the high overcast and leveling out at approximately thirty meters, the aircraft flew past almost before the sound was heard; a deafening roar much like the sound of a dozen artillery shells passing directly overhead. The Führer and several officers flinched in surprise. Upon recovering from the shock, Hitler swung the telescope to view the impossibly fast craft becoming a shrinking gray-green dot in the blue Prussian sky.

This is big, gasped the amazed British agent to himself. *That bloody thing must have been making over 500 mph. A plane like that could turn the tide of the war. With that kind of speed they could decimate Allied bombers and leave their fighter escorts in the dust. This aircraft could easily turn the coming invasion into a second Dunkirk.*

Now a different sound imposed itself on the scene. A conventional aircraft coming in fast from the east. As the spectators turned they were able to make out the familiar form of a Focke-Wulf 190 approaching at about thirty meters above the runway. This was the Reich's latest and fastest fighter, built by Messerschmitt's competitor. As the 190 was nearly abreast of the viewing area, the new propeller-less craft appeared in an earsplitting roar. The jet seemed to burst from nowhere to overtake the 190, then outdistanced it as if it was a tethered kite.

As the jet disappeared into the blue, all eyes tracked the 190 as it seemed to drone ploddingly onward. The pleased Führer impulsively clapped Messerschmitt on the shoulder and reached out to shake his hand, but the engineer gestured to indicate that there was still more to come. After a few silent minutes the faint presence of another aircraft could be heard approaching from the west. One more fast-moving propeller aircraft was coming in at treetop height. This time it was a North American P-51. The Germans had somehow captured one of the new Allied fighters and repainted it in Luftwaffe markings. This aircraft, purported to be the fastest fighter in the American arsenal, could attain a speed of 440 mph in level flight, faster even than the 190. Its sleek, pugnacious design supported its nickname, *Wildhorse*. As the P-51 approached the observation area, it too was overtaken in an aggressive diving pass by the new wonder plane. Hitler moved to the telescope in order to continue viewing his new prize weapon. The demonstration could not have been more dramatic. Here was a new aircraft able to best the latest technology of both sides as if they were slugs on a garden path.

A spontaneous celebration broke out in the viewing area. Congratulations were exchanged all around. The Führer was delighted. He actually hopped with enthusiasm. A great demonstration. A triumph for the Reich. And damnable bad news for the Allies.

Through his field glasses, the British agent observed the faces of the spectators. *The Boshe are swanning about as if they had already won the bloody war,* he grimly remarked to himself. *Bastards! Well, we'll see, won't we?*

A short time later, the aircraft landed and taxied triumphantly to the observation area. There, Hitler inspected the remarkable aircraft with great interest and offered his personal congratulations to the factory test pilot, Fritz Wendel. In an uncharacteristic display of magnanimity, the Führer announced to the group that he was extremely pleased with the demonstration of this new technology and it was innovations such as these which would assure inevitable victory for the Reich.

Hitler then drew the aircraft designer aside and they walked together toward the staff cars. "I have one question, Herr Professor Doctor Messerschmitt. Can this impressive new aircraft of yours carry bombs?"

The engineer responded immediately. "Yes, mein Führer, it certainly can. But of course, there would need to be certain special modifications."

The Führer, however, was no longer listening. He had heard only the word "yes." He then once again offered the engineer his hand.

"My congratulations, Professor Messerschmitt, and my thanks. You have given me my blitz bomber. And with it we will finally crush the Communist hordes in the east and make our Atlantic wall truly impenetrable. Yes! A most excellent birthday gift! A bomber that is invulnerable, that is what you have given me, my dear professor."

Hitler's birthday was only three days off.

Hitler then turned, accepted the salute of the assembled group, stepped into his six-wheeled staff car and sped off.

Blitz bomber? thought the shaken Messerschmitt. *I have produced an air superiority fighter aircraft and the man wants me to turn it into a dump truck?*

Early the next morning a rather lengthy coded message describing the previous day's demonstration was carefully folded and taped under the accelerator pedal of a small Opel truck. This vehicle left the base twice each week and traveled to the nearby town of Lötzen to pick up supplies for the officers' mess. A two-inch stripe of fresh gray paint marked the left front tire.

In Lötzen, the message was retrieved by a warehouse clerk and passed to a railroad conductor, who carried it aboard a troop train heading west. Once in France, the message was passed to a young woman in the train station who was presenting newly knitted wool socks to the soldiers as they disembarked from the train. The sock girl secreted the message in her basket and that evening delivered it to a member of the resistance. On the next moonless night, a canvas bag containing the message was snatched from the ground by a tree-skimming British Westland Lysander. The message was decoded at the intelligence center at Bletchley Park in London and taken by motorcycle courier to SOE headquarters on Baker Street.

Somewhere along its journey from the Insterberg Luftwaffe base in Prussia to British Intelligence in London, a duplicate of the message was made and routed to an NKVD operative in Zurich whose code name was "Lucy." A few days later the message arrived at the Commissariat for Internal Affairs (NKVD) in Moscow and flagged to the attention of Chief of Soviet Intelligence, Lavrenti Beria.

13

The US Carrier Hornet
1,000 miles from the Japanese Islands
April 18, 1942

Steaming east in rough seas at twenty-five knots, the yeoman found Captain Mitscher at his place on the bridge. He was wearing his trademark baseball cap, the first captain in the Navy to institute the custom.

"Message from the flagship, sir."

Captain Mitscher read Halsey's message: LAUNCH PLANES. TO COL. DOOLITTLE'S GALLANT COMMAND. GOOD LUCK AND GOD BLESS YOU.

"Wake up, we're goin'!" was the word echoed through both the enlisted men's quarters and the officers' compartments two decks above. The Army aviators scrambled to dress and shave, a major project for those who had succumbed to the romantic notion of growing a beard while at sea. When all had assembled in the carrier's ready room for Col. Doolittle's final instructions, many of the flyers' faces sported numerous razor nicks staunched by dots of white toilet paper.

"We can't be four-hundred miles from Tokyo," Capt. Bedford Crandall remarked to his copilot, Sam Caloon, in the seat beside him. "Last night we were well over one-thousand miles from the Jap coast."

Caloon merely shrugged.

Col. Doolittle explained that earlier that morning some Jap picket boats had been sighted. "They appeared to be fishing vessels but then we intercepted a radio message to the mainland originating from one of the boats.

"We must therefore assume that our position has been compromised. In order not to further endanger our mission or this task force, we've been given the order to launch at first light. If this carrier were to be attacked by enemy aircraft, our Mitchells would have to be deep-sixed to clear the decks for the Hornet's own fighters. We are presently seven-hundred miles from our target, six fifty by the time we launch. The extra two hundred shouldn't make much difference."

Few in the room bought that one.

"We've trained long and hard for this mission, now let's give those Japs a taste of their own medicine!"

There were no cheers or shouts. Only a quiet sense of resolve.

"I'll be the first plane off. Wish me luck, gentlemen."

No one spoke in response.

"Then, good luck to us all."

As the crews were dismissed, the engineers bolted from the room and up to the flight deck. They all had the same idea; get those fuel tanks so full of 100 octane that they couldn't hold another drop.

The overcast was punctuated by tattered clumps of cigarette-ash dark clouds, which discharged intermittent squalls of cold, stinging rain on the ground crews hurrying to remove canvas engine and canopy covers.

Two white lines had recently been painted on the flight deck to help the aircrews line up properly for their takeoff roll. The thin line was to align the nose wheel of the bomber. The thicker, outboard marker was to line up the left main gear. This track would provide the right wing of each aircraft six feet of clearance from the carrier island.

Since Col. Doolittle was first in line, he would not only confirm that a fully laden B-25 could indeed take off from the short deck of a carrier, but he would be doing it from the shortest length of runway.

The Hornet swung into the wind as the crews nervously boarded their planes. They were well aware that any unairworthy aircraft would have to be pushed over the side to clear the way for the bomber behind it. To conserve fuel, engines could only be started when the aircraft in front had begun its take off roll. This was no place for a hard starting engine. There were last minute reminders from the launch officer written on a large blackboard which he held up to each aircraft. *Stay on the line. Stabilizer in neutral. Full flaps. Good hunting.*

With engines screaming into the forty-five knot gale produced by the aggregate of ship speed and wind velocity, Colonel Doolittle and his copilot, Lt. Richard E. Cole, simultaneously released the straining brakes and their Mitchell lurched forward. Remarkably, the fully loaded bomber vaulted into the air with a good thirty feet of deck to spare. The next aircraft, engines revving up to take off speed, was manhandled into position and given the signal to go. The second plane left the flight deck but then dropped out of sight, giving everyone a fright. The pilot had held the nose up too long, but corrected at the last moment and the Mitchell recovered and rose into the air. Nearly the entire crew of the Hornet, plus the bomber squadron's maintenance teams, breathed a sigh of relief as they stood to witness this questionable and unorthodox operation.

When it was *Boogie Woogie Baby's* turn, she taxied jerkily out toward the white lines. Capt. Crandall had carefully aligned her left main gear on the thick outboard line. Then he and copilot Caloon depressed the brakes and inched the throttles forward. At an rpm slightly over normal take off and a manifold pressure of fifty inches of mercury, she stabilized and stood shuddering on the deck like an overanxious thoroughbred. Bed Crandall slid back the side window and with a gloved thumbs up indicated to the launch officer that they were at prescribed rpms. The launch officer whirled his checkered flag in the air faster and faster, requesting even more power, trusting his ears to determine optimum take off revs. When finally satisfied with the sound, he raised both arms in the air and turned to watch the pitching bow of the carrier deck. The moment after the deck reached its furthest downward movement he swung both arms forward with the signal to go. Crandall and Caloon released the brakes and the screaming twin-engined bird plunged into the wind, receiving added momentum from the downward pitch of the tilted deck. As the *Baby* approached the end of its run, the deck began its upward sway and literally flipped the bomber into the air like a spatula under a perfectly browned pancake. Crandall's eyes stayed glued to the white line on the port side. Suddenly the line disappeared and was replaced by water—dark, angry, roiling seawater. They were airborne. The crew of *Boogie Woogie Baby* exhaled a collective "Whew!" Now they banked to starboard and awaited their comrades just below the overcast. When all sixteen Mitchells had successfully launched, Col. Doolittle's plane flew directly over the length of the Hornet, which had altered its course to an exact vector towards Japan and set his heading. All sixteen aircraft followed suit. The craziest part of the mission had been accomplished; launch a squadron of bombers from an aircraft carrier. Next up was the most sensible part of the mission: drop a few calling cards on the Japanese homeland. The crews gave little thought to the least sensible part of the mission; landing safely after they'd paid their respects to the Empire of the Sun. But so it is with heroes.

The airmen had been directed to leave all personal effects such as wallets, photos, and letters behind. These were collected and locked away in a steel cabinet aboard the Hornet. The navigator of the *Boogie Woogie Baby*, however, did not fully comply with the order. In his pocket he kept an empty pack of cigarettes with a folded photo cut from a two-year-old *LIFE* magazine under the cellophane. After double-checking their heading and calculating a preliminary ETA to the IP, he removed the empty package of Luckies from his breast pocket.

"Hey," shouted the engineer, Sgt. McCabe. "Don't nobody light up. We're leakin' gas all over the place."

"Don't worry, Roscoe, packs empty. See," said Nick. "Just makin' use of the cellophane."

Tolkin taped the empty Luckies pack with the magazine photo to the bulkhead of his workstation. From behind the cellophane, the striking face of the young nurse once again reassured him. The first time he had seen the photo, he was captivated by the girl. When he stumbled upon the photo a second time while thumbing through an old issue of *LIFE*, he impulsively tore out the page. How many times since had Nick Tolkin thought about this girl? *What is she like? How tall is she? She looks tall. Is she funny? I mean, does she have a sense of humor? She might easily be cold and stuck up, with those looks.* But somehow he didn't think so. *She's got a good heart. It's only a magazine, but there's something about her. I just know she's got a good heart.*

The smell of gas intruded upon his reverie.

"Hey, Roscoe," Tolkin shouted, "we must really be leaking. The whole compartment stinks."

"I know, I know! Near as I can figure that aux tank in the crawl space over the bomb bay is holed pretty bad. Pua says he can see streams of gas runnin' out the back of the bomb bay. That tank shoulda took us up to the Jap coast but we've been out less than an hour and it's nearly half empty."

Oh shit, thought Nick. *Fuel problems. Better let the skipper know.*

Nick made a few calculations on the circular slide rule and confirmed the bad news. Fuel consumption which should have been 70-75 gallons per hour was being burned and leaked at a rate of 98 gallons per hour.

Nick presented the situation to the flight deck.

"Okay, Nick," said Crandall, "plot us a course straight in. We got no choice."

Nick nodded and set to work. The original plan was to come from the southernmost part of the Japanese islands and hit Tokyo from the southwest. This plan was based on the theory that the defenses would be protecting against an attack from the east. The fuel situation now dictated a straight-in attack. Let's hope the gunners aren't waiting for us, was the silent prayer of the crewmen.

When the new heading was given to the flight deck, Nick turned to lend a hand to Pua and McCabe, emptying the extra five-gallon cans of gas into the tank rigged to fit in the lower turret. Over a dozen cans stowed in every available corner and crevice were employed. This was an idea of one of the Hornet's airdales. *God bless that guy.* With his screwdriver, McCabe punched holes in the empties so they'd sink when jettisoned. No point in providing a shiny trail back to the Hornet.

Two hundred miles out, the overcast opened up and weather turned CAVU—ceiling and visibility unlimited.

"We're going to arrive around high noon on a crystal clear day," Nick informed the pilots. In the moment that information sunk in, each man had the same thought: *the Jap gunners would be salivating.*

With a steady, reassuring drone, the Mitchell's engines devoured the miles of open ocean, leaving each of the crew to quietly contemplate their role in this improbable expedition. Shattering the reverie of his crewmates, Tolkin announced, "We could be seeing land any time now."

Within a half hour Caloon shouted, "There!" He pointed as a coastline appeared on the distant horizon.

"Providing that's not Korea," said Capt. Crandall, "we've got our target ahead of us. Nick, what're our chances of making China after we unload?"

"Very doubtful," responded Nick. "We either ditch in the Sea of Japan or put 'er down in Korea."

"Awright, Nick, you get your wish. We head for Russia. Plot us a track to those godless Commie bastards."

"I'm on it," said Nick.

It was several minutes more at wave top level when Caloon made another sighting.

"There! What's that?"

"Good eye," said Tolkin. "If that's not a factory smokestack, it should be the Inubo Saki lighthouse. Yokohama's there," he said, indicating left. "Tokyo's straight ahead."

As the *Baby* hedgehopped over the outskirts of the enemy's capital city, the crew could make out a schoolyard with a baseball field and a flagpole flying the rising sun emblem. Kids at recess could be observed waving at the *Baby* as she flew over.

At this altitude it was difficult to make out landmarks, let alone targets.

"Gotta take her up," announced Crandall and climbed to 1,500 feet. This was a trade off; better visibility for the crew but also a better line for the Japanese gunners.

In the distance on every side, isolated plumes of black smoke and ground fires could be observed. Clearly, the first of the squadron's bombers had made their presence felt. In response, the air was filled with black puffs of lethal flak seemingly fired indiscriminately into the air around them. The untested AA gunners appeared to be panicked and undisciplined.

The *Baby* carried three five-hundred-pound demolition bombs and clusters of incendiaries, making up a total of over 2,000 pounds of ordnance. The crew was hoping for four good targets.

"Doors open," declared Nick.

Up ahead, puffs of black smoke dotted the sky. Japanese antiaircraft gunners were overleading the Mitchell. Behind them, the crew could see tracers arcing. These gunners had spotted them but were not leading the aircraft sufficiently.

"Power plant dead ahead," shouted Caloon.

"I got it," answered Nick, now ensconced in the nose of the aircraft, his head aligned with the improvised aluminum bombsight. The Norden had been removed because of the low altitude attack plan and the high possibility of capture.

"One gone. The other away," shouted Tolkin as he toggled two five-hundred pounders.

"Gotta see this," said Crandall as he banked the *Baby* into a tight circle in order to view the effect of the drop. His eyes and the crew's were rewarded by the sight of a ravaged structure, flaming debris, and a toppling smokestack amidst billowing black smoke.

As the coal blossoms of flak grew thicker and the tracer fire intensified, a second target came into view. A factory of some kind. Nick dropped an egg but there was no time to turn and assess the damage. The crew was rewarded by a huge concussion which shook the plane.

"Musta been a dynamite factory," said the grinning Pua.

As the aircraft turned west, then northwest, a truck factory appeared ahead. The *Baby* dropped its last load, consisting of incendiary clusters, which seeded the roof of the main building and the tops of newly built trucks parked in the adjacent lot, their timed fuses patiently waiting to ignite. A close flak burst peppered the right fuselage and tail of the *Baby*, sounding like hail pummeling a tin roof.

"Doors?" shouted Caloon.

"Doors closed!" Nick replied.

"Then let's get the hell out of here," said Crandall as he maxed the throttle and dove for the deck, ducking under the increasingly closer antiaircraft bursts. Divested of her bomb load, the *Baby* felt lighter and wanted to run.

As they were hedgehopping on the western outskirts of town, Tolkin shouted, "Will ya look at that." Ahead and slightly east of their course was an airfield with dozens of aircraft lined up neatly along the taxiway.

"Ooh, ooh," shouted Pua. "Lemme, lemme. I don wanna go tru dis whole war without shootin' off dis gun."

Tolkin turned and set the machine gun in the lower aperture of the Plexiglas nose and then moved aside to allow Pua access to the fifty.

Crandall altered course slightly so that Pua could get a good alignment on the parked aircraft.

"Nakajimas," said Caloon. "Give 'em the works, George."

"Payback!" shouted Pua as he gleefully macerated the newly built line of fighter bombers.

It was all over very quickly after which Crandall, once again dropped to treetop level, followed a valley down to the rocky shores of the Sea of Japan, out over the whitecaps and away from the deadly black blossoms and neon stingers directed at them by the inhabitants of a shocked and angry city.

It was late afternoon when they made landfall. Worried that they might have reached the coast of Korea, they turned right, ninety degrees north, to make sure it was Russia. Some of the landmarks confirmed they were indeed over Soviet territory. They now flew low so that they would provide less of a target for what might be nervous Soviet gunners.

"That should be Slavyanka, according to my chart," announced Tolkin to the pilots on the flight deck. "Follow the shore line north and we should make Vladivostok."

With the gas gauges pegged on empty and the crew expecting to hear the sound a straw makes when you get to the bottom of a soda, the men scanned the terrain off the port side.

"C'mon, any big grass field will do. Keep your eyes peeled," Crandall urged his men.

"There! Look at that!" Sam Caloon shouted victoriously.

"Yep, that's an airstrip. Nice goin', Sam," said Capt. Crandall. The grass airstrip had a dozen or so green-winged biplanes parked beside a main hangar. Crandall set the *Baby* down softly and taxied toward the low buildings, ready to shove the throttles forward if the soldiers standing around the area had slanted eyes. The men who walked toward them were Caucasians and were smiling. With the engines cut, Crandall slid open his side window.

"Tovarich!" one of the soldiers shouted to the men in the bomber.

"Tovarich! We're Americans!" Nick shouted in return.

"Americanskiy!" acknowledged one of the soldiers, which brought smiles of relief to both the aviators and the men on the ramp.

"We made it, you guys," Capt. Crandall shouted to his crew. "If they give us some fuel we can fly all the way to Chun King."

"Where are we?" said Tolkin, pointing to the ground.

"Here Tavrichanka!" declared one of the officers, gesturing all around him.

With the *Baby* chocked, the aviators were shown to a small structure which served as the operations office. There, Nick attempted to convey to the officials that they were Americans based in China on a reconnaissance mission and had gotten lost. He requested fuel for his aircraft so they could be on their way again. On the insistence of a Russian officer, the aviators reluctantly surrendered their sidearms.

The Russian's response was, "You must here remain. Have interview. Now to make eat." He gestured to his mouth with curved fingers, nodding.

To the five aviators who had just completed an impossibly dangerous mission, the meal of boiled beef, cabbage, and caviar was a victory feast. Later, as darkness fell, they were ushered to nearby barracks where they were told they were to spend the night. The straw-filled mattresses and steel bunks felt like the Ritz. Mission accomplished, crew and aircraft intact. Tomorrow they'd be winging their way home. It was a grand feeling.

In the morning, a Russian colonel arrived and shared a hearty breakfast with them. Although he spoke no English, the men were comforted by his expression of camaraderie to fellow aviators. When their meal of caviar, bread, blini, and yogurt was finished, the Americans were ushered out to the ramp, past the *Boogie Woogie Baby* and onto a Russian-marked C-47, which flew them several hundred miles north to Khabarovsk.

Very reluctant to leave the *Baby,* the unarmed Americans had no choice but to comply.

In Khabarovsk, they were interviewed by a three-star general who, though quite affable, clearly did not buy the story of lost aviators from China.

They were then informed that they and their aircraft were to be held until their story could be verified and that any belongings left in their ship would be brought to them. The fortunes of the intrepid crew of aircraft number eight of Lt. Col. Doolittle's bomber squadron had changed somewhat for the worse. They were stuck. Out of the war for at least the time being, which to the crew meant they were virtual prisoners. But still, they were alive.

14

Boarding the train at Penn Station, Peggy steeled herself for yet another prolonged train ride, this time fleeing from all that was familiar towards the unknown. Spending time with Cece and visiting the house in which she grew up was only a temporary antidote to her harrowing Hollywood experience. But as the days passed, Peggy felt an ominous and growing unease. Hopefully this new adventure might provide the remedy she so desperately sought. Peggy understood that her compulsion to flee to the unknown was irrational. And that frightened her a bit. But better the unknown, she reasoned, than the rebuke fraught here and now.

Timmy had gallantly volunteered to drive her to the station. Dear Timmy. Peggy, of course, refused, and he, naturally, insisted. She refused more strongly and he insisted more vehemently. Finally, realizing it was better to give in than continue the futile conversation, she accepted his offer, reminding herself that he was just trying to be nice.

Why do I resent someone being nice? she asked herself. To make matters worse, Timmy gave her a present when he dropped her off at the station.

"Don't open it until you're on the train, kiddo," he told her with a sly grin, then jumped into his truck and, with a wave, sped off into the flow of traffic heading up 34th Street.

Now in her seat, she contemplated her exodus strategy. She chose to travel light with one bag checked in to Chicago, another smaller suitcase in the rack above her seat.

When she first arrived at Penn Station, Peggy found an agitated crowd with many frustrated people being turned away at the ticket booths. Restrictions had been imposed due to the war and a "priority" was required in order to travel to many destinations. When she requested, "One way to Sweetwater, Texas," Peggy was relieved to find that the Department of the Army letter sent to her by General "Hap" Arnold and signed by Jacqueline Cochoran provided the "priority." This allowed her to purchase a ticket and travel.

As the train began its slow crawl out of the station, still underground, windows dark, Peggy reached into her traveling bag and opened the box that Timmy had given her. It contained a watch. A pilot's watch. A canvas-strapped Bulova with large numerals and clearly marked minute indices, luminous in the dark. There was also a note.

"Dear Peggers, a little something that will come in handy when you're flying. I had a friend get it for me at the PX at Floyd Bennett. It has a real neat 'hack' feature that'll let you time things to the second. I was told it's the latest thing. Good luck. I know you'll make a great pilot. Tim."

Peggy removed the tiny lady's watch she wore and strapped on the Bulova. *I love it,* she said to herself. *Must have cost a week's pay. I love it.*

There were several young women aboard the train. Peggy surmised that some, like her, were headed to Sweetwater—aspirants to Jacqueline Cochoran's flying group. She observed that a couple of girls occupied private sleeping compartments. Girls from wealthy families, no doubt.

During the first leg of the train's journey west, Peggy kept mostly to herself, reading and rereading magazines, checking her new watch and gazing out of the window as the countryside flew past. When she raised her eyes to the sky she would imagine touching the clouds. She spent her nights sleeping in her seat, dreaming about good times that were a distant memory or better times that might lie beyond the bleak and dismal present. Peggy didn't go out of her way to engage any of the other passengers. But at Union Station in St. Louis, when she joined a few of her fellow travelers getting off to stretch their legs, two young women introduced themselves. Mildred Barnes and Anna Velez were both heading to Sweetwater and hoping to fly for the Army Air Corps. They seemed like good eggs, so Peggy introduced herself.

"Peggy Cohan, private license. I was in the fashion business in New York."

Mildred was an Army brat whose father was a flight instructor at a base near Washington, DC. She had two years of college and had taken a joy ride at a county fair and fell in love with flying. She was surprised and proud of the fact that her dad encouraged her.

Anna's dad managed a farm for a gentleman farmer. She was up in an old crop duster when the flying bug had bitten. Peggy related her tale of going up with a photographer friend, leaving out a few irrelevant details. She acknowledged that, like Mildred and Anna, it was an immediate love affair. Despite her intention to keep to herself, Peggy was forced to concede that the three of them had much in common. The sky had the power to do that.

As the girls warmed to each other, they soon found themselves engaged in a good old-fashioned gabfest. They spoke of their beaus back home, proms, staying out late, their first drink. Their first several drinks. Peggy, who had until now been holding back, surprised herself by volunteering the fact that she had once done a "little modeling." The girls seemed impressed. The conversation then turned to the dreamy-looking soldiers on the train and eventually deteriorated into some catty gossip.

"Did you notice the girl in the sleeper one car back?" Mildred asked conspiratorially.

"No, I guess I didn't," was Peggy's response.

"I did," said Anna. "Very hoity-toity." She cocked her head and looked down her nose, affecting her best upper-class disdainful grimace.

"Well!" Mildred continued, "That's Pamela Briggs." Provoking no reaction, she continued. "Briggs?! Briggs's Street Cars and Trolleys."

"Oh!" both Peggy and Anna responded. Peggy, however, was simply going along. She hadn't heard of Briggs trolley cars.

"Fabulously rich," Mildred continued, "looking to do her part for the war effort, I suppose."

"And she'll be nice and rested when she does it, considering that luxe sleeping compartment she's occupying," Anna added cattily.

"Board!" shouted the conductor and the girls, still smiling over Mildred's proletarian remark, returned to their seats.

Peggy intended to eventually disengage from the two girls and return to the solitude of her window seat, but the young women sought her out and insisted on continuing their conversation.

And so the tedious ride through Missouri, on to Dallas, then Abilene, was eased immensely by the compatibility of the three fly girls. They chatted their way across the endless Texas horizon. *These girls are nothing but optimistic about the future*, thought Peggy. *I wish I could be so carefree.*

When they finally arrived at the Sweetwater station, Peggy, Millie, and Anna met on the platform and were walking together to claim their checked bags.

Anna happened to turn and notice a Negro couple disembarking the train. The woman was having difficulty negotiating the steep metal steps. As she was being assisted by her husband the reason for her difficulty became obvious. She was very pregnant and clearly not feeling well. Three women passengers who were exiting at the same door made no effort to hide their annoyance at being impeded. The Negro couple's three suitcases were obstructing the steps. The man was unable to deal with his luggage while he was tending to his wife. The young women, who were most likely heading to the Sweetwater flying program, impatiently clambered over the suitcases, knocking one off the steps and down to the platform where it sprung open and spilled its contents. The young ladies strode past the distressed couple, finding their plight amusing. Other passengers walked past, and turned to look, but, likewise, did not stop to help.

Anna and Millie headed over to the couple to offer assistance. They stacked their own suitcases off to the side of the platform so that the woman could sit and regain her composure, allowing her man to retrieve their bags from the car's steps. Peggy knelt to gather up the couple's spilled belongings and returned them to the suitcase.

"How're you feeling, dear?" Millie asked the woman.

"Bit better, thanks," she said, trying to rise. "I think I'm okay now."

"Best sit for a couple of minutes more," Anna urged. The woman nodded and sat back. Millie reentered the train and brought the woman a drink of water in a paper cup.

Eventually, the girls escorted the couple through the terminal and deposited them on a bench just outside the station.

The man stood and spoke to Peggy, Millie, and Anna. "This be the Snyder bus. I want to thank you kindly for your help, misses."

"Yes," said the woman, obviously feeling better. "Thank you kindly."

"You're welcome. Sure you're okay?"

The soon-to-be mom nodded that she was.

"Then, goodbye."

As Peggy, Millie, and Anna walked back to the station to claim their luggage, Millie turned and waved. "Good luck. Hope it's a girl."

"Split a taxi to the base?" asked Anna.

"Sounds good," replied Peggy.

Peggy's two suitcases fit easily into the trunk of the cab, but Millie and Anna had packed a bit more heavily. Their luggage filled the trunk, the seat next to the driver, and even required an oversized trunk of Millie's to be roped to the roof.

After a long ride, at the end of a dusty turnoff, a large sign straddling the front gate of their destination came into view. It proclaimed that this was Avenger Field, Aviation Enterprises, Ltd. The girls had arrived at the place that would be their home for the next thirty weeks.

When the cab pulled up to the guard shack, an Army sergeant scrutinized their letters and their faces as if he was certain they were a trio of fifth columnists. Finally, they were waved in and directed to Bay E-4. The cab dropped them off in front of a rather dilapidated line of barracks.

"This one's E-4, ladies," said the driver. "I'll give you a hand with your trunks."

Inside the stark wooden structure, they found two bays with a grimy toilet and shower room between them. There was also an inexplicable elongated porcelain trough. For laundry? Each bay housed six metal bunks. Six girls to a bay? Twelve girls to one bathroom?!

"Too late for sheets and pillow cases," a corporal informed them. "Supply's closed for the day. Sign in tomorrow."

As Anna, Millie, and Peggy were getting settled, picking out their bunks and staking out closet space, another cab pulled up. It was followed by a panel truck. The three girls went to the window and observed as Pamela Briggs, the trolley car heiress, sat in the rear waiting patiently for the driver to open the door for her. She exited the car and stepped onto the porch wearing heels, a tan suit with a pill box hat, pearls, and a fox stole draped about her shoulders. In one gloved hand she held a leash fastened to the collar of a small white dog. The stylish young woman knelt down, scooped her pet up in her arms and stood assessing the building. The expression of encountering a bad smell flickered across her face.

"Come along, Franklin," Miss Briggs said to her pet, "Mummy has to inspect her rooms." The dog was a Sealyham, which looked exactly like the President's dog, Fala, a Scottie. The difference was that Fala was black and Sealyhams were white.

When she entered the bay, Peggy, Millie, and Anna were seated on their bunks.

"Oh," said Miss Briggs, "I'm sorry. I was told E-4. I didn't realize these rooms were occupied. I'll return to the gate and rectify the mistake." As she spoke, the cabbie and the trucker entered with her trunks. "Stop. Stop," she said to the men. "Wrong rooms. Some kind of mix-up. I need to go back to the idiot at the gate and get this mess straightened out."

Anna, Millie, and Peggy exchanged smirks as Pamela Briggs made a regal exit and reentered the cab. The three women ran to the window to watch her drive off.

As it turned out, Miss Briggs couldn't find anyone who could clear up the mix-up and so spent the night with her luggage and little dog occupying an upstairs wing of the Blue Bonnet, Sweetwater's only hotel.

The three girls in E-4 would spend their first chilly night in Sweetwater sleeping on bare mattresses and utilizing their own coats for blankets.

When Peggy woke she experienced a nearly forgotten sense of optimism. *This is all new,* she realized. *A clean slate!*

"Rise and shine, ladies! Up and at 'em," barked the corporal from the barracks door.

The girls dressed hurriedly. "Let's go, ladies!" They were ordered out to the blacktop between the buildings. "C'mon, c'mon." Told to line up. "Move! Move! Straighten it up." And given their first instruction in close order drill.

"Left! Left! Left, right, left. Your other left, Red!"

They were marched in a ragged line to the administration building and told to line up for check-in. The girls were still in their civilian clothes; slacks and blouses, some in skirts and bobby sox. Peggy wore a white shirt, her gray Katharine Hepburn slacks, and saddle shoes. Decidedly unmilitary. They were told uniforms would be issued tomorrow. When they completed the sign in, they were marched to the flight line and told to wait at ease for further instruction.

A tall oafish-looking army officer with a crew cut and prominent ears appeared and called the group to attention. Checking his clipboard, he announced, "This will be your check flight. Fundamentals, basic competence. Just making sure you belong here. Cohan, Margaret, you're first."

"How'd you get my name?" Peggy asked. "I signed in just a few minutes ago."

This fact seemed of no interest to the instructor who acted unaccountably annoyed and impatient.

"The rest of you are at ease," he barked. "You got anything to wear?"

"Uh, no," was Peggy's response, hoping that she had divined his meaning.

"Over there. Hurry up," as he gestured to a long table stacked with flying gear inside an open hangar. "Next. Jones, Martha E., and Velez, Anna, find a suit and headgear. You're both on deck."

Peggy pulled on a pair of flight coveralls, which would have been slightly roomy on Bronco Nagurski, along with a musty canvas flight helmet and a parachute. Peggy buttoned up, then snugly cinched the belt on her coveralls. Slinging the chute harness over her shoulder, she ran towards the flight line to catch up with her flight tester. They stopped at a sleek two-place, low-winged Fairchild PT-19A monoplane.

"Have you ever flown this particular aircraft?" the instructor asked.

"No," Peggy answered.

"First, put on the chute. Loose. You'll tighten it up after the preflight. C'mon. C'mon. We'll do the preflight and I'll tell you about it as we go. First of all, I'm Lt. Floyd Dailey."

"Margaret Cohan," said Peggy, extending her hand and tossing him a "what a handsome man you are" smile. "Everyone calls me Peggy."

The lieutenant looked at her hand, then into Peggy's eyes. "We don't shake hands in the military. I will call you Cohan. You will address me as sir."

"Yes, sir," said Peggy without emotion. But in her thoughts she added, *You horse's ass.*

Lt. Dailey seemed satisfied with Peggy's preflight and they climbed into the aircraft with Peggy taking the front position. After some explanation of the instruments and throttle settings, he told Peggy that he would be communicating with her through a speaking tube. He would talk, if he had something to say, and she would listen. Since

Peggy could find no speaking tube in her cockpit, she assumed it would be a one-way conversation.

A mechanic came out to the aircraft and after removing a crank from the compartment in the side of the nose area, cranked the inertia starter. Lt. Daily set the magnetos to "on" and activated the starter. The engine kicked over easily and roared to life. Peggy smiled.

The nose of the PT-19A was much longer than Timmy's Piper Cub and so as she was ordered by her dour instructor to taxi out to the runway, she executed the little "s" maneuver that Abner had taught her in the *Jenny* so she could get a better view of the ramp immediately in front. The Army pilot in the rear seat took note, but said nothing.

"Take off. Climb to five hundred feet and begin a right turn. Then continue climb 'til you level off at two thousand. Take a heading of 240 degrees."

The agile little trainer scooted down the runway and effortlessly lifted itself into the air as the shimmering concrete of Avenger Field fell away. Below, the base was reduced to a few lines and buildings in the midst of the great expanse of Texas scrub.

Aloft, the lieutenant asked for a sequence of maneuvers that were remarkably similar to those that Timmy had showed her back home. Her handling was precise, her turns regulated. Peggy flew with the confidence of a student who had been given the answers to the final exam. Lt. Dailey then directed Peggy to gain altitude where he requested a power-on stall, from which his prospect recovered competently.

"We'll do power-off stalls at another time," he informed the young woman in the front seat. "The Army doesn't like risking its valuable equipment."

Peggy nodded that she understood, adding *Horse's ass* silently.

Peggy's landing was controlled and precise. It was obvious that the girl could fly. Peggy eased along the taxi way toward the parking area and then swung the aircraft around so it sat on the ramp in its previous parking spot. She looked back at her instructor for acknowledgement to cut the engine. When he nodded, she cut both magnetos and the engine died. A ground crewman chocked the aircraft as Peggy and the Army lieutenant deplaned.

"Well," said Peggy to Lt. Dailey, "am I in?"

"I'm grading you a satisfactory," Dailey said with all the enthusiasm of a man signing away the family homestead. "But that doesn't mean you are 'in.' They'll decide that over at operations. And, Cohan, one more thing."

"Yes?" asked Peggy, turning toward her instructor in expectation of a compliment.

"The chute and the coveralls go in the hangar where you found them."

"Yes sir," Peggy said charmingly. Once more, she amended her reply with a silent, *Horse's ass.*

As Peggy returned to the hangar the rest of the girls were waiting in the shade of the structure.

"How'd it go?" asked Millie. The others edged in to hear Peggy's reply.

"Good, I guess," said Peggy. "Pretty straightforward, I'd say."

Anna and another girl were still up on their check out ride.

In the hangar a young woman in khakis sprinted toward Peggy as she was removing her chute to replace it on the table from which it came.

"You Peggy Cohan?" the young woman asked breathlessly.

"Yes."

"Well, they want you right away over at Woofted operations."

"Thank you. I'll be right there." *What in the world is a Woofted?* wondered Peggy as she stacked her chute, helmet, and coveralls and hurried toward operations.

When she entered she saw a small crowd of journalists brandishing press cameras and one film camera surrounding the famous Jacqueline Cochoran in her office. The publicity-savvy aviatrix was holding court. She joked with the journalists, pausing to allow herself to be photographed, always providing a dazzling smile and her best side to the camera lens.

After a few more questions she held up her hands for silence and announced, "The real story today is our next class of future pilots. I'd like you to meet a few of them. You might even wish them good luck." Jacqueline Cochoran's enthusiasm was infectious. "Let's go outside. You can meet our ladies near some of the aircraft they will eventually master."

As Jackie herded the reporters out of her office past Peggy and the two clerks, she lagged behind and whispered into Peggy's ear. "Wash your face, dear, and then come join us for the photo session." She then began to walk away but stopped after two steps and turned to Peggy once again. "And, by the way," she said, flashing her dazzling smile, "Welcome to the Women's Flying Training Detachment or *Wooftd*." The lightbulb went on as Peggy beamed back a sincere thank you to Miss Cochoran as she strode out to the waiting reporters.

One of the clerks showed Peggy to a lavatory, marked "Ladies' Latrine," where she could scrub off the grime of the open cockpit flight. She then hurried out to join the group. When the press posed the young women around a Vultee trainer, a couple of cameramen centered on Peggy. Her natural affinity for the camera lens was obvious. Eventually, the *LIFE* photographer asked to shoot Peggy by herself, even adding a smudge of grease swiped from the aircraft's shock strut, just to add character to the right cheekbone of the young, aspiring fly girl. It was placed in nearly the same spot that she had washed a few moments before.

When the *LIFE* and Pathe reporters finally had their fill, they were escorted to the officer's club by Jacqueline Cochoran for lunch and more public relations. They left Peggy standing in the midst of eleven young women pilots, in various phases of training, all of whom were glaring daggers at this brazen rookie.

They were all there to fly but, still, no woman appreciates being upstaged.

During the next three days, new girls arrived at Sweetwater from all over the country to fill the ranks of Jackie Cochoran's new class of trainees, all of them vying to become part of Jackie Cochoran's program. They were processed, flight tested and, if they met requirements, given a permanent barracks assignment.

Three of these newbies found their way to E-4. Janine Fort from Nashville, Tennessee, Rita Davis from Columbus, Ohio, and Suellen Tackaberry of Santa Fe, New Mexico. Three earnest young women joining Peggy, Millie, and Anna, with the identical goal: to fly for the US Army Air Corps.

First Lt. Emmett Cahill, wearing freshly pressed khakis, Air Corps issue sunglasses, and a service cap with a forty mission crush, climbed to the top of a maintenance stand and gestured for the women to approach.

"Come on, gather in and listen up. Right. All of you are experienced pilots. You've proven that by your records and by our personal observations of you in the air. You can fly, no question. We are now going to teach you how to fly all over again.

"It's not a question of a right way over a wrong way. We are going to teach you the Army way. Some of you may find it difficult to give up the habits and techniques that have worked for you in the past, but if you are unable to give them up, I promise that we will wash you out.

"In the next thirty weeks, we will make you Army Air Corps pilots. To do this, you will learn the discipline and teamwork that is required of a military man . . . uh . . . er . . . woman, as would be in your case. That's all. Dismissed!"

Pamela Briggs and five handpicked bunkmates were eventually accommodated in Bay B-2. The issue of her luggage and lap dog had been settled by Jacqueline Cochoran herself. "One trunk, no pets, six girls to a bay. Take it or leave." Pamela elected to stay but not before reminding Jackie Cochoran of what an unreasonable woman she was. After all, how many opportunities would the Women's Flying Training Detachment have to recruit such quality people to its ranks?

Cochoran rolled her eyes, patiently explained once again that those were the rules, and briskly ushered Miss Briggs out of her office while wishing her a sincere, "Good luck on your training."

B-2 inevitably was known as the debutante's bay and no one was surprised when it was adorned with new non-GI curtains, an electric fridge, and some custom carpentry that expanded the closet and storage space beyond the regulation wooden wall lockers and footlockers.

The girls in B-2 were mostly from the right side of the tracks and a couple of them, like Pamela, actually owned the tracks. But in this training program, being well off or socially prominent mattered less than being able to master the fundamentals of controlling an airplane.

On day two, uniforms were issued to the women. Their flight suits were tan wool gabardine coveralls from the stock of male sizes and were invariably too long and too large. The girls called them zoot suits because they fit like the popular style of blousy, droopy pants worn by the hepsters back home. The ladies in B-2, however, sported flight suits that fit perfectly due to the efforts of a local seamstress pressed into service by Miss Briggs for a long evening of emergency alterations.

The new girls in the other bays cinched their belts tight, rolled up their cuffs and sleeves, or took a nip and tuck with needle and thread themselves and made due. For non-flying situations, the girls were issued officer's garrison caps, pink general's trousers and white blouses. These tended to fit much better. Apparently, there were many small-boned generals in the army.

During the initial weeks of training, the women marched everywhere they went and stood frequent inspections between flying and ground school. Demerits were issued for any infraction, whether it was an improperly rolled mattress on bedding day or a sloppy altitude on an initial approach. It was obvious that the instructors were equally concerned that the trainees become good soldiers as well as good pilots.

The tally of demerits was posted each week so that the trainees could know their standing in the class. This created a competitive atmosphere. Pamela Briggs decided that she and the ladies of B-2 would earn top ranking in the class. She fervently believed that those to whom much is given are deserving of even more.

After dinner one evening Pamela Briggs, carrying her tray, approached Anna Velez in the dining hall. She proffered her tray and said, "Oh, Velez, dear, would you take care of this?"

Velez, confused, accepted the tray and watched as Miss Briggs sauntered to the exit where her friends were waiting, little smirks on their faces. *"Muchos gracias,"* Pamela said sweetly in the direction of Anna as she and her group exited the hall.

"What was that all about?" Peggy asked, walking toward the clean-up station with her tray.

"That haughty bitch," Anna said, fuming. "She handed me her tray and like a dope, I took it."

Millie joined them and observed, "She considers everyone the help."

"No," said Peggy, "she knows what she's doing. She's out to get your goat. Ever since the latest gig list came out with you at the top of the class."

"No! . . . You think?"

"Of course," Peggy said, "She wants to rattle your brain. She's after the top spot."

"Okay, good," said Anna thoughtfully. "Now, I know what she's up to . . . she's got a fight on her hands."

"Atta girl," said Millie. "Say, would you mind terribly dumping my tray for me, *muchos gracias*."

In Primary Training the women flew the PT-19A and the L-4A, learning army landing procedures, navigation, and proper preflight walk-around checks. Peggy was very comfortable in both aircraft despite being much more familiar with the 65hp L-4A, which was identical to Timmy's Piper Cub.

In subsequent weeks, Peggy's "free as a bird" view of flying was replaced by a highly structured and disciplined set of rules and directives. Briefings were timed precisely each day for mission instructions and weather. Tardiness of even a minute or two was not tolerated. A dressing-down in front of the other women for some small infraction like a button undone or a conversation extended for a moment too long was the rule.

Attempts at achieving individuality, like earrings, a colored scarf worn as an accessory, or even non-regulation socks, were immediately banished. Even underwear was to be regulation khaki.

"Well, to hell with them," said AnnMarie Cassault, the daughter of a Macon, Georgia, farm equipment dealer. "They may paint my heart olive drab but, by God, my panties are gonna be pink!"

The rest of the girls, solidly behind this position and in a form of united disobedience, followed suit. The ladies of 43-W/2 would, underneath it all, by God, be wearing pink.

Peggy was the first in her bay to solo in the PT-19. As tradition dictated, she was tossed, fully clothed, into the wishing well in front of the operations building. The "wishing well" was more like a fountain in which the trainees floated their hopes and tossed a coin. A successful first solo earned a dunking for the pilot and the opportunity to retrieve a coin from the bottom. This coin was considered a prized souvenir by the girls and doubled as a screwdriver to open panels during preflights.

One day out on the flight line, as Peggy was walking towards the hangar to stow her chute, she was encountered by Pamela Briggs.

"You're Peggy Cohan, aren't you?" She asked affably.

Peggy didn't slow but continued her pace to the parachute racks. "Yes, that's me."

"Cohan, what is that, Irish?" said Pamela as she strode along with Peggy.

Peggy didn't answer.

"Like George M. Cohan?" Pamela persisted, "The Yankee Doodle Dandy. Am I right?"

"It's possible," was Peggy's response, still walking.

"Well," Pamela said, "that means you'll be happy to hear that they're serving baked potato tonight at dinner."

Peggy stopped, turned to Pamela, adjusted the parachute strap on her shoulder and, looking squarely into her eyes, said, "Pamela, go fuck yourself." Peggy walked off.

A wide-eyed Pamela Briggs could only manage a feeble, "Well!"

Peggy stowed the chute as the tiniest of smiles crept along the corners of her mouth.

16

After a long and tedious training day, the girls of Bay E-4 changed into their pajamas and hit the books. The subject: electrical systems. Though the three new girls had arrived only days after Peggy, Millie, and Anna, they regarded them as upper classmen. Consequently, they assumed that Peggy, Millie, and Anna were experts about the aircraft and particularly, electrical systems.

"During refueling, the aircraft must always be grounded," read Tackaberry from the textbook.

"To the airframe," added Janine Fort.

"In case of a spark discharge caused by static electricity," read Rita Davis. "Which could ignite any gas fumes," said Anna Velez, completing the directive.

All six girls nodded, satisfied that the safety procedure had just been committed to memory.

"Just remember, all electrical systems on the aircraft are grounded to the skin and the airframe," Millie added, turning the page to the next chapter. "They'll ask you that."

It was then that the runner arrived. "Message for Margaret Cohan." It was from Jacqueline Cochoran. It read:

> Peggy, could you please come over to operations in the new conference room and lend a hand. We have Senator Zebulon Manville of North Dakota and his party visiting us. He seems

favorable to our program and we want to make a positive impression. I'd like you to serve as one of the hostesses. Wear a nice dress and fix your hair. Please try to arrive before eight.

Peggy read the message and looked up, mildly abashed.

"What is it?" asked Millie.

"It's from Jackie," answered Peggy. "She wants me to wait tables. For some senator. I won't do it."

"I think you ought to do it," said Millie.

"No, it's demeaning." Peggy shook her head. "Not gonna do it."

"Maybe you should do it," Anna urged.

"Uh-uh! I'm a flyer, not a cocktail waitress."

As she was saying this, Anna and Millie rose, grasped Peggy under each of her arms and steered her towards the shower room.

"She's kinda our commanding officer," Millie pointed out. "I think it's like an order."

Showered and now in a flower-print dress borrowed from Tackaberry, shod in loaner high heels, an upswept hairdo expertly styled by Millie and Rita, and adorned with lipstick and mascara and a silver necklace donated by Janine Fort, Peggy Cohan had undergone a startling metamorphosis. The five fairy godmothers stepped back and viewed their effort. The pretty girl, who had been downplaying her looks for so many months, had been transformed into a knockout. And the timing was perfect. It was ten minutes to eight.

When Peggy arrived at the operations building, Jacqueline hurried over to her.

"I must say, darlin', you clean up nice." She could see that Peggy didn't take it as a compliment. Jackie indicated another girl in the room. "Vera, Vera honey, could you come over and meet your cohostess for the evening?"

Vera, a great-looking gal with flaming red hair, strode over.

"This is Peggy Cohan. Just completing basic. Peggy, meet Vera Chesney. She's in advanced, five weeks in. I do appreciate both your help. There's the bar," she said, pointing to bottles and glasses atop four filing cabinets. "We've got some good bourbon, scotch and rye, beer, ginger ale, root beer, and soda water, whatever you'll need. The hotel in town even made us some canapés and little sandwiches. And there's plenty of ice in those buckets over there. Your job is to keep it flowin', got me?"

Vera said, "Roger, that!"

When Peggy offered a half-hearted nod Jackie noted her reticence.

"Now, Peggy, before you begin, I'd like a word." Jacqueline steered Peggy down the hall and into an unoccupied office filled with extra furniture and a spare typewriter.

"I can understand if you consider this job beneath you but I want to explain something. Women flying airplanes, especially military airplanes, is a frightening concept to most of the men around here. You and I know that a woman can fly every bit as well as a man, even better I might say, but let's stick with just as well. Now, women's roles have been pretty much laid out since Biblical times. We want to change all that, but we're never going to do it by just being good. We're going to do it by being smart. Why, women only got the vote twenty-two years ago. Someday I can even see a woman becoming President of the United States. But that day isn't today or tomorrow. Right now, it's up to us to start the process of changing men's minds and more than a few women's minds. And we're going to do it by flying airplanes. Now, men's minds aren't so easy to change. They're scared. Mostly timid little boys hiding behind their muscle and swagger. They need to cling to their male superiority. That's to our advantage. We don't cling to any fears or illusions. We know what we can do. But we have to play it smart.

"Now, this Senator Manville, he's an older man. Why, he was born way back in the eighteen hundreds. He still wears shirts with detachable collars. For some reason this old boy supports women aviators and making use of women for the war effort. Make no mistake, he regards us as cute oddities. A novelty. We're like his little daughters whom he is allowing on the roller coaster. Well, Peggy, I'll take it. Any support for women to fly Army planes is good support. No matter how misguided, I'll take it. Now, I hear you're a natural pilot and that's great, but tonight I need you to be a sweet, darling, attentive, respectful, brainless bit of fluff. Do that and you'll further the cause of women flyers better than if you were Amelia Earhart herself. Are you with me?"

After an enlistment speech like that, all Peggy could do was nod and say, "I'm with you."

"Good."

Jacqueline Cochoran's assistant, Jane Medford, poked her head into the room and said, "Jackie, they're here!"

A broad glowing smile and a look of guileless charm suddenly appeared on Cochoran's face.

"Oh, thank you, Jane. Isn't that wonderful. I must go and greet the Senator." She headed down the little hall and into the large conference room, practically chirping with delight.

Peggy offered drinks and canapés to Senator Manville, a short, gray-haired, rosy-cheeked, and slightly paunchy fellow who introduced his staff. They consisted of his two aides, a pair of bespectacled humorless fellows who, shunning alcohol, requested soda pop. They quickly earned the nicknames Frick and Frack. There was also a dowdy secretary rounding out the entourage. She ate nothing, drank nothing, and wore a suspicious scowl on her face while clutching her purse and steno pad to her breast as if it was her lifejacket on this speedboat to hell.

Peggy smiled and served drinks and behaved as if this evening in the company of the great and powerful senator was the highlight of her life. "Acting!" Peggy thought, "Acting!" She smiled shyly at an unctuous compliment offered to her by Frack. Or was it Frick?

As the party chugged along, punctuated by a toast to Hap Arnold and George Marshall and Senator Manville with special acknowledgements of his wisdom and intellect, someone from somewhere produced a deck of cards. The Senator, in an expansive mood, suggested a few hands of poker. Jackie and Jane were both willing but said that they weren't too sure of the rules. The Senator and Frack . . . or was it Frick? . . . assured the two women that it was easy and it would be their pleasure to teach them the basics.

"Oh, would you, sir?" said Jane, which drew a sideways look from Jacqueline as being possibly a bit over the top.

No harm. Zeb was delighted to play teacher. After a brief discussion of the rank of winning hands, they elected to play for quarters, just to make it interesting. Of course, amazingly, the Senator won nearly every hand. "Just good luck," he averred modestly.

"Oh, no," asserted Jackie and Jane, assuring him that perspicacity and acumen were the traits at work here.

Peggy walked behind the players, plying them with refreshments, acting and smiling. Senator Zebulon, who was holding a pair of nines, was raising. As Peggy refreshed Jackie's scotch and double soda, she noticed the three jacks and pair of tens that the woman held. A full house with three of a kind.

"Oh, you win again," said Jackie, tossing her wretched hand on the table, just carefully enough that the cards stayed face down.

On the next hand Peggy observed that Jane was dealt a jack, ten and nine of diamonds, and an ace of clubs and a two of spades. She discarded the ace and deuce and drew two cards. Peggy moved to replace Frack's root beer with a new glass and fresh ice and observed Zeb seeing Jane's bet and then raising. Jane then put in her quarters and called. Zeb threw down a triumphant pair of aces, sixes, and a queen.

"Oooh! Too good!" lamented Jane and slammed her worthless cards face down on the table. She had drawn an eight and seven of diamonds for a straight flush. A one in a million hand and she'd discarded it so that Senator Zeb could claim the pot.

"I guess this is my lucky day," Zeb cackled, quite pleased with himself.

With a grin of greedy contentment, Zebulon Manville raked the Liberty quarters toward his vest.

"You are really amazing," said Jane. "Why, you know, Senator, you could make a good living as a professional gambler."

Miss Tuttle, the secretary, found this statement shocking. Manville, on the other hand, was in the midst of a Walter Mitty fantasy and loving every moment of it.

It was nearly eleven p.m. when the Senator's car pulled up to the building and the party concluded. Zebulon was up some seventeen bucks. It was obvious the senator didn't want this night to end. He kissed Jackie's hand and called her "my dear" and, with a sigh, exited the building to the waiting Cadillac. He was joined by Frack, Frick, and Miss Tuttle.

"I think it went well, don't you?" Jackie said, unable to keep herself from grinning. A shared hearty laugh brought the curtain down on the successful evening.

As Peggy and Vera were leaving, Jackie said, "Thanks, ladies. I kinda owe you one. G'night."

17

Commissariat of Foreign Affairs
Office of the Foreign Minister
Moscow

With rumors of an American bomber landing safely in the Soviet Union, the outraged leadership of the Japanese empire immediately contacted their consulate in Samara.

Hidekei Shigemitsu, the Consul-General, conveyed his country's demand that the aircraft be impounded, and that its crew should be placed under arrest and promptly extradited to Japan to stand trial for war crimes.

The communiqué, which characterized the Americans as "barbaric gangsters" and "war criminals," arrived by diplomatic pouch at the Soviet foreign office in Moscow. When the matter was brought to the attention of Soviet Foreign Minister, Vacheslav Molotov, he asked his staff the present location of the American bomber crew.

He was informed that the crew had been comfortably settled in a private house in Komsomolsk on the Amur, some three-hundred kilometers north of Khabarovsk, the town in which they were subjected to their initial debriefing.

"I see. Now, consider, is the Soviet Union going to turn the soldiers of its American allies over to the Japanese? And willingly risk the

Lend-Lease material and supplies being sent to us?"

The junior diplomat shook his head, tentatively indicating a negative.

"Correct. We will not. Therefore, here is what we will do. Put the Americans on a train and send them west. It will be weeks before they turn up here in Moscow. In the meantime, convey our sincerest regrets to the esteemed Nipponese consul and explain that at present the Americans are in transit and we are unable to locate them. We will inform their foreign office straightaway if and when we determine their whereabouts. Send that."

A rare smile appeared on the face of the usually dour Soviet diplomatic chief. Still grinning wolfishly, Molotov leaned toward his junior attaché.

"Pavel, do you perceive the essence of the art of diplomacy?"

The young man shook his head. He guessed he was about to find out.

"The art of diplomacy," Molotov expounded, "is telling your opposite to go to hell, but saying it in a way that makes him look forward to the trip."

"Yes, sir," acknowledged Pavel Grigorovich, as confused with the explanation as he was with his chief's sudden and inexplicable good humor.

Half a world and nearly a dozen time zones away, Jane Medford knocked on an office door.

"New directive from Hap Arnold," she announced as she entered the room and placed the order on Jackie Cochoran's desk.

"What now?" asked Jackie.

"We are reminded to tell the trainees not to seal the letters they write home. It seems they've got to be censored. Spies are looking for timetables and naming of types of equipment and other sensitive information."

"Oh, what a bother. You mean we've got to read all their letters? The stuff to boyfriends and husbands?"

"I'm afraid so," Jane said. "At least for a while."

"None of us have time for that," said Jackie, frustrated. "Wait." Jackie paused. "Got an idea. How about that instructor who hurt his shoulder on his motorcycle. Bartley. He's not doing anything."

"Perfect," said Jane. "I'll let him know he's got a new job. Base censor."

"That'll teach the big lug to fall off a motorcycle." Jackie winked at Jane, who clearly appreciated her boss's solution.

The preflight inspection was considered a very important piece of army pilot training. Instructors graded meticulously and there were rumors that they sometimes would create a problem just to see if the trainee could catch it.

Anna Velez, currently the top-ranking trainee, was performing a preflight on a Stearman. She scrutinized every bolt and rivet. Felt for bumps in the main gear and tail wheel sidewalls, checked for cracks in the windscreen. Made sure brake lines were dry, control surfaces secure. Taking her time, doing it right. When her instructor walked to the hangar to grab himself a Coke, one of the Bay 2 debutantes sauntered over and engaged him in conversation. She generously supplied the nickels for both their Cokes as she flirted with the man. Enjoying the interaction he resolved to check Anna's inspection as soon as he finished his refreshment.

When Anna climbed up for the cockpit check, Pamela Briggs strolled to the wing of the aircraft, ducked under, and with a diagonal cutter, snipped the safety wire securing the clamp supporting a hydraulic brake line. She came out from under the wing and, using it as a shield, nonchalantly sauntered away from the aircraft.

When the inspector finally finished his Coke and his tête-à-tête and returned to the trainer, he discovered the broken safety wire and registered three demerits for Anna's lax preflight. Those gigs dropped her to fifth place in the class.

When the new rankings came out, Anna was upset, but philosophical. "I can't imagine how I missed that. Guess I'll have to be more careful in the future."

Her bay mates tried to console her but it was unnecessary. Anna had already put it behind her and was thinking about the next day's training.

While joining the others in consoling Anna, Peggy saw the incident as less of a setback for Anna and more of a stroke of luck for herself. With Anna receiving three demerits, it brought Peggy closer to the top of the class, one gig behind the base's resident socialite, Pamela Briggs.

Lt. Milo Bartley was the instructor who Peggy continually badgered to teach her techniques beyond the standard curriculum. She flattered and cajoled him into letting her practice aerobatic maneuvers like wingovers, power-off stalls, and outside loops. He even condoned crosswind landings when traffic was light. Bartley was reluctant to provide the non-regulation instruction. Peggy somehow managed to get him to go along, pleading her case while standing too close, bumping against him, and gazing meaningfully into his eyes. When the gullible young lieutenant dropped himself and his motorcycle, separating his shoulder, he ceased being useful to Peggy.

One day Peggy visited the main hangar during lunch time, where a complete set of technical manuals for all the aircraft were stored. She wanted to check out the specs on their next aircraft, the Vultee BT-13. Peggy spent her lunch hour poring over technical details, flying characteristics, and cockpit layout, getting a jump on the orientation process. It made good sense to stay ahead of the schedule.

On her way out, she passed a group of women sitting in the shade on the floor of the hangar, obviously waiting for their instructors. As she approached, Peggy realized it was Pamela Briggs, her debutantes, and a few new acolytes. Pamela was holding court.

"Now, this shabby outfit might be fine for some, but if you want to be in the company of quality women of social position, intelligence, and culture, then Miss Nancy Love's group is the place to be."

One of the girls offered a timid rebuttal. "But Jackie Cochoran is a famous woman flyer. She won the Bendix."

"My dear, she didn't win anything that her nouveau riche husband didn't buy for her," reposted Pamela with great disdain.

As Peggy walked past, Pamela continued, her voice rising. "For some women—common, no background, no prospects, poorly educated—Jackie Cochoran's group is perfect. Common types are comfortable with other common types. Jackie Cochoran may be an acquaintance of Eleanor Roosevelt, but she's still common."

Another girl offered weak dissent. "Then what are you doing here in Wooftd with Jackie?"

"Oh, honey, if there was some way I could transfer to Love's ferry squadron, I'd be gone before you could blink your eyes."

What load of bull crap, thought Peggy as she walked through the hangar and out to the ramp.

On the way to her appointment in the Link Trainer she was hailed by Janine Fort. "Peggy, got a minute? Can we talk?"

"Sure," said Peggy, checking her watch. "What's up?"

"I saw something the other day. I feel funny mentioning it. I'm not even sure what I saw," said Janine.

"What?" asked Peggy. "What did you see? Or think you saw?"

"Remember when Anna tanked her preflight the other day?"

"I do, so?" Peggy now gave the hesitant girl her full attention.

"I was in the Vultee cockpit trying to memorize the instruments, getting a little jump on next week, you understand."

"All right, go on."

"I saw Pamela sneak up on the Stearman as Anna was climbing into the cockpit. Then she came out fast and walked off like she did something."

"Where was Watkins while all this was going on?" Peggy asked.

"Here's the thing," Janine continued, uncomfortable at telling her story. "I saw Watkins at the Coke machine chatting it up with one of the debutantes. Doesn't that seem suspicious?"

"I'd say it does," said Peggy. "But it might not mean anything."

That evening Peggy and Janine spoke with Anna and repeated the story. Anna became quiet and said, "Y'know, I specifically remember sliding my finger along that length of safety wire. I'm almost sure it was in one piece when I checked it." Anna then shrugged and said, "Whatever we think might have happened, there's nothing I can do about it now. Right?"

Peggy and Janine both nodded in agreement with Anna.

"Still," Peggy said, "I hate to think that she got away with something. Oh well, maybe something will come up to even the score."

"Good evening, Cohan," Lieutenant Bartley said to Peggy on the porch of one of the ground school buildings as she was heading to class.

Oh, no, thought Peggy, *I suppose I have to talk to him.* "How's the arm?" she asked, feigning concern.

"Actually, it's the shoulder," he corrected, moving the sling with effort.

"Oh, yes, of course," Peggy replied. "So, keeping busy?"

"Yeah, pretty much. I teach aerodynamics to the new Primary girls. Had it pretty cushy until Madame Cochoran assigned me the job of censoring the mail. Lot of work reading all those letters, cuts into my beer drinking time."

"Let me get this right," Peggy said, "you read our letters?"

"Yup, why do you think they tell you not to seal them?"

"You must get into a lot of personal stuff, "Peggy mused.

"Yeah, boring! I'm supposed to look for and cut out places, dates, schedules, mention of specific aircraft. And also morale. Her nibs wants to see anything that might be considered a morale problem."

"How long do you have to do this?" Peggy queried.

"About six weeks. 'Til the wing heals."

"Well, its been nice chatting," Peggy said, checking her Bulova. "But, gotta go. Class, you know."

"Maybe I'll see you around," said Bartley, hopefully.

"Yeah, sure," said Peggy. "Maybe." *Maybe never,* she thought to herself.

At mail call that evening, Peggy was surprised to receive two letters. One was from her mother; she folded it and placed it in her pocket, unopened. The other was from Cece; she read it immediately. Peggy seldom received mail and Cece's lively words brought Peggy news of the world she had left behind. Even though Peggy had sought refuge from that world by joining the Women's Flying Corps, she was surprised that she still had interest in what was going on back home. Cece wrote of the successes and failures of her modeling rivals, the state of hemlines, the new platform shoes, and the latest hits on the Hit Parade. Frances Langford had several records at the top of the charts, the Ozzie Nelson band was big, and a new boy singer named Frankie Sinatra and a trio of girls called the Andrews Sisters was making a big splash on the home front.

And then there's me!" Cece wrote. *"I've been singing on the radio. A couple of shows let me do a song. Now, I'm going to make a record and if it turns out that people like it, I'll get to make more. It's all very exciting. Oh, and by the way, my new stage name is Cece Collins. They thought that Castelagno sounded too much like Mussolini's cousin. Hope you're lovin' your flying and that you don't go anywhere where you can get shot at. Love and hugs, friends to the end. Cece.*

Peggy reread Cece's last paragraph and a broad grin broke out on her face. *She's on her way,* thought Peggy. *Good for her.*

Back in the privacy of the barracks Peggy took out her mother's letter and opened it.

It read:

"My dear Peggy, sorry it's taken me so long to write. There are so many things so much I want to say but I didn't know how to begin. I'm sorry about so many things. What can I do? How do I make it up to you? I know I wasn't a good mom but if you would only try to understand . . . "

Peggy didn't continue reading. She tore the paper into bits and flung the shredded missive to the floor. She found herself short of breath, unnerved, angry, sad. When she finally managed to regain some composure she took a deep breath and resignedly knelt down and picked up the torn pieces. *I'll deal with this some other day,* she vowed. When all the scraps had been salvaged and carefully stored in the envelope, Peggy examined the bulky packet and looked up. *Now that's an idea,* she announced to herself.

Later that evening, Peggy, flashlight in hand, told her bay mates, "I'm going out for a bit. Need some air. Be back in a little while." The other women, engaged in chatting or immersed in their textbooks, barely acknowledged her exit.

Peggy let herself into the unlocked operations building, went straight to the spare office where she found paper, and inserted it into the typewriter. After several drafts with spelling errors and typing mistakes, she finally produced an acceptable letter.

It read:

Dear Miss Love,

I am currently a trainee in Jacqueline Cochoran's flying detachment. I find myself amongst women of highly questionable character. It is my feeling that Miss Cochoran's lack of breeding and common background has attracted the worst elements to this training program.

I consider the women here crude, vulgar, and possessed of inferior moral disposition. I am convinced that the graduates of Miss Cochoran's program will prove to be unqualified and a detriment to the US Army Air Corps.

I, therefore, respectfully request to be transferred to your contingent at the Air Ferrying Command. I feel I would fit in very well with you as leader and role model.

Sincerely, Pamela Briggs

That should do it, thought Peggy as she pulled the paper from the machine. In the glow of the flashlight, she scribbled a vague impression of Pamela Briggs's signature. Then, while the ink dried, she typed the address on the envelope: Miss Nancy Love, c/o Newcastle Army Airbase, Wilmington, Delaware. Purposely omitting the return address, she put the unsealed letter beneath some other envelopes in the outgoing mail bin.

Bartley read the letter and as a dutiful censor brought it to Jane Medford, who showed it to Jackie, who put it in a file and shut the drawer.

"I've got more important things to do right now," said Jackie to Jane. "I'll deal with this some other day."

In addition to their flying instruction Jackie Cochoran's women were required to become competent in Morse code. The practice of sending insults to each other punctuated with off-color words and phrases sped up the learning process.

Out at the range, the women practiced firing the Colt 1911 .45 caliber automatic, a heavy and difficult handgun to control. While Jackie's students were essentially noncombatants, any aircraft that carried sensitive equipment such as advanced radio devices or a Norden bombsight required the crew to carry and be qualified to fire the weapon.

From the Chemical Warfare instructor the trainees received a lesson on the utilization of their gas masks. Once properly fitted, the women entered the gas chamber. The instructor then activated a gas canister and as the room filled with the acrid mist the girls were directed to breathe normally and trust the mask. The instructor then directed the girls to remove their masks in order to experience a brief exposure to the chemical. With their masks off, eyes and throats smarting from the noxious cloud, the girls edged anxiously toward the exit. It was then that the instructor blocked the entrance and announced that it happened to be his birthday and he would grade everyone an excellent if they would honor him by singing "Happy Birthday." The women sang, choking, tears streaming, the fastest rendered version of the song on record. The army, it would seem, enjoyed its rare moments of humor.

Peggy and her colleagues were taught to taxi the Army way, with precise distances between planes. Nearly every aspect of flying and life had a specific Army procedure. There seemed to be checklists for everything. The memorizing of checklists for walk-arounds, preflights, start-ups, and shut-downs was discouraged. The trainee was taught to hold the actual checklist in hand and methodically go down the list. No shortcuts.

When in the air or taxiing, the women were taught to use precise military jargon while using the radio. No personalizing of messages, no jokes, no chatting, business only.

Formation flying was a discipline new to nearly all the women in training. Getting purposely close to another aircraft was unnerving for some and a few girls washed out because they couldn't get used to the tactic. The majority, however, mastered it. They eventually became comfortable with the maneuver of forming up, split S-ing and rejoining in a tight formation.

For many girls who learned to fly at rural, low traffic airstrips, military landings were a difficult technique to achieve. Approaching into the wind and using the sideslip maneuver to line up with the runway was the common, expedient way to land. This was the method Peggy had formerly utilized. The Air Corps demanded a precise downwind leg, a ninety degree turn to a base leg, and then a turn to the final approach. All at prescribed speeds and altitudes.

Different. Difficult. But eventually the women learned. And then what was learned became second nature. At that point, they had become military pilots.

When the class successfully completed primary, they moved to basic and the BT-13, a more powerful aircraft, nicknamed the *Vultee Vibrator*. At first the speed, responsiveness, and increased torque of the "hotter" aircraft proved tricky, but it was soon mastered. They learned navigation principles, cross country techniques, and instrument flying.

From basic, they transitioned to advanced training with the AT-6 Texan and its 550hp Pratt and Whitney "wasp" engine. It was the hottest bird most of the women had ever flown. Lots of torque. They also learned to fly the twin-engined Cessna AT-8 with a hp rating of 450. The technique of dual throttles was a new skill to the majority of the trainees.

At thirty weeks these once green civilian pilots had mastered the Army curriculum and were ready to graduate. The Wooftd appellation had been changed while the women were in training and was now called the WASP, Women's Air Force Service Pilots, a name approved by General Hap Arnold himself.

At the graduation ceremony most of the women could barely believe it was all over. The weeks had literally flown by. In their new Santiago blue uniforms with blue berets, bearing the officer's eagle, they stood in formation. Jacqueline Cochoran, with obvious pride, pinned silver wings on each graduate.

The wings were purchased by Jacqueline at the PX. She had the central shield of standard air corps pilot's wings removed by a local jeweler, who soldered a new shield with a banner in place. The banner was inscribed with the squadron designation and the shield bore the number of the class. In Peggy's and her bunkmates' case, 318th, W/2.

When Peggy received her wings and congratulations from Jackie, she experienced a new and profound sense of pride. This was an accomplishment that was not cadged or schemed. It had nothing to do with looks but was totally earned by hard work. What's more, she did it as part of a team, supporting the women around her and receiving their support in return. An entirely new experience for Peggy Cohan.

"Front and center WASP graduate, Muriel Hannigan," ordered Jane Medford. The top woman in the class strode forward, executed a crisp about-turn, and took her place beside Jackie Cochoran.

Jackie nodded to Muriel and quietly said, "Miss Hannigan, you may dismiss the squadron."

To the graduating class, students, instructors, and ground crews all standing at attention, she uttered a single word: "Dismissed."

The graduation ceremony was concluded amidst applause, cheers, hugs, and berets tossed in the air. The women who had bested thirty-eight determined pilots earned the privilege of uttering one word at graduation. Muriel was embraced by Jacqueline Cochoran. Anna Velez was second in the class, while Peggy placed third with her nibs, Pamela Briggs in fifth. The cross-country problems proved the undoing of Pamela Briggs. Hannigan, on the other hand, displayed the instincts of a homing pigeon during the complex exercises. Peggy, normally extremely competitive, was surprised that she felt quite content with the final results.

The girls were now anxious to receive their assignments, which would be posted outside the operations building. Peggy was assigned to pursuit aircraft along with Millie, Rita Davis, and six other girls. They were ordered to report to the Bell factory in Romulus, Michigan, near Detroit. Anna and Janine, along with several other girls, were given multi-engined aircraft and assigned to Bakersfield, California, and the Boeing field. Tackaberry and five girls from the debutante's bay were sent to the ferry squadron at New Castle, Delaware, to Nancy Love's command.

Pamela Briggs and three girls near the bottom of the class were sent to the gunnery range at Amarillo, Texas, where they would tow targets for antiaircraft gunners.

Later that day, in her office, satisfied that another class of women had been successfully trained and graduated, Jacqueline leaned to open her lower desk drawer. She removed the Briggs letter to Nancy Love and tore it into tiny pieces, closing the book on 43-W/2.

20

Komsomolsk
Easternmost Russia
Bordering the Sea of Japan

The American aircrew was ensconced near Komsomolsk in a large, slightly rundown home once owned by a prosperous pre-Revolution farmer. There the Americans attempted to settle in and resign themselves to their internment. The impromptu interrogations by Soviet officials had now become less frequent. Though the same questions were asked, Capt. Crandall and his men doggedly stuck to their story: while on a reconnaissance mission from China, they got lost, ran low on fuel, and were forced to land in Russian territory.

The Russians listened patiently but it was clear that they were unconvinced of the forthrightness of the Americans. *Could they be spies? Albeit, extraordinarily incompetent spies. Or could they be what they claimed to be?* In typical Russian form they elected to wait and see.

From the beginning the Americans were provided with sufficient food and while the menu lacked variety, the boiled beef, potatoes, cabbage, caviar, black bread, bologna, and yogurt provided was hearty and nourishing. The airmen were also supplied with Soviet cigarettes, which consisted of long hollow paper tubes half filled with very strong tobacco. They were "Ducat" brand and had an aroma reminiscent of old socks.

Then, without warning, the American crew was ordered to abandon their quarters in Komsomolsk, board a train, and begin the nearly 10,000 kilometer journey across Siberia.

Two sleeping compartments were set aside for the Americans. This provided a considerable degree of comfort in addition to essentially isolating the airmen from the other passengers. During the long and tedious trip their needs were grudgingly seen to by a cadre of low ranking army personnel, who took turns along the route serving as interpreters and wardens.

"Hey, this is some fun, eh?" Pua would say enthusiastically during the early days of the journey.

The other airmen stared at him disapprovingly.

"What? I like trains. So?" he'd retort.

As the train rumbled through the breadth of Russia, the Americans viewed miles of barren steppes, dense forests, the strikingly beautiful shores of Lake Baikal, and witnessed some of the most desolate and inhospitable terrain on the planet stream past their compartment window.

"Where are we going?" Captain Crandall repeatedly asked their caretakers. "C'mon, guys, tell us."

The response was not very informative and always the same. "West. We go west."

At a station stop, when the airmen were given permission to disembark and stretch their legs, Nick Tolkin, the navigator, managed to filch a printed train schedule. He showed it to his crew.

"End of the line is Moscow," Tolkin declared. "Near as I can tell we're headin' to Moscow."

Even tentative knowledge of their potential destination was a comfort to the men.

They never made it all the way to Moscow. At a small town named Zuyero, just short of the capitol, the Americans were ordered off and taken by a horse cart to a house at the edge of the village.

A short time after occupying the house in Zuyero, the story of the Tokyo Raiders came out. Allied news sources recounted a daring raid by sixteen American B-25 medium bombers that struck a savage blow to the heart of the Japanese empire. The Japanese account characterized a tentative and cowardly hit and run attack on a quiet residential area of Tokyo perpetrated by four aircraft from Mainland China in which all but one was destroyed by crack Japanese gunners. Whichever account one chose to believe, it was now obvious that these men had taken part in that raid, establishing that they were indeed Allied airmen, not spies.

Quietly proud that their secret was out, the B-25 aircrew expected to be promptly repatriated to the States. Unfortunately, this did not occur. In light of the treaty the Russians had signed with Japan and their desire to avoid incurring the ire of the Empire, they chose a middle course in the disposition of the American flyers. Russia would impound the aircraft and intern the crew for the duration of the war. And so, the American aircrew was resigned to spend the summer and probably the rest of the war in Zuyero as wards of the Soviet Union.

In the fall the crew was visited by a Red Cross official and a junior member of the consulate staff in Moscow. The visitors brought some cartons of American products including several Red Cross packages. These contained candy, Hershey bars, chewing gum, playing cards, pairs of knitted gloves, paint sets, and prayer books. In addition, they received parcels of local food, a crate of phonograph records, magazines, and cartons of American cigarettes. Most welcome of all was mail. The letters were from the crew's relieved families, who had been notified that their boys were safe. The airmen were enormously buoyed by the visit and the promise by the State Department officer that they would post the crew's letters back to the States. The officials vowed to return soon with more—packages, news from home, and perhaps a timetable for their repatriation. That was the last time the airmen met with a representative of their government.

Along with the Zuyero house, the Americans were provided with an interpreter. His name was Kamenny Nalchik Stolsky. With his tentative grasp of English, he served as butler, scrounger, aide, and liaison to the outside world. He was also their sole source of sustenance. Kamenny did not drink or smoke, but did possess one weakness. Gum. He loved the Beeman's chewing gum. This fit in very well with the gum-chewing aircrew, which unanimously preferred Wrigley's. The Beeman's was all for Kamenny. The flyers had two names for their majordomo. The first was "Due Time" because his reply to demands, requests, and questions was invariably, "In due time." The second was "The Snitch" because the crew believed that everything they said or did was reported and compiled in some oversized Kremlin dossier.

Aside from the feelings of abandonment and the boredom of isolation, life for the internees was fairly tolerable. They enjoyed the services of a housekeeper and cook who diligently looked after them. The access to leftover food was a great incentive for these servants to ingratiate themselves with the airmen.

Meals consisted of the ubiquitous boiled beef, cabbage, bologna, eggs, and black and red caviar. Occasionally they might be served chicken, usually boiled, and upon rare occasions, mutton. While neither the fare nor the accommodations were precisely to the liking of the Americans, no one complained. They understood that they were eating better than most of the local population.

One morning, dropped off by a farmer and his cart, Kamenny arrived with his regular food acquisitions. Along with the package of food he carried a large wooden box into the house. It was a Victrola record player. The stateside collection of records provided by the consulate aide could now be played. The once useless black disks suddenly became a real touch of home.

"Where'd you get it?" Caloon asked Kamenny as he installed a needle and cranked up the player.

"I get from people who make business. I get."

"Well, however you got it, thanks a whole lot," said the second officer.

The boys gathered around as Sam gently put the needle down onto "Moonlight Serenade" by Glenn Miller. The Tommy Dorsey had been cracked in transit but there were still a couple of Bing Crosbys, a Benny Goodman, the Andrew Sisters, and a nifty nonsense song called "Mairzy Doats" by some girl singer named Cece Collins. The sounds of home filled the house and for the first time in a very long while, a bit of the boredom and emptiness lifted from the hearts of the airmen.

One day the tranquility of the sleepy town of Zuyero was shattered. The booming of distant guns could be heard. Big guns.

"What's that all about, Kamenny?" demanded McCabe.

"What? I hear nothing."

"Are you deaf? That's artillery, man."

Finally, Kamenny reluctantly confirmed that the Germans had advanced to within artillery range of the capitol. Moscow was under siege. The sound of the relentless bombardment was clearly audible on the days when the wind was from the west.

A few weeks later Kamenny announced that the American aircrew had been ordered to move south from their present location to a town in the Kuban. The Soviet foreign ministry determined that Russian prestige could be damaged if the American "guests" were inadvertently harmed while in their care.

After a train ride of a mere 800 kilometers, the American aircrew and their belongings were deposited at the front door of their new home. It was a large structure standing alone in the countryside, resembling a rustic, small town American lodge hall.

21

Bell Aircraft Corp.
Romulus, Michigan
March 20, 1943

"This is the Bell P-39d Aircobra," Lt. Wallace Wood, the short, baby-faced instructor, proudly announced to the five women pilots gathered around him. He affectionately patted the fuselage of the aircraft. Lt. Wood stood approximately 5'4" and fit in well with the average height of the women surrounding him.

Pursuit aircraft were the domain of the short aviator. Unlike bombers that had plenty of headroom and the kind of legroom that could accommodate your Gary Cooper and Jimmy Stewart types, pursuit ship cockpits were invariably cramped. The Bell P-39 cockpit was the exception. With its automobile-type door and roomy, well laid out interior, it proved to be a comfortable workplace. The banty rooster of a pilot assigned to check out Marie LeClaire, Rita Davis, Betty Willis, Margaret Cohan, and Mildred Barnes relished the luxury of the extra room.

"As you receive transition training on this aircraft you should note that there have already been nine women who have a class IV rating and are cleared to ferry this pursuit ship. The P-39 has an undeserved reputation for being a killer of pilots. It is not a killer. It is merely an unforgiving aircraft. Carelessness will get you into trouble with the Aircobra. But isn't that true of any aircraft you fly?"

The assembled women nodded in unison.

"You'll notice this aircraft has tricycle type landing gear, most likely different from the other pursuit ships you have flown. This configuration will provide better visibility taxiing and it will require you make some adjustments to your landing techniques. But there'll be time enough for that. First you are going to take turns taxiing the aircraft to help you get a feel for the controls and the instrument panel. I have a set of tech orders for each of you. You can take them back to your billets tonight after our session. I suggest you study the material thoroughly. Any questions?" Then, checking his clipboard, he said, "LeClaire, get in and we'll start. Cohan, you're up next."

"So, Lieutenant Wood, sir," said Peggy, exaggerating the "sir" in a slightly mocking tone. "Tell me again why the boys don't like the Aircobra?"

The instructor reacted to Peggy's flirting insolence with a sideways glance, but then let it go and answered her question.

"Two things; the drive shaft runs between the pilot's legs. That's because they put a big gun in the nose and had to put the engine behind the cockpit. A lot of the guys don't like that long steel drive shaft doin' three thousand revs so close to your...I mean, under their seat."

"Ooooh, sounds exciting to me," said Peggy with shameless enthusiasm.

Lt. Wally blushed bright pink.

"What's the other thing?" Peggy quickly countered to allow the instructor to regain his composure.

"Oh," said Lt. Wally, "the supercharger. They decided the 1150 Allison didn't need a supercharger. So at altitude it just has no poop. Over 15,000 feet she's a slug. Not very good for dog fighting."

"That's it?" said Peggy.

"Well, there is one more thing," said Lt. Wally.

"And that is?"

"Uh, spins. When the Cobra gets into a spin it's not easy to get her out of it."

"Really, can you show me?" said Peggy, affecting her most sincere and earnest acolyte's expression.

"You mean a lesson on spins? Why? You're practically qualified," said Lt. Wally.

"Yes, but you know so much about this plane and you're such a great instructor. I bet you could teach me so much more." Peggy locked her eyes on Lt. Wood while she tossed her head as if to get the hair out of her eyes, even though her present hair style was much too short for any stray locks.

Later, when Peggy and the lieutenant were sitting together at a table in the base canteen, she continued her questions. This type of fraternization with a student was frowned upon, but Peggy was insistent and Lt. Wood liked her company. After all, she was a damn pretty girl. They shared coffee and sinkers while Peggy pressed on.

"So, how come they made you an instructor? Were you really in combat? What was that like? Did you shoot anyone down? What plane did you fly?"

The answers came grudgingly at first, then flowed in a sudden outpouring of painful memories.

Yes, he'd been in combat. Flew a P-40. Had two confirmed victories and one probable. Saw his best friend auger in. Ka-blewie! Nothing left. Put together Jimmy's things and mailed them to his folks. No letter. Couldn't. Somebody else would have to do that. Then the nightmares. And now, being afraid to go up, knowing that I was next. Next patrol I got jumped by a couple of Japs. Where was my wingman? I'm hit. The controls are sluggish, losing coolant, overheating. Oil pressure, tapioca. I'm a goner. No! Stay low, nurse it back. Maybe…make Kun Ming before she seizes up. Finally, there's the strip. C'mon, bring 'er straight in. The belly hits. Oh, God! I ground loop. Dirt flying around in the cockpit. I forgot to put down the gear. You believe that? Why ain't I dead? I should be dead. I should have been killed, too.

Lt. Wood looked up into Peggy's face and asked, again, "Why?"

Peggy was unprepared for his emotional outpouring. What had begun as her well-practiced cajoling of a man in order to get something from him had become an uninhibited emotional release. Peggy saw tears well up in the man's eyes. His hurt was real. This was no longer a game. A game she loved to play because she almost always won.

Peggy looked around. The snack bar was deserted except for some noisy painters over at the other end of the room. No one was watching. No one had taken any notice. The lieutenant's privacy was intact.

She reached under the table and placed her hand on his knee. In the past this had always been a calculated action. The guy would get rattled, then hot and bothered, and Peggy would get her way. But this time Peggy was not thinking about herself. This time the touch was a consoling touch. And Lt. Wood understood it was. He had never before spoken of this. Shared the burden. Not even to his family. Not even to himself. The tears welled up in his eyes and streamed down his cheeks. He took a deep breath, shuddered, and let it out long and slowly as the first seedling of relief emerged. He turned and gazed into Peggy's eyes. She returned his look. What she saw was gratitude and she squeezed his leg once more to let him know she understood.

The slightly flustered lieutenant pulled out a handkerchief and clumsily blew his nose.

"Whew!" he said, shaking his head. He took another deep breath and asked, "Now, anything else you need to know?"

This prompted them to share a relieved chuckle.

"All right," was Peggy's response. "What's the 'wingman' thing and what does the wingman do?"

"Boy," said Lt. Wood in mock exasperation, "with you the questions never end. In a two plane echelon," Lt. Wood held up his two hands to represent a pair of aircraft. "One is the leader or hunter and the other protects his six."

"Six?" asked Peggy.

"Yeah," said Lt. Wood. "Like on a clock face with twelve being dead ahead. Your six is where you are most vulnerable, so your wingman, usually a new guy in the outfit, watches your a… backside while you're free to execute the mission. It's called zone protection. He usually hangs back 500 to 1,000 feet at altitude and keeps the bogeys off your back. Think of a sixty degree cone of airspace behind the leader."

"Okay, makes sense," said Peggy.

"You turn, he turns. You go inverted, wingman goes inverted. Always keeps you in sight and sticks to you like glue."

Lt. Wood demonstrated by flying his two hands in corresponding moves, one hand always mimicking the action of the other.

"It's a proven combat dog fighting tactic," Lt. Wood explained. "Not that you'll be flying combat anytime soon."

"Hey," said Peggy. "A Girl Scout's gotta be prepared." She smiled and raised her hand in the three-fingered scout salute.

Late that afternoon and twice more the next day, the formerly perpetually dour Lt. Wood went up with Peggy and taught her some aerobatics and techniques to recover from a spin. He was pleased with her ability to accept his instruction and apply it. *This girl is an apt student, picks things up quicker than most of the men,* he thought, feeling a bit of pride in his protégé.

Back on the ground, the lessons continued. "Altitude!" the Lieutenant stressed. "Altitude is the thing, and with it you can get speed. And speed is life. That German, Von Richthofen, said it: altitude is good, but speed is life. It'll save your a . . . save you in a dog fight. And remember, don't get yourself into a flat spin with this bird. With the center of gravity where it is, behind the wings and cockpit, it's tough to get the nose down so you can recover."

Peggy nodded solemnly at his warning.

"If you're really stuck and full rudder, forward stick, throttle bursts don't do it; I've been told that rotating the control stick like you're stirring a big vat of mashed potatoes might get you out of the spin. But that's a last resort, got it?"

"Got it," replied Peggy.

"And don't forget," Wood persisted. "This bird needs to land hot. Of course, you know that. You've been flying it. Remember, there's something about the aerodynamics of the Cobra that will stall her out without warning if you're slightly under landing speed. Okay?"

"Okay. One more thing," Peggy said. "How's the gun sight work?"

"Oh, you don't have to worry about that, ferrying," Wood replied.

"But, how's it work?" Peggy persisted.

Lt. Wood sighed in mock forbearance. "Projects a reticle on the windscreen."

"I know," said Peggy. "I've switched it on. But how's it *work?*"

"The outer ring marks a 400 yard lead. The dot is zero lead. To shoot down a fast-crossing target you fire when the target touches the outer ring, in line with the dot. Get it?"

"Okay, I think so. Thanks, Wally. You've been a doll."

"No kid, thank you! There's nothing more I can teach you," Lt.Wood said as he extended his hand.

Peggy moved close to him, put her arms around him and gave him a big, outrageously nonmilitary hug.

When student and instructor parted and the blush had drained from his face, Lt. Wally mused, *Whew, that girl is somethin'. Besides being a real looker, she appreciates a damn good instructor.*

22

Willis, Cohan, Barnes! Jensen, Davis, Prudhomme. Ferry orders!"
The Bell operations clerk called out the names at the small group of
women chatting outside the building.

Rita Davis raised her hand, "I'll tell 'em," she said, volunteering to
walk over to the barracks where the other women were probably still
asleep after returning from last night's cross-country.

The orders read: *E. Willis, M. Cohan, M. Barnes, P. Jensen, R. Davis,
J. Prudhomme. Receive one P-39 aircraft and deliver it to Fairbanks,
Alaska, via Fond du Lac, Wisconsin, Pierre, South Dakota, and Seattle,
Washington.*

"That's quite a haul," said Peggy, "a three or four-day trip."

"Wonder what they want these fighters in Alaska for," said Betty
Willis.

"Most likely to ship 'em to the guys in the Pacific," said Millie.

"That doesn't make any sense," said Peggy. "Fairbanks is inland. If
they were replacement planes for the Pacific then they'd be going to
Seattle or San Diego. More likely, they're for Alaskan defense."

From the ramp of the Bell Aircraft factory, eighteen newly built
and test-flown P-39s turned onto the main strip and took to the air.
These aircraft, each bearing a 175-gallon centerline external tank, were
painted in olive drab with the red star of the Soviet army emblazoned

on the fuselage. They were the first of two hundred and twenty Lend-Lease fighters beginning the long overland journey to Alaska and ultimately, Russia.

After days of flying in bad weather and poor visibility, sleeping on hard airport benches and baggage area dollies, all twenty-four pilots landed their aircraft at the Fairbanks Airdrome in Alaska. The Army had set up operations on one side of the runway and had put up prefab structures for offices and personnel. Concrete foundations for several hangars were in the process of being poured. The Army was quickly turning the Fairbanks strip into a fully functional airbase.

Their B-4 bags in hand, the pilots reported to the officer in charge. With their aircraft parked, chocked, and presumed to be delivered, the women were anxious to initiate their return trip.

"Uh, there's been a snag," announced the balding major who manned a desk labeled "Adjutant. Major Simpkins, Donald."

"You see, the flight with the Russian pilots didn't make it. And it doesn't look like they're gonna get here anytime soon. The new orders, for you six and the other eighteen over there in the truck garage, is to fly these aircraft to Ladd Field in Nome and then the rest of the way to Russia. You're going by way of Ozerny, Yakutsk, Tomsk, and Magnitogorsk. From there you'll be assigned a specific base."

"Are you crazy?" was the response of Betty Willis.

The other five women simply looked at each other, too shocked to speak. But, "are you crazy" was, in the view of Miss Willis's colleagues, a perfectly appropriate response.

"This has got to be a mistake," Peggy finally said once the initial shock of the Army man's announcement wore off.

"It's no mistake," said the major peevishly. "Now, I realize you're not regular Army so I'll let it go. But those are your orders."

"Wait, wait, we're not supposed to leave US territory," Mildred Barnes pointed out excitedly.

"That's right! It's in our charter or something," added LeClaire.

"Nevertheless," Simpkins harrumphed, "tomorrow at six, you and the other pilots take off to your first refueling stop, Ladd Field in

Nome. Then it's on to Ozerny, on the Chukotskiy peninsula. Those are your new orders. Is that clear? Now, that's the building we've cleared out for you pilots," he said, pointing to a rough structure beyond the newly poured footings of the new hangars. "Go over, they'll set you up with a cot. And get some sleep, you're going to need it. That's all. You are dismissed."

"This isn't right," Pat Jensen told her mates as they walked across the newly plowed ramp to the indicated building. They all mutely agreed.

I don't really care that much about where they send me, thought Peggy. *Hey, it might be an adventure, but they sure picked a crappy way of breaking it to us.*

Six days later, after stopping over in some of the most primitive locations imaginable and traversing nearly the entire width of northern Asia, ten P-39 Aircobras set down on the grass runway of the newly activated Kotluban airbase in the Kuban of southeast Russia.

Watching their chocked Cobras being refueled at journey's end, the ferry pilots milled about on the ramp.

"This isn't the middle of nowhere, it's the end of nowhere," Betty Willis declared to the assembly of pilots around her.

"We must have flown over five thousand freakin' miles," Rita Davis added.

"These people look like Eskimos to me. Maybe we're near the North Pole. It's certainly cold enough," Pat Jensen muttered as she shivered under her flight jacket.

"I wonder if we're near the war?" Peggy Cohan questioned out loud. "Bet we're fairly close to the war."

"Never mind the war," Major Felker said. "Just stay together and we'll be taken to our quarters. Don't wander off, hear?"

"Wander off?" Willis asked. "To where?"

PART 2

The Ukrainian spring was punctual in 1943, transforming winter-hardened roads into rivers of impassible ooze. It would seem even the earth conspired against the army of the Reich in this third year of the invasion. Both sides could sense the tide was turning. Though the siege of Leningrad persisted, Paulus's army was stalled at Stalingrad. The German assault had lost its vitality. For the past two years the Russians fought a dogged defensive campaign; engaging the enemy, bearing horrific casualties, then repeatedly falling back to regroup. But this spring, the time for defense had ended. It was time to attack, time to drive the enemy from the homeland. The great counteroffensive of what would be called the Great Patriotic War was imminent. Until then, it was every loyal Russian's duty to impede and harass the enemy in every way possible.

High above the contested landscape, a tremulous line of fragile aircraft plunged resolutely westward through the cloud-cluttered night, their five cylinder 110 hp radial engines growling at the earth a thousand meters below. The pilot in the lead aircraft peered apprehensively into the night through churning propeller blades while nervously checking and rechecking the magnetic compass. It was the responsibility of the lead aircraft to guide these flimsy biplanes to their target. Simplistic Soviet doctrine decreed that the other planes in the string need only follow the aircraft ahead of them in order to be guided to their destination. And so at seventy mph, like some great airborne caterpillar, the undulating line of antiquated bombers surged toward its objective. There was no moon this night and only the subtlest contrast of black versus blacker allowed the flyers to distinguish sky from ground. Beacon fires along the way, lit by local partisans, enabled the determined aviators to confirm their course. These missions were flown every night, weather permitting, with many of the aircraft flying as many as five sorties before dawn. Mobile restaging areas manned by partisans were clandestinely assembled along the flight path so that aircraft could be fueled, rearmed, and quickly returned to action. Despite all the logistical effort and dedicated manpower, the damage inflicted was usually minor, consisting of an occasional destroyed vehicle, a few bathtub-sized craters gouged in the frozen earth, and an interrupted night's sleep for the Hun. But even that was something. In this war, a war for the Rodina, the Motherland, any discomfiture inflicted upon the fascists was something.

At a prearranged signal the dozen antique bombers separated into two lines of six. A computation of time, air speed, and wind by the lead navigator confirmed they would shortly be over their target.

All at once the sky ahead came alight as lances of enemy searchlights stabbed upward, slashing the gloom in hopes of revealing a target for poised Nazi gunners. The two lines of aircraft obdurately pressed forward towards those ominous beams while the pulse rates of the aircrews quickened. Occupying the rear seat of one of these aircraft sat a passenger whose heart rate accelerated at a slightly greater pace than the others. This experience was entirely new to her.

Earlier that evening the women pilots of the 466th Light Bombardment Squadron, many still in their teens, were chatting easily about the mission ahead of them. They joked, laughingly referring to this night's foray as a "midnight sleigh ride" as they donned their bulky leathers. In a gesture of camaraderie crossed with mischief, they invited the American girl along for the ride. Since only four aircraft would carry a navigator/gunner, there were eight that would fly tonight with an empty rear seat.

"You come, fly, see we make bombing," one girl said, grinning wickedly, as she pounded her fist into her open palm.

"The American might enjoy the 'outing,'" one of the other pilots added in Russian to the amusement of the rest.

Now at 3,000 feet, headed directly into the maw of a poised Nazi flak circus, Peggy Cohan, American ferry pilot, was beginning to realize that this "sleigh ride" might be a genuinely idiotic idea. From where she sat, this game looked dangerous and certainly anything but routine.

The young American was one of a group of ATC ferry pilots. Only three days before, they had delivered ten Lend-Lease Bell P-39D Aircobras to the 122nd Air Brigade Airdrome in the southern Ukraine. The odyssey had taken six days of dawn to dusk flying and saw several of their original complement forced to drop out along the route. Upon completion of the delivery, the Americans were scheduled to retrace the ALSIB route and immediately return to Nome. Unfortunately, the transport designated for their return sat red-balled at an airport near Moscow. Thus, the extension of the journey into the heart of Russia, once viewed by many of the young aviators as an exotic adventure, now became a monumental inconvenience.

Despite a polite reception, the Americans chose to keep mostly to themselves at the Soviet airdrome. This was partly due to the language barrier and partly at the discomfort of finding themselves in the midst of so many dedicated Communists. Most of these college-educated young Americans viewed Communists as one stripe above bomb-wielding anarchists. But Peggy Cohan, more curious about her Soviet sister aviators than concerned about ideology, elected to visit a nearby squadron area to get a closer look at the exotic aircraft and perhaps meet some of the women who flew them.

Airplanes had always held an almost mystical fascination for Peggy. She found herself irresistibly drawn to the complex machines, seeing them as miraculous steeds capable of galloping through the air. She was especially curious about any type of aircraft she had never seen before. As Peggy approached the clumsy looking PO-2s, resembling the Curtis *Jenny* she had once flown back home in Flushing, she was regarded warily by the Russian ground crews and pilots. Peggy was surprised to discover that the entire bomber squadron was made up of women. Not just flight crews, but mechanics and ordnance specialists as well. When Peggy attempted to engage them in conversation, they responded guardedly. The Russian women were well aware she was one of the group that had recently brought in the new Aircobras, a far more advanced aircraft than most of the equipment at the Soviet airbase and decades beyond the primitive stack-winged PO-2s. Even the vaunted Shturmovik fighter bomber seemed like a Model-T next to the sleek and lethal-looking Aircobra.

Eventually Peggy's openness won out over their reticence and the language barrier and she began to communicate with the Russian women. She was, after all, a sister of the sorority of the air. Close in age, most of these girls, like Peggy, were still in their teens. A few English words here and there plus the universal sign language of flyers soon punctured the Russian reserve and a spirited, good-natured exchange ensued.

A broad-faced Slavic girl with ruddy cheeks explained their mission.

"We fly in dark. Bomb Fascist. Take new bomb. Bomb more. Five," she displayed five fingers. "Sometime six fly," she said, adding a thumb to complete the count.

"All night?" Peggy asked.

"Da! . . . All night. No fly rain or snow." She shook her head and moved her hand downward, wiggling her fingers to mimic snowfall.

"Soon we make bombing. You come? You sit. Like fancy lady in troika." The Russian girl then mimed her impression of a grand lady, aloof and bored with her surroundings, fluttering her hand as if it were a fan. This prompted a chuckle from the entire group. "You come? Yes?"

"You fly with me," one of the women said. "I, Natalia Spasenskaya." The broad-faced, curly-haired blonde with large gray eyes tapped her chest and smiled. "I make, how you say . . . wetness riding," with her hand she made a slow, flat gesture.

"Smooth?" Peggy guessed.

"Da. Smooth. Hokay?"

"Okay," said Peggy impulsively, surprising herself that she had agreed to tag along on a combat mission. She consented partly out of curiosity but mostly from the sense that the invitation was a bit of a dare. Peggy always had difficulties turning down a dare.

Now, here she was over enemy territory descending into the lights and sights of the German gunners. Peggy tensed her grip on the welded steel brackets on each side of her seat, oblivious to the two katyusha: twenty-kilogram mortar shells stowed there "to throw down on head of fascist." Heading into the midst of the slashing lights, the noise, and the arcing scimitars of antiaircraft fire, the acrid smell of cordite assaulted Peggy's nose. She had a box seat on the lethal drama being enacted before her in the night sky. This "sleigh ride" was turning out to be nothing like the outing described by the Russian girls. This was frightening.

As the line of biplanes approached the air space above the probing beams and intermittent streams of tracers, Peggy observed a strange tactic. Her pilot cut the power of their bomb-laden aircraft. For a moment she thought that the PO-2s engine had failed, but then she realized that the other five aircraft in her formation had likewise throttled back and were together gliding quietly toward the German positions. When they were approximately 1,000 meters from the drop zone, one of the lead PO-2s banked away sharply from the formation and revved its engine. The German searchlights immediately slashed toward the sound. Peggy watched as the biplane jinked and side-slipped frantically to evade the probing lances. When the lights painted a portion of wing or fuselage of the decoy, the ack-acks responded instantly, directing their fire ahead of the glimpsed aircraft. But each time the streams of tracers and explosive blooms found only empty air. *That's some gutsy pilot*, observed Peggy as she sat watching the macabre game.

Suddenly, her own craft lurched upward, in reaction to the release of 1,200 kilograms of high explosive from the underwing racks. Peggy breathed a sigh of relief despite being choked by clouds of acrid smoke and burnt cordite. Under reduced power, their heavily-laden aircraft had been dropping steadily and the dark ground was looming uncomfortably close. Behind them, a timpani of fiery blossoms rumbled along the earth. Peggy stared in rapt fascination at the explosions, only to be shaken from her reverie as her pilot pounded on the fuselage to remind her of the two bombs stowed on either side of her seat. Peggy had forgotten them. She nodded an exaggerated "yes" and proceeded to haul the heavy missiles out of their improvised racks. Lifting nearly forty pounds of steel and high explosives while seated was no easy task. She eventually managed the chore by undoing her seat harness and, crouching on her seat, raised and jettisoned the small bombs over each side. Two satisfying explosions a few moments later confirmed that her offerings had been received. After a few moments more, beyond the reach of the searchlights, the PO-2 engine revved loudly once more and nosed up into a slow banking turn. Numerous fires on the ground indicated that their mission had been effective. Along with many small fires, a delayed chain of massive ground explosions evidenced that an ammunition stockpile or fuel storage area had been set off. That was very good news. After the long Russian winter, the Germans were short on both ammo and petrol. This raid would deplete the Nazi war larder significantly.

So this is combat, Peggy mused. I must admit that although people are trying their best to kill me, it certainly is exciting. But I do think it's time to scram the heck out of here.

Skirting the area of searchlights and concentrated antiaircraft, Peggy's PO-2 turned east. Suddenly a burst of flame lit up the dark sky high on their starboard side. A Russian aircraft had been hit. It exploded in midair. The crew had no chance, even if they had been equipped with parachutes. As the fiery debris spiraled to the ground, Natalia turned to Peggy and solemnly shook her head. There was nothing they could do but continue back to base.

Then out of her peripheral vision, Peggy noticed another streak of flame. This time much lower in the sky and to their left. Another Russian aircraft in trouble. Peggy could make out the distinctive shape of a PO-2 diving toward the ground, its engine trailing flame. As the crippled aircraft landed roughly in a field, it rolled briefly, and finally tilted crazily up on its nose. Peggy noticed movement in the cockpit illuminated by the rapidly spreading fire, then observed a form scrambling free of the cockpit, which was now nearly engulfed in flames. Miraculously, the pilot managed to roll out onto the wing, crawl to the ground, and drag herself clear of the inferno.

Peggy reached forward, nudged her pilot and pointed to the burning wreck. Natalia once again shook her head in helpless resignation at the sight. But when Peggy conveyed with her fingers that the pilot had run from the ship, Natalia banked sharply and turned back towards the crash sight. Illuminated by the flames, the downed pilot could be seen some yards from the crash, kneeling in the field, head lowered. When she noticed her comrades approaching, the downed pilot rose unsteadily and waved frantically skyward in an attempt to warn them away. It was no use. Natalia Spasenskaya was determined to rescue her comrade.

They came down hard in an uneven pasture. While still taxiing on the rough, terrain towards the crackling wreck Peggy jumped from the wing and sprinted to the downed aviator. With great effort, Peggy hauled the large, disoriented woman to her feet and began half-dragging, half-carrying her toward the idling biplane. Natalia suddenly appeared and together they maneuvered the dazed woman to the waiting aircraft. As they arrived, lights from beyond the far side of the field pierced the dark. The faint, clattering roar of a diesel-powered vehicle racing towards them could be heard above the crackling flames and the *pop, pop* of the PO-2's idling engine. As Peggy and Natalia hurriedly heaved the wounded woman up onto the wing and into the rear cockpit, a German half-track burst through the tree line and sped towards them. The Nazis were less than two hundred yards away. A machine gun began to chatter in concert with the *crack, crack, crack* of rifle fire and the shouts of men; it was background noise to the raging fire and the *clickety-pop-pop* of the idling PO-2's five-cylinder engine.

With their semi-conscious passenger safely lodged in the rear seat, Peggy lowered herself as delicately as she could onto the woman's lap. As she did, Peggy was horrified to watch Natalia, on the wing, suddenly lurch backward and fall from view. She had taken a rifle bullet in the leg just as she was raising it to climb into the cockpit. Natalia Spasenskaya fell back, helplessly sprawled on the wing, desperately clinging to a support wire to prevent herself from sliding off to the ground. Peggy reacted instantly, ignoring the angry buzz of bullets all around her. She vaulted forward and dropped down onto the wing next to the injured Natalia. Then in a nearly superhuman effort, Peggy took hold of the girl by her leather flight suit, hauled her upright, and dumped her head first into the open forward cockpit. She could feel the lethal presence of the German riflemen bearing down on them as she scrambled back to the rear cockpit. Landing hard on the injured woman, Peggy shoved the throttle forward as her toes probed for the rudder pedals. The yelp of pain uttered by the barely conscious form beneath her was ignored.

As the truck attempted to head off the now taxiing aircraft, the Germans found themselves blocked by the furiously burning wreckage. They were forced to veer around it in order to continue the pursuit. Peggy ducked her head as another volley of shots rang out, but inexplicably, none seemed to come close. The flaming wreck had momentarily blinded the riflemen. Nevertheless, they continued to fire in the general direction of the sound.

It was a miraculously short takeoff. Less than one-hundred feet. As the PO-2 rose tentatively from the uneven ground, Peggy was impressed by the considerable lift provided by those broad, Russian-built wings. *Abner would have appreciated it too,* she observed, in a fleeting and disconnected thought. As the ship clawed for altitude, a dark skeletal tangle of tree limbs loomed before them. All Peggy could do was to push on the already maxed throttle and haul back with both hands on the fully rotated control column. The aircraft literally flew through the bare uppermost branches of a stand of birch trees bordering the field. Ominous thuds, snaps, and crackles attested to the inelegant egress. The erratic vibration of the now unbalanced propeller confirmed it. But they were in the air, swaddled in darkness and putting distance between themselves and the Germans. She checked the compass to assure herself that she was heading east and then took a couple of exaggerated deep breaths in an attempt to calm herself. All she had to do now was find the Russian airdrome in the dark and land this torn and shaking relic without killing herself or her two injured passengers.

As Peggy pointed the craft into the quadrant of sky which hinted faintly of the arrival of dawn, she was gratified to see movement in the front cockpit. With great effort, Natalia was slowly snaking her body into an upright position while simultaneously trying to avoid contact with the flight controls. When finally properly seated, she turned back to Peggy and gestured in a slightly southerly direction. As Peggy nodded that she understood the new heading, the injured girl slumped forward, once again losing consciousness. All Peggy could do for her was lean forward over the Plexiglas windshield to secure the girl's seat harness and hope that she would survive the flight; there was a lot of blood. Not long after the course correction, Peggy began to pick out some vaguely familiar landmarks in the dim predawn light. The Dnieper River. Chimney smoke. The irregular rooftops of a small village. And, then, there it was in the mist, the Regimental Airfield. Since there was no radio to announce her presence, she would have to land as carefully as possible and keep her fingers crossed that Russian antiaircraft gunners would recognize one of their own.

Peggy lined up on the lantern-outlined strip and brought the vibrating PO-2 in nose high, attempting to bleed off as much air speed as possible. Concerned that her landing gear might be damaged, she lifted the nose to an even greater angle and flared out into a virtual stall, cutting the throttle as she touched down. Her instincts served her well. The right main gear had been sheared off by that enemy-held tree line. The bare axle dug into the half-frozen soil, followed by the right wingtip, driving the lumbering PO-2 into a spar-shattering ground loop. But the aircraft's momentum was so reduced that instead of flipping over completely, the tail elevated nearly to vertical, then fell back heavily onto the tail wheel.

Almost immediately the aircraft was surrounded by fire trucks and an ambulance. Ready hands lifted the two injured women from the aircraft and bore them to the ambulance. Peggy, who finally managed to convey to the medics that she was unharmed, was greatly relieved that both her passengers showed signs of consciousness.

After a prolonged and frustrating attempt to describe the night's activity to a young, male Russian officer, Peggy cadged a ride on a flatbed truck to the wooden barracks where the American ferry pilots were quartered. Quietly making her way in the dark amidst her sleeping countrymen, she located her wooden bunk, wriggled out of her borrowed flight suit and boots, and fell back onto her coarse wool blanket, barely mustering the energy to lift her legs onto the bunk. *So much for Russian sleigh rides,* mused Peggy as she contemplated the improbable reality of her recent adventure. She slept deeply, dreaming of soaring noiselessly through blue skies and sun-brightened clouds of pink cotton candy.

Peggy awoke to the smell of freshly baked bread. She rose and dressed quickly in the chilly barracks and joined her American colleagues in the common room for a breakfast of black bread, sausage, caviar, and strong tea, which was brought to the Americans on covered trays by four sullen uniformed Russian women. She said nothing to her colleagues of her previous night's excursion. Later that morning Peggy searched for the base hospital in order to learn the fate of her two passengers of the previous night. She found the Balnitza without difficulty. Upon entering the small central hall she looked to the left and saw that it was occupied by several male soldiers. Peggy turned to the opposite wing. Only two occupants were in evidence. It was Natalia, who recognized Peggy. Her face lit up with a broad grin when she saw the American girl. She had a large purplish bump on her forehead with a small Band-Aid in the center of it and her left wrist was tightly wrapped.

"No break bone," Natalia cheerfully announced as she threw back the blanket to reveal the clean white dressings on her left thigh. She proudly displayed her ability to wiggle her toes. The injured woman in the bed next to her turned out to be Major Svetlana Sorkovna, the highly decorated squadron commander. She was solidly encased in a cumbersome and obviously uncomfortable plaster cast. The stucco envelope encircled most of the large woman's upper torso and there was a stout wooden brace imbedded in the plaster to support her upper arm and hold it straight out from her side. Dislocated left shoulder, several cracked ribs, fractured lower arm, and fractured wrist. But alive. She also suffered second-degree burns on her hands and face and her two blackened eyes were framed by the stubble of eyebrows and eyelashes which had been singed away. She resembled a giant panda that had smoked an exploding cigar. Despite her disfigurement and obvious discomfort, Major Sorkovna displayed a broad gold-toothed smile as Peggy introduced herself. She insisted on attempting to embrace the American girl and kissing both her cheeks, though it was obvious that the movement caused her considerable discomfort.

Peggy drew a chair up between them and the three women chatted and giggled together like old friends, happily reunited. They even found hilarity in their frequent gaffes in English and Russian. Everything seemed funny to them this bright morning. These women were now joined by the special bond reserved for those who had together outwitted death. They were unwilling to part company, even at the insistence of an imperious nurse, who pronounced the visit to be over. Peggy reluctantly bade her two new friends a heartfelt farewell, sensing the likelihood that they would never see each other again.

"*Da svedanya, tovarich* Peggy."

"*Da svedanya*, Svetlana, Natalia."

Later, back at the American quarters, over a lunch of canned beef and potatoes, Peggy was cajoled into recounting her last evening's exploit. The entire base had been buzzing about it. Now it fell to Peggy to provide the details. Her American colleagues listened in fascination, frequently interrupting the improbable tale with questions.

"Wait, you're telling me that you actually bombed Germans?," probed Lt. Baker.

"Were you scared?" asked Millie.

"How fat was the Major?" Rita wanted to know.

The male American pilots seemed openly annoyed and skeptical as Peggy recounted the details of her wild ride. Many male aviators in the Ferry Command resented the policy of allowing women to fly. It meant that more of them would be available for combat duty.

The next day a Lisunov Li2D, the Soviet-built version of a US C-47, arrived to take the Americans to Alaska. Everyone was eager and relieved to be finally heading home. As Peggy was gathering her belongings, Major Felker, the ranking ATC officer, called her aside and informed her that she would not be returning to the US with the others. He had just been told to convey to Peggy that she had been ordered to remain at the airbase in Russia for an indeterminate amount of time. Felker was apologetic, admitting that he was at a loss to explain the order. All he knew was that it had come from very "high up." Later, as Peggy stood alone, watching the young Americans hurrying out to board the transport, she pressed her tongue tightly against her palate in an attempt to stifle the tears she felt welling up in her eyes. She was determined not to let them see her cry. Yes, it was clearly irresponsible to accept a ride on a Soviet bombing mission. She would freely admit that. But then, hadn't she helped save the two Russian pilots? Why, then, was she being punished? Exile to Russia? Why couldn't she return with the others and be punished back home in the States? Major Felker was unable to answer her questions.

Millie, Rita, and a couple of other women acknowledged Peggy with a weak wave as they boarded the transport. The majority of flyers avoided eye contact. With her chin held high, Peggy bravely offered a thumbs up as the twin engines of the Lisunov alternately coughed staccato puffs of sooty exhaust before settling down to a confident thrum.

"This really stinks!" muttered Peggy into the prop blast of the taxiing transport. "It stinks to high heaven!"

Her departing colleagues couldn't have heard her remark. But if they had none of them would have disagreed.

Alone, ten thousand miles from anywhere, and it's cold. Peggy shuddered as the sense of isolation assaulted her soul. *What am I doing here? Am I crazy? How did I get into this dumb mess? What's wrong with me? One mess after another.*

2

Moscow, the Kremlin.
The offices of the First Secretary of the Ukrainian People's Party.
Spring 1943

A disturbing report, thought Nikita Khrushchev, as he sat in his temporary Kremlin offices. It was an intelligence memo describing a new and advanced aircraft being developed by the fascists, purported to employ a remarkable new technology capable of faster speeds than anything in the Soviet or Allied arsenals. A development that could give the Nazis a decisive upper hand.

"Rest assured, Vasily Nickolaievitch, our designers behind the Ural barrier are well along on the identical technology," the bald, round-faced commissar lied to his subordinate. "The principle is turbine dynamics—something our lads have been tinkering with for some time." Khrushchev leaned forward confidentially. "We have every reason to believe that the Germans stole it from us."

This bravado-laced assurance comforted the commissar's aide, who nodded appreciatively at the revelation and the fact that his chief had confided in him.

As concern in his aide's face was fading, Commissar Khrushchev pondered the reason behind NKVD chief Beria's uncharacteristic generosity in sharing such a piece of intelligence with him. Khrushchev had always sensed that Beria was his enemy and it was only Stalin's overt regard for him that kept their interaction civil.

So, the Germans have a miraculous new airplane, Khrushchev thought. *What am I supposed to do about it? What can I do about it? Sabotage? We have neither the men nor the expertise. A bombing mission? Not one aircraft can be spared. Besides, few of our operational bombers have the range to reach the heart of Germany. No, there's little I can do now with our spring offensive about to be launched. I'll have to worry about this particular nettle some other time.*

Khrushchev took the file and dropped it solemnly into a side drawer of his ornately carved, pre-Revolution cherrywood desk.

"This one will have to steep, Vasily," he said as he jangled his key ring, located the appropriate key, and turned the lock. "Now, what new developments with the Fritzies?"

"Not much change, comrade commissar, as the Rasputitsa is hampering their ability to maneuver. We continue processing prisoners at Stalingrad, and more supplies are getting through to Leningrad. Our buildup near Kursk is proceeding on schedule. Otherwise, the situation is generally static. Oh, and General Novikov has requested your attendance at the presentation of some medals. Some of our women aviators have had some unusual successes."

"I don't see how I can spare time for decoration ceremonies. There is so much more pressing ..."

A sharp knock at the door interrupted the commissar's ruminations. His junior aide, Drushenko, leaned into the office and announced solemnly, "Comrade Khrushchev, excuse me, but the first secretary would like to see you immediately."

Stalin! He wants me? Immediately? Khrushchev rose briskly and hurriedly gathered papers from his desk in hopes of preparing himself for whatever questions the absolute ruler of the Soviet Union might pose to him.

As Khrushchev hurried along the narrow red-carpeted hallways of the Kremlin, it was willpower alone that forced him to calm and slow his pace in the face of the adrenaline urging his short legs to break into a run. A summons from Stalin. He was well aware that no living being in all of Russia could be confident of seeing the next day's sunrise after an encounter with the Russian head of state.

Khrushchev's office was on the second floor of the triangle-shaped state senate building erected by Katherine the Great in 1776. The massive red brick structure stood in the northeast corner of the huge Kremlin compound. The first secretary's offices were on the floor below and adjoined the cavernous senate chamber. When Khrushchev presented himself at the foyer to Stalin's offices, the uniformed aide instructed him to go upstairs to the third floor where the first secretary was expecting him in his living quarters.

Stalin usually commuted to his dacha in Kuntsevo, seven miles beyond the Moscow city limits, but during these desperate times the first secretary of the central committee spent his nights in a special suite of rooms prepared for him within the Kremlin walls. Most of the *Politburo* had fled the city when the first angry peal of German guns rumbled in the distance, but Stalin defiantly chose to remain, and thus became an implacable and courageous symbol for the people of Moscow.

"General-Major Khrushchev, you are expected. Go right in," said one of the armed guards standing outside the door to Stalin's quarters. The other soldier opened the sturdy ornately carved door and closed it behind Khrushchev as he entered.

Stepping through a tiled entrance hall, Khrushchev was struck by the stark contrast between the former quarters of the Imperial family and the homey atmosphere of a Georgian parlor. A small brocaded sofa squatted on one side of the room, flanked by two overstuffed chairs. Each armrest and seat back bore a white, delicately stitched lace antimacassar. Behind the sitting area, several bookcases lined the high wall, upon which hung a large painting of Lenin. His eyes were ablaze, jaw jutting with revolutionary fervor.

On the opposite side of the room, illuminated by two tall windows, which commanded a view of the Kremlin courtyard, stood a broad, solid cherrywood dining table surrounded by matching chairs. The table, used for the formulation of war strategies, was strewn with at least a score of rolled maps. On a smaller elaborately-carved table near the entrance stood a tasseled lamp beside a heavy brass samovar and several glasses in silver holders. Two ornate picture frames sat amidst the glasses, displaying the smiling photos of Stalin's second wife, Nadya, and their little daughter, Svetlana.

The floor of the large room was covered by three oriental rugs that delineated each area. One lay under the sofa and two armchairs, the largest under the conference table and the smallest beneath a worn and shiny brown leather chair and inlaid table. The table bore a green glass reading lamp and a bulky square humidor of pipe tobacco beside a fourteen-inch stack of papers. This was the seat from which Stalin digested the myriad detailed reports from every corner of his country—documents that unfailingly found their way to the attention of the Soviet head of state.

Khrushchev had never been in Stalin's quarters before. He had been received many times at Kuntsevo, the comfortable but unimposing dacha where Stalin and his family lived. The furnishings in Stalin's country home were modern, up-to-date, and cosmopolitan, as would be expected of a Moscow-dwelling, high government official. This room, on the other hand, seemed to live in the past. The predominantly red decor, cluttered with too many hangings and personal mementos, gave the impression of a curio shop with a distinct Moorish flavor.

"Nikita Sergeyevitch, is that you?" boomed an affable voice from the other room.

"Yes, comrade Stalin, it is I," Khrushchev answered a bit too quickly, betraying the fact that his leader's voice had startled him.

"I'm coming out now. Tell me what you think."

The commissar of the Ukraine turned to face the sound of the voice, not knowing what to think. And then he saw him. Stalin entered the room smiling, a disconcerting contrast to his usual stern demeanor. He was modeling what appeared to be some comic opera uniform. The jacket was a bilious, light green color, with a single line of oversized brass buttons down the front. The dark green trousers bore two broad red stripes with gold piping running down each leg. The wide shoulder boards on the jacket resembled a pair of bookshelves, displaying two enormous gold stars encircled by an excess of baroque brocade. The tall service cap was likewise festooned with gold-thread embroidery. Miraculous tailoring disguised the fact of Stalin's stunted left arm, which was a full three inches shorter than the right—a result of a beating he had received as a boy from a drunken and abusive father.

"Eh? Well, what do you think?" said Stalin as he raised both arms and executed a slow turn.

"It's . . . most impressive, Comrade First Secretary. . .but, eh, what is it for?"

"It is the uniform of a generalissimo, Nikita Sergeyevitch. Which, of course, I am during this time of war. When I meet with the American president and the British prime minister the world will be watching. I must be dressed appropriately. The plain green tunic of a son of the revolution simply won't do. See here." Stalin gestured Khrushchev over to the map table where two books lay open. He then pointed to a photograph in one of the volumes. It was a picture of a younger Winston Churchill dressed in the uniform of the first lord of the admiralty. The highly embroidered outfit was topped by a cocked hat with a white plume.

Before Khrushchev could comment, Stalin said, "What if he wears this uniform at our upcoming meeting in Yalta? And see here," he said, indicating a photograph in the other book of a younger Franklin Roosevelt as under secretary of the American Navy. "I certainly wouldn't want them to think any less of me because of my dress. We understand very well the meaning of simple Soviet cloth, but these aristocratic types might not. They must see me as a modern head of state fully equivalent to their own stations in life. In parlaying with these two I can relinquish no advantage. It was Beria's thought and, I think, a shrewd one. So, what do you think, my friend? Is it excessive? Be honest. Be brutal if you must."

"Comrade Stalin, you are every inch the generalissimo." Khrushchev's earnestness made the usually reserved Stalin break into a broad grin.

"I'm glad you like it, Nikita Sergeyevitch. I like it, too."

I never said I liked it, thought Khrushchev as he was guided to a nearby chair.

"If you give me a moment I will change. There are some matters I would like to discuss with you," said Stalin as he left the room. "I want to keep the 'generalissimo' crisp and unwrinkled when he confronts the aristocrats."

When Stalin returned, he was once more wearing his familiar dark green tunic. He walked to the humidor, claimed his pipe, lit it, and sat down on the sofa beside Khrushchev.

"I understand . . ." Stalin paused and reapplied a match to his pipe to get a better light. He puffed twice, then again, and nodded with satisfaction. Stalin continued his train of thought. ". . . that Novikov has requested a high ranking presence at a ceremony of some awards to some women aviators. I would consider it a personal favor to me if you would attend this ceremony in your capacity as member of the Politburo and commissar of the Ukraine.

"You see, my friend, one of these brave women is an American; an aviator engaged in delivering aircraft to us from America. How she became involved in the action against the Nazis is complicated but really does not matter. What is important is that her behavior was truly heroic; I'm told she single-handedly saved the lives of the formation commander and a senior pilot by returning a damaged aircraft to its base after a highly successful raid on the enemy.

"Novikov has recommended she be made Hero of the Soviet Union. I have approved his recommendation. I believe this gesture will appeal to the American president and he will immediately grasp the political value of such an event as presented by his country's press. You know, his wife is an avid advocate for women's rights and this recognition could make him much more receptive on the matter of a second front.

"When I meet with Churchill and Roosevelt I must obtain an agreement for the initiation of a new campaign by the English and Americans. Such an action will force Hitler to withdraw reserves from the Motherland and set the scene for our summer counteroffensive. I must make them realize that their North African campaign has little value to Russia. Hitler's soft underbelly, Churchill calls it. Bah! I call it idiotic dithering. Only an outright invasion of mainland Europe can benefit us.

"Go to the decoration ceremony, Nikita Sergeyevitch. Smile when Novikov pins the medal on the brave American woman's breast. Better yet, you do it. Then smile for the press cameras. We will hope it is a well-shaped breast and that she is pretty. But if she is not, smile any way."

"I will make the arrangements to attend the award ceremony, comrade Stalin," Khrushchev said.

Stalin nodded and patted the rounded cheek of his Ukrainian commissar as if he was a bright child who had just gotten himself potty trained.

"Now, next subject; the turbine aircraft the Nazis have developed. This weapon could prove to be a great threat to our counteroffensive. I am told this propeller-less aircraft can fly 100, even 200 kilometers per hour faster than anything we have in the air or on the drawing board. Nikita Sergeyevitch, this is not your area of responsibility, I know, but it is a matter of such importance that I want your keen mind thinking about it. That is the reason I had Beria send you a copy of the intelligence report. He did so reluctantly; that Beria, how he hoards his secrets. We must neutralize this weapon; perhaps by a suicide team parachuted in; the abduction of their key engineers; something bold. I'm sure you will determine the appropriate action.

"In the meantime I have suggested to comrade Lavrenti that he devote as much attention to this very real threat to our future survival as he does to the transporting of disloyal Ukrainians to the Gulag. He has commandeered so many trains that much needed troops must sit idly on sidings as he sends entire villages east. It's times like these that I am forced to question his zeal. But this is hardly an issue that should concern you," Stalin said matter-of-factly.

The matter of ethnicity had always been a troubling issue to Khrushchev. Many Ukrainians thought of themselves as more

European than Russian. There were even some villages that welcomed the German invaders, gave them aid, and even offered to fight with them. The aid was often accepted but Hitler cautioned his commanders to be wary and reminded them that Ukrainian collaborators, even useful ones, should never be considered anything but the enemy. Now, as the German advance had been halted, these people were considered traitors in their own land and left to the mercy of the sadistic and powerful head of the NKVD. Khrushchev himself was a Ukrainian, born in Kursk, and he understood completely the threat in Stalin's subtle and seemingly matter of fact mention of Beria as an overzealous but loyal minion. Stalin was famous for his deftness at playing his underlings off against one another.

"Would you care for a glass of tea, my friend?" Stalin asked affably.

"Thank you comrade Stalin, but if you don't mind, I must return to my duties."

"Very well." Stalin sighed heavily and extended a hand to Khrushchev. "Sometimes your loyalty to me is difficult to bear. Thank you again for coming, Nikita Sergeyevitch." Khrushchev nodded humbly.

"Oh, one last thing," said Stalin as Khrushchev was reaching for the door handle. "Any change in the fighting in your sector?"

"Unfortunately, no change, comrade Stalin. Despite all our efforts we remain stalemated."

"Then greater effort must be applied, Nikita Sergeyevitch. Greater devotion to duty. If our fighters are required to make the ultimate sacrifice for the Motherland then this is what they must do."

"But comrade Stalin, our losses have been . . ."

"Remember, Nikita Sergeyevitch, the death of a son or a father is a tragedy but the loss of ten thousand fathers and sons are merely statistics. Greater effort, Nikita Sergeyevitch, greater effort!"

Stalin had already turned his full attention to the pile of correspondence on the table beside his chair as Khrushchev exited.

3

Despite the new surroundings, life in the Soviet dormitory eventually became tedious for the five American airmen. Their present quarters, which once served as a meeting hall for the local farming collective, had fallen into disrepair since the war. At first the men kept themselves busy battening the leaks and cracks, patching the roof and covering broken windowpanes. During the long, frigid winter the main priority was cutting firewood and stockpiling it. When time permitted they even managed to scrounge some furniture to make things more livable. Two offices adjoining the hall were claimed by Crandall and Caloon. Utilizing scrap lumber, the men contrived rough wood partitions along the opposite wall so that Nick, McCabe, and Pua could also have their own private spaces.

Conditions were makeshift, but there was little complaint; the American airmen were well aware of the hardships the Russian people were enduring. The war with Hitler's Germany was not going well for their hosts, but compared to the locals, the living conditions of the American crew was lavish.

Now, as the days grew longer and springtime approached, the urgency to stockpile heating fuel diminished. The boys had time on their hands with little to do to fill it.

They decorated the area around their respective bunks with photos cut from magazines. Pua had a large color photo of Waikiki pinned to the wall beside his cot. In the foreground was a distinctly non-Hawaiian family cruising in a '41 Chevy convertible. Sam Caloon had a black and white photo of a Southern college campus cut from an old *Collier's*. McCabe put up a pair of cute coeds in a shiny black Studebaker with the Golden Gate Bridge in the background. Capt. Crandall boasted that real-life versions of both girls and convertible were waiting for him back home. The men carried no photos of their own. In fact, they had no papers of any kind. Their only identification was their dog tags. Except for handkerchiefs, cigarettes, and McCabe's comb, all their personal effects were locked up in a cabinet on the Hornet. Only McCabe carried a comb despite the crew cuts provided by Kamenny and his antique mechanical clipper. Roscoe's red hair was much too short for the teeth of a comb but he carried it in his back pocket purely out of habit. The stylish pompadour once sported by the American crew chief was a mere memory.

Though there were no prison bars to restrain the American aircrew, they viewed their isolation as something akin to solitary confinement. Of the men in the dormitory, only Tolkin, the navigator, made an effort to adapt to his surroundings. He went out of his way to engage the house staff and initiate conversations with neighbors when he could. Since Nick's family back in the States were of Russian heritage, there was a familiarity to the sound of many of the Russian words. This exposure enabled him to pick up a smattering of the language. The other aviators, however, scrupulously resisted any form of interaction with the locals and kept themselves aloof. They chose to regard the Russians as primitive and inferior. This attitude was promoted by the their commanding officer, Capt. Crandall. He viewed Communists as sinister and deceitful, caring little that the Russians were fighting their common enemy. To Crandall these godless Reds were the enemy of every true blue American and he never missed an opportunity to lecture his crew on the subject.

"Let's ask if we can do something," Nick would say. "Any kind of work. As long as we're useful."

Bed Crandall's usual response was, "We're doing nothing to help these Commie bastards."

"But they're fightin' the Germans. We're fightin' the Germans. We'd be helpin' America."

There was a logic to this which some of the other men in the crew could appreciate. But they kept silent. Crandall was the skipper. He was calling the shots. And hadn't he gotten them all safely through up until now?

On one occasion, during a rainy spring morning, Nick attempted to offer his mates a Russian lesson. On an art pad from one of the Red Cross paint sets, Nick wrote out his captain's last name. Crandall.

"Skip," said Nick, "take a look at this."

Crandall grudgingly gave his attention.

"This is your name spelled in Russian. They don't have a 'C' so you would use a 'K.'"

He wrote a "K."

"The 'r' is this; looks like a lower case 'p.'"

He wrote "Kp."

"Then we add an 'a,' which is the same as our 'a.'"

He wrote "Kpa."

"Then an 'n' which is a small capital 'H.'"

Кран

"Now, a 'd' which is this capital 'A' but with its top cut off . . ."

Кранд

" . . . another 'a . . .'"

Кранда

" . . . and finally the 'L.' Which is kinda like the sign for pi."

Крандал

"There it is. Crandall in Russian."

"My name has two ls."

"In Russian you don't need it if you don't pronounce it."

"That just shows you how off the beam these people are," said Crandall.

"Hey, Nick, do me," said Pua.

"Sure," said Nick. "This box with no bottom is a 'p.'"

He wrote п.

"Then this 'ooh' which looks like a 'y.'"

He wrote пу.

"Then the 'a,' which again is the same as our 'a.'"

He wrote пуа.

"That's it. Pua."

"Hey, neat," said the gunner.

Caloon and McCabe came over.

"Looks like chicken scratches," said McCabe.

"Don't make any sense to me," Caloon added, shaking his head.

Nick pleaded, "C'mon, fellas, it's really easy. Take a look." He wrote on the paper.

"Nah," said Caloon, "it's too strange and too hard."

"But guys, all you have to do is learn the letters."

"Nick," said Caloon, "you learn it for us. Then write 'em a letter. Tell 'em to get us the hell out of here."

"Hey, guys, it's easy, really," Nick pleaded with his colleagues. "C'mon."

No one was listening.

The endless string of long empty days seemed as if they would go on forever until one morning the sound of aircraft overhead jarred the tranquility of the countryside.

A continuous procession of aircraft could be seen streaming over the dormitory and dropping down to their west, presumably to land. It was obvious that a new airbase was being established closer to the front lines. Perhaps the tide was turning in favor of the Russians. Perhaps they were actually pushing the Nazis back.

"Why don't we ask if they can use our help?" Nick sounded the familiar refrain that evening at supper. "They probably could use us. Setting up an airbase is a complicated job."

The others looked to Crandall expecting his usual reply. The captain surprised everyone when he said, "Yeah, they might at that . . . and in the process we might run across an opportunity to bug the hell out of here. Don't ya see it guys; airplanes! If we find out exactly where we are we might be able to grab one of those ships and head for the border—Iran, maybe."

"But we only saw fighter planes, Bed," said Sam, "and those are gooney-lookin' old biplanes. We couldn't all get out in one of those."

"How do we know they won't bring in some bigger stuff later on? Hey, when some brass hat visits he usually comes in a big ship. Anyhow, I think it's worth a try. See Nick, you finally got your wish. When the Snitch shows up, we're gonna offer our services."

"Kamenny, you slippery dog," shouted Lt. Caloon as their Russian plenipotentiary entered with an armload of paper packages, bread, and some loose vegetables clumped together in a string bag.

"I greet you, captain of brave American raiders. (Many of the newspaper articles described the men as the Tokyo Raiders.) I trust you slept well?"

"Thank you, Kamenny, ol' buddy," the captain said in an overly solicitous tone. "I did sleep well. What can you tell us about all the aircraft landing to the west of us during the past few days?"

Kamenny paused as he was unpacking the groceries and looked blankly into the captain's eyes. Then, shrugging and looking overly innocent, he said, "Aircraft? What aircraft? I not notice aircraft."

"Cut the shit, Kamenny," said Caloon. "There's a new base setting up a few miles west of here. Any fool can see that."

"Any fool?" Kamenny nodded profoundly. "Perhaps a special fool is required."

"Kamenny, if there's a base there are lots of things we could do. We'd like to help out. We're going stir crazy just sitting around like this. It's been a year."

"Stir crazy," repeated the confused Russian as he cocked his head at his own wrist and gave it a few limp turns as he puzzled for meaning. "Sitting around?"

After another day of unrelenting badgering by the Americans, Kamenny grudgingly agreed to at least inquire at the airbase. If indeed such a base existed.

They were given their answer several days later.

"Nyet!" said Kamenny, emphatically shaking his head. "Colonel of all aircraft planes and pilots, tell good greetings to brave comrade flying soldiers of American army, but have full complement of workers and flyers. Helpers are not in need. Must refuse generous offer of helping with thanks."

In the following days more airplanes were observed heading for the base. At night, a new wrinkle, the drone of aircraft taking off.

"Night missions!" Capt. Crandall observed. "They're goin' after the Krauts at night. All night long. Those Heinies are getting no sleep."

"Neither are we, brudda," added Pua.

On one particular afternoon, the sound of aircraft brought Tolkin and Caloon out on the porch of the dormitory. The two men strained to get a better view of the new arrivals.

"Those're kinda familiar lookin', don't ya think?" said Caloon.

"You're right, they're ours, I'll bet. Look a lot like P-40s but they're different. Sleeker. Hey guys," he shouted to the others. "C'mon, get a load of this. American planes."

"Yeah, with red stars on their sides."

"Hey, it's still good to see something from the States."

When the sky was finally clear of aircraft the men abandoned the porch and dejectedly returned to the tedium of their normal routine.

On the next day when Kamenny arrived, cheerily producing some tins of caviar and a couple of freshly killed chickens, the airmen once again pressed him on the issue of the airbase.

"We want to see this colonel ourselves," said Capt. Crandall.

"Yeah, face to face," said Nick. "We want to talk turkey with the man in charge, show him we mean business."

"Yeah! There's lots of things we can do. I can wrestle bombs and service the machine guns. I can even break down the old Lewis guns these comrades are usin'," Pua put in vehemently. "A busy base can always use more hands. C'mon, who does this colonel think he's bullshittin'?"

"Take us to the base, Kamenny," Crandall demanded. "We want to see the man himself. It's not like we don't believe you spoke to the guy and argued for us but we just want to hear it from the horse's mouth."

Kamenny paused, cocked his head. "You want speak with horse?"

One week later, when the Americans were convinced their request had been ignored, a battered, green flatbed truck pulled up to the dormitory with Kamenny at the wheel.

"Come, you guys," Kamenny shouted and waved, all the while sporting a smug grin on his broad, baby face. "We make visit in personal, with mouth of horse."

Crandall and Caloon sat up in the cab with Kamenny while Nick Tolkin rode on the flatbed with the two sergeants. They headed west along a rutted dirt road in the general direction of the new airbase.

"Here goes nothin'," Crandall muttered to Caloon.

At least it's a change of routine, thought Tolkin, as he and the two sergeants endured the relentless pounding administered by the hardwood planks of the flatbed.

After traveling approximately seven kilometers, military vehicles and uniformed troops began to appear on both sides of the road. Narrow roads had been cut into the woods left and right of the main thoroughfare and structures could be glimpsed set back into those woods. Nick noted that the structures must be virtually invisible from the air.

After stopping at a checkpoint at which Kamenny produced a folded piece of paper for the sentry, they were waved on by the guard, who slung his submachine gun over his shoulder. The guard pointed out the smaller of three low buildings on the far side of a broad, aircraft-ringed grass field.

The Americans dismounted in front of a building with a sign bearing Russian letters and some numbers. Nick attempted to translate, deducing that this was the 122nd Army Air Brigade Headquarters which was comprised of the 588th, 496th, and 386th

Air Regiments. And confirmed that the brigade commander was Colonel I.N. Petrovitch.

When Kamenny read the sign for them, Tolkin translated further.

"So this Colonel Petrovitch is the base commander?" Tolkin asked.

Kamenny nodded. "Da," he said, indicating that Nick was correct.

As the aviators were ushered into the CO's offices, they were eyed suspiciously by the uniformed men sitting at the desks in the larger outer office.

Just as the Americans were beginning to feel distinctly uncomfortable at the furtive glances and generally chilly reception, the door to one of the offices was thrown open by a short, barrel-chested officer. He wore a broad smile highlighting two gold front teeth and spoke grandly to the American airmen. Judging by the cluttered shoulder boards, they were meeting the CO.

"Welcome, American comrades," he said magnanimously, moving from one man to the other to shake hands and then grasping each flyer's shoulders firmly with both hands. He nodded curtly to Kamenny. "Please come to enter," he then said, gesturing to the door from which he had emerged.

The men filed in and found a large, round oak table surrounded by seven straight-backed dining room-style chairs. The table was set with plates and utensils and glasses sitting in fitted metal stands.

"You take tea? Please to pour for yourself. See, we have zakuska. Very nice." He was gesturing to platters of smoked fish, pickled onion rings, several types of herring, and platters of red caviar. There was even a chunk of Spam sitting on a small plate. It was neatly cut in two with the empty tin sitting beside it as if to verify that it was the real thing.

Quite a spread considering it was barely eleven in the morning. The Americans dug in with gusto to the apparent delight of their Russian host. The food spread before them was a welcome change from the rather repetitive diet of boiled beef, potatoes, and cabbage that they had been served so regularly.

After the airmen had eaten their fill and complimented the Russian commander on his sumptuous largess, it was Captain Crandall who finally brought up the business for which they had come to the base.

"Sir," he said, taking a firm tone with the Russian CO. "We are an American combat crew. We flew a B-25 Mitchell medium bomber. For fear of running out of fuel, we were forced to land on Russian soil. Both our countries are at war with Germany. We are allies, yet we are prevented from returning to our unit."

Kamenny translated sporadically as Petrovitch indicated, with a nod, or a quick shake of his head, when he comprehended the American captain's words or when he required clarification.

"We have been interned by the Russian government for reasons that make no sense to us. We have been idle for a year. Do you understand what it's like for a well-trained combat crew to sit idle for so long?"

The Russian colonel nodded politely but his eyes betrayed the empathy he felt for the men before him.

"We ask that our aircraft be returned to us and we be allowed to leave—we want to get back into the fight." He paused for the Russian's reaction. When there was none, he continued. "But if for some reason that is not possible, then at least let us help in the fight right here. The vile Germans are a blight on humanity and must be eradicated, and despite our political differences, we must ally our two nations to this sacred cause."

Impressive! thought Nick Tolkin. *Old Crandall sure sounds like he means it.*

When Crandall finished stating his case, the Russian pushed his chair back from the table and stood up.

"My comrade aviators, I have feeling for your condition. There is strong reason we can no send you to return. Reason is nonaggression treaty our leader, first secretary Stalin, has made with Japanese." He nodded to Kamenny to translate further. "Returning you to battle make possible anger of Imperial army who are presently being close by in Manchuria. Second front to be soon made open. Defense in west with same time defense in east, very bad. You make request; to help with fight against Germans, we must with all respectfulness . . ." He turned to Kamenny for the word, shaking his head "no."

"Decline," said Kamenny.

"Decline. You lack to speak Russian language, this make problem, make work difficult. Even so, we are at full numbers. Manpower is maximum. More workers only, er . . . make . . . how to say . . ." he turned again to Kamenny.

Kamenny blurted out, "Cock-up." Petrovitch eyed Kamenny strangely and then said, "Much confusion."

"So, American friends, I speak you, *nyet*. I am sad. It is impossible."

The colonel then opened a low cupboard and brought out a liter-sized vodka bottle and some fluted shot glasses.

"But, let us part while being friends. I have large respect for courage of you, gentlemen." He uncorked the vodka bottle and all the glasses were filled. He poured quickly and expertly, without spilling. "I make toast. To his honor, President of America, Roosevelt."

All drank in the Russian manner; the glass drained in one gulp.

Caloon then poured himself a shot and raised his glass. "To Uncle Joe Stalin. That's what we call him back in the States."

"Uncle?" The colonel pondered for a moment as Kamenny translated. The colonel brightened. "*Da!* To 'oncle' Stalin."

Nick watched Crandall through the corner of his eye and detected no hesitation as the group downed the second drink. As the last of the empty glasses were placed on the small tray and the Russian colonel made a little nod, as if pleased with the proceedings, the air was shattered by the anguished wail of an air raid siren.

"You must to shelter immediately," the colonel barked, in English, his affability disappearing, replaced by the authoritative demeanor of a commander. As he exited, he shouted something in Russian to one of the soldiers in the office, who sprinted for the door and beckoned the Americans to follow.

They exited hurriedly following the young soldier into the bright sunshine as the angry chatter and roar of a strafing aircraft filled the air. No time to find cover. The raid was upon them as the Americans flung themselves to the ground amidst the clatter and snap of flying dirt and machine gun fire. Eyes squeezed shut, they felt the dark presence of a pair of Nazi aircraft swoop over at what seemed like rooftop level. When the shadows had passed, the Americans raised their heads and looked for each other. Their initial terror diminished as familiar faces greeted each other wearing grins that only young men who believe fervently in their own immortality could muster.

As they rose and brushed themselves off in half-comical embarrassment, they spied the still and torn body of the young Russian clerk lying akimbo in the dirt before them, a pool of bright crimson spreading over the dark red soil under him. There was no question that he was dead. None of the Americans had witnessed a man killed in combat before and the sight chilled their hearts. But the moment was fleeting as they realized that they were still out in the open. Sprinting toward the cover of the nearest building with the image of the bloody and lifeless form fresh in their minds, they realized in that instant that making a hot dog takeoff from an aircraft carrier or dropping a load of bombs on some surprised factory workers is not really war. War is a dead boy bleeding out on a patch of dirt far from home. A boy who should have had at least fifty more years of living ahead of him.

The shock and heat of a nearby explosion jarred them back to reality. A building beyond the colonel's offices had taken a direct hit and erupted in smoke and flames. The Americans rose to move toward the structure only to see at least a dozen Russian soldiers already racing toward it. As the swiftest of them reached the front steps the world around them burst into a maelstrom of flying dirt, wood chips, and bloody uniform cloth. The stunned Americans watched as every man in the group of rescuers was cut down.

After a second pair of attacking aircraft roared overhead, guns decimating everything in their path, the Americans sprinted to the group of fallen men to offer whatever aid was possible. One of the injured, hit in both legs, pointed to the burning building and shouted urgently, "Balnitza! Balnitza!"

"I think that's the hospital," Nick shouted. The crew scrambled toward the structure despite the heat and dense smoke. More plumes of smoke and flame could be seen spewing from beyond the tree line. The flight line had been the object of the initial attack.

The Americans and Russians rushed into the ravaged portion of the structure to find burning debris pinning patients and hospital staff. To the left of the entrance an operating room had taken a direct hit. Mercifully, the surgery was empty at the time. Beyond, several patients could be heard shouting for help and struggling to free themselves from fallen debris.

The Americans and Russians set to the task of extricating the survivors. Together, they worked frantically, lifting burning and splintered lumber from medical staff and patients. In some cases, several men were required to lift the heavy beams off the victims.

The rescuers ignored the heat and burning structure around them, toiling side by side with soldiers and firemen, who worked furiously to control the fire and extricate survivors. A smoldering roof beam fell and thudded end first to the floor between Kamenny and Caloon. It balanced nearly upright for a moment, then slowly tipped, coming to rest against the sidewall and Sam Caloon's back. The copilot barely noticed the slight bump but when the burning wood set his leather jacket afire, he frantically wrenched it off, tossed it aside, and returned to the task of helping the victims.

Those who could walk were assisted out of the building. Others were carried outside bodily. The crews worked until everyone, alive and dead, had been removed from the destroyed wing of the hospital. To make some of the injured more comfortable, the Americans reentered the structure and brought out mattresses and pillows, some of which were wet and scorched, for the injured lying on the ground outside. It was then that they discovered that some of the patients were women. There were only two women occupying the far wing of the hospital. Fortunately that wing had escaped being damaged and both patients were lifted to safety through a window.

At the all-clear, soldiers who had taken refuge in shelters arrived and provided litters to carry the injured into the undamaged operations building where only minutes before, the colonel had received the Americans.

Kamenny, who had been lying on the grass with his exhausted American charges, sat propped up with his arms extended behind him and declared, "Hey, American raiders, we pretty good firemens, no?"

The sweaty, soot-blackened, and exhausted aviators watched solemnly as the stricken wing of the wooden hospital smoldered sullenly, flames extinguished but still radiating heat. The Americans were so exhausted they could barely crawl out of the way of the newly arriving fire trucks.

Eventually Kamenny and the Americans began the long walk back to "Melody Ranch," the name they christened the former Communist meeting place and their present home. Their truck had been commandeered during the emergency.

"At least we got a good feed out of it," Sgt. Pua muttered to no one in particular around mile four.

That night the men once again heard the distant drone of engines. Most ignored the sound and simply slept on. Nick Tolkin, however, was roused to full wakefulness. *Son of a gun,* he thought as he listened. *They're flying missions; these moxie Russians aren't about to let the Krauts put 'em out of business.*

Several days later Kamenny arrived, bearing a message from Colonel Petrovitch. If the Americans cared to visit the base again at a future date he would be pleased to provide them with a tour of the facility.

"Sure, why not," said McCabe after Kamenny explained it to them a second time. "We might get another of those swell feeds."

4

The base had been badly damaged in the German attack. The Luftwaffe's original target was the west Stalingrad area, where Russian forces were harassing Wehrmacht troops who had broken out of the encirclement. Since the primary target was obscured by clouds, the strike force separated into three smaller groups to hunt for other opportunistic targets. By chance, six He111s stumbled upon the Soviet Airdrome in the Kuban, managing complete surprise.

Six P-02 bombers, two Shturmoviks, and a Pe-2 medium bomber were destroyed, along with a maintenance hangar and the four TI-53s inside. Asphalt revetments were severely cratered, essentially barricading several aircraft that had somehow weathered the attack under camouflage netting. Some troops caught in the open were killed and one of the base's two food storage bunkers and the machine shop were damaged. Fortunately, only one Aircobra was lost, caught in the open during a retraction test. The other Lend-Lease Aircobras had been safely ensconced under camouflage or in underground bunkers dug out of the wooded hills surrounding the base. The attack on the hospital resulted in the deaths of six soldiers, five patients, and two medics. Fortunately, the damage was kept to a minimum thanks to the efficient work of base fire crews. It was reported that there would have been many more casualties in the hospital bombing if not for the timely actions of some civilian visitors who repeatedly entered the burning structure to rescue the injured.

An entire country of brave people, thought Peggy Cohan as the story of the hospital rescue was recounted. The hospital roof had been plainly marked with a red cross. Nazi pilots obviously found it to be an irresistable target.

A few days before the attack, Peggy was ordered to report to the base commander's office, at which time he informed her that she was to receive a high honor from the Russian army and that this was the reason that she had been ordered to stay behind. Though relieved, Peggy would have gladly forgone the medal or scroll or whatever it was they intended to present if she could be permitted to return to the States. She prudently kept this sentiment to herself. These people are fighting for their very existence, she understood. *They need to give me a medal far more than I need to receive it.*

No date had been set for the medal presentation, so Peggy settled into a somewhat comfortable routine among her fellow Russian aviators. Expressly forbidden to go on any more bombing forays, Peggy was, however, given permission to help check out pilots in the new Aircobras.

Among the aircraft ferried to the Russian squadrons was an ungainly-looking trainer version of the P-39. It was designated the "TP-39" and provided a second seat and dual controls for an instructor, positioned forward of the normal cockpit in place of the nose cannon and machine guns. The "TP" was so disliked by American pilots because of its appearance that many of the planes were eagerly "disposed of" to Russia along with the Lend-Lease combat versions. The Russians, however, loved the trainer since it greatly expedited their transition rates.

Although the TP had no offensive capability, it did allow pilots to learn the aircraft's systems in the air with an instructor at hand and affect transition much more quickly and safely than going from ground training directly to solo flight. This form of training was especially valuable to those pilots who had been flying the PO-2 biplane. The two aircraft were worlds and world wars apart.

Peggy eagerly accepted the task of utilizing the TP-39 to transition the Russian pilots.

Some students assigned to her turned out to be from her adopted bomber squadron, including Natalia and Major Svetlana, neither of whom had completely recovered from their injuries and therefore were limited to ground instruction. Peggy's schedule called for a group of five women in the morning and three women and two men in the afternoon. Characteristically, the Russian males grumbled to the adjutant about the foreign female instructor, but Major Simonev advised them to accept the training or face the consequences. Peggy employed the methods of her own transition to the Aircobra back at the Bell factory in Detroit.

The P-39 was only one of the many hundreds of Lend-Lease pursuit aircraft sent to the Russians, including T-6s, P-40s, and British Spitfires. All viable fighters, but the P-39 was easily the Russians' favorite. Designed by Bell to be a state-of-the-art pursuit ship in 1939, the Aircobra never lived up to the expectations of Yank pilots. The sleek aircraft was thickly armored from its nose to aft of the cockpit, and the extra weight made it perform as if it was underpowered. At altitude, American pilots found it sluggish and unresponsive; the unimpressive Allison engine failed to live up to its intended specs. It would obviously never become a dominant dog fighter. The odd placement of the engine was another negative for US Army pilots. Located aft of the cockpit, it effectively balanced the big cannon and four machine guns nestled forward of the windscreen. Chronic overheating problems and an inclination to go into a spin during aerobatic maneuvers further cemented the Aircobra's negative reputation. "Flying Coffin," "Widow Maker," and the "Awful Auger" were just a few of its derisive nicknames.

As much as the Americans disliked the Aircobra, the Russians loved it. Air units were assigned to specific Army divisions and their role was chiefly in support of infantry and armor. At low altitude, the P-39 was at its best. It could decimate enemy positions while remaining relatively immune from ground fire because of its thick, protective underbelly. The Russians found the big nose cannon to be a superb tank buster and, at low altitude the 1150hp Allison engine performed beautifully. Aleksandr Pokryshkin, the leading Russian fighter ace, was running up his victories in a Bell P-39. To Pokryshkin and most Russian pilots, the "Kobra" was a charmed and formidable aircraft and was referred to as "britchik," or "little shaver." Shaving was their euphemism for strafing.

Peggy's charges first familiarized themselves with the P-39 in a series of run ups and taxiing sessions. The students were delighted with the visibility afforded by the tricycle landing gear, which made taxiing and parking much easier. When all of her students had experienced the Aircobra on the ground, Peggy initiated actual flight instruction. Aside from some slight reticence on the part of a couple of her male students, the transitions went smoothly, and Peggy's fledgling Cobra pilots all soloed on or before schedule. Two new P-39 squadrons were being rapidly assembled, one of which was to be made up entirely of women. When Peggy had successfully transitioned her third group of trainees, the two-seater was reassigned to another squadron with less experienced pilots.

With the transitions completed, Peggy was asked by Petrovitch to continue training the pilots. Now, flying a single seat Cobra with full armament, Peggy and her girls practiced combat tactics, techniques for getting out of spins, and some dog fighting tricks she had picked up back in the States. Her students were eager to learn and diligent in their efforts to master the hot new aircraft, especially the aerobatic and dogfighting techniques. Doctrine dictated Russian flying procedures and permitted none of the freedom or improvisation of modern air warfare employed so effectively by the Luftwaffe over Russian skies. The pilots, however, were well aware that the unauthorized skills that Peggy was teaching might shift the odds in their favor when facing an airborne enemy. Until now, these odds had been overwhelmingly on the side of the Luftwaffe.

After one particularly long training session, when all the aircraft had been recovered and refueled, Peggy noticed that her students seemed to be hanging around. Normally the weary pilots would head up to operations and stow their gear immediately after performing their post flights.

This evening a group of women approached Peggy and surrounded her. *What's up?* she wondered. *A union meeting? A bitching session? Well, if they want to survive in combat, they'll just* . . . Peggy was interrupted by Olga Slochyn, one of her most adept students. She held a small cloth package tied with twine.

"For you," said Olga, with the rest of the women moving close, as she ceremoniously presented it to Peggy.

Peggy took the package, touched at the gesture. She nodded to the women around her and said, "What is it?"

The women smiled and exchanged knowing glances. Even the girls who spoke no English at all were engaged by the scene.

"Open," said Olga, nodding and pointing to the package.

Peggy undid the knot and unwrapped the parcel, which contained a white silk helmet liner. A prized possession. These were not regular issue, but meticulously handmade by family members and sent to the girls at the front. Leather flying helmets were brutal to a woman's hair. The silk protected hair from matting and becoming kinked. It also kept a flyer's head warm at altitude, unlike the leather cap under which a girl's wet hair would frequently freeze.

Peggy was touched. She had seen the white silk head coverings before and was aware of how highly coveted they were. Finding it difficult to speak, eyes moist, all she could do was nod. Fighting to control her emotions, she reached out to embrace the women surrounding her.

When all had been thanked, some with tears glistening on their cheeks, the group dispersed, pleased with the outcome of their collective gesture.

"I think she liked it," observed one of the girls in Russian as they walked to the equipment hut.

Peggy didn't speak. She was unable to. The white cap that she held in her hands represented a poignant symbol of approval. What's more, it was earned and deserved. For Peggy, the thin silk head covering was more meaningful than an Academy Award.

"Today we will learn the concept of the 'wingman,'" Peggy told this afternoon's assembly of trainees. "Olga," said Peggy to the girl in the group who had a little English. "How do you say 'wingman?'"

"*Krylo* is wing," Olga replied, flapping her arm.

"And man?" asked Peggy.

"Man is tselovek. We woman," she said, pointing to her chest. "Not man."

"Okay, I get it," said Peggy. "How about 'person?'"

"Person, *tsyelovyek*," Olga said with a satisfied nod. The other women quietly concurred.

"Okay, now, six o'clock."

"Six o'clock?" questioned Olga, pointing to her watch.

"Da," replied Peggy.

"*Shest chahsohr*" Olga answered.

"There it is," said Peggy, pointing forward. "Twelve." Now, pointing behind. "Six o'clock, the *krylo tsyelovyek* protects the leader's *shest chahsohr*. All right, let's go flying and I'll show you how it works."

Peggy led her flight of six Cobras over the Sea of Azov and demonstrated the relationship of the wingman to the leader. She then divided her charges into pairs of leader and wingman and had them take turns. Peggy flew as wingman with each girl and then exchanged places. Her pilots caught on quickly. While the girls were practicing, Peggy and her final wingman flew above and apart from the formation. While she was checking out the last girl, she had Olga drill the formation by shouting different enemy sightings into the radio to train her charges to react instantly. For example, when Olga said, "Enemy, four o'clock high," the pilots who had now learned the clock system would instantly break and split apart, thereby presenting an attacker with many targets to choose from. This would hopefully cause a momentary break of concentration. Once clear, they could reform into the leader-wingman configuration so at least one of the aircraft might bring its guns to bear on the attacker.

As they practiced, Peggy was at altitude checking out Rufina, her final student. The girl was directed to fly as if in combat with Peggy as her wingman, sticking to her "six" despite the most extreme aerobatics. Once satisfied that Rufina understood, they exchanged places and it was Rufina who was taxed to stay on Peggy's tail. At first the girl was a bit tentative, but after a series of drastic aerial gyrations which proved to Rufina that the Cobra would remain in one piece, she tenaciously stayed glued to Peggy's "six."

"*Horosho*, Rufina, good work. Now, let's locate the others and head home."

The two Cobras were descending through broken clouds in the general direction taken by the rest of the flight when Rufina pulled up alongside Peggy and urgently pointed down and to the left.

Below, four black objects could be seen. The training flight throttled back and headed west along the shore of the Sea of Azov. Some 1500 yards behind them and closing from slightly above were four—no, five more black objects. *Uh-oh. Not ours. Those are Nazi fighters.*

"Enemy, six o'clock! Break! Break!" Peggy shouted into the intercom as she kicked the rudder and simultaneously shoved the throttle and control column forward.

The malevolent shapes of five Me109s took form before them in the air. These enemy interlopers were far from their normal patrol routes and closing in on the now scattering formation of Cobras. Luftwaffe hot dogs looking for some easy scores. *Well, not my girls,* thought Peggy as she singled out the lead German. *My God, this is real.* Peggy shuddered, her heart beating wildly as she fought for calm. *Center him in the windscreen,* Peggy reminded herself, grateful for the altitude that enhanced her speed and allowed her to close the distance to the predator.

The Heinies had split up in individual pursuit of the now scattered Russians. The fighter in Peggy's sights doggedly pressed towards its prey. Peggy could see the flicker and smoke as the 109 fired at the juking Cobra. Missed. A second and third longer burst likewise missed.

Still out of range, but desperate to distract the German, Peggy positioned the 109 at the extreme edge of her optical sight and fired a long burst of her machine guns. Despite the great deflection angle, she was surprised to observe a thin, sputtering stream of white trailing from her target. *Coolant! Wow, lucky shot. Can't believe it.* The surprised Messerschmitt broke off and dove, turning out to the water.

"Rufina, finish him," Peggy shouted into the intercom and pulled up to find the others.

The appearance of Peggy and her wingman was a complete surprise to the Germans. They had expected easy pickings. Now, suddenly, they were outnumbered and outgunned. With the loss of advantage, they elected to run. The rearmost German turned inland and sped north at full throttle. Two 109s dove for the deck, crossed the coast, and headed south out over the water. One of the initially pounced-upon Cobras had managed to buy some altitude and now had a good angle on the pair of fleeing Germans who flew straight and level, perfectly silhouetted against the glistening sea.

With one pass the Russian girl raked her tracers through both aircraft, registering obvious hits. The lead German, his control system shot up, fought to rein in his stricken ship while the engine of his partner began to smoke. These two made the cardinal error of bunching up while under attack. The pilot of the erratically flying aircraft threw off his canopy and frantically scrambled clear, his chute deploying only seconds before he splashed into the sea. His plane quickly followed, striking the choppy water, bouncing once into the air as a wing broke from the fuselage. The plane finally plopped flat into the sea like a badly skipped stone.

His companion was in worse trouble. Fighting for control, his engine now on fire and too low to bail out, he abruptly nosed over and struck the water with a furious splash. No movement could be seen in the cockpit as the aircraft bobbed in the chop for a few moments, then slid sideways into the depths. The blue Azov swirled over the spot of entry to obliterate all evidence of man or machine.

A fourth German was attempting to flee in a climbing turn. Two Cobras, still well out of gun range, were in pursuit.

The women, inexperienced at dog fighting, sporadically fired their guns at the German as he juked and rolled, expertly keeping himself out of their plane of fire.

As the two Russians closed in on the German, he executed a sudden split-S maneuver, causing both Cobras to overshoot badly. Had there been a single Russian, this adroit change of position would have allowed the German to turn the tables and put his adversary in his sights. Prudently, the 109 pilot scrammed for the deck and elected to fight again another day. By the time the Russian women could recover, he was hightailing northwest to safety.

"Where did he go?" Anna queried in Russian into her intercom.

"We had him," Mariam said. Then in English, she asked, "What happened?"

"He was a good pilot," Peggy answered. "Very experienced. We were lucky. Anybody hit? Everybody okay?"

One by one, they acknowledged. All were undamaged and unhurt.

"Okay, then. Nice shooting, ladies. Let's form up. We're heading home," Peggy ordered into the radio. She attempted to disguise the quaver in her voice brought on by yet another unexpected exposure to combat and her relief in not losing any of her charges.

Later, close to the airdrome, Peggy broke radio silence and asked in what she hoped was a more composed tone, "Who got the double?"

A voice responded, "Polina, it was."

"Nice shooting, Polina," Peggy said. "Rufina? Did you get that Heinie?"

"Da, I get," answered the girl.

"He go down on sand. I see," Olga confirmed.

"Nice shooting, ladies."

"But two fascist go free," a voice on the intercom complained.

"Still, very nice shooting. Your new squadron's first three kills. Excellent!"

As the day's outcome sank in, Peggy realized that she had successfully convinced everyone, including herself, that she knew what she was doing.

Upon their return to base, the training flight's approach intervals were precise, their turns crisp, their touchdowns smooth and businesslike. No longer untested green beaners, these women fighter pilots were becoming combat veterans.

When the Kotluban Base awoke on this May morning, it was confronted by a scene out of deepest winter. The world had been completely whited out. More than two feet of wet snow had fallen during the past twelve hours, coating everything in a thick angora jacket. When the early shift of mechanics and armorers arose, they were forced to dig out of their huts and tunnel through huge drifts to the flight line and bomb storage areas. Large, damp flakes were still falling furiously as they worked and a new coating was deposited almost as quickly as it was cleared. As the cloaked sun rose in the sky, an eerie, milky glow shimmered in the air. The temperature variance created a thick fog, which hung over the entire base as the wind died. Visibility had dropped to zero. This rare and unexpected spring snowfall had taken the meteorologists completely by surprise. The base was utterly snowed in, with a lull predicted during the daylight hours and another substantive snowfall forecast for after sunset. Massive drifts of wet snow blocked runways and taxiways. Though the mechanics managed to excavate their way to the aircraft and clear laden wings and fuselages, there was very little likelihood of air operations for the next twenty-four to forty-eight hours.

With reluctance, the base commander ordered a temporary stand down while snow removal crews worked to free up the base.

The aviators of the 486th were allowed to sleep in. Those who woke surveyed the situation and immediately returned to their beds. The endless string of day-night operations had left exhausted base personnel yearning for an extra hour or two of rest. For them this improbable winter spectacle was a godsend. Later that afternoon, when more of the aviators were up and about and the word spread of the 48-hour stand down, a sense of giddiness and reprieve pervaded. In the absence of scheduled missions, someone in the 486th suggested having a party. The idea raced through the snowbound airdrome. *A party. How exciting.* The war permitted little time for social contact, but that didn't mean young people on the base hadn't noticed each other. Dedication to the Motherland was one thing but youth was still youth. This was an opportunity for a young woman to wear a dress. To put a ribbon in her hair. To be a girl. To perhaps share the company of some of those dashing male airmen. Who knows, to perhaps even find a beau. A party. Even Petrovitch, the exacting group commander, knew better than to get in the way of such a powerful idea.

The large maintenance hangar was selected for the festivities. Originally a cow barn, it had been impressed into service when the airdrome was built. The large open structure featured a concrete floor that allowed it to serve perfectly as a maintenance hangar. Only three aircraft were occupying the hangar at the time: two Shturmoviks, red-lined for sheet metal repairs and hydraulic work, and the hangar queen, a Pe-2 bomber. The Pe-2 was habitually in need of some repair, this time a gear retraction adjustment. These aircraft were promptly pushed out onto the freshly shoveled ramp and covered with white tarps, clearing the space for the gala.

Food began arriving in the late afternoon. Bottles of vodka in straw-filled wooden crates appeared almost magically, along with tins of herring, bologna, sturgeon, and the ubiquitous caviar. Then, as if to consecrate the gathering, large portraits of Lenin and Stalin were affixed to the walls along with a red banner declaring "All glory to the brave fighters against the fascist hordes." Flags bearing the emblems of the various units were displayed along with the standard of the Soviet Union, all combining to lend a festive air to the former cow barn.

A hastily assembled band—consisting of two accordions, a pair of violins, a cello, trumpet, trombone, snare drum, balalaika, and saxophone who doubled in clarinet—began tuning up in a far corner of the hall. The group was rough but eager, referring to themselves as the "Hotsy Totsy Symphonica."

Most of the men arrived early and looked dashingly handsome in freshly brushed uniforms, shined buttons, and polished boots. Their hair was slicked back and neatly combed—a marked contrast to the usually tousled and matted appearance caused by countless hours spent in close-fitting leather flying helmets. The boys stood together chatting self-consciously, attempting to look bold and debonair as they kept a watchful eye on the curtained entrance for the first glimpse of the girls.

When the first girls arrived and poked their heads through the newly-installed beaded curtains, all conversation ceased among the men. They were eager to survey the "talent" for tonight's festivities. Upon realizing that they were the first, the women immediately balked and turned tail. Some minutes later a second group went through the same ritual, but before they could exit, too, some more girls arrived and crowded in behind them. This blocked their escape and gave them no choice but to proceed into the hall. A few wore their uniforms, but most were clad in dresses under their heavy army coats. Those dresses had been carefully stored away for just such an occasion.

Remarkably, the girls were transformed into beautiful young women, radiant and feminine. The contrast of the women in their usual bulky and loose-fitting flying gear to these dressed and coifed young ladies was nearly incomprehensible. *These girls had legs!* The men's appreciation was obvious and extremely satisfying to the women who had spent much of the day primping.

The bulk of their activity that afternoon had been devoted to hair. The cooling systems of a trio of Pe-2 bombers had been pressed into service. Mechanics had run up their engines to generate gallons of hot water. Luxuriously hot water with which the women aviators were able to wash their hair. The water was relatively clean since no anti-freeze had been employed by the Soviet air force since they had run out of the necessary glycol nearly two years before. The monthly bath train wasn't due for a week so the formation commanders chose to ignore this unorthodox use of aircraft coolant. Considering the results, the effort was well worth it. Gone were the weary-eyed and disheveled-looking women aviators in their voluminous flying togs. The former maintenance hangar was magically transformed into an elegant peacetime dance hall filled with vivacious young girls whose shining faces took the men's breath away. When the music began, the bravest of the boys strode forward to sweep the prettiest of the women onto the dance floor.

Also in attendance was Lieutenant Lilya Litvak, the Yak pilot who was on her way to double ace status with seven kills to her account. She had arrived two days before from the Stalingrad area on an escort mission. Lilya was a petite, pretty young woman with a tiny waist that showed off her curves to good advantage. It was said that she bore an uncanny likeness to the popular Russian film actress, Olga Seranova. Lilya wore her flying uniform and boots, but adorned her short blonde hair with colored ribbons made from dyed strips of parachute silk. Lilya danced gaily with several men but it was clear to all that her special interest was senior lieutenant Alexei Lavochin, the second in command of Shturmovik squadron 255.

Peggy Cohan arrived with her two friends: Svetlana, still encased in her arm and shoulder cast, and Natalia, limping slightly and supported by a cane. Peggy wore a slightly oversized flower-print dress borrowed from one of the girls. Her hair had grown out since her flight training bob and despite her attempt to deglamorize herself by not doing a stylish hairdo or wearing lipstick, she looked stunning. Like many of the girls who had no silk stockings to wear, Peggy had a pencil line drawn down the back of her legs. The effect gave the impression of the seams of extremely sheer rayons. She was quickly asked to dance. After refusing several young pilots, the tall and very determined senior lieutenant Lavochin, ignoring her protestations, firmly grasped her hand and whisked her out onto the floor. Resignedly, Peggy relaxed in the arms of her dashing partner. She looked so attractive on the dance floor that some of the brave fellows who had invited the first group of girls to dance now wished they had waited.

As the evening unfolded and the prodigious draughts of vodka were taking effect, several of the men strode out to the center of the floor. They stood in a circle, arms crossed, eyes straight ahead. Peggy turned to Svetlana with a quizzical look.

"*Kazotska,*" Svetlana declared with delight.

Then the music began, slowly as the dancers squatted, bouncing in time, arms crossed at their chests. In perfect tempo the dancers kicked each leg straight out and immediately brought it back to avoid falling. The delighted spectators clapped in time as they observed the dancers flaunting the laws of gravity. Now, as the music and rhythmic clapping accelerated to an impossible pace, the dancers were hard-pressed to keep up. Inevitably, the first soldier fell, then another and then a third. The audience clapped and alternately roared its approval and groaned derisively as the men faltered and dropped out.

The young pilot with whom Peggy had been dancing suddenly jumped in with the remaining two dancers. He was fresh while they were breathless, red-faced, and bouncing unsteadily. When one of them extended his hand to the floor to keep from falling, the crowd hooted good-naturedly. When he subsequently plopped, exhaustedly, to the concrete they cheered him. The two remaining *kazotzkas* continued for several more minutes. One man was fresh while the other, flushed and gasping, was clearly spent. When he finally went down he was cheered, lifted up on the shoulders of his comrades and offered a guzzle from a large vodka bottle in a wicker casing. He drank like a man parched.

These Russians are different from any people I've ever known, thought Peggy. *Usually so stoic and seriously dedicated and then in a blink they are silly and passionate and more than a little bit crazy.*

Now, in the center of the floor, only the young senior lieutenant was left. He was tiring, but still keeping up with the music and rhythmic encouragement of the revelers. This now included Peggy, who had become as vocal as the others. For a while it seemed as if he would go on forever. when he began to falter and finally, exhausted, sat down heavily on the hard hangar floor. His mates, laughing, rushed forward, picked him up, and tossed him into the air several times. He was then carried to where Peggy was standing and set down upright in front of her, where an unopened bottle was thrust into his hand. He pulled the cork with his teeth and spat it to the side, then took a prolonged guzzle as the crowd cheered. Peggy sensed that he had dedicated his performance to her and so in acceptance of his gesture, snatched the bottle from his hand, raised it high and took a long deep draught of her own. The giddy crowd cheered and applauded her action. In that moment Peggy ceased to be the helpful foreigner. As the scalding liquid cascaded down her throat she realized she had become one of them.

Peggy's tall senior lieutenant introduced himself, speaking closely and breathlessly over the laughter and applause of the spectators. "*Imya*, me," pointing to his chest, "Alexei Lavochin." He spoke his name as if he were bestowing a rare honor upon Peggy.

He's as conceited as he is good looking, she thought.

"Me," Peggy responded as she gestured to herself. "Margaret Cohan."

"Ma-ga-ret," the pilot mimicked. "Co-han?"

"Yes," Peggy nodded. "You can call me Peggy."

"Paggy?" he repeated curiously.

"It's my nickname. Peggy!"

"Nick name? Ah! Nickname! Me, *Loshka*. Nickname."

Peggy extended her hand. "How do you do, Loshka."

"I pleased, Peggy," he said as he bowed and kissed her hand.

The band began a slow tune and Peggy and Loshka strode arm in arm to the dance floor, where they joined the others. The young Russians observed the pilot and the pretty American girl in his arms and nodded approvingly. They made a good couple. Lavochin was on his way to becoming an ace with four kills to his credit, an impressive accomplishment for a ground attack pilot, and the American girl had already proven her mettle in the past few weeks. *Yes, they were an attractive couple. A heroic couple.*

Only one person in the room had reservations about this potential pairing: Lilya Litvak. And as the dashing Lavochin drew Peggy even closer to him, Lilya's jealousy turned to wrath.

He's got ideas, Peggy realized as they danced. Perhaps it was the vodka or the music that made Peggy relax in his arms and wonder without much concern, *Just where is this going?*

When the number was over and the dancers were still applauding, some of the young men who sat this one out were jockeying for the next dance. Since there were twice as many male pilots, each girl had at least two offers. One towheaded sublieutenant headed for Peggy but a withering glance from Lavochin made him retreat with a curt little bow and an about-face.

Another slow number had Peggy and Alexei dancing closer than before, with his arm encircling her waist in a very possessive manner.

This guy is sure of himself, Peggy thought. *I can certainly understand why. Tall, dark, and handsome, and a great pilot.*

Natalia, Peggy noticed, is utterly preoccupied with some lantern-jawed captain over in the corner by the work stands. The famous Lilya Litvak, who is dancing with a tall young pilot, seems to be glaring at me. *What's with her? Unless . . . this guy . . . of course! Lilly thinks she's got a claim on my Loshka.*

At the realization, Peggy snuggled a bit closer to her partner, causing Lilya to dance closer to hers. Her eyes never left Peggy and Lavochin.

Alexei leaned down to Peggy and whispered, "You want go quiet place? With Loshka?"

"Whatever do you mean?" Peggy asked, smiling. "What quiet place? Where?"

"Cerkov," said Alexei. "We go Cerkov."

"Okay, Alexei, I'll go to the Cerkov with you, *da*. But I've got to tell my girlfriend, Natalia. Okay. You wait. Okay?"

"Hokay," said Alexei weakly as Peggy turned and weaved her way across the dance floor to where Natalia and her captain sat.

"Natalia," Peggy said, "tell me what..."

Natalia held up a finger to stop Peggy from speaking and said a few words in Russian to the captain, which must have amounted to "be a dear and get lost for a few minutes, will ya?" He immediately rose, made a slight bow, and obediently got lost in the crowd. Natalia then turned to Peggy and nodded for her to resume her question.

"What is 'Cerkov?'" Peggy asked her friend.

"Cerkov is house to make pray." She put her hands together, miming prayer.

"A church?" said Peggy. "Oh, all right. Thanks. I'm going with Alexei to a church. I guess I'll see you later." She turned away to find Alexei in the crowd.

"Peggy! Is mistake," Natalia shouted to the already disappearing girl. Natalia began to laugh. When her captain returned, she was still laughing.

"What is funny?" asked the captain in Russian.

"Life, my dear comrade captain," said the still chuckling Natalia. "Life is funny."

Holding hands, Peggy and Alexei made their way through the crunchy snow past the camouflaged aircraft hangars and the maintenance sheds toward the woods. Despite the fog, the snow's reflection bathed the scene in a soft, eerie glow. Narrow paths had already been worn in the snow, providing access to the work areas. As the couple ventured deeper into the woods, a dark structure loomed ahead. It was a long, low building with a sod roof and what appeared to be a steeple at one end.

This must be the church, thought Peggy. As Alexei held the door open for her and bade her enter, Peggy felt a twinge of discomfort. Was it conscience? Was it disrespect? Even though Peggy was not religious and this was not her faith, she felt a moment of reticence.

When Alexei turned on the lights, Peggy was much relieved. The "church" was in reality a parachute packing shed. The steeple was simply a tower built into the far end of the structure to haul up chutes to dry or straighten out the lines and risers before packing on the long wooden tables.

Alexei took Peggy in his arms and kissed her. Peggy surprised herself by her response. His kiss and embrace, rather than heated and randy, was respectful and full of ardor. She responded in kind and threw herself into the passion of the moment without inhibition or reservation.

Alexei took off his tunic and undershirt and then removed Peggy's coat, unbuttoning each button unhurriedly. He then reached down and lifted her dress over her head. As she stood there in her panties and bra, excited and receptive, Alexei admired her for a moment, then stepped away. He quickly turned off the tower lights and the main lights. When he returned to Peggy's side, only a single dim entrance light remained. Alexei then pulled a parachute from the stack of newly-packed chutes and yanked the ripcord. The pilot chute popped out and Alexei drew out the remainder of the silk and spread it out on the packing table.

He returned to Peggy, picked her up in his arms, kissed her passionately, and lay her down on the opened chute. Quickly pulling off his boots and undoing his belt, he climbed up on the table and lay beside her.

Silk sheets, thought Peggy as she embraced him and returned his passion.

Later, they returned to the party as a new dusting of snow began to fall. On the way they encountered another couple on the path to the church. Once back inside the temporary dance hall, Peggy and Alexei faced each other, flushed and beaming, the intimate bond between them fresh and resonant. They danced as if they were alone in the hall. When Peggy indicated that she wanted to speak to her friend, Natalia, Alexei bowed and gallantly kissed her hand. Peggy reached up and stroked his cheek with the back of her hand.

As she turned to search for Natalia in the crowd, she mused to herself, *That was the most elegant quickie since the beginning of the world.*

When Peggy spied Natalia, still with her captain, she said,

"Church! Church! For praying!" Peggy put her hands together in mock prayer. All Natalia could do was laugh. Eventually Peggy joined her. Captain Lantern Jaw stood patiently by, quietly having no clue.

It was late and the party was breaking up. As Peggy and her friend were leaving, Natalia called over her captain and gave him her handkerchief. He accepted the purple-flowered favor and carefully placed the prize in his tunic. Now male and female flyers went their separate ways. Everyone understood that the nonfraternization rules had been set aside for the evening but they were fully in effect once the young people left the building.

As Peggy was straightening up after retrieving Natalia's fallen cane, she found a short young woman standing close by. It was Lilya Litvak who barred her way. She smiled at Peggy but with her mouth only. Her eyes were cold and serious.

"You Americansk Peggy," she said, her finger a barely contained spear pointing at Peggy's heart.

Peggy nodded.

"I Lilya Litvak," she announced, her smile becoming a sneer.

Peggy nodded again.

"Soon one day we make flying together. I like learn from expert Americansk pilot."

"Certainly," Peggy responded, not able to muster as much bravado as she wished. "I'll look forward to it. I hope it's soon," Peggy added with her composure barely regained.

Lilya reached out, took Peggy's hand and shook it as if an important business venture had just been concluded. She then turned abruptly and walked away.

That was more of a challenge than an invitation to go flying, Peggy realized.

Natalia took her cane from Peggy's hand, shrugged her shoulders, and shook her head as if to say, "Forget about it. It's no big deal."

"Come," said Natalia. "Talia need make *spaht*, sleep."

Once Natalia was snugly tucked in, Peggy headed for her own quarters. As she walked across the base in the falling snow, she was taken by the beauty of this white serenity.

Oversized snowflakes danced in the air before her as if hoping to extend their brief crystalline existences. As Peggy walked, they coated her shoulders and woolen cap and perched on her cheeks, melting into droplets fresh and cold. Peggy stuck out her tongue and caught one, relishing the gift. *I'm happy*, she realized, her hazel eyes aglow. *It's been so long.* She inhaled the cool air and pondered why she had to come so far to begin to feel comfortable with herself. *I have always been such a show off, always craving attention. Now all I want to do is fade into the background. And yet, I always wind up in the middle of things. What is it about me? When I get what I want, I don't want it. That's a little crazy, isn't it? But for right now, this moment, I'm happy.*

Peggy was fast asleep in her bed before any more such paradoxical thoughts could drift through her mind.

6

The American aircrew's next visit to the regimental airdrome was by invitation. They made the trip in another flatbed truck. Kamenny's resourcefulness no longer surprised his charges. As before, Caloon and Crandall sat in the cab with Kamenny, while Nick, McCabe, and Pua steeled themselves for another tailbone-punishing trip in the truck bed. After a bruising ride the vehicle finally arrived at the base. Once they passed through two checkpoints, they were directed to the headquarters building and were cordially greeted by a uniformed officer.

"Welcome, American comrades," Major Konstantin Simonev, Colonel Petrovitch's executive officer, said in surprisingly good English. "My colonel has asked myself to make you cordially greeting in his absence. He wishes you to share with us this celebration occasion—the decoration of several heroic aviators and the great honor to be bestowed upon our regiment: the elevation to Guards Regiment of the Army of the Soviet. He gives one small request; that you make observance only and not to speaking or making contact with journalists who will be present. Is agreement?"

The Americans nodded assent to the terms.

As they walked toward a large work stand, which would provide a good view of the proceedings, the major called out, "Sergeant McCabe, if you will to wait one moment, I have item which belongs you."

McCabe lingered behind as the Russian officer walked to a small Jeep-like vehicle and retrieved a paper-wrapped parcel. It contained McCabe's A-2 flight jacket. The scorched leather sleeve, shoulder, and back had been removed, matched precisely, and expertly replaced. A new silk lining had been installed and the frayed cuffs expertly repaired.

"Hey, thanks, Major," McCabe said, beaming, as he pulled it on. "Better'n new. It's already broke in." He flailed his arms like a mental patient who had just slipped his straight jacket.

McCabe hadn't complained about his lost jacket but privately he missed it desperately. More than merely a lucky charm, he felt as if he had lost a part of himself. Upon zipping it up he felt whole again.

"Hey, Major, thank your people for me, will ya! *Spaseeba,* a whole lot."

"I shall convey message. Now, I must repeat, you are invited to make observing of medal giving which is to be two hours from this hour, at noon hour. When journalist and dignitaries make departing, you are permitted to participate in small celebration. Vodka, cakes, caviar, *katushas.* Is acceptable?"

The Americans nodded again.

"*Da. Horosho.* Here work platform will afford excellent visualizing." He glanced over to the reviewing stand. "You will now excuse myself . . ." He turned and strode toward the newly built cloth-draped platform.

Beside the platform Kamenny was standing with a Russky colonel who seemed to be reading him the riot act. Remarkably, Kamenny stayed calm. He kept nodding repeatedly and making little placating gestures with his hands. This officer was not the base commander. This fellow, it turned out, was the base political officer, named Yankovlevitch. On an equal footing with the old man, but there to look out for the party's interests. He didn't care for the Americans one bit and was vehemently opposed to their presence. "Conspicuous foreigners" was his concern. *What would the commissar think? Were they running a lax ship?* He wanted them gone. Off the aerodrome, back in their own quarters, with the door locked.

Kamenny was barely holding his own when Major Simonev joined the pair. After speaking heatedly for a few moments more the major called an enlisted man over. After a few brief words, the soldier and Kamenny turned and hurried toward a nearby supply tent. When they exited, the private bore an armful of clothes that he handed to the Americans. They were mechanic's coveralls. The American airmen were asked to wear Soviet issue coveralls to cover their US uniforms. A concession that apparently placated the politico.

Kamenny explained the whole thing to the Americans as he helped them on with the heavy cotton gear. They might be a bit warm but who cared, especially if it allowed them to view the big ceremony. For men who had been cooped up for nearly a year, this outing was like a trip to Coney Island.

Five Yak fighters that had arrived at dusk the previous day were currently in the air circling the base in the event of another German intrusion. The Russian big brass arrived promptly at fifteen minutes before noon in a Petlyakov four-engined bomber. The lumbering aircraft taxied to a ramp area covered with perforated steel plate; the American-made steel surface that thwarted the ubiquitous mud.

With the propellers barely stopped, a door on the side of the aircraft opened and a three-step platform was placed on the ground. Shortly, four officers exited the plane, followed by six armed soldiers. They were greeted warmly by Colonel Petrovitch and his key officers. Kamenny explained to the Americans that the short, round-faced two-star general was NS Khrushchev, the top political officer of the southern district and a member of the Politburo, said to be a confidante of Stalin. A very big party cheese. The other, General Novikov, was the air commander of the southern district. Khrushchev and Novikov were accompanied by their aides.

The cordon of armed soldiers snapped to attention as the two general officers followed the base commander to the reviewing stand.

On the newly built wooden reviewing stand, Peggy Cohan and her two sister aviators stood at attention in the warm air.

I wish they'd get on with it, she thought as she fought the slight nausea caused by the heat and the combination of the winter tunic she wore over her flight jacket and regular uniform. Someone realized at the last moment that her leather flying jacket offered no place to pin a medal so she was loaned a Russian officer's tunic for the occasion. The combination of a belted tunic, over a leather flying jacket and US-issue khaki blouse and service cap made her look like an odd Russian-American hybrid.

Remember, don't lock your knees or you'll pass out in the sun. They taught her that in Texas. *Lord, I hate this.* Stealing a glance at the two grim-faced young women beside her, Peggy could see that they were just as uncomfortable as she was. The photographers from Pravda and TASS were jockeying to capture the women flyers, who stood at attention, making every effort not to look too uncomfortable.

Peggy wished to be anywhere but here. *Oh, for the freedom and anonymity of empty blue skies, hair and face tucked out of sight under leather flying helmet and oxygen mask. A world apart where a person can't be peered at or reduced to a mere object of decoration.* So many painful memories flooded back. So many unpleasant aspects of her life were recalled in the glare of the flashbulbs.

The five American airmen and Kamenny viewed the ceremony from the vantage point of three work stands pulled to the side of the ramp. From there they had a good view of the reviewing stand and the Russian troops turned out on the taxiway in front of it.

It looked like three women were the heroes of the day. Two seemed to be disabled—one leaned on a cane and the other had her arm and shoulder in a bulky brace. These two were robust-sized women. A pair of keepers, one would say back home. The third one, despite the bulky tunic, looked slender and very young. Even at a distance one could see she was pretty. Kamenny produced a pair of ornate opera glasses. Where he had appropriated those nobody knew, nor would ask.

As the glasses were passed along, it was during McCabe's turn that he announced, "Hey, Nick, your girl's up there."

"My girl? What you talkin' about?" said the navigator.

"Yeah, yeah. It sure looks like her," said McCabe, thumbing the focus for a bit more clarity. "If it ain't, it's her twin sister."

"Who? Who you talkin' about?" replied Nick, positive he was the butt of one of McCabe's pranks.

"Your pinup in the Luckies pack," McCabe explained. "Here, see for yourself." He handed the glasses to the navigator. "Looks like the exact same tomato to me."

Nick put the glasses to his eyes, found the third woman on the wooden stand and gasped. "Can't be!" He rotated the focus ring with his finger, turning the image fuzzy and then sharp again. "I don't believe it." It was her. She looked uncomfortable on the platform. As Nick peered at the young woman he could see that she was wearing an American service cap while her colleagues wore the woolen head gear of Russian officers. She was also wearing American style pants and shoes and he could make out an Army Air Corps necktie and a glimpse of a leather flying jacket under the Russky tunic. *It's the face of the nurse in the magazine photo and she's an American.* Nick Tolkin was stunned at the thought that his good luck pinup and companion was here in Russia, also ten thousand miles from home.

"Holy cow! Can it really be her? It is! Holy cow!"

Captain Crandall snatched the glasses from his stunned navigator's grasp. "Give it here. Lemme see ..." He then laughed. "The spittin' image, Nick. You'd best go right over there and tell her that you love her." He dragged out the word "love," which made the entire situation even more humorous to the other airmen.

"I gotta meet her. I gotta speak to her," said Nick as he jumped to the ground from the metal stand.

"Whoa, Nellie," said Sam Caloon. "Best wait 'til this medal hoedown's over. I don't s'pect these Russians and s'pecially that fat little general over there take too kindly to your bargin' in on their little rodeo. These Russkys got no religion, you know. So I s'pect they take their medal shindigs pretty seriously."

"But I've got to meet her," pleaded Nick. "Kamenny, you've got to arrange it."

"If it is possible, it will be arranged," Kamenny replied. "All in due time."

At Major Simonev's nod, the regiment was called to attention. General Khrushchev was trailed by Major Sergienko, his aide. Following them was General Novikov and southern district Air Commander Col. Petrovitch, as well as the Regimental Commander and Major Simonev, his adjutant. They were followed by the regiment's commander of party organization, Col. Yankovlevitch. The dignitaries approached the reviewing stand. The three officers trailed the visiting pair up the steps of the platform and joined the entire assembly at attention as the band rendered the "Internationale," Communism's sacred anthem.

Nikita Khrushchev shifted slightly as he stood in the midday sun. He flexed his shoulders in order to relieve the kink that was spreading up his back. It was a surprisingly warm day and he could feel a bead of perspiration trickle down the back of his neck and dampen his collar. His eyes wandered over the massed troops standing in precise ranks before him, their voices swelling in patriotic fervor. Aside, to the left, his eyes came to rest upon a small group of men standing leisurely on some maintenance stands. They didn't appear to be soldiers. Civilians perhaps. But they looked young and fit. Why, then, were they not in the military? Curious. *Once these interminable proceedings are over I'll ask Petrovitch who those rather lackadaisical characters are. Now if we can expedite this ceremony I will be happy to be on my way. I'm sure all of us would prefer to get back to the business of fighting Germans.*

Colonel Petrovitch stepped forward and addressed the regiment in Russian.

"Comrades, we are here assembled to recognize the valorous actions of our fellow warriors. To solemnize this occasion we are honored by the presence of Air Marshal AA Novikov and General Major Nikita S. Khrushchev, member of the Politburo, first secretary of the Ukrainian People's party and general commander of the southern district. We would be further honored if we could prevail on the commissar to grant us a few words."

On this cue the men and women of the 496th air bombardment regiment broke into spontaneous applause, which, of course, was well rehearsed. Khrushchev stepped forward, acknowledged his audience with a nod and spoke.

"Pausing as we do this day from our sworn and sacred duty of driving the fascist hordes from our beloved homeland, we look with pride upon the faces of our brave comrades who today are to be recognized for their special achievement. You who stand proudly before us; brothers and sisters in arms, we salute you. You have done your duty and you are deserving of the full measure of our gratitude. Be assured that our beloved leader, first secretary Stalin, is aware of your service and is well and duly pleased."

At this point, Khrushchev's aide, Sergienko handed him a banner tightly rolled against its shaft.

"Here is the banner which may now and forever be flown by your regiment."

With a dash of theatricality, Khrushchev unrolled the banner—red with a gold star surrounded by mottos—and with the help of his aide, displayed it to the assembled soldiers.

"You are hereby invested as a guards regiment of the Union of Soviet Socialist Republics. Colonel Andrei Ivanovitch Petrovitch, regimental commander, here is your banner. General Novikov and I salute you and your fine warriors in their efforts in this great patriotic war."

"I thank you," said the obviously moved Petrovitch. "We will make every effort to deserve this high honor."

Khrushchev added, "But the time devoted to celebrating your valor must be short. We are still far from our goal. Therefore, your future efforts must be doubled and redoubled for this is a vile and tenacious enemy we face; hateful and formidable in his unscrupulous guile. But in the end we will free our homeland from the fascist invader. Together we will inevitably prevail."

The regiment once again broke into spontaneous applause.

Khrushchev then followed Petrovitch and a young lieutenant

bearing a tray of cased medals down the steps of the reviewing stand. Standing front and center and apart from the regiment stood about a dozen aviators. All women. These were the pilots and navigators who had participated in the raid of three weeks ago which had destroyed both an enemy fuel depot and truck staging area filled with ammunition-laden vehicles. A major enemy fuel dump and ammunition cache had been eliminated in a single blind air strike.

For this the members of the mission were to be decorated with the Order of the Patriotic War, First Class. Petrovitch passed out the medals and shook the hand of each recipient. Beside him, a step behind the officer carrying the tray of decorations, stood General-Major Nikita Khrushchev, who nodded in solemn approval as each flyer received her honor.

The process was repeated once again for the attending ground crews of that particular raid. The forty or so mechanics and armorers also received the Order of the Patriotic War, but in its non-gilded second class form. After dispensing all of the medals, along with a personal "well done" to each recipient, the trio returned to the reviewing stand. There, the rotund commissar addressed the base commander.

"You are to be congratulated, Colonel. A fine looking group of young warriors."

"Yes, comrade Khrushchev, they are indeed. I thank you. You are most kind in saying so."

"Nonsense, colonel. It is I, on behalf of the Politburo, who should be thanking you for inspiring such zeal and efficiency."

Col. Petrovitch was pleased and flattered by his guest's remarks. It could never hurt to be in the good graces of the party, even though he personally was not a member. Commissar Khrushchev was known to be an honest man. A party official who was straightforward and incorruptible and who did not use his position for personal advantage. Khrushchev's observation was correct. These young men and women were, indeed, a fine cadre of soldiers. The colonel's shoulders straightened perceptibly and he held his head a bit higher as he allowed himself the feeling of satisfaction.

"I have but one small query," Khrushchev whispered to the commandant.

"Please, comrade general, ask."

"Those men over there, observing us from atop the work stands. Who are they? They don't appear to be soldiers. Why are they there?"

Col. Petrovitch answered tentatively, betraying his nervousness. "They . . . they are . . . Americans, comrade Khrushchev."

"Ah, then they are journalists?"

"Er, no, comrade Khrushchev. They are internees. They are the crew of the bomber which landed in Tavrichanka over a year ago. They are part of the American squadron that bombed Japan. You might remember..."

"Yes," said Khrushchev, after a slight pause. "I do recall the incident."

"They have been quartered at a small dacha nearby and have requested to be put to work on the base. They feel the need to be useful in the war against the fascist, which is their country's enemy also. I have not granted their request but on the basis of some evidence of good character on their part I have permitted them to visit the base for this special occasion. To view firsthand the might and excellence of our military capabilities."

Khrushchev could tell that the colonel was worried that his cordial treatment of the Americans would be looked upon unfavorably by his political superior. Indeed, the colonel was upset that the Americans had been spotted. Khrushchev usually enjoyed allowing his subordinates to stew before he finally revealed his personal feelings on any given matter. In this case, however, the commissar let the worried commander off the hook quickly.

"My dear Colonel, I will leave it to you to decide the disposition of these men. I assume you have interviewed them and are satisfied they are no security threat to us. As for myself, I would appreciate it if you would arrange for me to meet with these Americans. I would like to speak to them, discern their nature. If you could arrange such a meeting after the investment I would appreciate it. Oh, and, if you would, include the young American woman who is to be decorated. I have never met any Americans except on official business. And none of them were young. I would like to meet some young Americans."

"It will be arranged Comrade Khrushchev," Petrovitch said with a curt nod.

"Now, with your permission, sir," said Petrovitch, "our regiment would like to offer a declaration."

Khrushchev nodded for him to proceed.

Petrovitch in turn nodded to Simonev, his adjutant, who barked an order to the assembled troops. On command, they dropped to one knee and as Simonev joined them they uttered these words.

"We, the cohort of the 496th Guards Regiment, do solemnly pledge our loyalty and total allegiance to our leader, First Secretary Stalin. We shall faithfully stand behind him, our father, our inspiration, until the fascist hordes are driven from our beloved homeland. We hereby solemnly swear."

Khrushchev stepped forward and gestured for the troops to rise. "I shall personally inform the First Secretary of your heartfelt expression of fealty." He gestured again for some kneeling stragglers to rise. "We have more business, I believe," he said as he turned to face the three women on the platform.

Finally getting around to us, thought Peggy, relieved that the tedious series of ceremonies was at last concluding.

As the Colonel, his aide, and Khrushchev turned to face the three women, Peggy could sense a certain instability in Natalia. Supported by one crutch, Natalia's legs betrayed an increasing unsteadiness. She nonetheless fought to remain at rigid attention. Khrushchev noticed her difficulty and quietly said to the Colonel, "With your permission Petrovitch, may I direct this soldier to stand at ease?" Without waiting for the colonel's assent he softly said, "Lieutenant, please stand at ease." Natalia gratefully relaxed her body and reached out to the railing behind her.

Well, thought Peggy, her eyes still forward, *at least the fat little general seems like a decent man.*

The photographers swarmed the scene, flash bulbs popping once again as they gobbled up the moments of the ceremony.

Natalia, who managed a sort of semi-attention, was awarded the Order of the Red Banner by Khrushchev, who pinned it on her tunic. Khrushchev shook her hand and then gave her a kiss on each cheek. He then moved to Major Svetlana, and told her that the Motherland was proud of her. Beside the Order of the Patriotic War and Order of the Red Banner already in place, he pinned the Order of Alexander Nevsky on the loose tunic draped over her body cast. He then shook her hand but because of the cast he could only give her a kiss on her right cheek.

"How's the arm?" he asked.

"Better every day, comrade general," replied the Major.

"Excellent!" said Khrushchev, visibly pleased with her answer.

Now it was Peggy's turn. The press edged forward as Khrushchev stepped to face the young American girl. He smiled at Peggy. A very proud grandfatherly smile. NS Khrushchev was very much the showman. *The First Secretary will be pleased to hear that she is indeed pretty, he observed silently.*

"You have my personal gratitude and the gratitude of First Secretary Stalin along with the workers of the Soviet for your brave and selfless act. I understand by your heroic actions you have restored two valued fighters to us and our great patriotic struggle. For this, Margaret Cohan, you will be enshrined forever in our hearts as Hero of the Soviet Union."

The aide stepped forward and presented a velvet-covered tray that bore two leather medal cases. As Khrushchev opened the diminutive red case that resembled a jewel case, the photographers readied themselves to capture the moment.

He removed a small gold star suspended from a small red ribbon and spoke so that all assembled could hear. "By order of the Supreme Soviet, I hereby invest you as 'Hero of the Soviet Union.'" He then pinned it on the girl's tunic, high up and close to the shoulder. The Hero of the Soviet Union was Russia's highest award and no medal could be worn above it. He pinned it on slowly, giving the photographers ample time to record the moment.

"Your ordeal is not yet over, young woman," he said softly to Peggy, who understood none of it. "Every Hero of the Soviet Union is also invested with the Order of Lenin."

He then reached for the larger case and removed a full-sized medal suspended from a wide red and yellow ribbon bearing the stern likeness of VI Lenin cast in platinum. *Oh, no,* thought Peggy, *another one?* Khrushchev pinned the second order on Peggy's chest below and to the left of the first. He then shook her hand, grinned broadly and, standing on tip-toe, moved forward to place a kiss on both her cheeks. The girl bent over slightly to accommodate him. As the flashbulbs seemed to pop endlessly, Khrushchev, prolonging the moment, whispered to Peggy in Russian.

"This photo will be in many periodicals. Your face will become famous if only for a little while. I hope that pleases you."

Fortunately, Peggy again did not comprehend. She did not share Khrushchev's idea of fame and was uncomfortable at being the center of attention. He spoke again, softly, to Peggy alone. "You are changed forever young woman. Your brave heart is now companioned with a Russian soul." Peggy's face revealed her lack of understanding. Khrushchev saw and nodded, smiling. "It does not matter, the deed is done."

For most everyone else, this was a wonderful moment. Good for morale, good international public relations, and best of all, the recognition of genuine valor.

Khrushchev, Novikov, Petrovitch, and the rest of the officers on the stand then began to applaud the three women. The entire regiment joined in the applause. In typical Russian fashion, those who were being applauded, in turn, applauded the regiment. As Svetlana and Natalia awkwardly attempted to applaud—Svetlana, her arm in a rigid cast, and Natalia clapping with one hand against her crutch—Peggy joined in as well, much to the delight of the regiment, the press, and Commissar Khrushchev.

"You may dismiss your command, Col. Petrovitch," Novikov told the regimental commander. "If there is someplace suitable, I am sure the press would like to interview our newly vested heroes."

In the shade of a camouflaged maintenance tent, the three women fielded the reporter's questions, most of which were directed to the American girl.

To Peggy Cohan: "Why were you on a Soviet bombing mission?"

"Simply as an observer."

A reporter representing a Swedish publication asked, "Do you feel that Soviet bombing techniques could be improved?"

Col. Yankovlevitch stiffened.

"No. As far as I can see they are quite efficient."

Both Petrovitch and Yankovlevitch relaxed with Peggy's answer. But the Swede continued pressing. "But as an American technical advisor surely you must have some suggestions for improvement?"

"The extent of my expertise is solely in the P-39 aircraft. I'm simply helping transition some Soviet pilots in its operation. And I must say they are very quick to learn."

Petrovitch and Yankovlevitch again exchanged pleased nods.

After a half hour more of questioning from journalists representing Pravda, TASS, the Soviet Army's own publication, Reuters, and a Swedish weekly, Khrushchev stepped forward and tactfully brought the interview to an end. He dismissed the press, reminding them that these women were soldiers and had already spent too much time away from their military duties. Khrushchev then saluted the three medal recipients, turned, and exited the tent.

When the three newly decorated women arrived at the squadron area, the briefing hut was crowded with people. They were greeted with cheers and applause.

"Bravo!"

"Long live the brave hearts of the 466th Bombardment Squadron!"

"Well done, Natalia!"

"Well done, Svetlana!"

"Well done, *tovarich* Peggy."

Peggy was picking up more and more of the difficult Russian language. That last remark, referring to her as "*tovarich* Peggy," had great meaning, for it attested to her acceptance by these proud and dedicated aviators.

On a table in the center of the tent stood several vodka bottles. *Uh-oh, more tasting,* thought Peggy. *These Russians would toast the spines on a cactus if the darn things grew around here.*

The women were led to the table in mock solemnity. Their medals were removed from their tunics. The young bespectacled meteorologist, Yakov Bolkanin, placed Major Svetlana's Alexander Nevsky medal in a large glass, actually more the size of a small vase. He dropped Natalia's Red Banner medal into another, and finally, Peggy's Gold Star and Order of Lenin in a third. To the amusement of all, including Svetlana and Natalia, who had witnessed this ritual before, Bolkanin filled the ample glasses with vodka. He then announced that no self-respecting Russian would think of wearing their medals without having consumed the vodka in which they were submerged.

Svetlana and Natalia, grinning, each raised the large beaker of clear liquid to their lips. As Peggy did the same, the onlookers began to chant *Skven:* "Drink! Drink! Drink! Drink!" The two Russian women drained their glasses and triumphantly slammed the empty cups down on the table. They joined in the chant as Peggy was only half finished with hers. When the glass was finally drained, she likewise slammed it down. As she did she surprised herself and all around her with a loud and extraordinarily deep burp, producing cheers and laughter. The corps of aviators swarmed the three women and offered embraces and congratulations.

In the Regimental Commander's office the group raised their considerably smaller glasses in a toast offered by Commissar Khrushchev. First they drank "to Stalin," then "to the three beautiful women, two Russian, one American, who were decorated this day. The exemplar of the soul of Russia: to suffer and endure and prevail. I drink, young women, to your Russian souls."

The commissar threw his head back and drained his glass in one swallow. The others followed suit. He then moved to the table and punched a dome of freshly baked, wafer-thin bread, picked up a large shovel-shaped shard, and dug into a mound of chilled black caviar. He placed the entire thing into his mouth, closed his eyes, grinning as he savored it.

"And now, Petrovitch, if I could impose on your hospitality, I would like to meet with the American aviators. If it could be arranged. Quickly, since I must be on my way back to the front. And, yes, the young American woman, too. Our newest hero of the Soviet Union."

"They have been summoned, comrade Khrushchev," said Petrovitch. He then turned to Simonev, nodded, and watched as Simonev exited the tent.

The young Americans were ushered into the presence of the round-faced commissar a few minutes later. Kamenny nervously offered his services as interpreter.

Capt. Crandall had bridled at the request for them to meet with the Russky big shot. He felt that their summons had been more of an order than a request and believed that they should decline the meeting. Tolkin and Caloon advised their captain to go along. They argued that such a meeting couldn't worsen their position and it might afford an opportunity to plead for their repatriation at a high level. Swayed by this logic, Crandall relented.

He entered the tent warily with his crew.

The rotund two-star general stepped forward and introduced himself simply as Nikita Khrushchev. "And now," he said through the uncomfortable interpreter, "I would like to learn your names."

Bed Crandall stepped forward, braced to attention and saluted. "Crandall, Bedford A., Captain, United States Army Air Corps, sir!"

"Crand-dall, Bed-frad," Khrushchev repeated.

"Sir, that's Bedford Crandall." He pronounced his name slowly. "Bedford being my Christian given name."

After a brief interpreter confab, the Russian nodded and repeated the name correctly.

"Sir," Sam Caloon said, stepping forward and matching the brace of his captain. "Samuel Caloon, First Lieutenant, United States Army Air Corps, sir."

"Samuel Caloon," Khrushchev repeated, then turned and spoke to the interpreter.

"The general wishes to clarify the nature of this meeting as unofficial and social," explained Kamenny. "He merely desires to meet the soldiers of our American allies. Therefore, saluting and standing at attention is unnecessary. Unless it is your preference."

The posture of both Crandall and Caloon relaxed and they stood easy, feeling a bit foolish but decidedly more comfortable.

Nick Tolkin then stepped forward and introduced himself. When Khrushchev heard his name, he reacted with a tilt of his head and spoke a few words to the interpreter.

"You are Russian? The commissar asks."

Khrushchev's eyes flashed a momentary spark of annoyance at Kamenny's frivolous use of the word "commissar" but instantly regained his affable and benign demeanor.

It was then that Peggy, wearing her leather flight jacket, entered the tent, shepherded by Major Simonev. She was somewhat breathless, having traversed most of the distance from the far side of the base at a run. All they said was that the General wanted to speak to her personally, immediately. As she entered unsteadily, the effects of the vodka impeding her gait, she walked to the moon-faced officer and saluted. Khrushchev beamed at her in a very comforting and fatherly way. He then stepped forward, said something that sounded friendly and took her hand. "Thank you for coming," Kamenny translated. Peggy nodded and smiled, having some difficulty standing still due to the growing effects of the vodka.

Sam Caloon nudged Nick in the ribs and whispered, "It's your pinup girl, in the flesh. And she's had a snoot full."

There was no need to inform Nick. As she entered, his heart beat in double time. All he could do was stare, mouth slightly agape. *Wow,* he thought, *she's even lovelier in person.* He was acting like a teenage boy seeing his first Duesenberg.

Khrushchev, now holding Peggy's arm, introduced her to the group. "Here is American aviator, Ma-garet Cohan," the interpreter translated for Khrushchev. "Our newest Hero of Soviet Union and countrywoman to you."

"Hi ya Margaret," said Capt. Crandall as he shook her hand.

"A real pleasure to make your acquaintance," said Sam, lapsing into a charming, honeysuckle drawl.

"Hu-hullo," was all that Nick could muster as she reached to take his hand.

"You have blue eyes!" Peggy blurted as she met his gaze.

"Yeah, looks like one of those sled dogs, don't he? I'm McCabe, crew chief," the tech sergeant announced. "Boy, is it swell to set eyes on an American girl!"

"George Loomis Pua, and that's double ditto for me," announced the grinning dark-skinned gunner as his big paw enveloped Peggy's.

What a treat to hear American voices again, thought Peggy. *And American faces! Oooh, they look swell. I wish the room would stop spinning.*

"So, you are meeting for the first time," the interpreter translated. "Then I have done a good deed. Bringing countrymen together. Now, tell me, my new American friends. About your backgrounds. Where you live in America. Your families."

"We live in Connecticut," said Crandall. "I attended Yale, joined up in my senior year. My father's an officer of a local bank."

Khrushchev looked impressed. Then pointed to Caloon.

"My people hail from South Carolina. I attended Spartanburg Junior College and my daddy grows tobacco."

Khrushchev's eyes then fixed on Tolkin.

"My parents live in Brooklyn, New York. That's part of New York City, but not Manhattan. I attended City College and was majoring in engineering when I enlisted. I've got another year to go before I graduate. My father's a tool and die maker at the Grumman plant."

Khrushchev and Kamenny were conferring on the meaning of "tool and die maker" when Nick added "machinist."

Khrushchev then brightened and said, "Ah, machinist, *da*. Question, Officer Tolkin. Name to ear is Russian. Is family Tolkin from Russia?"

"Yes, sir," said Nick. "Both my parents are Russian. They met in the United States."

"Ah," said the commissar, satisfied that his surmise was correct.

McCabe explained that he was a high school graduate from San Francisco and that his father was a policeman there.

George Loomis Pua told the Russian that he was from Hawaii, the place that had been attacked by the Japanese. He was from another island called Molokai where he graduated from high school. Both his mother and father worked in the Dole pineapple processing plant on the island.

Khrushchev, along with the other men in the tent, then turned to Peggy. She, with slightly slurred speech, told them that she was from Long Island, New York, had been working in the fashion industry, and had taken up flying as a hobby since she lived so close to an airport. Her father died when she was a little girl and her mother worked for an insurance company. "And," she added, "I'm presently in Russia helping pilots transition to the P-39D Air Cobras that my colleagues and I ferried all the way from Alaska to here for the Russian Air Corps."

The last portion of her convoluted statement came out even more slurred. Khrushchev turned to Simonev and winked. "They made her drink for her medals. Poor girl, she's not used to Russian vodka."

When Simonov completed the translation, Khrushchev nodded as if satisfied with the information provided and said, "Thank you, young friends. I have now an improved understanding of our American allies. It is most interesting that two of you, as I comprehend, are from wealthy backgrounds and the other four are of the working class. Yet you are friends and interact comfortably. I find that heartening. Thank you all for visiting with me."

Then, with a glance at his watch, "I fear I must be on my way. Back to the business of pursuing the war. Duty calls."

"General," Crandall rather brazenly stepped forward, partially blocking the commissar's path to the exit. "We were wondering if you could help us. Sort of put in a good word. Y'see, we surely want to get back to our units. It's been over a year that we've been here in Russia. Could you help us get back?"

Khrushchev turned to Simonev and spoke rapidly in Russian, asking for a clarification of Crandall's request. Simonev tersely explained their circumstance.

"I do not know what I can do," Khrushchev responded thoughtfully. "Perhaps . . . I make no promise," the commissar said after the translation. "But I shall look into it. Col. Petrovitch assures me that you are men of good character. I would concur. You have my word that I will see what can be done. That is the best I can do. Now, I must take my leave of you."

"Thank you for your hospitality," he said warmly to Col. Petrovitch, grasping the officer's shoulder. "We must return to less pleasurable tasks. Da svedanya, Hero of the Soviet Union. Da svedanya, brave aviators. Comrades, a farewell salute."

After shaking hands with each of the Americans, Khrushchev saluted smartly, nodded to Simonev and exited the tent. Simonov remained for a few moments, exhaling a deep sigh of relief, then after a short bow to the Americans, hurried out to the ramp after the commissar and Colonel Petrovitch.

"You think we told him too much?" asked Caloon.

"Nah, we told him nothing specific. Besides, he's on our side, ain't he?" said McCabe.

"So, Margaret, just how long have you been here?"

All eyes turned to the American girl. Nick Tolkin's eyes had never left her.

"About four weeks, I guess. And, everyone calls me Peggy. S'cuse me, I need to sit down." Peggy's slurring had become more pronounced.

"All right, Peggy it is," said Sam Caloon.

"I really need to sit down," Peggy repeated, her head tilted, groping for a chair that refused to remain still. Finally seated, she asked, "How 'bout you fellas. What're you doing in Russia?"

Sitting in the briefing chairs, the men formed a semicircle around Peggy and related the story of how they were part of a B-25 raid on Japan.

"I know about that," said Peggy, forming her words with difficulty. "Was on the radio an' all the papers. You fellas are big zeroes... h-heroes."

"We are? No shit," said the surprised Hawaiian gunner. He quickly added, "Please excuse my French."

"Do you know how many of our guys made it?"

"Most, I think, if I remember rightly. But I think all the planes crashed. 'Cept for yours, I guess."

"Yeah, but the Russians got the *Baby*. Our plane was the *Boogie Woogie Baby*," Crandall added.

"Why are you . . . why don't they send you home?" Peggy asked in a serious tone.

"Don't know," Sam Caloon shrugged.

"Some kind of red tape," McCabe put in. "Hey, ya get it? Red tape!"

Peggy chuckled, slapped her knee and pointed to McCabe as if to say, "Good one!"

"How about you, Peggy?" Nick asked.

"Me, I guess I'll get to leave soon. Most of my girls are checked out on the Cobras. Now I understand that they wanted me to stay for the medals. I imagine it'll be fairly soon."

"Say, Peggy, I was thinking, maybe sometime after work I could buy you a cup of tea? What do ya say?" asked Bed Crandall.

"No," said Peggy, "that won't work at all." In a tipsy giggle, she said, "Round here, tea's in a glass. No cups." She chuckled mightily at her own joke.

It was then that one of Col. Petrovitch's officers entered with Kamenny and motioned for the men to follow him. As they were filing out they waved a farewell to Peggy.

"So long, Peggy."

"Nice meeting you."

"Bye."

"See ya around."

"When?" said Nick Tolkin. "When are we gonna see you again?"

Peggy offered an exaggerated shrug. "Don't know," she said as they all exited the tent and followed Kamenny toward the waiting truck. After traveling a few yards, Peggy turned and shouted, "I'm over in the visitor's barracks or at the 466th."

Nick turned and gave a thumbs up, a broad grin on his face.

On the walk to the truck, Nick confronted his pilot. "Hey, Skip, just what're you up to? Huh?"

Crandall smiled wickedly. "Rank hath its privileges, Nick, you know that."

Out on the ramp a pair of Yak fighters took off as the engines were started on Khrushchev's converted Ilushyn. They would provide escort on the 500-kilometer journey to Engel's, central command of the Stalingrad front. One of the escort pilots was Lilya Litvak.

During her stumbling, meandering route to her quarters, Peggy noted how good she felt having met those great American boys. *Now, bunk, do me a favor and hold still.*

7

As the P-8 bomber lifted from the Kotluban Aerodrome and climbed to altitude, Khrushchev's mind immediately turned to the war and the defense of the Motherland. He settled back in his large wicker chair and reached for his suitcase of papers. The long-range bomber had been converted into a transport complete with a small galley, a curtained area behind which were two full-sized beds, and a line of fold-up aluminum seats along the fuselage. Khrushchev found the metal seats cold and uncomfortable, so he had a wide wicker chair with cushions brought aboard and secured in place. The commissar overheard the crew jokingly referring to it as "the throne," which for some reason pleased him.

As he sat on his throne discussing the developments at Stalingrad and other communiqués with his aide, Sergienko, he came upon the copy of Beria's report on the new German turbine aircraft. Recently updated, intelligence now confirmed that the planes were in production and that training schedules were already approved. Predictions were that the first squadron should be operational by mid-summer. Stalin had personally asked him to take action on this situation but up until now no remedy had come to mind. Some action must be taken. "But what? Sabotage?" he mused out loud.

"Paratroops!" Sergienko offered gravely. "We could drop commandos on their factory; use explosives to destroy everything."

Khrushchev shook his head. "Have you seen our paratroops? Every airborne operation we have undertaken thus far has been a failure. Even the action against the Finns was a fiasco. And should we succeed in destroying their factory they'd only build another. No, it has to be something else. If we could get our hands on one of the planes or even a motor, our engineers could build them. Then we could build our own countermeasure. In a fair fight our boys would make mincemeat out of the Fritzies."

"But, Comrade Khrushchev," interrupted the puzzled aide, "I thought we were on the verge of development of this technology?"

"Yes, true, we were but we've hit snags. Our engineers are at a dead end," Khrushchev explained weakly all the while avoiding eye contact with his aide. "It's just a question of the motor. The fascists have found the magic elements that continue to elude us. If only we could get our hands on one of those motors!"

"Then we should steal one," Sergienko announced brightly. "Land on their base. Load it into an aircraft like this one and fly off with plenty of fighter escorts clearing the way."

"A fairly daring suggestion, Vasily Nickolaievitch." Khrushchev smiled at the naïve and simplistic solution of his aide. But yet . . . his eyes twinkled as he thought it through. "The raid would have to be deep into German territory. I'm not certain where the factory is but it is certainly somewhere west of Gdansk. Besides, what if we were successful? The entire world would then know that our technology was inferior to the Germans . . . having to steal it rather than develop it ourselves. It's a matter of prestige, Vasily."

"Yes, Comrade Khrushchev, you are right."

His aide's ready acceptance of the prestige issue made him think even harder. *How could we obtain a working turbine motor and not lose face?*

As the aircraft droned forward on its route to Stalingrad front command, the thoughts of the Commissar of the Ukraine drifted back to the American aircrew and the young American woman he had presented with the Gold Star medal. She was very attractive but slim, almost frail, much less robust than the typical Russian woman. But there was something else about her. Despite her slightly inebriated condition, something in the eyes. A steely determination. He had noticed it at the medal investment. It was clear that this young woman believed that no task was beyond her. In that way, she was very Russian. Very Russian indeed. It was in that moment Commissar Khrushchev saw the plan which could make the German invention available to the Soviet cause without loss of face.

"Turn the aircraft around," he ordered suddenly. His aide stared at him dumbfounded. Khrushchev repeated the command. "Have the pilot turn us around. We are returning to the airdrome. He can say that the engines are running improperly. But we must return."

The lumbering P-8 banked to the right and made a slow one-hundred and eighty degree turn back toward Kotluban. Two surprised escort pilots duplicated the turn and took their positions off the wings of the larger craft. They would all be spending the night back at the aerodrome.

The pilot of Khrushchev's bomber radioed the base and announced that he was returning because of some engine "irregularities."

"Do you wish to declare an emergency?" ground control asked the pilot.

The pilot responded casually, "No, I expect to be making a normal landing." The pilot then conveyed to ground control that Commissar Khrushchev was requesting to speak to Col. Petrovitch personally. In a few minutes the colonel was located in the Shturmovik fighter bomber area and brought to the radio.

"Is there some problem Comrade General?" asked the Colonel.

"No, no problem, really. You know how these transport pilots baby their airplanes . . . and their passengers. But I thought that while I am at your base, I would like to meet with those American airmen once more. Our little get-together was most informative, but I realize I have a few more questions and now there is an opportunity to ask them. Are they still on the base?"

"Commissar Khrushchev, I believe they are no longer here; back to their quarters a few kilometers north of us. But I can easily send for them. I might even have them here by the time you land."

"No. No need colonel. But if you would kindly arrange transportation, I would prefer to go to them."

"Certainly, Comrade General. All will be arranged."

"That's kind of you, Petrovitch. I will see you shortly, then."

Khrushchev handed the microphone and the headset to the copilot and returned to his wicker chair in the body of the plane. The pilot and copilot glanced at each other, said nothing, then directed their attention to the instruments, controls, and the slanting rays of the late afternoon sun.

Back at the base, Col. Petrovitch ordered a staff car readied and directed one of his junior officers to drive to the billets of the American airmen and inform them that they were about to be visited by General-Major Khrushchev, first secretary of the Ukrainian People's Party. Also, an appropriate supper should be provided.

"It seems the mountain comes to Mohammed," the colonel said aloud, but since he didn't appear to be addressing anyone in particular, no response seemed appropriate.

8

The table was set with a remarkable array of food. A rare feast for the Americans. Some of it was familiar, like the boiled beef and chicken, but in addition there was roast pork, sturgeon, red and black caviar, and several types of herring. Blini and blintzes, along with bowls heaped with boiled potatoes and dishes of sour cream and yogurt, graced the table along with cakes and pastries. There was even a type of champagne that was a welcome change from the ubiquitous tea and vodka. It was obvious that Petrovitch was pulling out all the stops for his high-ranking guest.

The visit had transformed Kamenny into the most unctuous of headwaiters as he welcomed the commissar and seated him at the head of the table.

Khrushchev was jovial and obviously hungry, which delighted Kamenny. The single cook who saw to the gustatory requirements of the airmen was suddenly augmented by the addition of two female helpers in the kitchen and two more to serve. This night's feast completely eclipsed the lavish spread set for them by Colonel Petrovitch. The men ate with gusto as the staff served, cleared, and replenished platters with dogged efficiency.

When appetites had been satiated, Khrushchev proposed a toast to Stalin. In the Soviet Union, Khrushchev explained, the first toast was always to Stalin. This was followed immediately by a toast to Roosevelt and then to "all brave men and women who each day overcome great odds in their fight against the enemies of mankind." Kamenny was cautioned by the commissar to translate his toast precisely as spoken. The Americans and Kamenny joined Khrushchev as he toasted the Allied freedom fighters.

It was then that the round-faced commissar quieted and became serious. He leaned forward and spoke more softly, as did Kamenny who mimicked his tone.

"My American friends, I have sympathy for your situation. Unfortunately, at present there is little that can be done for you. It is a sensitive matter of a diplomatic nature. There would be sizeable risks. We are presently at peace with the Japanese Empire. Jeopardizing this peace would be foolhardy and potentially disastrous. However, I feel for your plight. Young men, energetic and eager to join in the defeat of your country's enemy. Our shared enemy. If you would be willing to undertake a mission of great importance and, I must add, considerable danger, then upon completion of this mission I would personally intervene to see to it that you are repatriated. Do you understand? Your service to the Soviet Union and, I must add, the Allied cause, would serve to mitigate the risk of diplomatic discomfiture."

"Sir, just what kind of service do you have in mind?" asked Captain Crandall who spoke after a short silence.

After the translation, Khruschchev smiled. "A direct question. I like that," said the commissar, leaning forward. "The service would be a simple intelligence gathering mission. The fascists have been developing a particular piece of technology. We have likewise been exploring a similar avenue. We would like to know if the Fritzies are as advanced as we are on this development. We therefore would like to procure a sample of their latest effort to compare with our own. It would be your task to obtain such a sample. A dangerous task, certainly, but then, you are all brave men. Once this mechanism is in our hands I would see to it that you are all returned. To Connecticut, Southern Carolina, Brooklyn, New York, Molokai in the Hawaiian Islands, and San Francisco. You see, I remember what you have told me."

When Kamenny had translated, Caloon asked, "What sort of technology is it?"

"I will only tell you at this juncture that it is used in an aircraft."

"Would we have to go behind enemy lines?" Sgt. McCabe asked.

"Yes, definitely behind enemy lines," Khrushchev confirmed. "But I must tell you that we would take great pains to deliver you safely and, of course, extract you safely."

After a long pause, Capt. Crandall said, "I don't know, sir, we'd have to think about it; talk it over. Could you possibly give us any more information?"

Khrushchev responded, shaking his head as Kamenny translated. "I cannot give you more information at this time, but I do urge you to consider carefully the proposition. Send word of your decision through Col. Petrovitch. Please do it promptly. So, American aviators," Khrushchev said, leaning forward and tapping his cupped hands on his knees as he rose. "I must leave you now."

A young officer entered as Khrushchev stood up. He handed a folded piece of paper to Major Sergienko, who read it and immediately showed it to Khrushchev. A broad grin broke out on the commissar's face.

"Wonderful news, comrades. From Stalingrad. Several Romanian units have surrendered and Chuikov has flanked the Fritzies' main force. Paulus is beaten and he knows it. I must be there for the kill. Tomorrow. Early. I bid you, good evening."

Two waiting staff cars then returned Khrushchev and his party to the base where a wing of the officers' barracks had been prepared with a feather bed. NS Khrushchev would enjoy a good night's sleep before his dawn departure to Stalingrad command.

"What just happened?" Crandall asked.

Kamenny explained. "It would seem that the fascists have been routed at Stalingrad. Victory in the south is within our grasp. It is best possible news."

Back at the American billet, long after lights out, the airmen animatedly discussed the commissar's offer.

"Whoa, guys, I want to hear what you've all got to say," said Crandall, "but remember, I'm still in charge of this crew. The final say is mine."

"I bet it's a radio ranging device," mused McCabe. "I heard that the British are working on something like that."

Peggy didn't remember much of her medal party when she woke the next morning. She was fully clothed. Her Soviet felt-lined boots were neatly placed at the foot of the bed and her borrowed tunic was carefully hung up, the medals properly reaffixed. *Headache, my God, what a headache!* she thought as she struggled to sit up. *But, wow, what an adventure.*

9

A day after the medal ceremony the routine on the base had returned to normal. The new day found Peggy checking out a new group of students on the flight characteristics of the Aircobra. Though her final flight of the day had been completed and she had dismissed her charges, Peggy remained out on the flight line to deal with a stubborn male mechanic who didn't seem to understand a nose gear problem. Requiring repeated cycles for the gauge to register "locked" was not acceptable. Peggy insisted that the malfunction be written up in the log but was having difficulty conveying this to the mechanic. He seemed to feel that if it eventually worked, where was the problem? *What a knucklehead,* thought Peggy. *Why do men always resort to senseless posturing around women pilots? It was the same back in the States.* The mechanic finally agreed to accept the log entry but only after Peggy invoked the name of Redenko, the maintenance chief. Then, while offering an effusive expression of thanks to the mechanic for finally doing what was supposed to be his job, she noticed the five American airmen walking toward her on the ramp. Peggy waved and they returned her wave, grinning. *Great, I didn't dream the American boys. They're real.*

The Americans stood together for a while on the ramp, chatting and joking as if they were old school friends. It was good to hear those familiar voices. Wonderful to hear an American girl laugh.

When they finally thought to head indoors, the sun had set and the sky was growing dark. Peggy brought the men over to the visitors' billets. Since she had been the only occupant since the last group of escort pilots had gone, she was pleased to have the company.

"Would anyone care for some tea?" she asked.

"Sure, that'll be fine," said Nick.

"I've gotten to the point where I actually like it," said Peggy, lighting the flame under the samovar and finding five extra glasses. "They drink tea from a glass, did you notice?"

"Yeah, you mentioned that," muttered Crandall. "Don't forget, we've been here since April, '42."

Peggy shook her head. "Wow!"

Over tea and American cigarettes, they brought each other up to date.

"We've got bombers in England, big ones, with four engines; B-17s and B-24s. We're beginning to take the war to the Germans," Peggy explained. "Over in the Pacific, we've had some naval victories and I think the Japs are starting to regret that they ever thought of Pearl Harbor.

"And you boys, you were actually part of Jimmy Doolittle's raid on Japan?"

The men nodded modestly, but obviously delighted to have achieved some celebrity.

"How many made it, do you know?" asked Sam Caloon.

"I seem to remember . . . one or two were captured by the Japanese. But that was after they landed in China. None, I think, were shot down by the Japs. And I do recall that the President gave Jimmy Doolittle the Medal of Honor and made him a general."

"How do you like that, the old man goes from light colonel to general while we squat in the Soviet Union eatin' borscht," grumbled Sam.

"Hey, what's wrong with borscht?" Nick countered defensively.

"If he got the medal," said McCabe, "that's gotta mean that we're heroes, too."

"Hey, Skip," Pua said. "You were talkin' about running for the Congress someday, weren't ya? That medal oughta be a big help, won't it?"

Crandall nodded thoughtfully. "Might be, might well be worth a few extra votes."

"Hey, Peggy," Sam Caloon said, pointing to the small gold star on the Soviet tunic which she now wore in place of her leather jacket. "They gave you a medal the other day. A pair of 'em, in fact. What's the scoop on that?"

"Oh, I just hitched a ride on one of their night missions and when the pilot got shot, I flew the plane back," Peggy replied modestly. "Two-place biplane. You've seen them on the ramp. Simple to fly, just like a Stearman. The trick was finding the base."

"And you received Russia's highest honor for that? There must be more to it," Crandall insisted. "C'mon. Give."

"Well, yes, we did rescue the squadron commander and the mission happened to be a big success. We got lucky and managed to knock out lots of fuel and ammo."

"Ah," Crandall nodded. "Now, that makes sense."

"Frankly," Peggy confided. "I think there was more publicity in it than heroics. There were lots of reporters on hand. The *London Times* fellow told me he was surprised that Margaret Bourke-White of *LIFE* magazine wasn't there, they made such a big deal. The tea's ready. Hand me your glasses. I'll pour."

As Peggy poured the steaming, aromatic tea from the old brass samovar and handed out the large square sugar cubes, she studied the faces of the young aviators. How distinctly American these boys looked. How comfortably familiar. The exceptions were Sergeant Pua, who resembled some of the ethnic Tartars, and the navigator, Tolkin, who, despite those blue eyes, matched the coloring of most of the Russians. *And sometimes, that Tolkin, I catch him staring at me; but still, they're all swell, even the Captain, who I think is a little bit in love with himself. They're terrific guys.*

As Peggy filled the last glass she said, "Let me show you the way the Russians drink their tea." She made a show of placing a sugar cube between her teeth and sipping her tea. "You don't put it in the tea. The cube melts as you drink. Try it."

Nick and McCabe tried the sugar cube trick but both shook their heads.

"Nope," said McCabe. "Don't like it."

"Ugh," said Pua. "I swallowed the sugar."

"It takes a bit of getting used to," Peggy observed with a smile.

"Hey, Peggy," McCabe said with a mischievous look in his eye. "You wanna see somethin' really cute?"

"Sure," said Peggy, playing along. "Show me something cute."

"Nick," McCabe said, "show her."

Nick froze, reddening in embarrassment.

"He's got your picture in his pocket. He's had it since back in the States. Go on, show it," goaded McCabe.

Peggy smiled, sensing she was in on some good-natured American ribbing.

"No . . . I . . . I . . . don't have it," stammered Nick.

"Yeah, you do," McCabe said as he reached for Nick's breast pocket.

Nick slapped his hand over the pocket but Pua and Crandall stepped forward, relishing the situation, and pinned Nick's arms to his sides as McCabe unbuttoned the pocket and withdrew the empty Luckies pack. He presented it to Peggy in front of the chagrined navigator.

"That's you, ain't it?" asked Pua.

Peggy looked at the cropped picture beneath the cellophane and recognized the nurse photo from what seemed a lifetime ago.

"Yes, it's me," Peggy acknowledged, experiencing a momentary twinge of discomfort. She fought the emotion and attempted to respond matter-of-factly. "I did some modeling a while back."

"How 'bout that," said Sam Caloon, who with Pua, Crandall, and McCabe, radiated boyish glee at having been party to such a sweet prank. Even Nick managed a half-hearted smile at the situation despite the blush still glowing on his cheeks.

Peggy laughed along with the boys but simultaneously experienced a pang of empathy for Nick. *Poor guy. Must be embarrassing for him.* Empathy was a rare emotion for Peggy. It took her by surprise.

Peggy held out the Luckies pack to Nick while they were all still chortling. Nick swiftly pocketed it, buttoning the flap. Now that the photo was out of sight, the group returned to their conversation and and to their tea.

An uneasy thought flashed through Nick's mind as he sipped from his glass. *Hope she doesn't think I'm some kind of oddball, carrying photos of strange girls.*

The American house party reluctantly broke up when Kamenny arrived and announced that it was time to go. He emphasized his point by suggesting that their permission to work at the base might easily be revoked if they abused the ten p.m. curfew.

Some days later, the boys visited again and brought over their record player. Peggy invited some of the girls from the PO-2 squadron to listen to real "Amerikanskiy" music. After some bottles of vodka appeared, a party ensued. Few words were understood but in the universal language of young people, everyone communicated beautifully.

The airmen danced with the girls and McCabe gave a jitterbug demonstration with the aid of a navigator named Malvina who caught onto his moves with amazing speed. Malvina had danced in the *Ballet Russe* before the war.

Sergeant Pua and a tall pilot named Olga danced, at a very respectable distance from each other, to Glenn Miller. Sam Caloon made the observation that their appearance was uncannily reminiscent of the '39 World's Fair's Trylon and Perisphere. Crandall, Caloon, and Nick took turns cutting in on whoever of them was dancing with Peggy. Then someone put on "Mairzy Doats" and Peggy, who was chatting with Nick, found something familiar about the sound. The lyrics were nonsense but the voice . . . When it was over, Peggy picked up the disc and saw the artist's name, Cece Collins, on the label. *She did it*, thought Peggy. *That's swell, really swell. She did it! Good for her, she did it. I knew she would.*

"What's up?" asked Sam. "You look like you won the Irish Sweepstakes."

"Oh, nothing special. Just that it's a very funny song."

"Oh," said Sam as he nodded in agreement, thinking, *It's not that funny.*

Kamenny arrived a few minutes before ten to break up the party amidst groans uttered in two languages.

"Oh, almost forgot," said Sam Caloon as he was donning his flight jacket. "We brought you this Red Cross parcel. The cigarettes are missing but there's a Hershey Bar, some playing cards, and a paint set. We thought you might like it."

It was a taste of home and Peggy, indeed, liked it.

"Thanks, fellas," Peggy said, clutching her parcel to her chest.

After the young people bade each other good night and left, a very contented American girl devoured her chocolate bar and thought about her friend Cece. *I'm so glad for her,* Peggy mused. *At least something in this cockeyed world goes right.*

During the next few days, the Americans spent much of their off duty time in Peggy's quarters. Natalia and Svetlana accused Peggy of being selfish in the way she hoarded the five handsome Americans.

On one particular evening when Peggy had arranged to get some cakes for their tea and the men prevailed upon Kamenny to get them the makings for some sandwiches, the subject of home came up.

"How long do you have to be here?" Nick asked Peggy.

"I expect I'll be leaving any day now. Soon as they can send a transport for me. I'm strictly short-timing," was Peggy's reply. "I've already transitioned twenty-nine pilots to the P-39. Might be one more group to check out. It's been great and these people have been really nice to me, but I'm ready to leave. How about you fellows?" asked Peggy. "What's keeping you here?"

Crandall explained that it was something to do with some Jap-

Russky treaty. "We're interned for the duration it seems. Unless we can figure a way to make an escape." Crandall then told her about their making a plea to the round-faced two-star.

"You know, the one who flew in to pin on your medals. He was a real baloney bender. Came up with a cockeyed scheme for us to steal some German technology for him and then he'd help us leave. Maybe. It just seemed too risky. Getting my crew killed for some German gadget; not worth it."

"Yeah," Caloon added, "that jabber don't jibe!"

"I decided against it. He's gonna be disappointed. Hey, tough titty. Oh, sorry. But at least we have something useful to do now. Your Colonel's got us working. Feels good, too. He's a pretty right guy."

"You mean Petrovitch?" said Peggy. "Yes, he's okay. Accepts women on their ability. Unlike a lot of these old fuddy-duddy officers."

"Maybe it's fuddy-duddy to your way of thinkin'," said Caloon, "but I don't think I'm so keen on women flying airplanes, either. 'Specially in combat. It doesn't seem right."

"Yeah," agreed Crandall, "with these Russians, their backs against the wall and all, maybe, but it seems to me there are just certain things that women shouldn't be doin'. They're just so much better at other things."

"Like what other things?" said Peggy, testily. "Cooking, and cleaning?"

"Yeah," said Crandall, "and other things." He nudged Caloon in the ribs. "Besides," Crandall continued, "they lack the strength and coordination of a man. That's a proven fact."

McCabe nodded as Crandall spoke but Pua and Nick seemed skeptical.

"All I know," said Pua, "is that my momma can lop the tops off a bin full of pineapples faster'n any man at the plant."

"I think a person can do what they can do," Nick added, "and what sex they are shouldn't matter one bit."

"Just look around, fellas. Everything on this base proves you wrong. You just got to be willing to see it." Peggy gestured out toward the flight line. "So, let's change the subject," Peggy announced cheerily. "Just what is it that Petrovitch's got you boys doing?"

"Well, the skipper helps the weather officer, takin' readings and makin' copies of the forecast. Pretty cushy, eh, Bed," added Sam Caloon. "I'm working with the maintenance officer. Keeping the board up to date on ready strength."

"Our two sergeants operate one of the engine change hoists. They've actually topped the base record for a Shturmovik engine replacement."

"And Nick. He's working in maps and charts, making photocopies of old ones for the next day's mission. Right up his alley, too. Y'know, these Russkys are really short of navigators."

"And what exactly is the dangerous mission the commissar wanted you to take up?" Peggy asked. "Can you tell?"

"Oh, something behind German lines, really off the wall, sure to get us all killed," Crandall explained.

"Seems to me your bombing mission from a carrier to Tokyo was pretty darn risky."

"Yeah," Caloon agreed, "but we had the *Baby,* our plane. Heck, as long as we had our plane we could pull off anything."

"So," Peggy said, "if you really want to get out of here, make a deal. Ask for your *Baby.* If he needs you bad enough he'll give you your plane back. Heck, I wouldn't mind coming along for the ride."

"You would?" asked Tolkin.

"Sure, why not. That's what us heroes do," said Peggy, affecting a mock-heroic stance.

Crandall and Caloon stood in the base commander's office at rigid attention and rendered a smart salute. At the colonel's gesture they stood at ease.

"Sir, tell the general that we'll do it. We'll take on his project. But we have two conditions." The translation was dutifully made.

Within the hour the message was on its way to Engels and the headquarters of General Major NS Khrushchev.

When the communiqué arrived, Col. Sergienko read it and placed it on the large pile of mail and documents for his chief's night reading and returned to his chore of preparing the days directives for signature. He paused, glanced a second time at the short message on the yellow paper. Impulsively, he rose and strode into the general's office and handed it to Khrushchev.

"What's this?" said Khrushchev, who, immersed in some bad news from Leningrad, felt almost relieved to be interrupted.

"Just in. I thought it might be a priority, sir."

Khrushchev took the short telegram-sized communiqué, tilted his reading glasses up on his forehead, rubbed his eyes, then flipped down his glasses and read it.

"Hah! Good man, Vasily. At least something goes rightly this day. What's this? Conditions?"

"I don't know, Comrade General."

"Send immediate reply. State conditions. What kind of conditions?" He looked at his aide quizzically.

"I'm sure I wouldn't know, sir," answered Sergienko.

Seeing his aide's complete ignorance on the subject he elected to confide in him.

"These men, the American internees, you remember their plane landed in the east?"

"Yes, sir, I do recall . . ." said Sergienko.

"They are going to steal the secret of the German propeller-less plane for us. See, they've agreed."

"I see," said Sergienko. "Isn't that dangerous?"

"Dangerous? Going to a Nazi airfield and stealing the secrets of turbine propulsion? My dear Vasily Nickolaievitch, it's suicide. But if they succeed . . . ah, if they succeed. Our dear friend Lavrenti would be apoplectic with jealously. Send immediately. State conditions. Go."

In two days the American airmen's conditions arrived:

1. The return of our B-25 bomber, the *Boogie Woogie Baby*.

2. Peggy Cohan to be permitted to accompany us.

"What is this 'Boogie Woogie Baby' nonsense?" Commissar Khrushchev asked with slight annoyance. "And Peggy Cohan . . . who?"

"Sir," Sergienko explained, "the Americans frequently give their aircraft names. I believe they want their old aircraft, the bomber they flew to Tavrichanka to use for the mission."

"Ah, yes . . ." nodded Khrushchev.

"Peggy Cohan is the young American woman you decorated, if memory serves."

"Yes, I remember. I'm surprised she hasn't been returned to the Americans."

"My understanding," said Vasily, " is that no transport has been able to be diverted for such low priority use during the past weeks."

"Really. Very well," nodded Khrushchev. "Vasily. Tell them we agree on both conditions."

"You are going to return the aircraft to them, sir?"

"No, of course not. Who knows where it is after all this time. We'll just tell them it was destroyed. We'll provide some aircraft. But it must be American to support the ruse."

"They want to take along their countrywoman."

"What does that mean, Vasily?"

"Don't follow you, sir?"

"It means they are planning to escape. Once they have their airplane, mission be damned."

"Sir?"

"These Anglo-Saxons affect a sort of cloying chivalry towards women. If they were truly intending to execute the mission, they would never put their countrywoman in harm's way. No, they most certainly are considering this an opportunity to escape."

"Then the mission is cancelled?"

"Not at all," Khrushchev answered slyly. "We must merely employ safeguards, special safeguards to insure the fulfillment of their task. Send immediately, Vasily. Conditions agreed to. I'm an easy man to negotiate with, am I not?"

The first secretary of the Ukrainian Party's grin, Sergienko thought, bore a striking resemblance to the cartoon wolf in the grandma disguise.

Four days later an odd sight appeared above the Kotluban airdrome. A twin engined C-47 transport with US Army markings made its approach to the broad grass runway led by a MiG-3 fighter. A second Mig flew on the C-47's right wing. When the C-47 touched down, the Migs flew off, leaving the transport to roll to a halt at the end of the strip. At the copilot's window a red Soviet flag on a short pole emerged and flapped briskly in the breeze. A light truck escorted the aircraft to a revetment at the edge of a stand of trees where camouflage netting was waiting to be erected.

When the Americans were brought out to view the aircraft, Major Simonev declared proudly, "This plane for you. From . . ." He nodded his head conspiratorially toward the north. " . . . from Kremlin."

"Uh-uh, this is a mistake. No, that's not our plane," declared Captain Crandall.

"A gooney bird? No, sir. That's bunk! This is a cargo plane. That's no Mitchell," added Caloon.

"For you," insisted Simonev grandly.

"The general promised," Crandall argued. "Hell, the deal's off. We want the *Baby*."

The Russian major smiled patiently, his English comprehension diminishing even as they continued conversing.

"This plane. You take. This you plane. Is good Amerikanskiy plane.

Strong. You learn fly. Check out. You plane. Is good. No baby. Big plane."

The aircraft was in cargo configuration with large double doors at its left side. It was freshly painted in US Army Air Force camouflage and proper stars and bars on wings and fuselage. It looked as if it had just rolled off the line at Douglas.

"But we want our plane," Caloon insisted.

"Yeah, we want the *Baby*," McCabe added vehemently.

"*Da*, you plane," Simonev nodded and smiling, walked off as if he was a used car dealer who had just sold the dog of the lot.

After a morning of takeoffs and landings, the Soviet checkout crew departed and left the Americans alone with the C-47. They continued practicing after their noon meal until the relatively basic systems of the transport had been mastered. In flight they were aware of the constant presence of two Russian fighters at a slightly higher altitude monitoring their progress.

"If we run for it I think those Yaks are there to shoot us down," said Crandall.

"What's the matter, don't they trust us?" replied Sam.

"Yeah, well, we don't have enough gas to go anywhere," Crandall observed.

"You gotta admit," announced the copilot, "she handles nice."

"No power. No guts at all," grumbled Captain Crandall, although the extraordinary stability and flight characteristics of the craft were not lost on him.

Crandall and Caloon occupied the front seats, while Roscoe manned the engineer's station, leaving Nick and Pua to lounge contentedly in the cavernous hull of the cargo ship. The boys were happy to be flying again, especially as a team.

"This sure beats those rattletrap Shturmoviks. Man, that cold wind whistles right through the Plexiglas," observed Nick.

"This ain't bad," announced Pua. "I could cut me a little panel in one of those doors and rig up a fifty."

"Where you gonna get a fifty?" countered McCabe. "These Russians won't let us near a gun, 'cept for you, Nick, and that's 'cause you're one of them."

"Fuck you, Roscoe," said Tolkin.

"Fuck you more, Nick."

"Fuck you both," chipped in Pua. "C'mon, huh? We're landing." This ended the adolescent exchange.

Later in the operations center Major Simonov inquired as to their progress.

"You fly okay? Learn good?"

Lt. Caloon nodded wearily and answered, "*Da*, we fly good."

"Is good!" beamed Simonov.

"But this isn't our airplane. Don't you get it? The general promised our airplane."

"Is good airplane. Big to carry," the ever-positive major insisted.

A pilot entered and said something in Russian. The major held up a finger to indicate he'd be right back as he and the pilot consulted a map on the large central table.

"They prob'ly cracked her up," Roscoe muttered.

"What?" said Crandall.

"The *Baby* . . . our plane. Bet they cracked her up. These guys are animals."

"I'll bet you're right," said Caloon. "That's the reason they can't give her back to us. They cracked her up."

"Fuck!" Pua said as he shook his head with the realization that the *Baby* was probably lost.

"Hey, look. Peggy's outside," said McCabe.

Peggy was standing beside the front porch of operations as the Americans converged at the window. She was dressed in a Russian belted tunic over her leather flight jacket and jodhpurs and boots, the standard uniform of the Russian flyers. On her head she wore a white silk flying helmet that made her look like a bride or a novitiate nun. She had just completed instructing a group in split-S maneuvers,

Immelmanns, and simulated combat situations in the Air Cobra, or *Cobrastitsa*, as the Russians called it.

"Hi, Peggy. We're going to visit with the CO. Where you going to be?" asked Nick.

"I'm off duty," Peggy replied, pulling off her silk topper and running her fingers through her hair. "I'll wait for you boys here. Okay?"

"Great! We won't be long, I hope," said Crandall.

When the flying officer saluted and exited the colonel's office, the Americans were waved in by Petrovitch, who also gestured Simonev to join them. The Americans saluted. Petrovitch returned it and gestured for the men to sit. Simonov remained standing.

"Colonel, I have to tell you. We're not happy. We were supposed to get our airplane. The general promised," Crandall began.

"This aircraft is given. What more is to say?" Petrovitch spoke, conveying his helplessness in the situation. "Is good airplane. Strong. No?"

"Yeah, yeah, real good. We get it. The ole' switcheroo. So, colonel, when do we get going? What's the mission?" Capt. Crandall asked. Simonev translated although it was clear that the colonel understood.

Petrovitch eyed Crandall and then the other men with a bemused expression on his face. He spoke in Russian.

"You are eager. Good. You have achieved mastery of airplane? Yes?"

Crandall nodded curtly after Simonev conveyed the colonel's words.

"*Horosho!* Good!" Petrovitch declared. "Soon you will have briefing. I myself not know particular of your . . . *rabotesh* . . . eh, mission. But is surely of great importance."

"But when will we be briefed, sir? If you don't mind telling us," said Crandall.

"In due time," said Petrovitch.

The Americans cringed at the phrase. They'd come to hate that phrase during the past year.

At a knock at the door, Petrovitch called out, "Vkhodyt!" This meant "enter" in Russian.

Peggy stood in the doorway.

"Ah, *tovarich* Peggy. Come. The morning instruction is concluded?"

"Yes, Colonel. They flew well."

"*Horosho*, good," said Petrovitch. He seemed genuinely pleased that his people were measuring up. "And so . . . is something you wish?"

"Oh, no, sir," said Peggy. "I just saw the crew and thought you were briefing them on the mission."

"The mission, I fear, is still mystery to all, but you will be briefed, I am sure, in due time. Is all?" Looking from face to face. "Then, you are dismissed."

The Americans saluted the Russian colonel and exited the building.

"Hey, Peggy, what d'yuh know, what d'yuh say?" said Nick.

Peggy smiled as she acknowledged the distinctly New York greeting.

"Everything's just fine. How 'bout you fellas?"

"We're getting the runaround," answered Caloon.

"Yeah, what're these Reds waiting for? We're ready," grumbled McCabe.

"What do you think it is?" said Nick.

"Some sort of secret weapon the Germans got. We're supposed to cop it. Ain't that what the fat general said?" reminded Pua.

"Seems right," Peggy confirmed.

"Whatever it is, it's gonna take a cargo plane to carry it. Did ya think of that?" said Nick.

"That means it's big," Peggy mused.

"Gee, I hope not too big," said Caloon.

"Well," Pua said, "I gotta check a coupla' cylinders. See you guys later. Acey, deucey, Peg."

Pua then headed out in the direction of the ramp.

"Time to try'n pop some Panzers," announced Nick as he checked his watch. "Got a mission. I'll see you later, Peg."

"A mission? You shouldn't be flying combat, Nick," Peggy said sternly.

"No big deal, Peg. They're milk runs, really. Besides, the Shturmovik squadron's hurtin' for navigators."

"Well, you better keep your head down," warned Peggy.

"Hey, I'm sure gonna try," Nick replied, grinning.

"Nick," said Peggy, as he was walking away.

"Yeah? What?" asked Nick, stopping and turning toward her.

"Should you be flying missions when you're getting ready to do the job for the commissar?"

"It's just a late afternoon sortie. Try and catch a unit out in the open, maybe pop a tank or some trucks. No big deal," Nick explained.

"Well, take care of yourself, Nick. Maybe consider sitting a few out once in a while," Peggy said, almost admonishing him.

"Well, I'm flattered by your concern, *Principessa*. I'll certainly take your words under consideration."

"What did you call me?"

"*Principessa*," said Nick. "It means princess."

"I know what it means, Nick."

"Well then, see you later *Principessa*," said Nick with a smile as he headed toward the Shturmovik squadron.

As Peggy watched him walk off she wore an odd expression on her face.

"So, Peggy, can I buy you a cup of tea?" asked Crandall, exuding his most dashing country club charm.

Sam and Roscoe took their captain's remark as a cue to leave.

"Gonna give the Hawaiian a hand," announced McCabe.

"And I'm gonna supervise," added Caloon. "We'll see you later, Skipper, Peg."

Peggy waved to the departing pair as Crandall stepped closer to her.

"How 'bout we take a walk over to the canteen for a cup. I'm buyin'."

"All right, Captain Crandall. I'd be pleased to have tea with you," Peggy replied.

The pilot's canteen, or *stalovaya,* as it was called, was a makeshift structure with rough-hewn tables and chairs. Russian ground crews had built it and furnished it in their spare time. On one wall loomed a large painting of Lenin, and beside him hung a smaller, color photo of Stalin. Around the room, banners were posted with various squadron designations, along with a wooden propeller from a Policarpov biplane. In a place of honor, the guards banner awarded to the regiment was reverentially hung. At each end of the rectangular room stood a potbellied wood stove. Tonight, the balmy evening required only one of the stoves to be burning.

Inside, on wooden stools, at an aluminum counter contrived from the right wing of a downed He111, Peggy and the American pilot sipped their tea and chatted. The conversation turned to the crew of the *Baby* who, in Crandall's view, comprised the best qualities of a combat team. Crandall spoke of Pua's boundless enthusiasm and warrior mentality, and McCabe's positive outlook on life and his supreme confidence in his ability to repair anything. He characterized Nick, whose relaxed and easygoing manner disguised, in Crandall's view, a very keen intelligence.

"Nick seems like a swell guy," Peggy observed. "I feel like I've known him for ages."

Peggy noticed that Crandall stiffened slightly at her remark so she added, "I guess that's because we both come from the same hometown."

"I guess so," said Crandall, now seeming a bit anxious to get off the subject of Nick.

"Then there's good ol' Sam," Crandall went on. "Terrific ol' boy, that Sam. He would have made aircraft commander months ago if we were still flying combat. He's a great pilot. Steady, mature. I'm lucky to still have him as my second in command."

"What about you?" Peggy asked. "What's Bedford Crandall all about?"

"Oh, I have my ambitions. My family expects a lot of me, you know. Some day this war is going to be over and I'll be glad when things get back to normal. I mean, in a war situation all Americans have to work together. There's no choice since we're thrown in with all types of people; people that in more normal times one wouldn't dream of associating with. I mean, some social levels should never be breached. If you know what I mean?"

"I'm not sure I do," said Peggy, sensing the extent of the captain's snobbishness and finding his world view reminiscent of Miss Pamela Briggs back in basic.

"It seems to me," Crandall continued with utter certitude, "that the lower orders are more comfortable associating with their own."

"You actually believe that?" asked Peggy.

"Oh, yes, definitely. Sociologists would tell you the same. It's a known fact."

"Hmmm!" Peggy intoned. "That so."

"Absolutely. Some people are destined to do the work, to follow." Crandall went on. "Others are born to lead. It's a responsibility of the class which I fully accept."

"Don't you think the war might have changed things?" Peggy asked. "I mean this so-called natural order of yours?"

"Not at all. When this is all over, I'll take my place at the bank; capital investing is the area in which I'll most likely specialize. Big capital projects; municipals, dams, bridges. That's where the real money is. But it takes a big thinker to handle that sort of thing. Then, I've also given some thought to politics. A well placed lawmaker . . ." he leaned forward and lowered his voice, " . . . can do a lot of good in the financial world."

"No doubt he could," said Peggy, silently taking issue with Captain Crandall's elitist view of his exalted place in peacetime America.

"*Privyet,* Peggy, Captain," said Natalia.

"So nice to see you this evening, Captain Crandall," said Marina, in nearly flawless English. She had obviously practiced.

The two women, wearing their flying leathers, had entered the canteen and noticed Peggy and Crandall at the counter.

"Care to join us?" Crandall asked unconvincingly.

"*Nyet,*" said Natalia, brandishing a small thermos bottle. "Must to prepare for evening flying. Warm drink for chill, *chaska* chai." She held up her cup. "*Da svedanya.*"

An identical container was held by Marina, who said, "Good evening, Comrade Peggy, Comrade Captain, see ya 'round."

Peggy and Crandall smiled at her attempt at colloquial English and nodded to the two women as they topped off their bottles from the large samovar at the end of the counter and departed.

"She speaks very well, doesn't she?

"Yes," agreed Peggy. "I think she was a university student before the war."

"We ought to introduce her to Nick. They could practice together, what d'you think?"

"Might be an idea," Peggy agreed halfheartedly.

"So, Peggy, what did you do before the war?"

"Oh, I was a model. Mostly fashion. Magazines, newspapers," Peggy explained.

"Sounds fairly exciting."

"Yes, it was fun and the clothes were lovely," mused Peggy, "but like anything it can become tiresome. Besides, the war makes the fashion business pretty unimportant. Wouldn't you agree?"

"Well," Crandall said, "you can thank our President Roosevelt for this war. We'd all be better off out of it, but the man had to meddle in Europe's business."

"You really think we could have stayed out of it? What about Pearl Harbor?" Peggy asked.

"Well, some say President 'Rosenfeld' provoked the Japs so he could get us into a war."

"That doesn't make any sense," Peggy replied.

"Well, that's all right, Peggy," he said, condescendingly patting her hand. "Don't you worry about it. Politics are not really a woman's area. So, tell me, Peggy, your name, Cohan," Crandall asked, switching the subject. "That's Irish, I would presume?"

"Actually, it's not. My parents were Jewish. It was changed from Cohen. My dad thought it would be better for his business. He was a lawyer."

"Really," Crandall said, the surprise in his voice extending to his face. "Well, er, you are certainly the prettiest Jewish girl I ever . . . I mean, been with . . . I mean, met."

"You are the flatterer," Peggy said, affecting the accent and demeanor of a Southern belle, all the while deciding that the American captain was an insufferable jerk.

"No, I mean it," said Crandall, leaning closer to emphasize his sincerity. "With a touch of makeup and the right clothes you could fit in anywhere, really."

"Why, Captain Crandall, you're too kind," was Peggy's response, fighting to control her rising anger. "Well, thanks for the tea, Captain," she said, putting down her cup. "I think I'll be heading back to my billet." Peggy began to rise from the stool. As she did, Crandall rose with her, moved close and placed his hand on hers.

"Say, Peg, why don't I come along? Keep you company. What do you think?" asked Crandall, lowering his voice meaningfully.

"Can't," said Peggy. "Already got company. Seven new girls who came in with that flight of Yak fighters. I'm not alone anymore. And I think they're all making use of that bathtub of mine."

"C'mon, Peg, you know there's something going on between us. Admit it. You can feel it, I know. Don't fight it," Crandall urged. "Give in to it."

"Well, perhaps you're right. Why fight it," Peggy said dramatically, "I might know a place where we can be alone. How's that for an idea?"

"Sounds great," said Crandall eagerly. "What're we waitin' for?"

Peggy took Crandall's hand and led him out of the canteen into the gathering dark, past the maintenance dugouts and several camouflaged aircraft and toward the large maintenance barn. From there, Peggy, still gripping Crandall's hand, led him along a narrow path through the woods to the parachute packing shed. As she pulled him along Crandall thought, *She's eager all right. I knew it.*

"There," said Peggy, "that's where we're going. To the church. They call it the 'church'," Peggy added mischieviously.

Church? wondered Crandall, who followed Peggy into the building. Once inside he looked up and said, "Oh, I get it. Church! Now, come here Miss Cohan." Crandall held Peggy by the shoulders and attempted to kiss her but she twisted away.

With her arms freed, Peggy unzipped her jacket, then reached up and seductively opened the first two buttons on her blouse. Crandall's eyes widened. Then impulsively, she reached down, loosened Crandall's web belt, and brazenly undid the top button. She led him over to a long table, then suddenly backed off from the aroused man and darted away, saying:

"Let's lose these lights. More romantic, don't you think? In the meantime, Bedford, make yourself comfortable. Be right back." She sang the last three words as she shut the bright overheads and the single bulb at the entrance, plunging the large room into darkness.

The only sound that could be heard was the thud of first one shoe, then the other, followed by the metallic clinking of the metal buckle of Crandall's belt. Crandall assumed that Peggy must be having trouble finding her way after she had turned off the overheads.

He sat in his shorts atop one of the rigging benches in heated anticipation of her return. For a moment, he thought he heard a rustling sound close by and then felt a sudden draft of air but soon all was silent. The pilot sat in the dark for several long minutes before realizing that he was alone in the shed. After considerable fumbling, he located the light switches and verified that, indeed, Peggy was gone. What's worse, his trousers were nowhere to be found.

Angry and humiliated, he fabricated a makeshift kilt out of a canvas parachute case and stormed across the base to where Kamenny awaited them each night to chauffeur them back to the ranch. It was a drafty and uncomfortable ride for Captain Crandall that evening.

When Pua asked, "What happened to your pants?" Crandall's answer was, "Shut up!"

The others simply shrugged and exchanged smirks.

The next morning Caloon, after looking vainly for Peggy in her quarters, went over to the women's bomber squadron area and was greeted by the smiles of most of the Russians. They understood that he had probably been sent to retrieve the trousers. One of the women, barely able to conceal her glee, directed him to the canteen. When he entered, it was crowded with aircrew. The young aviators turned, grinning, all savoring the bawdy prank. On the wall, suspended by two nails through the belt loops, were Crandall's pants, displayed as though they were a war trophy. They were hung slightly to the left of Lenin's portrait. Lenin seemed to be staring disapprovingly at the tan trousers.

When Caloon saw the pants on the wall and then viewed the faces in the room, he burst out laughing. The Russians instantly joined in and shortly everyone in the room was enjoying the joke.

When Caloon climbed up on the counter and retrieved the trousers, he turned and held them over his head as if he was noble Jason retrieving the Golden Fleece. The crowd roared its approval. Affecting a mock heroic pose, he strode from the canteen, the khakis draped over his shoulder, amidst cheers and applause.

When he brought them to the weather shack where Crandall was waiting, the Captain asked, "Where'd you find them?"

"In the canteen," Caloon said simply.

"That witch! Did anyone see you?"

"Nah," said Caloon, "Nobody was around."

Crandall's shoulders relaxed in relief.

Only once was there an allusion to the incident. At a weather briefing a few days later one of the female pilots said "krasiviye bryoo-kee" to Crandall. He responded to her pleasant tone with a nod and a cordial, "Yes, so nice to see you, too."

Krasiviye bryoo-kee means "lovely trousers."

Once trained and deemed combat ready, the new P-39 pilots and their Air Cobras were immediately assigned to a Shturmovik squadron as a special unit and turned loose on the enemy.

With her task of transitioning Russian pilots to the Aircobra completed, Peggy suddenly found herself without much to do. She habitually spent time in the squadron areas where she engaged many of her former students upon their return from missions. Since Nick had been serving as lead navigator and rear gunner on one echelon of Shturmoviks, Peggy was frequently on hand when he returned from a mission. She found that she looked forward to his ready smile and enjoyed chatting about the day's flying and their shared background growing up in the same city. Their encounters became a highly anticipated part of her day.

"Hey, you ever go to Coney Island?" asked Nick as they strolled from the flight line.

"All the time. We took the Flushing line to the El. All the way out to Coney," answered Peggy. "You ever been on the Wonder Wheel?"

"Oh, lots of times. And Luna Park, and the parachute jump," added Nick.

"Oh, that was fun. I can still feel my stomach in my throat when it dropped. And what a view!" said Peggy, smiling at the reminiscence.

"An' how 'bout the hot dogs?" asked Nick. "I could eat four at a time, easy."

"Mmmm, Nathan's Famous! They were swell."

"Sauerkraut or just mustard?"

"Both," Peggy replied as Nick nodded, impressed.

"Did you ever go under the boardwalk?" Nick asked slyly.

"What kind of girl do you think I am?"

"I dunno, but I'd like to find out, doll," Nick twitched his mouth a la Bogart. "But, really, how come I ain't never seen you?" Nick asked, affecting a very Brooklyn accent.

"I was there," was Peggy's response. "You just never noticed me."

"Well, you can bet that next time I'm there, I'll be sure to keep an eye out for a tall blonde with great gams and lots of medals." Nick punctuated his compliment with a mock leer.

"Oh, say, Peg," he said, reaching into his shirt pocket. "Do you want this?" He handed her his Luckies pack with the photo under the cellophane.

"The nurse shot," Peggy said, examining it in her hand. "Don't you want it anymore?"

"Nope. What's the point? I got the real thing right here in front of me."

Peggy looked deeply into Nick's eyes. Then, she crumpled the pack and picture and tossed it into a sand-filled butt can beside the path.

Nick smiled and they resumed their stroll toward the canteen.

It seemed that every time the Shturmovik squadron returned from its late afternoon mission, Peggy was on hand to greet the airmen and chat with Nick.

One evening Natalia, no longer in need of her cane, sat beside Peggy in the canteen. "What is? You like Russian boy, Tolkin, or American captain? You maybe like both? Together?" She laughed lustily.

"No," answered Peggy, shaking her head. "We're friends, that's all. The captain, he loves himself too much and Nick, he's just a nice guy."

"Nice guy. Da. Nice guy with have strong *plicho*," said Natalia, as she gripped her shoulder. "Also, very good *zopa*," Natalia continued with a lascivious look.

"*Zopa?*"

Natalia half turned and gripped her own ample buttock.

"Oh," Peggy replied. "I'm sure I hadn't noticed."

"You notice!" Natalia replied, smiling lewdly.

"Well, he's just a friend. A friend. Nothing more."

"Ah," Natalia said, eyeing Peggy sideways. "A friend. Nothing more. Okay. You say this. I believe."

One evening with the sky still glowing a burnished red and large thunder clouds moving in from the west, the day's final sorties of Shturmoviks were returning from their forays over the German lines. The P-39s had been recovered earlier and the pilots had been through debriefing and were headed to the equipment shack beside squadron headquarters to stow their gear. Peggy once again was on hand to greet the pilots, many of whom had been her students, and joined their conversations about the day's flying, close shaves, victories, and the ones that got away. Now, as the Shturmoviks were being parked and put to bed in their revetments, Peggy walked down the ramp looking for Nick.

As the Shturmovik crews filed past Peggy's familiar figure on their way to debriefing, most acknowledged her with a nod or a smile. Their mission had been successful. Off to hunt for Panzers, they instead encountered a nice fat supply column, which they decimated with their machine guns and cannon. And, happily, with no aircraft lost.

In the fading light, Nick eventually appeared, balancing a heavy burden on his shoulder. The mechanic accompanying him also carried two heavy objects.

"Hey, *Principessa!*" Nick called out to Peggy. "I was hoping you'd be here."

"Glad to see you, Nick," smiled Peggy. "What'cha got there? Present for me?"

"Naw, actually it's a present for our Hawaiian boy. German machine gun. See, I bought it from one of the partisan guys who refueled us. He took it, near as I could understand, from a crashed Heinkel."

The mechanic put down the two weighty ammo cans next to Nick, said something in Russian, and continued up to operations.

"Hey, Dimitri, *spaseeba!*" said Nick.

Dimitri turned, waved, and continued his walk.

"Two cans of ammo with the deal. Pretty good, huh?"

"You bought it?" Peggy asked, incredulous.

"Yeah, only twenty dollars. I was gonna buy souvenirs in China, but since that's not going to happen . . . nice, isn't it?"

"Oh, it's beautiful," Peggy said with mock sincerity.

"Eye of the beholder, Peg. Eye of the beholder."

As Nick and Peggy stood discussing the aesthetic merits of the machine gun, Bed Crandall and the other Americans arrived. Ignoring Peggy, Crandall said icily, "C'mon, Nick, Kamenny's waiting."

"What'cha got there?" asked McCabe.

"An MG42, I think," answered Nick. "It's for poi boy, a present."

"Oh, man, it's a beaut!" said the Hawaiian. "You got bullets an' everything."

"Yeah," said Nick. "Merry Christmas."

"Oh boy," gushed Pua. "Look, it's got a swivel mount, too. Musta been from an airplane."

"A He111, I'm told," said Nick.

"Oh boy," Pua repeated.

"We should stash it in the plane for tonight," said McCabe.

"Naw, I wanna take it back to the ranch. I wanna look at it."

"So long, Peggy," said Nick as he headed toward Kamenny's truck.

"See ya around, " said Sam.

"Take 'er slow," said McCabe.

Pua and Crandall did not say good night. Pua was too involved with his new toy and Crandall acted miffed and aloof. *Still sore,* Peggy thought. *He'll get over it.*

Peggy strolled to her dorm in the cool evening with a feeling that, at this moment, everything was right with the world. When she entered her room she found Natalia filling the large wash tub with hot water and a small one on the stove, heating up.

"*Da svedanya,* Natalia. What's up?"

"You not memory?" Natalia said. "Tonight shampoo night! *Da?*"

Peggy suddenly recalled. Tonight they were to wash their hair with the last sliver of that wonderful Amerikanskiy soap.

"Of course, I remember," Peggy lied. "Tomorrow we will have clean hair."

"And all others," Natalia said with great satisfaction, "will be, as you call it, stinky."

14

The Messerschmitt Repair Facility
Kovno, Lithuania
May 1943

On a dirt road at the far side of the base, two men stood beside a light truck viewing the skies.

"He's nearly at the drop point," Fritz Weber announced as he followed the speeding aircraft through his Zeiss binoculars. He grasped the bulky optics in his left hand while providing support with the tips of the fingers of his right, the hand that was swathed in an elastic bandage immobilizing his severely sprained wrist.

"Now we will see," Professor Messerschmitt said as he peered through his own field glasses at his Me 262 prototype making its run.

"Verdammt! Premature release! I can make out the bombs. Both systems have failed!"

"I have an incomplete bomb release reading in the cockpit," crackled the youthful voice from the speaker in the truck parked behind Messerschmitt and Weber.

Weber put down his glasses, reached back into the vehicle, and took the microphone. "Confirmed. We see the ordnance. Premature release, it appears. Do not operate salvo switches. Make a low pass over our position for confirmation of ordnance released. We want to see those shackles as they failed."

"Verdammt! Damn, bloody damn," was all Willi Messerschmitt could say. "If he's clear of bombs tell him to land. I will be in the office trying to decide if I should inform the Führer. Ask Willi to join us, please. We must figure a solution to this."

Test pilots Willi Linz and Fritz Weber sat in Messerschmitt's office wrestling with their dilemma.

"A totally new design is required," said Messerschmitt. "The ordnance is unstable at these higher speeds but we can't modify the bombs, there are too many already stockpiled. It must be a totally redesigned attachment and release system."

"I was certain the Bf 110 shackles would do the job," said Fritz Weber.

"They failed in each test," said Linz, shaking his head.

"It's a simple problem but we don't have the engineers and designers," added Messerschmitt.

"Couldn't some be diverted from some other . . ."

"Every project is critical," said Messerschmitt, cutting Linz short. "Think, think!" said Messerschmitt. "I could design it myself but I have too many commitments and then I'll need engineers to build and install the mechanism. If only the Führer could have seen it for what it truly is; an air superiority fighter. But no, he wants a bomber. Thinking that belongs in the first war." The aircraft designer shook his head in frustration. "Engineers, designers, machinists. Where can I find them?"

"Herr Doctor Messerschmitt," said Willi Linz tentatively, as if he was still a student in gymnasium.

"Yes," answered the aircraft designer patronizingly.

"There was a precision machinist in our town, he was a friend of mine. His name was Kleinman."

"Ya, and so?" Messerschmitt responded impatiently.

"He was a Jew and deported to the Burchfeld camp, I understand," Linz continued.

"So? What can I do? You know it is my policy to stay clear of politics."

"Well, it seems to me that there might be lots of men like Kleinman in such camps," Linz explained.

Messerschmitt's mind suddenly grasped the concept. "Could they be found? Could they be separated out from all that humanity. Is it possible?"

"If there's anything I know, it's that the Reich keeps meticulous records," Fritz Weber added. "Yes, Herr Doctor, I believe it is possible."

One week later, Dr. Messerschmitt stood behind an improvised wooden workbench and addressed a ragged assembly of concentration camp prisoners.

"You are engineers, draftsmen, electricians, machinists. You have been brought here for a specific project. What we require is an electrical bomb release mechanism with an integrated mechanical backup system. Our initial attempts at modifying an auxiliary fuel tank release from the Bf 110 bomber have proved unsatisfactory. The system elements are here on this table for your inspection. The higher airflow encountered on our new aircraft causes flexing of the components or their mountings resulting often in premature and erratic release.

"You are here to design and manufacture a new release mechanism. Time is of the essence. If you succeed, there may be other projects. I will do what I can for you. I make no promises. You begin immediately."

The listless group of men stood silently, afraid to react. Was this some sort of sadistic game? Once they were useful, educated, respected men of the world. Then the world decided to discard them. Was this a reprieve? Could it be trusted? Did it matter? Do what the Nazi tells them. Perhaps there's a chance, a chance to live. A chance for the entire family to survive. Eight hopeless men contemplated the glimmer of hope that flickered faintly before them.

The group was directed to inspect the components on the table and then ushered off to some sheds hastily built along the side of a hangar. Inside, drafting tables, a machine shop, aluminum and steel stock, and some electrical components were provided. The prisoners were charged with not only the design and fabrication of the fixtures but the production of kits so that line mechanics could install them on the growing fleet of Me 262 aircraft.

15

Fog, thick and impenetrable, greeted the early risers at the Kotluban airdrome this morning. Operations would be delayed. Weather had predicted the fog, but expected a wind in the mid-morning to provide visibility for the day's flying. That wind never materialized. The fog curtain hovered over the base, if anything, becoming more dense by noon.

Reluctantly, Colonel Petrovitch ordered a stand down; an opportunity to perform some necessary maintenance, replenish stockpiles of bombs and ammunition, and afford the aircrews some much needed rest. The only consolation was that the identical weather conditions would hamper the Fritzies.

After a late breakfast of black bread, an egg, coffee, and some porridge, Natalia, Svetlana, still in her full body cast, and Marina Bershanskya, the girl who could speak a little English and was eager to practice it, were invited by Peggy to her quarters to chat and do some much needed laundering. This rare lull in operations was fortuitous since the base had endured eighteen straight days of day and night missions. Everything was to go into the wash, even the clothes on their backs. They had all day for it to dry.

As the girls first sorted and then soaked their clothes in two tubs of warm water with good, strong proletarian soap, a third smaller washtub was heating on the stove. Each brought their own government issue washboard, small enough to fit in a regular-sized bucket.

"Let 'em soak for awhile," said Peggy, with an impish glint in her eye as she tore the seal on a deck of Red Cross-provided Bicycle playing cards and riffled the deck with her thumb. "Do any of you ladies know the game of poker?"

The Russian women, sitting in their underwear, exchanged glances and shrugged.

"No? Well, you're about to learn."

Peggy started with the best hand, putting the ace, king, queen, jack, and ten of diamonds on the table in sequence.

"This is a royal flush," she explained. "Same suit, same color. It beats a straight flush," she said, putting down the 3, 4, 5, 6 and 7 of clubs. "Then we have four of a kind," she said, showing an example. "A full house," she said, laying down three of a kind and a pair. Then, she showed them three of a kind.

Peggy described all the winning hands. Then showed them two terrible hands, each with the highest single card being the winner.

"Is similarity to *skaat*, game grandfather to me, play often," said Marina.

"Okay," Peggy acknowledged, "and good English, Marina."

The girl smiled at the compliment.

"We are dealt cards and based on how good we feel our hand is, or bad we think someone else's is, we bet."

"What we bet?" asked Svetlana.

"Money," answered Peggy. "*Kopeks, rubles.*"

"Got not *rubles*," said Natalia, shaking her head. "Send rubles to home, for mother and little ones."

"All right, we'll use chips," said Peggy, looking around for something to use as a chip. "Buttons," she said, pointing to her jacket, "or crackers." Peggy pointed to a tin of biscuits.

Svetlana shook her head. "Button for clothings, cracker for to eat."

"What will we bet?" asked Marina.

Peggy looked around her room for something in quantity, considering going outdoors and collecting pebbles.

"Wait, wait. Is two pairings stronger than three numbers same?" Natalia queried.

"*Nyet,*" Svetlana corrected, as she pulled the cork on a bottle of vodka she had brought in her laundry basket. "Three same numbers higher over two pairings. Correct, Peggy?"

Peggy nodded absently. *Correct, Lana.* "I've got it, ladies, we're not going to bet. We don't have to bet. We're going to play strip poker."

As Peggy explained strip poker, the Russian women found the concept first unbelievable, then appalling, then strangely intriguing. After some further explanation by Peggy, they grasped the concept well enough to put on flying gloves, boots, socks, caps, and scarves before the game began.

Natalia was the big winner and amidst giggles and groans, Svetlana's last sock and Marina's underpants were lost to the pot. Peggy, who was monitoring the game and not really playing earnestly, was bare-chested like Marina but still retained her panties.

On the next hand Svetlana bluffed, was called, and lost again. She, however, refused to give up her large underpants.

"*Nyet!*" she said, setting her jaw.

"C'mon, Lana, it's the rules. Take 'em off," said Peggy.

The women egged her on sadistically, their fervor enhanced by the ingested vodka from the nearly empty liter bottle.

"*Nyet!*" Svetlana repeated vehemently. "I formation commander. I no become naked."

"Lana! We play. We take away clothings. You play. You take away clothings," reasoned Natalia.

The other women concurred, banging on the table, laughing and making derisive noises.

Intimidated by the chiding of her sister aviators, she said, "Hokay, I take off. I take off plaster," tapping her chest.

"You can't do that," said Peggy.

"And so, why?" asked Svetlana imperiously.

"You must be in plaster for six weeks, doctor has instructed," said Marina.

"Doctor, pha!" was Svetlana's reply. "I have wear five weeks. I take off plaster."

Disbelief turned to amusement as the girls watched Svetlana reach down to her waist and begin to crumble the edge of her plaster cast. When she could no longer get a purchase on the remnants of the plaster shirt, the others joined in to free the large woman from her hard, white chrysalis.

Once the cast had been split and pried apart and bare-chested Svetlana had been successfully hatched, the girls simultaneously voiced the identical reaction.

"Feh!"

"Oh, God."

"Argh!"

"Lana, you stink," said Peggy.

"I happy," said Svetlana, oblivious to her rank condition.

The ladies quickly rinsed their laundry, wrung it out and set it aside to be sorted later. They were determined to give Major Svetlana a bath. And so three slightly tipsy nearly-naked laundresses filled a galvanized tub with hot water for the cleansing of their similarly tipsy superior officer. The girls busied themselves heating water and pouring it over the ecstatic woman. At last the cast was off. To Svetlana it seemed as if she had endured months of encapsulated discomfort. Actually, it had only been five weeks and four days. In a small bit of irony Major Svetlana ended up removing her underpants after all.

Since their clothes were drying very slowly in the damp air, the girls rigged a pair of clotheslines above the stove and succeeded in drying out a set of flying gear for each of them—slightly damp but good enough to wear. The three tipsy women left Peggy's quarters that afternoon with empty laundry bags and most of their clothes hanging limply on the outdoor line in the fog.

It was late afternoon on the next day when Peggy headed over to the flight line in anticipation of visiting with the crews and seeing Nick. As she headed to the revetments, she could hear the Shturmoviks in their patterns and making their landings. A few had already been recovered and their crews were walking along the path to operations and debriefing.

Peggy passed one pilot and offered a nod and slight wave. He simply shook his head and continued. Peggy walked up to two more pilots and gestured.

"Good flying? Thumbs up?"

One of the pilots put his head down and looked away. The other man put his gear down and said to Peggy, "*Syem atkhadit, shest obratniy.*"

Peggy thought she understood but didn't want to. To emphasize his message, the Russian repeated his words and then held up seven fingers of his gloved hands and gestured west. Six fingers returned. Finally, he held up one finger and pointed it to the ground. One of the planes didn't make it.

Up at operations it was confirmed. Stepanenko, the squadron leader and his American "observer" had been shot down. Two pilots reported seeing the stricken Shturmovik losing altitude, trailing smoke. Neither observed a crash. The only positive news was that the aircraft had been lost in the no man's land east of the German positions. Yes, a sad loss, indeed, but tomorrow was another mission. A new squadron chief would be picked and the war against the fascists would continue. This was the terse and pragmatic message of Major Simonev to the aircrews. He dismissed them and noticed Peggy at the rear of the hall.

Simonev took her aside and attempted to console her.

"Not to give away hopefulness, *tovarich* Peggy. Airplane still have control when go to ground. Perhaps no crash. Not to give up hopefulness for your countryman." He patted her shoulder tentatively and steered her to the door of the briefing room. "Go sleep. Tomorrow we know more. Maybe good news. Now you go sleep."

Peggy walked slowly to her quarters feeling stunned and disoriented. She attempted to analyze her feelings but was unable to do so. He was a nice guy, but as a combat flyer he knew the risks. All these kids know the risks and they accept them. *So, it happened to*

Nick. It's a shame. It's more than a shame. It's terrible. Awful. I can't bear it. It's so unfair. So wrong. I feel so bad. Oh, my God.

As she entered her room, Natalia, Marina, and Svetlana were there. She ran to her friends and was embraced in a bear hug by Natalia. Peggy began to cry. The shell of bravado that Peggy had so carefully constructed over the years had crumbled. In Natalia's arms, Peggy let go and cried uncontrollably. Svetlana extended her arms and embraced both Peggy and Natalia, her newly freed arm applying weak pressure. The three Russian women shed their tears with Peggy. They remained that way, standing, holding each other, providing a flesh and blood bower of solace for their friend. They understood. Perhaps better than Peggy.

On the next day, after duty hours, the American aircrew visited. They were shocked and incredulous at the loss of their crewmate.

"I tole him to lay off the missions," Pua groused fretfully.

"We got our own mission comin' up. What're we gonna do for a navigator? Huh? He had no right to leave us without a navigator, right?" McCabe rambled. His misdirected anger at Nick understood by all to be an expression of sadness at the loss of his friend.

"He was a good navigator," added Caloon.

"None better," said Capt. Crandall.

"The best!" put in Pua.

"I wanted us all to come home together," said the captain. "I really wanted that."

"Tea?" asked Peggy, happy to distract herself by the physical activity. She had regained her composure and hoped she wouldn't break down again, especially in front of Nick's crew mates.

She could feel that Crandall was more than a little reserved toward her but she could also tell that he felt Nick's loss as much as the others. How petty and unimportant was her little prank. At the time she felt so pleased at the thought of putting the conceited male in his place; it was quite the triumph. Now it seemed so childish. When the boys finally left with Kamenny to their off base digs, Peggy was relieved. Her self-control generated by pure willpower was beginning to slip.

She felt herself tearing up again. She couldn't help herself. That night she wept once more with her last waking thoughts questioning: *What's wrong with me? I never behave this way.*

Early the next morning, Peggy appeared at operations and patiently waited for a lull in their activity. After the details of two missions had been finalized, Major Simonev disengaged from his commanders and came over to Peggy.

"Any news?" she queried in Russian.

The major shook his head in negative response. "Not to give away hopefulness," he once again told Peggy in English. "Is too soon to know something," he said, attempting to keep up her spirits.

Peggy ambled across the base to the flight line where she watched the early squadron return and then walked back to her billet, still unable to comprehend the depth of loss she was experiencing.

At mid-afternoon of the following day, a battered truck roared onto the base honking its horn repeatedly. In the uncovered cargo bed six partisans and a man in flight gear stood shouting, whistling, and waving their arms. Inside the cab, beside the mustachioed driver, sat a grinning and waving Captain Georgi Stepanenko, the missing commander of the Shturmovik ground attack squadron. He waved to the cheering base personnel in the manner of Czar Nicholas on a visit to the provinces. Standing in the rear of the truck, a very animated Nick Tolkin, still wearing his flying leathers, waved and hollered as if his team had pushed the ball over the goal line in the final seconds of the big game.

Peggy was indoors when she first heard the ruckus, then from her porch saw the truck. She ran to join the airmen and airwomen surrounding it. Captain Georgi and Lieutenant Nick were lifted to the shoulders of the throng and borne to the ops building. The partisan rescuers were likewise swarmed and welcomed as heroes. Up on the porch of ops the base commander and his adjutant each embraced the prodigal airmen, who in turn acknowledged the enthusiastic assembly of aviators and ground crews.

When the two repatriated airmen ceremoniously shook hands, a new round of cheers and applause ensued. After a few more minutes the celebration was ended by Major Simonev, who reminded the celebrants that there was still a war on.

As the crowd dispersed, Peggy walked up to Nick. He grinned broadly and extended his hand to her. Instead of shaking his hand, she threw her arms around his neck and embraced him, holding him tightly.

"Hey, Peg," he said, speaking softly into her ear. "If I knew I was going to get this kind of reception I'd a gone missing a long time ago."

At midday a lone, twin-engined P-8 bomber set down at the Kotluban base. Within the hour, the American crew had been summoned to the mission briefing hut. Col. Petrovitch and two Russian officers were waiting when they arrived. The Americans were introduced to Major Milovan Djilas and Lt. AI Begina. Djilas was a tough-looking man in his thirties, sporting a blond crewcut. As he moved, his stocky, well-muscled body flexed ominously beneath his tunic. Begina, in contrast, was more youthful, slender, and wore steel-rimmed glasses; the image of the intellectual. Begina, Djilas's aide and recent university graduate, was to serve as translator. Djilas was in charge of a Soviet commando unit that specialized in operations behind enemy lines. While Begina cordially shook hands with each of the Americans, Djilas sat sullenly. The strongman made no eye contact with any of the other men in the room, including the base commander. Clearly, he viewed this meeting as a waste of his time and hoped to make the encounter as brief as possible. He seemed to be a man with more important things to do.

As the group sat quietly in uncomfortable silence, Peggy entered, acknowledged the men with a nod, and took a seat. When the colonel nodded for Djilas to begin, he immediately opened a briefcase and produced a stack of maps, papers, and photographs. Djilas briskly unfolded one of the maps and began speaking curtly to the group.

His annoyance at having to give this briefing was obvious. Colonel Petrovitch interrupted with a short burst of Russian which could only have been an admonition to the sullen commando. Djilas glowered at the rebuke, then exhaled and began his presentation again, this time more slowly and with less of the angry edge in his voice. As he spoke and Begina translated, the young Americans leaned in toward the exhibits.

First, there were two photos of a very odd, shark-like, twin-engined aircraft. One photo showed the aircraft on the ground, and the other was more blurry, as it was taking off.

"This is latest invention of fascists. You will notice there are no propellers," translated Begina.

"Rocket engines?" interjected Crandall.

"*Nyet*," Djilas corrected.

"We believe it is turbine propulsion. Internal combustion. Using kerosene or light diesel oil, " Begina explained.

The audience seemed unimpressed as Djilas continued.

"This aircraft possess great speed. We estimate speeds in excess of 600 kilometers per hour."

"That's nearly five hundred miles per hour," Nick observed.

Now the audience was impressed. Even Petrovitch, who had been standing impassively, arms behind his back, registered increased interest.

"Your task is to acquire specimen of turbine motor for study by Soviet engineers."

"Oh, is that all," quipped McCabe.

Begina translated for Djilas, who nodded.

"Yes, that is all," was Djilas's reply. The sarcasm was lost on him.

"And just how do you propose we make this acquisition?" Sam Caloon asked cynically.

Djilas unfolded one of his maps and pointed to a spot.

Begina translated. "Here is labor camp in Lithuania by Kovno. The fascists have moved small aircraft parts factory to grounds of camp. They do this to place factory out of range of Allied bombing. Also a concrete runway has been built. It would seem that new turbine aircraft requires concrete runway. Junkers and BMW factory send unassembled engine components by train from Konigsberg to be assemble. They employ German supervisors and workers but recently have impressed prisoners, Jews and Poles who possess technical ability, into the assembly process. Reports also indicate these technicians are developing external bomb release mechanisms so turbine aircraft can be utilized as bomber. They call this 'Blitz Bomber.'"

"Whew!" Pua shook his head. "Man, at five-hundred miles an hour, he'd be gone before you could pull the trigger."

"So, what do we do? Just land, pick a nice engine, and take off with it?" asked Crandall.

"*Da*," said Djilas when Crandall's words were translated. Begina continued the explanation.

"We make air raid. It shall come unexpected from east. The Allies avoid to bomb prison camps. That is why so many factories are on grounds of camps. Before raid we parachute commandos into area. Many will be Lithuanians who know land and will have ability to blend into countryside after operation. Commandos will subdue small garrison of guards, most who will have taken refuge in bomb shelters. You will at this time land, seize engine, then fly east. Commandos will disperse into countryside and disappear. Is done!" Begina seemed smugly impressed with the plan he had just laid out.

As the group exchanged glances, Djilas presented one last map: the camp and the factory area with the concrete runway dividing the two.

"Here," Djilas pointed, "is barracks of guards and here is bomb shelter. We must bomb carefully so not to destroy worker huts. Most recently women and children have been brought to base. They are families of new technicians. Is unusual, but we believe families have been brought as hostages to assure quality of work and discouragement of sabotage. When all elements will be coordinated we will contact you. You must be prepared to move quickly. This is operation what requires precise timing. I not intend to lose any of my men due to incompetence of untrained foreigners."

At this, Colonel Petrovitch said something curt and final to Djilas who nodded, lowered his eyes, and grudgingly accepted the rebuke.

Interrupting the silence caused by the interaction of Djilas and Petrovitch, Crandall spoke. "If you can get us in, Chief, we'll get you that motor, by God."

When his words were translated, Djilas looked at Crandall, as if to take his measure. He nodded, then looked toward Petrovitch and nodded once again.

His look conveyed to Petrovitch that he held a glimmer of hope that these people might do the job after all.

17

I don't want her along," insisted Captain Crandall to his crew as they stowed the engine dolly in the fuselage of the C-47. "She's annoying and will only get in the way."

"Aw, c'mon," said Nick, "don't be that way."

"Yeah, Skipper," chimed in McCabe. "She's American like us. We ought to get her out of here. You know, the plan?"

"Nope, she'd be trouble. Women don't belong. No! Am I in charge?" Crandall asked. "Or am I not?"

No one responded.

"Well, you know I am and I say she doesn't come."

"Bed," Caloon said, taking his captain's arm and walking toward the cockpit. Lowering his voice he continued pressing his point. "You want everyone to know she got your goat? The guys on the engine hoist don't know about the pants thing. Neither does Nick. If you don't let her come, they'll wonder why and start asking questions. My advice, Skip, is forget it. Act like it didn't get to you, just a stupid prank. If it gets out . . . well, don't give those crazy dames the satisfaction. See what I mean?"

He could tell Crandall was wavering so he pressed on.

"C'mon, be the bigger man. Nothin' bothers the cool American skipper, right? Dames come and go. Right?"

"Well . . ." Crandall grudgingly acquiesced. "Okay, I'll be the bigger man."

"That's right, Skip," agreed Caloon. "You're above it. And if we're buggin' out, it's right to take her."

Crandall ended the exchange by walking forward and sulkily taking the left seat in the cockpit. Caloon walked back to the three crew members fussing with the already secured dolly. He rolled his eyes at the trio and made a head nod to the flight deck.

"It's okay. She's comin'. Just let's keep it cool."

The men exchanged satisfied glances and filed out of the aircraft, followed by Caloon.

"He'll be fine," said the copilot. "Just some last minute nerves."

An odd message, this one, thought Major Simonev as he sorted the directives from the daily dispatch case. Upon rereading, he deduced its meaning. It read:

> FROM: *Col. BG Vakhmistrov, Special Operations Coordinator, Leningrad front*
> TO: *Col. IN Petrovitch, Commander 122nd Air Battalion*
> MESSAGE: *Apple pickers to proceed to Yaroslavl, most expedient route, no later than 5 June 43.*

We will miss the Americans, Simonev thought as he carried the folder of communiqués into his colonel's office. *In many ways they are much like us.*

Petrovitch was in conference with three of his squadron commanders discussing attrition rates and replacement schedules. The colonel ignored his aide as the folder of communiqués was placed on his desk. After putting the "apple picker" message in his chief's second drawer and closing it, Simonev briskly exited the office.

As Simonev was resuming his work on the strength charts, there was a knock at the door. He looked up but before he could respond the door opened and Colonel Yankovlevitch, the political officer, burst into the room.

"You are planning an operation without my knowledge? Why was I not informed? Who are the 'apple pickers?' I demand to know. Is he in there?" Colonel Yakovlevitch moved to the door but Simonev rose and blocked him.

"He is in with the squadron chiefs. They'll be finished shortly. Colonel, I assure you, this is nothing. A minor project, utilizing none of our manpower. It's nothing, really; calm yourself, sir. A simple reconnaissance venture having nothing at all to do with our sector's mission. Here, sit. Colonel Petrovitch will explain. There is nothing to it, you will see."

A sulking Yankovlevitch, slightly placated by Simonev's assurances, squirmed in the chair beside the desk.

Simonev then cocked his head and asked, "Have you read the dispatches?"

"No," stammered the Colonel. "I simply heard . . . ."

"How would you know of 'apple pickers?' That was in the directive. Do you read them before they come to us?"

"No, I certainly do not!" Yankovlevitch lied indignantly.

"What is the point of our office making copies and sending them to you?" Simonev asked, barely hiding his annoyance.

"Perhaps the routing sequences," Yankovlevitch offered weakly. "They often become confused . . . ."

It was then that the door opened and the three commanders exited the colonel's office, much to the relief of Yankovlevitch, who nodded absently to them as they passed and entered the inner office.

"Ah, Dimitri Andreivitch, so good to see you. Come in, sit. What can I do for you?" said Col. Petrovitch affably. In his experience, the most effective way of dealing with this non-military party hack was to feign an excess of respect and collegiality and hope that his heavy-handed meddling would be kept to a minimum.

"Simonev," he said brusquely. "Some tea for myself and my fellow colonel."

"At once, sir," Simonev responded obsequiously.

Petrovitch gave a brief sketch of the mission, explaining that it was an attempt to garner some intelligence from a Nazi base in the Baltic vicinity. Trolling for possible advances in technology was the way Petrovitch put it, and employing our foreign visitors for the incursion.

Yankovlevitch, placated by the explanation and the tea, nodded and relaxed. He was pleased by the idea of utilizing the Americans to do a dirty and dangerous job for the Motherland.

But when Petrovitch incidentally mentioned that General Khrushchev was involved, Simonev registered a mental "uh-oh." *Too much information for this weasel, I fear.*

When the mollified Yankovlevitch exited and Simonev and Petrovitch's eyes met, they nodded to each other, content with the outcome of their little encounter with the politico. But in Simonev's mind that "uh-oh" echoed like the peal of a distant bell.

In the predawn hours of a mid-June morning, Peggy Cohan dressed in her hybridized Soviet-American flying clothes, made up her bunk, packed her B-4 bag, and strode resolutely out the barracks door and into the crisp air of the nascent morning. On the distant ramp an American-marked C-47 waited in the darkness to carry her to her next adventure.

Peggy paused at the top step of her billet to contemplate what she was leaving behind. Strong friendships had been forged with the warriors of the Soviet regiment. She would miss the company of these brave people. Ordinary people with all-too-human frailties, who willingly put their personal goals aside to join the fight for their homeland. She considered the two closest to her; Natalia and Svetlana, and the pride she felt in their friendship. It all sounded so corny but there was also the satisfaction in being part of a team fighting for such an important cause.

Listen to me, I hardly recognize myself. Me, the girl who knew all the angles. I've become a Girl Scout.

Peggy shook her head, hefted her B-4 bag and muttered under her breath, "Too much thinking." She purposefully trudged toward the waiting transport. *What did I pack in this bag?* she mused. *Seems heavier than when I first arrived.*

Peggy had been instructed to inform no one of her departure or speak of the mission. It pained her to leave her friends without saying good-bye. Instead, she left two small packages on her bed. They were wrapped in brown paper and tied with twine. One was addressed to Captain Natalia Spasenkaya, the other to Lt. Col. Svetlana Sorkovna. Svetlana's package contained Peggy's last lipstick, almost new. Natalia's held a Bulova pilot's watch, fully wound and showing the correct time.

Peggy smiled as she contemplated a newly glamorized Col. Sorkovna issuing the day's orders to the flight crews and Natalia checking her wrist and, perhaps, thinking of her American friend.

The C-47 lifted from the broad grass runway of the Kotluban Aerodrome before the first glow of dawn appeared in the east. Slightly behind but quickly overtaking the transport, two Yak fighters assumed their respective escort positions: one on the left wing and one a thousand feet above the right wing of their charge.

Kamenny Nalchik Stolsky, the Americans' principle provider for more than a year, stood beside his flatbed. He watched his charges fly off, leaving him without a job. Jobs in the Soviet Union that did not involve mortal danger were hard to come by these days. He decided not to report their absence for a while, reasoning that since this very secret mission had been initiated by the General of the Ukrainian Front any discussion might compromise the end result. Yes, he would wait. Content to have come to this decision, he hoped that his boys would enjoy the two large bolognas and two loaves of hearty Russian bread that he packed for their journey. Kamenny unwrapped a stick of Beeman's, placed the piece he had been chewing in the wrapper, and tucked it in his pocket for later. He placed the fresh stick in his mouth as he watched the diminishing points of light disappear in the dark western sky. *Keep safe, my irrepressible American friends*, was his short prayer.

Three-thousand meters above the dark terrain, Lilya Litvak sat in the cockpit of her Yak fighter, number 44, marked in yellow behind the red fuselage star. She and her wingman, Katya Budanova, had volunteered for this mission. What had first appeared to be a routine escort assignment had an unusual addendum to the orders. If for any reason the cargo craft strayed from its course and seemed to be attempting to escape, the transport was to be shot down.

The nineteen-year-old Lilya liked the symmetry of the situation. Doing one's patriotic duty and, at the same time, settling a score. For on that plane with the Americans rode Peggy Cohan, the woman who had taken what did not belong to her and laughed. *Laughed at me! Perhaps it will be I who laughs last,* thought Lilya as the radio crackled and a Russian voice addressed her.

"Commander of escort, synchronize compass to forty degrees northeast."

Lilya pressed the radio button on her control stick and acknowledged as she made the adjustments to her instruments. She thought, *Strange, an unaccented Russian voice. I was not aware of any Russians on board with the Americans.*

Lt. Gregori Slyusalev, an intense and humorless man, was added to the team at the last minute. The slender, bespectacled translator was fluent in English and Lithuanian and the Russian brass insisted that he accompany the Americans on their mission. Slyusalev also rather imperiously demanded a seat on the flight deck that relegated McCabe, the flight engineer, to the cargo compartment with Nick, Pua, and Peggy.

Curious thing, mused Capt. Crandall. *Why's the translator wearing a sidearm? Maybe he just feels more comfortable wearing it. Some tough guy thing probably to counteract those steel-rimmed peepers. But with those Yaks in the air and this armed jerk on the plane, it's going to make bugging out near impossible. Looks like we may have to play this game according to Hoyle.*

In their final briefing the Americans were informed that their initial destination would be Yaroslavl, some 200 kilometers northeast of Moscow. Their route, however, would need to be circuitous in order to avoid the corridors of German aircraft presently assaulting the capital. The foreign markings on their aircraft might even put them at risk of attack by Russian defenders. Best to give Moscow a wide berth and avoid any contact. The total flight would be slightly more than 1,000 kilometers, lasting around four hours. The C-47's range was nearly 6,000 kilometers and could make Yaroslavl easily, but the two Yak escorts would require a refueling stop at a field near Spassk-Ryzanskiy, rejoining the transport as quickly as possible. The lack of armed escort left the transport totally defenseless during this period. The gap would have been an ideal time to bug out but Crandall rejected the prospect of gunplay in the cockpit. In terms of the transport's defenselessness, Staff Sgt. Pua had worked to rig up a remedy for that. In the days preceding the mission Pua had fabricated a gun mount and a Plexiglas window in the broad cargo door and was at this moment securing the captured German gun in its ring mount. He designed it so that he could sit on the floor and effectively protect the left flank of the aircraft.

When Lilya Litvak saw the gun protruding from the door she experienced a pang of uneasiness and instinctively maneuvered her aircraft to put the C-47's wing between herself and that gun. After a while she resumed her position off the left wing, comforted that the gun in the slipstream was pointed innocuously down and to the rear.

"Hey, poi boy," McCabe called over the drone of the engines. "Make sure you don't shoot off our wing while you're Kraut huntin'."

"Don' worry, chief," Pua assured McCabe. "I put in a stop. See!" Pua swung the gun toward the wing but its movement was impeded by an aluminum fixture. "Pretty neat, eh?"

McCabe rolled his eyes and nodded half-hearted approval.

Outside, Lilya dropped the nose of her fighter in instant response to the gun's movement. She warily resumed her position off the transport's wing, relaxing only as the gun returned to its unmanned and slack position in the slipstream.

Inside the aircraft, Nick and McCabe were attempting to reason with a stubborn young woman.

"What do you wanna go to Germany for?" asked Nick.

"Yeah," Roscoe joined in, "the Krauts are almost as bad as the Japs."

"Stay in Yaroslavl. Safe. Wait for us. C'mon, you won't miss anything," Nick added.

Peggy sat on a jump seat with her back against the fuselage while the two Americans sat on either side and continued their attempt to dissuade her from completing the trip.

"Did Crandall put you up to this? He wants to get rid of me, I know. Well, you can save it, boys, I'm coming. The commissar said it was okay and I'm coming. See, I'm all packed." Peggy indicated her B-4 bag stowed up near the flight deck. "They sent the P-39 trainer to another base. I'm out of a job. They won't let me fly missions. I'm tired of sitting around. My girls are transitioned. I'm coming, that's it!"

"But it's gonna get dangerous. Really dangerous," Nick pleaded.

"We don't even know if we can find an engine. And if we do, it might be too heavy to horse into this tub," argued McCabe.

From his position at his machine gun, Pua nodded in agreement.

"You too, George?" Peggy said. "You don't want me along either?"

Pua looked hurt at her accusation.

"We can handle it," assured McCabe.

"Oh!" Peggy shook her head in frustration, then rose from her place between the two men and sat, arms crossed, on the deck beside her B-4 bag. Discussion over.

The door to the flight deck opened and Capt. Crandall emerged. "Our escorts are leaving us to buy some gas. We'll stay on this heading and altitude and I expect they'll join up in no time at all. Nick, forget about Plan B," he said, tilting his head toward Slyusalev up front. "Meanwhile, we'll keep our eyes peeled and George, make use of that window of yours."

He returned to the flight deck where the dour-faced translator could be seen at the flight engineer's position.

"Oh, and George…" said Crandall as he was stepping through the door. "If you're gonna load that pop gun of yours, now'd be a good time." Crandall closed the compartment door behind him.

A rotte of seven Ju87 Stukas from Panzer Jager Staffeln 77 based at Rylsk were heading home after a successful mission. They were flying low to take advantage of the scattered morning light.

"We plowed the road, didn't we boys!" a German voice announced over the radio.

"What a party!" another pilot chimed in.

"Like shooting ducks on a lake!" a third added.

The Stukas had encountered a supply column from the east attempting to reinforce the Moscow defenders in the early morning hours. Since there were no tanks or antiaircraft guns defending the convoy the operation had been a turkey shoot. The initial attack stopped the lead trucks which blocked the narrow stretch of road allowing the Stukas to decimate the stationary convoy with cannon and machine guns. After repeated passes left no signs of life, the spent and victorious Stukas turned towards home.

Major Eugen Koch attempted to calm down his energized command. "All right lads, we had a good time. Now, radio silence and tighten up this formation." He hated to spoil their fun—after all, they had done well—but discipline must prevail.

The now tightly formed echelon of Stukas droned west without commentary, until . . . .

"Enemy aircraft approaching from the left quadrant; high."

Major Koch was annoyed. Hadn't he ordered radio silence? "Who said that?" he snarled into his microphone, wanting the identity of the jokester.

"I see him, too," another voice confirmed.

"Russkies?" someone asked.

"I see only one aircraft."

"Stay on course. There may be more and we're low on fuel and ammunition," Koch ordered. "Hans, how is your fuel?" the major asked.

"It could be worse. Why, Herr Major?"

"Go and have a look. Don't engage. Just sniff around."

"*Ja vohl*, Herr Major." Lt. Hans Voss broke from the formation and began a banking turn, climbing towards what he could now make out as a lone twin-engined aircraft.

"We have a single aircraft. A transport with . . . American markings, I think, Herr Major, an easy kill. Will you give permission?"

"Yes, go ahead, Hans," replied the Major. "You've earned it today."

Savoring the rare knockout of an enemy aircraft, Lieutenant Hans Voss closed on his prey. Ammunition was short but the counter showed a few rounds remaining in the pod cannons under his wing. One or perhaps two well-aimed shots would surely do the job. For best results, though, he should get close to the unarmed enemy.

Over the intercom, rear gunner Oberfeldwebel Dieter Stepanik, pleaded, "Leave some for me. I hardly got a shot off all morning."

"All right, Steppi, I'll follow him down and let you administer the *coup de grace*," Hans Voss generously replied. Sergeant Stepanik smirked in anticipation. It was obvious to Voss that the Americans had seen him because they were turning away. All the better to put a few good ones into the wing root. But, best to get a bit closer. He flipped up the cover of the gun button and . . . just a little . . . bit . . . closer.

Inside the transport, the crew watched as the Stuka loomed ever larger.

"Do we head for the deck, boss?" Caloon asked as the enemy approached.

"If we dive, he'll fire for sure. I'm guessin' he doesn't know what to make of us," answered Crandall.

"Maybe he's out of bullets."

"I'll just stay in this turn and give Pua the best possible shot at him."

Close. Yes. Voss could actually see the faces in the cockpit. *Dead men.* And then something moved at the side of the fuselage. This movement was the last thing that registered in Lieutenant Voss's brain as the jury-rigged machine gun in the transport's side fired a lethal stream of 7.62mm slugs, which raked the bulletproof windscreen, shredded the Stuka's Plexiglas canopy, and shattered the skulls of both the pilot and his still smirking rear gunner.

"Gotcha, ya bastard," Pua muttered to himself.

The Stuka continued its climb past the transport and held its course as if someone alive was at the controls.

Looking over their shoulders, the men in the six remaining Stukas observed the puzzling scene. The encounter should have been over and done with by now. When the stricken Stuka finally heeled over on its left wing and went into a loose spin, they realized that something had gone wrong. Major Koch ordered his flight to turn and engage the enemy plane.

"Uh-oh!" said Crandall. "Here comes the whole pack of 'em." He kicked the rudder pedal and pushed the yoke into a diving turn.

"Hang on," Caloon shouted to the crew in the body of the aircraft. "We're going to try and lose 'em in the weeds."

Looking through the window, Peggy observed, "Those are Stukas!" She struggled to stay in her seat by clinging to a cargo strap during the aircraft's violent maneuvers.

"Those antiques are slow as shit, ain't they?" McCabe asked hopefully, himself straining to remain upright.

"Not in a dive, they're not," replied Peggy. "That's the one thing they do well."

Following procedure, the Stukas formed an orderly line to take turns firing on the transport. The first fired its wing pod cannons and missed, then its machine guns and missed again. It pulled up and obediently went to the rear of the line. Meanwhile, the second Stuka was firing its machine guns, futilely missing well behind the juking transport.

The Stuka was designed to hit slow moving vehicles on the ground. An air-to-air target was a new and puzzling problem to several of the green Stuka pilots.

When the third attack missed completely, Squadron Leader Koch growled into the radio. "Move away! Clear the target. You are making a botch of this. I will finish him. Everyone clear out."

Eugen Koch understood that a considerable lead was required to hit a moving aircraft. With a sense of frustration at the ineptitude of his charges, he placed the pip of his gun's sight several meters ahead of the juking transport as his thumb found the gun button. He would put an end to this embarrassment as quickly as possible.

Inside the transport Nick, Peggy, and McCabe watched helplessly as the streaks of machine gun and cannon fire raged around them. Pua struggled to remain in his crouch while attempting to bring his weapon to bear on their attackers.

The realization that at any moment they might be plunging to a fiery death gripped the three passengers, their sense of terror heightened by their helplessness.

While straining to remain upright inside the maneuvering aircraft and at the same time trying to glimpse their attackers out of the small cabin windows, Peggy reached out and gripped Nick's hand. McCabe, supporting himself by holding onto a cargo loop, grabbed Nick's other hand and held on tightly.

As the Stuka closed on the helpless transport, a volley of tracers from two 12.7mm machine guns ripped into the surprised German's right wing. At the same time, the staccato bark of a 20mm nose cannon echoed, tearing the wing from the fuselage of Major Eugen Koch's Stuka. It snap-rolled violently and cartwheeled out of control toward the ground.

Lilya Litvak didn't bother to watch her target's demise. She instantly pulled her Yak into a climb to engage the remaining Stukas who had turned tail when her wingman, Katya Budanova, dove through the formation. Katya's guns shattered the empennage of her first target, sending it into a fatal spin. The four surviving dive-bombers flown by inexperienced pilots were no match for the expert Russian women. Though the frantic Germans attempted to flee in all directions, flying low and zigzagging, they were coolly dispatched by the much faster Yaks.

Lilya and Katya were among the best at what they did and bent to their task with cold, businesslike efficiency.

A satisfied smile appeared on Lilya's lips as she resumed her position off the left wing of the transport and watched Katya return to her place in the high cover spot.

Captain Crandall wiped the perspiration from his forehead and spoke to the interpreter. "Tell that pilot, thanks. We owe him and his partner." The unnerved translator conveyed the message.

Lily's answer was translated simply, "Pleased to provide assistance."

"Those is some helluva couple'a pilots," Pua said, breaking the tense silence by stating the obvious.

With the terror of the attack abated, Nick said to McCabe, "You can let go of my hand now, Roscoe." Roscoe dropped Nick's hand like it was a hot magneto wire.

Peggy also self-consciously let go of Nick's hand.

"Oh no, not you, Peggy," Nick said. "You can keep holding on."

Peggy looked into Nick's blue eyes and smiled, pleased by her friend's ability to make a flattering joke under such stressful circumstances.

21

Crandall greased the landing on the concrete runway of the Central Aviation Institute outside of Yaroslavl. On the approach the crew could see a structure that had once been the control tower cringing in ruins beside the runway. Several wrecked hangars, a few burnt-out husks of aircraft, and what was once an administration building likewise gave evidence of a Nazi air raid back in the spring of '42. Except for a small recovery crew, grouped beside a horse-drawn cart bearing a large rusty fuel tank and what appeared to be a generator and air compressor, the base which had once been an aeronautical design center and active training facility seemed to be largely defunct. Most of the buildings had been abandoned when the institute, its staff, and its faculty were moved east over the Ural Mountains and set up beyond the range of Nazi bombs.

On the far side of the runway, a squadron of sleek Yak 9 fighters sat on grass cloverleafs beside the taxiway. Beyond, adjacent to a wooded area, camouflaged tents provided temporary shelter for pilots and ground crews. Despite the German's halted advance on Moscow, the Institute's grounds were still considered a potential target.

Even before the engines were cut, Pua and McCabe, followed by Peggy, hurriedly deplaned to inspect their ship. Slyusalev, however, exited and, ignoring the others, strode directly toward the largest of the institute's buildings.

At the same time, the two Yak escorts made their landings side by side on the grass strip.

"I can't believe it," said McCabe, scanning the tail and fuselage while shaking his head. "No bullet holes, not a dent or a scratch."

"We sure are lucky," said a grinning Pua.

"Luck? Nonsense!" Crandall chimed in. "It was flying skill," he explained insouciantly, attempting but failing to keep a straight face.

"Actually, that was some pretty fair flying, Captain Crandall," Peggy remarked.

Crandall's smile faded into a suspicious glower as he reacted to Peggy's compliment.

"And you George," Peggy continued, "nice shooting! Where'd you learn to shoot like that? I thought it was all over for us."

Pua nodded then hastily changed the subject by pointing to the two taxiing Yaks approaching.

"Hey," said Nick with a wave, "let's go thank those fighter mutts."

When the two Yak pilots climbed out of the cockpits of their respective aircraft, they pulled off their leather helmets and revealed two grinning young women. The former crew of the *Boogie Woogie Baby* rushed toward Lilya and Katya, pumping their arms and patting their shoulders in exuberant thanks for the nick-of-time rescue.

Peggy held back, but then, after shaking hands with Katya, extended her hand to Lilya.

Lilya stared coldly at Peggy's hand, then into Peggy's eyes and, with a slight upward tilt of her chin, turned away.

Nick and Crandall noticed the snub but couldn't figure it out as they were directed by one of the ground crew to the nearby brick building.

Inside, Lieutenant Slyusalev was heatedly conversing with a civilian wearing a double-breasted suit. The translator was clearly registering some complaint. When the flyers entered the building another civilian, dressed more casually, directed them to a large room on the ground floor.

In the former dining area of the abandoned institute, tables and chairs had been moved to the periphery and stacked out of the way. A large shortwave radio was set up on one table. Two long tables with chairs had been placed near serving counters where two *babushkas* prepared to dole out a simple meal.

The American men and the two Russian pilots chatted enthusiastically, unhampered by the fact they understood very little of each other's language. After cheating death, a meal of black bread, dried herring, cabbage soup, and Spam was consumed by the flyers as if it was a feast from the gods. Close calls always create a hearty appetite.

As they ate, an army officer entered and announced that their respective aircraft had been refueled and rearmed. He then gestured to another table where maps were laid out and invited the flyers to consider the route to their next destination.

The translation was handled by Nick who, along with the others, was wondering why Slyusalev, the "translator," was not doing his job.

The Russian Army captain outlined the plan for the next leg of their journey as the group gathered around the table. He pointed to a town northeast of Moscow called Velikie Luki.

As Crandall and Nick searched for and found Velikie on the smaller charts, the captain continued his explanation in Russian, describing Velikie as the place where they would refuel and receive their final briefing on the mission. It was obvious that the Army captain knew little of what was planned beyond the stop at Velikie Luki. Slyusalev questioned the captain further in rapid-fire Russian, sounding imperious and impatient and ultimately disappointed with the limited knowledge the captain possessed.

Strange, thought Caloon. *A lieutenant ripping the backside of a captain. And getting away with it.*

Lilya and Katya pushed forward to get a better view of a larger map tacked up on an empty wall by the captain. The wall bore the outlines of two missing pictures, most likely the obligatory portraits of Stalin and Lenin.

When Peggy edged in beside the two Russian women to get a

better view, Lilya turned angrily and with both hands shoved Peggy backward. She said something sharply in Russian which Nick deciphered as "Keep your nose out of this. You aren't flying. You are just a passenger." Those words were the gist of her remark, with the addition of one extra word. A provocative word. The word *kurva*, which Nick knew meant "slut" in Russian.

As Nick turned his attention back to the chart, surmising that these two did not like each other, the enmity between the women suddenly escalated. To the surprise of the onlookers, including the *babushkas* in the midst of cleaning up, Lilya Litvak and Peggy Cohan faced off in the center of the room. Lilya then rushed Peggy, head down, butting her in the stomach and knocking her to the floor. Peggy rose immediately and strode toward Lilya, landing a roundhouse blow to the side of her face. The two women then came together, screaming and flailing at each other. The pair of nineteen-year-old girls continued their grappling until they sideswiped a table and fell to the dusty marble floor, where they rolled, clawing at each other, shrieking and pulling each other's hair. The stunned onlookers quickly recovered and moved to separate the pair.

Nick grabbed Peggy, pinning her arms to her sides and pulled her off Lilya. The Russian captain, likewise, restrained Lilya.

"Tramp!" shouted Peggy.

"*Minetka*," screamed Lilya.

The Russian officer barked at the two women. "What's this? We can't have this foolishness. Stop it at once. Stand at attention!" he ordered in Russian.

Both women ceased their struggling, though they continued glaring at each other. When the captain relaxed his grip, Lilya broke loose and lunged forward, swinging her small fist at Peggy. Nick saw the blow coming and while still restraining Peggy swung her out of the way to one side. Lilya's fist connected to the side of Nick's face with a solid smack. When Nick took the blow, both combatants seemed to calm, with the army captain once again moving in to restrain Lilya. He then angrily rebuked the two women in Russian as they glowered at each other beneath their brows. After a few more pointed words for the pair, he ordered the women to remain silent and stand at opposite ends of the group while he resumed the briefing.

Everyone in the room, jarred by the outburst, adopted an air of solemnity as they returned their attention to the charts. Pua and McCabe, however, had obviously enjoyed the fracas. Exchanging glances, they had difficulty suppressing grins during the captain's directions to their next refueling stop.

A landing field would be improvised in a grass meadow. Support and turnaround equipment would be waiting. This field was eight kilometers north of Velikie Luki and, he stressed, in German-held territory.

"Landmarks!" Slyusalev emphasized, now back on the job.

"Look for three crescent-shaped lakes, bordered by two prominent streams. The lakes and streams should still be visible in the fading light." The Captain pointed out the streams as the Polist and the Velikaya, tributaries of the Volga. "The field is less than a kilometer beyond the third lake."

The landings would have to be made just before dark. Runway lights would be provided and extinguished immediately after the aircraft were on the ground. There they would be briefed for the next leg of the mission. The flight from their current location to Velikie would take under three hours, approximately 575 kilometers. The heading would be 225 degrees. They would be flying at 200 meters altitude, hopefully avoiding any further encounters with enemy aircraft from the Leningrad front some 400 kilometers to the northeast.

He then announced to the group that the town of Shlusselberg, on Lake Lagoda, had been retaken, and the encirclement by the Nazis at Leningrad had been breached.

This news caused great elation to the Russians in the room while the Americans, unfamiliar with the geography involved, could only offer mild enthusiasm.

Back on the subject of their mission, the Russian captain suggested a take-off time of six p.m. to arrive at dusk in Velikie Luki. He further suggested that the crews use their day to get some rest. He then bade them good luck, saluted, and exited the room.

Nick, his crewmates, and the two Yak pilots now selected places around the large hall to sit or stretch out. As the navigator settled down in a spot beside a table, he smiled reassuringly at Peggy. She acknowledged him with a sheepish grin and offered an embarrassed "sorry about that" shrug. He noticed she had sustained a small scratch at her hairline with a slim trickle of blood already dried on her forehead. *Even after a fight and rolling around on a dirty floor, she's still somethin',* he thought. Lilya, at the opposite side of the room, could be heard talking animatedly to her wingman, Katya. Her expansive and jubilant tone suggested that she was declaring herself the victor of the altercation. Nick observed, however, that Lilya's eye was quickly burgeoning into one prize-winning mouse. Nick's own eye, which felt a bit tender, was in fact blooming into a fairly heroic shiner of its own.

"Lights to be off in the next one half hour," Slyusalev said, conveying the Russian captain's exiting words. The generator would be shut down then. "Best to make sleep inside building," he added as the aviators arranged their gear on the dirty marble floor and prepared to settle in for the night.

Peggy was too agitated to sleep, so she rose and exited the darkened area where the mission members had improvised their personal sleeping nests and quietly slipped out into the hall. There, by the light of a kerosene lantern, she sat on the floor and removed an envelope from her pocket. Peggy shook the torn pieces of her mother's letter out onto a clean space on the floor and in the privacy of the institute's hallway, began to reconstruct the mutilated message. The pieces were small and flimsy due to the lightweight V-mail stationary and so were flighty about remaining in place.

Her fight with Lilya had been unnerving. Peggy had never been in a fistfight before and the experience disturbed her. Such an encounter clearly showed that she had lost control of the situation and herself. A fact that she hated. On the other hand, the vented anger and pure physicality of the encounter had a cathartic effect on her. She was left with a feeling almost akin to relief. It might have been this feeling that permitted her to at last confront her mother's words. This time and this place might be her last opportunity to do so privately and without witnesses to judge the right or wrong of her reaction to them.

When the flimsy shards had all been assembled, she read the letter.

My dear Peggy,

Sorry it's taken me so long to write. There are so many things I want to say but I didn't know how to begin.

I'm sorry about so much.

What can I do? How do I make it up to you? I know I wasn't a good mom. If you would only try to understand: I was frightened. I was left all alone. I had a child to be responsible for. I didn't know how I would survive. I took it out on you. I didn't like you. I blamed you. I know that was wrong.

I hope you can forgive me. I want so much for you to forgive me. I'm so sorry. I look back and can't believe how I behaved. I want so much to make it up to you if you would only let me. Please, Margaret.

I've met a nice man. He's got a good job. He loves me, I think. And I think I love him but I don't think I can allow myself to love anyone until I can make it right with you. Please forgive me.

I'm so sorry, Margaret. Give me a chance. Please.

Your Mom

She was frightened! She was young! She wants a chance? *What about me. I was your daughter, you monster.* Peggy's mind roiled with anger. *Why weren't you looking out for me? You treated me like crap. You despised me. I was just a little girl. Your little girl.*

And now you've thought it over. You've met a man? So you are ready to make nice. Well, maybe I don't want to make nice. I've lived without you for this long, maybe I'd be better off without you. Peggy's eyes filled with tears. It was hard to breathe. The anger and hurt were overwhelming.

If I make it home I'd be smart to act like you don't exist. That's what you deserve, Stella. You don't deserve to have a daughter. And if I don't get home, you'll have to live with that, too. For the rest of your life.

"Hey, *Principessa,* whatcha doin up?"

A voice in the dark intruded on Peggy's broodings. Startled, she disconnected from the long suppressed emotions. It was Nick. "What do you want?" she said brusquely.

"Want? I don't want anything, kiddo. I just saw you were up and came out to say hi. Sorry, didn't mean to disturb you. I'll just go back and leave you be."

"No, Nick. Stay. Please." Peggy snuffled and wiped her eyes with the back of her hand. "I was just putting the pieces of this letter together. Got sorta torn."

Nick looked down at the paper shards. "What is it? A puzzle?" he asked.

"You might say that," Peggy answered. "It's a puzzle to me."

"Maybe I can help you, *Principessa.* I'm pretty good at puzzles."

"No," said Peggy, gathering up the pieces. "I've got it. It's a letter. From someone who was not very nice to me."

"And they're sorry?" asked Nick.

Peggy looked up at him, surprised at his perceptiveness. "Yes, they say they are, but I don't know if I should believe them. Or even want to."

"Well," Nick said, "if it's some mug, I'd say goodbye and good riddance."

Peggy smiled at Nick's gratuitous counsel.

"But," he continued, "if it's not, then make 'em show you."

"Show me what?'"

"Show you that they're sorry. By their actions, not their words."

Peggy looked into Nick's eyes and could see he was no longer joking.

"Words can mean almost anything, *Principessa.* The same words can have lots of different meanings. They can lie. What someone does is the truth. Usually, anyway. Don't waste time worrying about what to believe. Wait for the truth. Decide on the basis of the way they act. Then you can know for sure. After that it all depends on what you want to happen next. See. Simple."

"You are good at puzzles, Nick," said Peggy, putting her mother's letter back in her blouse pocket.

"Y'know," said Nick, "we ought to get some sleep. Tomorrow's going to be another big day."

"Right," said Peggy, rising from the floor.

"Peggy," Nick said in a matter-of-fact tone. "Can I ask you a question?"

"Sure," said Peggy, "of course."

"Uh . . ." Nick was hesitant. "Can I . . . can I call you in the city?"

A broad smile broke out on the face of the young female flyer. The question, "Can I call you in the city?" was a familiar cliché back in New York. A young man who had shared a romantic experience with a girl on summer vacation or camp or up at a mountain resort would ask this question. The answer would determine if their experience was merely a summer fling or something more lasting. Spoken in this present circumstance, it was both humorous and flattering and Peggy accepted it precisely in this way.

She answered the slightly apprehensive navigator with, "Yes! I would like it very much if you would call me in the city."

"Good night, *Principessa*," said Nick, turning away with the response he had hoped for.

"Good night, Nick."

22

As the transport passed over the shake rooftops of the town of Velikie Luki, four pairs of eyes inside the cockpit strained as they scanned the earth in the gathering gloom.

"Should be anytime now," said Nick from behind the left seat.

"There! That's a lake!" pointed McCabe from over the copilot's shoulder.

"And there's another, and, yep, believe I can see the faint outline of the third," observed Caloon in restrained triumph. "Good job, eagle eye!"

The C-47 throttled back and allowed the Yak fighters to surge ahead and descend into the cauldron of dusk below tree level. The Yaks were low on fuel. Below, faint flickers marked their objective. The two fighters set down on the undulating grass and taxied to the far end of the pasture, guided by a set of lanterns on a vehicle. The fighters were directed to a patch of flat grass at the edge of the meadow as the transport made its landing. It, too, was directed to the edge of the pasture where a ground crewman signaled a one-hundred and eighty degree turn and ordered its engines killed. Moments later, camouflage netting enveloped both the transport and the fighters as the runway markers were extinguished and darkness reclaimed the meadow.

The aviators exited their aircraft and were directed to the entrance of a camouflaged tent where several makeshift tables had been set up.

At the back wall some charts and a large, crudely-drawn schematic was displayed. Outside, a small generator hummed, powering the string of lights that illuminated the tent's interior. The light revealed one of the tables bearing several boxes of American C-rations and a large battered samovar standing amidst some glasses. A dozen or so unmatched household chairs, requisitioned from local homes, were provided for the aviators to sit, eat their rations, and view what would be their final briefing.

As the flyers entered, six men rose and regarded the newcomers. One, a tall, gray-haired man in a double-breasted suit wearing wire-rimmed glasses, appeared completely out of place. Not military, not party *apparatchik*. In contrast, the remaining five were dangerous-looking fellows; three solemn-faced, thick-set men in rough work clothes, along with two younger men dressed as paratroops and wearing jump boots. The faces of the two in uniform were familiar: the gruff Major Djilas and his young, bookish interpreter, Lieutenant Begina.

Djilas's hard blue eyes took the measure of each of the entrants in turn, and finally offered a curt nod to the group. Begina managed a tentative smile, pushed his spectacles back on his nose with his middle finger, and gestured for them to sit.

Djilas walked to the two women fighter pilots and made a quick bow as he shook hands with each of them. He then strode to Peggy and bowed once again as he shook her hand. This brief acknowledgement was a declaration of respect. He seemed to be aware of the accomplishments of these women. He then walked to the far wall of the tent, joined by his aide, and began the briefing. He spoke in Russian and Begina translated.

Interrupting, Lt. Slyusalev spoke in Russian, "Excuse me, Comrade Major, may I introduce myself. I am . . . ."

Djilas raised his finger menacingly, cutting off Slyusalev. He spoke curtly in Russian, his eyes flashing. "There is no need. I know very well who you are. I was born in Kamenetsin Podolskiy. The entire village, including my mother and two younger brothers, was sent east by the secret police, to God knows where. Be quiet, NKVD. And stay away from me. Far away from me."

Neither Nick nor Peggy understood the sharp exchange between the two men despite their smattering comprehension of the language. The other Americans were completely baffled by the exchange, but Lilya, Katya, and the partisans heard, exchanged glances, and prudently remained silent.

Slyusalev sat motionless, clearly unnerved, staring straight ahead. He was utterly convinced that if he mouthed one syllable in response Djilas would delight in killing him on the spot.

In this atmosphere the briefing on the plan to extricate a turbine engine from the Third Reich proceeded.

"As you know, there are essentially two separate bases," Djilas explained as Begina translated. "The first is the Messerschmitt repair facility outside of Kovno. Here, Lithuanian workers fabricate landing struts and wheels for the 109 and the new propellerless 262. The workers are treated well since there are many Lithuanians serving in Wehrmacht units. There are barracks for the workers here," he said, pointing to the structure with his bayonet, "and barracks for a small unit of guards, German and Lithuanian mixed, here and here. There are two factory buildings, an assembly shed and another for components. Here is a reinforced bunker," he said, indicating a square between the barracks, "which serves as bomb shelter. There is an antiaircraft gun installed on a tracked vehicle. The mobility of the gun is of great concern to us. The factory buildings are here," he said, the bayonet pointing, "and here, the living quarters." The bayonet pierced the paper. "Two buildings housing a small garrison and the workers. We have no interest in this side of the base. Except for the gun. We must pay special attention to this gun.

"Our objective lies on the other side. This concrete runway of 1,800 meters has been built beside the grass runway. The turbine aircraft obviously requires a long smooth runway."

At the mention of a turbine aircraft, Slyusalev visibly perked up. Djilas noticed the reaction but continued.

"There are three small shops where components for bomb hanging, release mechanisms, and the pylons to shield them from the air blast are being manufactured, then made into assemblies so mechanics in the field can install them. There is also a very large tent, dark red in color. A circus tent which was confiscated by the Nazis. We do not know what this tent is for but it is unlikely that it houses aircraft because of the lack of access from the runways."

Begina kept up his translation at the pace of Djilas's speech so the group was able to keep their eyes on the major as he spoke.

"The workers on this side of the base live in newly built barracks with women and children. They are guarded by a small contingent, all German. Obviously they do not fear the risk of escape since the families are essentially held hostage. Many of these workers are Jews and dissident Catholic technicians and engineers who were recruited from concentration camps in Poland and Latvia. There is a hangar, here," he said, pointing beyond the barracks, "set back against the tree line of a forest. Our reports cannot confirm any components in the hangar. Several 262s landed recently but they may have been repaired or modified and returned to their units. We do not know for sure. We have reason to believe that there is a turbine motor in this hangar. Our contact saw such a machine several days ago and our judgment tells us that it is still there. It may, however, be in a disassembled state, but even in pieces, it would still serve our purpose. Professor?" Djilas turned to the tall, gray-haired gentleman and Begina introduced him to the group.

"Comrades, this is Professor Arkhip Lyul'ka. He is a professor of aeronautical engineering and an expert on turbine propulsion."

Lyul'ka rose and offered a weak smile as he nodded a brief acknowledgement of the group. As he spoke, Begina translated.

"I am Arkhip Lyul'ka, Chief Engine Designer for the Sukhoi Bureau. I was requested to come here and provide you with a possible description and some understanding of the mechanism that is the object of your mission."

Out of the corner of his eye Djilas noticed the slight smirk of satisfaction that flashed briefly on the face of Slyusalev.

With a fountain pen, Lyul'ka drew an elongated rectangle on the back of a map and placed it beside the schematic of the base. He then divided the rectangle into four equal parts and added a narrow strip between segment three and four. He pointed to his diagram.

"Here you see what we believe to be a likely schematic of the turbine engine of the Hitlerites. This first section is the intake, where air is drawn into the system. Next is the compressor, a series of fan blades diminishing in size, where the intake air is squeezed. Next is the combustion stage where fuel is mixed with the hot compressed air and ignited. This explosively hot gas is directed to a turbine wheel that turns at high revolutions and then exits through the exhaust, a narrowed cone or nozzle. The exiting mass of gas creates the thrust forward which propels the aircraft."

At this point Begina ceased his translation and asked the professor for a clarification of the Russian word "thrust." "Reaction," answered the professor in Russian. Then he added, "Imparted energy." Begina translated these but confusion remained on the faces of the group. Finally, Lyul'ka said, "Push," and when Begina translated, the students finally registered understanding. Lyul'ka continued.

"You'll notice there are no pistons, no valves. There is only one moving part: the turbine, which is one with the compressor. Simple, no? Almost childish, yet the puzzle of the heat, high revolutions, and fuel have confounded us to this point. The engineers at Junkers and BMW have obviously solved this problem. A problem, I believe, of metallurgy. If you can procure an intact assembly for us it would render our capability second to none. The war would be shortened, lives would be saved. Russian lives and American lives."

The professor held his audience with the practiced grip of a skilled lecturer.

Then a raised hand. Peggy asked in English, "What if we can't find an entire engine?"

Begina translated.

Lyul'ka raised his finger. "An excellent question, young woman. We need sections two, three, and four. Especially four, the turbine, which we believe resembles a large metal fan with many small blades. One and five are merely air vents. If you can bring us any of these key components you will have brought us the knowledge to fight the fascists on their own terms. Any other questions? No? Then, Major, the hall is yours."

"Our plan is simple and direct," Major Djilas explained to the group. "Our bombers will attack the base, the transport will land while we keep the Fritzies pinned down. The Americans will load the turbine into their aircraft and fly east. During this time we are vulnerable from the air, which is why comrade Lilya and comrade Katya will provide high cover. If you notice any fascist heads peeping out of their bunkers we would appreciate it if you would give them a nice close shave."

Lilya and Katya exchanged glances and grins.

"Once again, we will bomb the base and drive the fascists to cover, while you, captain of the American transport, will land from the east and turn off to the right, here." Djilas indicated his schematic. "This is where you will be in close proximity to this maintenance hangar." He leveled his unsheathed bayonet. "What we seek should be in this structure," he said, pointing emphatically. "Here! Our men on the ground should have the troops neutralized so you may go about your business. The technicians and their families are billeted nearby in new barracks. The additional guards reside, here. These factory buildings were built to appear as prisoner barracks from the air because of the reluctance of American and British bombers to attack labor camps.

"Our people have been infiltrating the area for several days, hiding in the surrounding hills, living off the land. The Nazi decision to place this facility in a remote area works in our favor. We are poised to strike the base from all directions at the appointed moment. Cutting communications will be the first priority.

"These men," he said, indicating the men dressed as peasant farmers, "and I will board the aircraft concealed in the forest behind us and parachute into the area tonight. Professor, after the drop, you will be flown back to your facility, east of Moscow. I thank you for agreeing to come and personally providing us with a description of

292 · Kurt Willinger

the turbine motor."

The professor nodded in response.

"There is one concern remaining; the mobile antiaircraft gun. We anticipated one or two flak bunkers, fortified but immobile. These we could have targeted and immediately disposed of at first contact. Now we have no idea where this gun will be stationed. A problem. But not unsolvable. To the Yak pilots, I must caution, be wary.

"Pilot Crandall, with your permission I will give these charts to Navigator Tolkin. You see, our present position is indicated . . ." Djilas laid out the chart in front of Nick and pointed to a spot just northwest of Velikie Luki, " . . . here!"

Begina translated as the American officers leaned in to view the chart. Lilya and Katya rose from their chairs and joined the group in perusing the route to the objective.

"And here is the plot to the Nazi repair base at Kovno. It is slightly less than 475 kilometers. I would assume slightly more than a two hour flight. You must land when our bombers have cleared the area. They attack at nine forty-five. They will make only two passes. The initial pass will come from the east. The sun will be in their eyes. You must land precisely at nine fifty-five. Clear?" The Americans nodded in the affirmative.

Djilas then handed out two additional charts to the female fighter pilots and gave them their instructions.

"Your role is to protect the airspace. Only when the bombers exit the area are you free to engage the enemy on the ground. Anything and everything is a target except this hangar and the technician's quarters. Am I clear?"

The women nodded.

"I am at a loss as to why you American visitors have been chosen for this assignment but my orders come directly from General Chuikov, so I do not question, I simply obey.

"If there are no further questions, I would suggest you get some rest. Tomorrow will be an eventful day."

"Slyusalev," Djilas addressed the lieutenant directly. "Everyone here has a function but you. I do not know what your role is but I warn you, be useful to this mission or you will remain in Lithuania. Permanently." Begina did not translate.

"To the rest of you, good luck. Be aware, good men may die tomorrow so that you may complete your mission. I wish you all success. I salute you."

Djilas then snapped-to and saluted smartly. The group stood and returned his salute as he exited the tent with Begina, Professor Lyul'ka, and his three commandos.

As the men exited, Peggy dropped her salute, hurried over to her B-4 bag and retrieved two envelopes from a zippered side pocket. She then ran through the blackout curtains and into the night in pursuit of the professor and the commandos. Peggy caught up with them as they walked, guided by a man bearing a kerosene lantern, toward the IL4 bomber waiting silently under its camouflage netting.

"Professor," Peggy called out in English, "a moment."

The commandos turned but continued walking as Lyul'ka stopped and waited for Peggy to catch up.

"Professor," Peggy spoke as she approached him. She held out the letters. "Can you put these in the mail?"

"Pees-mah poach-tih pah sih lath she-heh-ah" was translated crudely as "letters post office send USA."

Lyul'ka smiled at her brave attempt at a Russian sentence and said, "I have small English. *Da*, yes, I will post your messages." He then took the letters from Peggy, held them as if they were very valuable and placed them in his breast pocket. "I will," he said and took her hand and pressed it between his hands. He then turned and strode toward the dim light of the lantern and the men clambering up the ladder and into the belly of the bomber.

"Thank you, professor. *Spaseeba!*"

The professor continued his walk toward the aircraft and without turning back to Peggy, raised his arm and waved, "You're welcome." At the base of the boarding ladder Lyul'ka turned, made a courtly bow and clambered up into the aircraft.

Back inside the lighted tent, the aviators were studying their charts and the layout of the base. With the help of Slyusalev they were able to join in the discussion of the plan and refine their logistics. When the subject of their final destination came up, Crandall suggested that if all went as planned they would bring their prize back to Yaroslavl. Slyusalev objected strongly and insisted that the engine be brought to a base closer to Moscow. He offered Dmitrov as a preferred destination. Crandall explained that the issue was irrelevant. If they managed to secure a turbine engine he could care less where they dropped it off. This seemed to satisfy Slyusalev.

Quietly, Caloon wondered to Crandall, "Why is this guy so hot to bring our cargo to Dmitrov? Smells kinda fishy, don't it, Cap?"

Crandall nodded in agreement. "Hey, right now we've got bigger worries than where we deliver the goods."

It was at this point that Peggy, who had been a mere spectator to the discussions, walked over to Crandall and spoke quietly to him.

"Captain Crandall, may I have a word, in private?"

Crandall eyed Peggy suspiciously and then glanced at Caloon beside him, who had overheard her request. Caloon shrugged and stuck out his lower lip in a grimace that conveyed: *Sure, what the heck, go talk to her.*

Peggy and Crandall walked together, through the curtains, out into the dark. Outside, Crandall, his arms folded in front of him, asked impatiently, "Well, what is it?"

"I just wanted to say . . . I needed to tell you . . . dammit!" Peggy stammered in frustration.

"What?" Crandall said, anxious to get back inside. "Well? What?"

"I'm not good at this," Peggy said, groping for her words. "I don't . . . I'm not an apologizing person by nature. So, you see . . . ."

Crandall cocked his head in exaggerated forbearance.

"I'm sorry," Peggy blurted. "I . . . I want to apologize. I behaved . . . awfully. It was mean and I should have never done that. I was having fun at your expense. I wanted to make you look foolish. So childish. It was wrong and I apologize."

Crandall turned his head in a cynical, sidewise glance.

"I'm really sorry, Bedford. I can understand if you stay angry at me but it's been bothering me. I wanted to say . . . I want you to know, I'm sorry."

Crandall, at a loss for words, peered into Peggy's face and despite the dark, was surprised to see the moisture welling up in her eyes. *She actually seems sincere,* he thought.

"It was a rotten thing to do, you know," said Crandall.

"I know. Rotten. Really rotten. And the way things are now I just had to say it. I was an air brain and I hope you can forgive me. I'm really sorry."

"Well," Crandall considered, "since you put it that way, it wasn't such a big deal."

Peggy gratefully held her hand out to Crandall and he took it.

"I'm so sorry, Bed. It was really mean."

Now, Crandall, unsettled by her embarrassment and feeling slightly magnanimous, said, "Peggy, what do you say, let's forget it. It's passed. Water over the sluice. Okay? Peg?"

"Okay, Bed. I appreciate . . . thanks."

As they stood together, the blackout curtains to the tent parted and Nick appeared. He observed the pair holding hands.

"Hey, what's going on? Oh! I'm sorry. I didn't mean to . . ." Nick turned hurriedly to reenter the tent.

"Nick," Peggy said, "it's okay, you don't have to leave."

"Lieutenant Tolkin," Captain Crandall barked. "Quit being such a horse's patoot. Now, let's go back inside. We've got to figure how to get to Kovno at precisely nine fifty-five, 'cause if we don't, Nick, it'll be your chestnuts in the fire."

The three Americans reentered the tent, Peggy first, then Nick, as Crandall held back the curtains.

After a final run through of the plan, the team, satisfied that all contingencies had been considered, prepared to bed down for the night. It was time to claim a soft spot on the ground and get comfortable. The lights would be extinguished shortly. Nick, reclining on his duffle bag, called over to Slyusalev who was ensconced nearby.

"Hey, comrade. You sleeping?"

Slyusalev lifted his head, raised up on his elbow and faced Nick. "*Nyet,* I no sleeping. What is?"

"Can you answer a question for me?"

"What is question?"

"The girls used a word, *minetka,*" Nick asked softly. "What does it mean?"

Slyusalev paused as if finding it difficult to pose the words. He then whispered the explanation. "Eh . . . *minetka* is woman who provide mouth intercourse."

Nick's eyes went wide. "Whew!" he said. It was then that the lights were extinguished.

The lone IL4 bomber bore resolutely into the dark moonless night which cloaked the war-weary European continent. As the last two warriors dropped from an open hatch in the belly of the aircraft, the pilot banked his ship to confirm that their parachutes had properly deployed. He then initiated a climbing turn and headed east, away from abattoir Europe and back toward the besieged Russian homeland.

On board, the lone passenger absently patted the breast pocket of his suit coat that bore two letters. One was addressed to *Cece Collins (Castelagno), 45 East 54th Street, NY, NY.* The last few lines of the letter read as follows:

> *I'm very happy for you, Cece. Ordinarily I'd be jealous as heck but for some strange reason, I'm not. I feel happy and proud. Almost like I made it, too.*
>
> *Somehow we got one of your records over here. If you could have seen how the kids here enjoyed your singing, even the ones who didn't speak English. They loved it. You make people happy with your singing. That's a real talent and that is why you deserve all the success in the world. Attaway girl.*

I love you and I hope to see you soon. Friends to the end. Peggy

The second letter was addressed to Mrs. Stella Cohan, 125-07 Main Street, Flushing, NY. Her letter ended with these lines:

It would be nice if we could put the past behind us. Perhaps that's impossible. But what would happen if we tried? We'll see. Peggy

The hopes of many were borne on the air this night.

23

Sofijia Porcrovicius held her breath as the sound of footfalls grew closer. What? A boar? A bear? Some large animal foraging for berries in the dim light of these early morning woods? She reached under the cloth covering her basket and gripped the handle a small well-worn knife as she pressed herself against the rough bark of an ancient pine. After an agony of uncounted, breathless moments he appeared. Not a bear, but a man. A man with a rifle.

She gasped. Not loudly. Merely a small inhalation. But the gunman stopped in his tracks and slowly scanned the space before him. *Surely,* she thought, *he could hear her heart pounding.* At first she was certain he had seen her but he looked past and continued his scrutiny of the area. Perhaps he would attribute the noise to a bird or fallen twig. After all, the light was still very dim and the new growth on the forest floor made it difficult to see.

But on his second scan he raised his rifle and leveled it at the woman's chest. Sofijia Porcrovicius raised her hands in silent capitulation, her basket hanging in the crook of her left arm, her right fist still clutching the knife.

"Who are you?" the gunman hissed in Russian. "Quiet or I will kill you." The gunman moved closer and wrenched the knife from Sofijia's hand. "What is in the basket?" he demanded. When her fright delayed her answer, he struck her with the back of his hand, knocking her down. Looking to one side, then the other, he leaned forward. "Who is with you?" he demanded in an angry whisper. "How many?"

Sofijia lifted her upper body from the ground and replied in Lithuanian-accented Russian. "No one is with me. I am alone. Only me."

The gunman slipped the knife into his belt and ordered, "Get up, walk that way." He tilted his head in the direction from which he had come. "Don't speak. Don't make a sound. Now go!" he ordered in a hoarse whisper. He jabbed his rifle toward the basket and, lifting the cloth with its muzzle, looked in and grunted dismissively.

Major Djilas was at the command post speaking on the "walking talking" device, positioning his troops. The Americans had included many of these so-called "walking talkings" in the vehicles sent over in the Lend-Lease program. When the devices were offered to Djilas, none were operational. However, a bright young corporal correctly deduced that their batteries could be reenergized by the generators of the foreign vehicles and succeeded in bringing them back to life. Now, with four functional walking-talkings, the major could communicate directly with his men encircling the German repair base. Much more efficient than sending runners.

Djilas eyed the woman as he concluded his conversation with the right flank element chief.

"What is this?" Djilas asked as the gunman prodded the woman forward with the muzzle of his rifle.

"I found her in the woods above the base."

Djilas nodded, then turned to the woman. "Who are you? What are you doing in these woods?"

Before she could answer, he reached out, pulled off her head scarf and handed it to her. Sofijia Porcrovicius at thirty-eight looked much older. She had once been pretty but the past two years had aged her markedly, her once long, golden-brown hair now shorn to a boyish length and tinged with gray. She raised her chin in more of an attempt at bravery than defiance and spoke.

"I am Sofijia Porcrovicius. I was searching for food for my family."

"In the woods?" Djilas countered skeptically. "Where do you live?"

"In the German camp. My family…"

"You work for the Germans?" Djilas snarled.

"We work for them," Sofijia confirmed. "My husband works for them. We are prisoners."

Djilas looked at the woman once more but this time with a slight tempering of the hard impatience in his eyes. "What food could there be in these woods?" he asked.

Sofijia proffered her basket and threw off the cloth. "Morels," she said. "Mushrooms. See, I have found a few nice ones."

Djilas leaned forward and looked into the basket. It held six or seven small mushrooms.

"For my children," Sofijia explained. "We get mostly cabbage and turnips. The mushrooms are a lovely change."

Djilas looked again into the basket as if to confirm what his eyes had already noted. "Madame Porcrovicius, your cheek seems bruised. How did you come to this injury?"

"It is nothing. Of no importance. A slight bump," Sofijia answered, attempting to avoid the issue.

"Arkady!" Djilas barked at his man. "Did you strike this woman?"

The soldier nodded once and hung his head in contrition.

"You will apologize to this lady at once."

Arkady nodded and turned to face Sofijia, "I am very sorry, lady. That I hit you. I apologize."

"Thank you," Sofijia said to the chastened trooper.

"Now go. Back to your sector," barked Djilas. "Be ready for the signal. Go."

Arkady shouldered his rifle and hurried off into the forest, confused but relieved at the odd outcome of this encounter.

"Madame Sofijia. If you would be agreeable, could you give us some information about the German base?"

"Certainly. I would be happy to help you in any way I can," Sofijia replied. "We are treated well, better than in the camp, but they are still

Nazis and they deserve anything that befalls them."

"Thank you, Madame Sofijia. Please sit," he said, gesturing toward a stack of wooden ammunition cases. "You know, my mother would often go out in the woods and bring my brother and I morels for our supper."

Sofijia tied her kerchief over her head as she nodded in understanding at the Major.

Sofijia explained that her husband had been a professor of engineering at the University in Vilnius. Then, after the annexation, he lost his job and they and their two children were deported to a camp just inside Poland. They existed there for over two years when they were suddenly shipped by truck to this place. Her husband was put to work fabricating some mechanism for a new German aircraft while she and the other women knotted and sewed camouflage netting.

"We work in a large tent from first light to dark. The food is poor and the children are growing thin."

"Here," said Djilas, handing her a tin of Spam. "Take this. It's… put it in your basket. Tell me, Madame Sofijia, how is it they let you roam free? You could so easily escape."

"My children, Petras and Vanda, are in their hands. We are free to come and go but not together. And an escape might well send us all back to the Polish camp. Here is much better, I can tell you."

"Do you know where they repair aircraft engines?"

Sofijia shook her head no.

"Then could you point out the functions of the various structures?"

"To the extent that I know them, certainly."

"Would it be possible to speak to your husband?"

"I would ask."

"What do you do in case of an air raid?"

"We haven't had one but we were told to go to our sleeping barracks immediately and stay there until ordered to leave."

"Anton!" Djilas called out.

A young man rose from a nearby group studying a map on the ground and hurried over. It was Lt. Begina, dressed in civilian clothes in the style of the local farmers, as were all the men.

"Anton," Djilas addressed his lieutenant. "Would you escort Madame Sofijia to within sight of the base. Wait with her as she points out the functions of the various structures." Djilas extended his hand and said, "I wish you and your family well, Madame Sofijia."

She nodded, offered her hand and with a weak smile, turned and went off into the woods with the young man in the direction of the base. It had been a long while since she had been spoken to so respectfully.

Djilas checked his watch and noted it was twenty minutes past eight. Almost time.

24

At precisely fifteen after eight, a flight of six Ilyushin bombers escorted by two Yak 1 fighters crossed the Belarus border into the occupied country of Lithuania. Approximately ten minutes later, a Douglas C-47 transport on the identical course crossed into Lithuanian air space.

The bombardier of the lead Ilyushin checked his watch and directed its pilot to slow to 390 km/hr. Favorable winds had brought them to their checkpoint over the Villiya River slightly ahead of schedule.

In the American transport the navigator, Nick Tolkin, also noted the discrepancy in schedule and had his pilot make the appropriate reduction in ground speed.

When the change in throttle setting occurred, Peggy moved forward to Nick's jump seat and asked, "Nick, what's going on?"

"We're just a little ahead of schedule," he answered. "I had Bed ease back the throttles so we'd hit our mark, that is if my numbers shake out."

Peggy nodded that she understood. "I'm sure they will."

Nick studied Peggy's face for a few moments. "You okay?" asked Nick.

"Fine," Peggy answered unconvincingly. "Nick, was it like this when you bombed Tokyo?"

"I guess," Nick pondered. "Pretty much. That was quite a while ago, you know. Why?"

"I just wondered. I feel so useless sitting back here."

"We're on this mission together, Peg. We're all part of the crew."

"I know, it's just…"

"Hey, Peg," said Nick. "Lemme ask you a question."

Peggy nodded.

"When we get home, can I buy you a hot dog?"

A broad grin supplanted the concern on Peggy's face. "I would love for you to buy me a hot dog, Nick."

"All right!" said Nick. "We've got a date. Only do me one favor, will you?"

"What?" Peggy asked with a smiling sideways glance.

"Don't wear those Russian riding pants, okay?"

Peggy chuckled. "Okay, I promise. I won't."

Peggy returned to her seat, her nervousness diminished, a small smile lingering on her face.

25

The Kovno steam hammers were active twenty-four hours a day, forging steel and aluminum landing gear components for Messerschmitt aircraft. Since American bombers were ranging farther into Europe, the fabrication of components was relegated to smaller installations like this Lithuanian site. The undercarriage elements would then be shipped by rail or truck to smaller assembly centers, thereby denying Allied bombardiers large factory complexes to target.

Now back on schedule and nearly within sight of their objective, the three trailing Ilyushins throttled back to create an interval with the lead aircraft. Seventeen miles and nine minutes and fifteen seconds out, the American transport trailed the strike force.

Over the months, a certain monotony had set in among the German and Lithuanian inhabitants of the base. They endured a brooding sameness to each day. The pressing matter of the war seemed distant. Exhortations of, "Work faster! Work harder! Work longer hours! We must make up our quotas!" were so constant and pervasive they lost all urgency. They faded into the background noise of Wehrmacht NCOs barking at their squads and the rhythmic and unceasing clang of the forges.

Sixty seconds out, three IL4 bombers, flying at 300 meters altitude and a speed of 265 mph, bore down on the base from the east. Twenty seconds behind, three more IL4s prepared to punctuate the initial attack. Bomb bay doors opened and when Soviet bombardiers acquired their targets the first wave salvoed their internal loads.

The ensuing explosions stunned the base inhabitants. Were these accidental explosions? A fuel or ammunition store? Forgetting their training, most ran out of doors or peered through their windows to observe the problem. With the realization that an enemy attack was in progress there was panic and confusion. The piercing wail of the air raid klaxon, too late to warn the base, only added to the chaos. Black smoke and gouts of flame from strikes on workshops and assembly sheds roiled in the air. A look to the east revealed a second wave of bombers bearing down on the base from out of the sun.

"To the bunkers. *Schnell, schnell!*"

The second salvo of bombs fell among guards and workers frantically running to their designated air raid stations. Concussion driven wood splinters and metal fragments slashed through the air. The dead and wounded lay in the pathways between buildings, becoming obstacles for the fleeing survivors as they sprinted for cover.

Two of the three-man crew of the tracked flakpanzer raced for their gun while the loader stood in the dining hall some hundred yards from his vehicle, his hands grasping his mid-morning cup of coffee and slice of black bread with shmaltz. He stared up at the ceiling in utter disbelief.

The base, under attack? Unglaublich! Inconceivable. We have never had an attack. Impossible! His muddled brain denied the testimony of his senses.

Before he could put down his *kaffe* and *brotchen,* a 200kg bomb struck the roof of the hall, entombing him and the kitchen workers in the flaming remnants of the ravaged structure.

"Where is Emil?" shouted the driver of the mobile antiaircraft gun as he brought the vehicle's clattering diesel to life.

The gunner, Feldwebel Helmut Neff, shrugged while struggling to drag a heavy wooden ammo box closer to his gun. As he placed the shells in the magazine, he shouted to the driver, "Go! Go! We cannot wait for that fat fool. Go!" Debris showered the vehicle as it lumbered into the open and elevated its gun towards the eastern sky.

Sofijia and Lieutenant Begina, standing at the tree line at the other side of the base, watched in amazement as explosions shattered the base's structures.

"I must go to our barracks. It is an order," said Sofijia.

"Not yet!" said Begina. "In a moment. First, tell me, the tent. What activity occurs in the large tent?"

"There is storage, finished parts to be shipped, oil drums. Wood for heating and the stoves. And the materials for the camouflage nets. We have a wide area where the women knot the nets and sew on the different pieces of colored cloth."

"Any motors? Airplane motors?"

"No," she shook her head. "No motors that I can tell. I must go!"

Begina scribbled in his notebook, thanked her, and gave her leave to return to her barracks.

"Do not run, Madame Sofijia. There is little danger where we are."

As Sofijia hurried toward the prisoners' dormitory, the final phase of the attack began. The first three bombers circled and repeated their attack from the north, once again targeting workshops and barracks. The flakpanzer had succeeded in scrabbling over the debris field to position its gun to face east against the presumed next attack. When the anticipated strike materialized from the far left flank, the driver frantically reversed treads to bring his gun to bear on the now retreating targets. Feldwebel Neff managed to get off two hurried and futile bursts in the general direction of the attackers. Suddenly, from the opposite direction, as he was replenishing the magazine, the second trio of Ilyushins roared over, unloading their underwing racks on the chaos below. Once again the out-of-position flakpanzer attempted to bring its gun to bear on the high-tailing bombers, managing an ineffective volley that burst futilely above and behind the attackers.

Now, as the wail of the air raid siren rose in pitch, a new assault struck the base. Two fighter aircraft repeatedly dove in strafing attacks on structures that had remained intact with special attention to the frantically maneuvering tracked gun. This action kept both the flakpanzer's crew and base personnel hunkered down under cover.

In the midst of the strafing, a twin-engined transport appeared in the east, and made a low direct approach to the grass runway. It touched down roughly, taxied to the end of the strip, and turned right onto the taxiway. It braked to a stop beside the maintenance hangars, engines still idling.

"Let's go filch us a big fat turbine engine," shouted Capt. Crandall as he set the transport's brakes and vaulted from the left seat. "C'mon, Sam," he said, leading the way from the flight deck.

Sgt. Pua had already popped the exit door and was positioning the step below the entrance. "Peggy, you're on the throttles and watch she doesn't overheat."

"Can't I come with?" she asked as the rest of the crew was hurriedly deplaning.

"No! I want a pilot on those engines and, besides, we may have to horse something heavy. Pua can't lift it all by himself."

Peggy nodded her grudging acquiescence.

The American crew sprinted for the maintenance hangars while Sgt. Pua stowed the machine gun and unlatched the larger half of the cargo door, securing it in the open position.

Above, one of the Soviet fighters pulled up, quitting the battle. It sped off to the east, leaving a lone Yak circling the newly arrived transport.

No longer under fire, Feldwebel Neff cautiously raised his head above the sides of his flakpanzer to view his surroundings. His driver lay dead or unconscious, while he himself had sustained a leg wound. Despite his injury he struggled to grasp a shell and drop it into the magazine of his gun, determined to somehow pay back the intruders. In the air, close by, he spied one of his tormentors making tight circles above the base. Hastily he removed his belt and applied a tourniquet to his injured leg while simultaneously struggling to swivel the muzzle of his gun in the direction of the enemy aloft. "*Verdammt,*" he cursed. As the Yak drifted through the pain-blurred view of his sights, he squeezed the firing grip in a forlorn hope of retribution. The gun fired as the Yak was in the midst of a tight turn. The projectile, fused for higher altitude, punched through the empennage of the aircraft, severing rudder and elevator controls without exploding. The stricken fighter twitched and jinked as its pilot frantically fought to control its descent.

Forgetting his pain, the gunner struggled to raise himself on his good leg and extended his arms in triumph.

"I have you," the victorious gunner exulted past his balled fists. "We got him, Otto," the sergeant shouted to his lifeless driver. "Do you hear me, man? We got him!"

His triumph was short lived as two peasant-dressed guerillas vaulted up the side of the disabled flakpanzer and simultaneously fired short bursts of their submachine guns into the tenacious non-com.

Armed men were now moving in on the base from all sides. The troops in the bunkers were kept pinned down by guerillas with submachine guns targeting the entrances. One man scampered up the radio tower. He destroyed the antenna and pulled down the cable, where it was cut into pieces and tossed into one of the fiercely burning fires.

Djilas's men now commanded the area on both sides of the runway, covering the bunkers where the bulk of base personnel had taken cover.

26

A downcast Djilas, submachine gun slung over his shoulder, met the Americans at the hangar door, shaking his head. Slyusalev pushed past the commando chief and burst into the hangar. The space was bare except for two empty engine dollies in one corner and some metal drums in the other. He snarled angrily at Djilas in Russian.

"This is for nothing? *Vot blyadstvo!* A great cock-up?" As Djilas's eyes narrowed, the NKVD agent hastily modified his tone. "A noble effort, yes, but we have no choice now but to withdraw."

"What about the other hangar?" asked Lt. Caloon.

Slyusalev translated Caloon's question and Djilas answered, once again shaking his head in futility. Slyusalev had no need to translate. "Also empty. No motors. Nothing."

Begina entered the hangar and spoke quietly to his major who, with a nod, gave his man leave to inform the Americans.

"We have sent for one of the prisoners, an engineer. Perhaps he can help us."

"Tell them, " said Djilas, "we cannot stay much longer. Our men have the Germans and Liths subdued but who knows how long that will last. I would gladly kill the lot but that would only put fight into them. We can't stay much longer. We are too long already."

It was then that a thin man, who appeared to be in his late fifties, wearing a frayed and ragged suit and wire-rimmed glasses, arrived running. He was shepherded by two armed commandos. The bespectacled man looked frightened but also determined to keep his composure.

"No harm will come to you," Djilas assured him. "We only want information." Begina began to translate to Lith but the slender prisoner raised his hand and nodded, indicating that he understood.

Some shots rang out in the vicinity of a nearby bomb shelter. Djilas turned to one of his troopers and cocked his head, directing him to see to it. He then turned to the man.

"Your name?"

"I am Zahlman Porcrovicius," he said, drawing himself up as best he could to the stature of bygone days. "Professor of Engineering."

"Then perhaps you can help us, Professor," Djilas said, his tone becoming less edged as he recognized the name. "We seek an engine. One of the new turbine engines. Where are they kept? Can you help us?"

"An engine," the professor said with a shrug. "They are all gone, shipped to the squadrons two days ago. We chrome-plated the turbine leaves to give them longer life. The regular steel, you know, without alloys, they burn. The chrome plating gives them longer life."

At this point the trooper who had been sent out returned and whispered to Djilas. "Nazi heroes, now dead Germans, sir." Djilas nodded.

"There it is," Djilas said, addressing the group. "Our effort has failed." No one translated. There was no need. The expression on his face made it clear their grand quest had been for naught.

"Aw, crap," said McCabe.

"We'd best get the heck out of here," Caloon added.

The men turned to exit the hangar area.

"Except . . ." said Professor Porcrovicius, finger in the air, his word halting the exodus.

"What?" said Begina. "Say it! What?"

"I know where there are two engines," the professor replied. "But . . . ."

"But?" said Djilas.

"They are installed on an aircraft."

"Where?" asked the Major incredulously.

"In the disguised hangar."

"Disguised hangar? There is no disguised hangar," Djilas responded angrily.

"Yes, cut into the hillside, there, beyond the large work tent," the professor pointed.

"Is this true?"

"Look for yourself," the professor replied as if he was speaking to a particularly slow student.

Djilas and the Americans sprinted past the troopers' barracks and beyond the old circus tent. From the hardstand, a closer inspection of a hillside berm revealed a low, sod-roofed structure with wide barn doors disguised by netting, branches, and dead foliage.

When McCabe and Nick ran forward to throw those doors open, a compact hangar with a concrete floor was revealed, its rear open to the forest behind. Astoundingly, in the center of the floor stood a shark-like Me 262B, a 2-place trainer. It bore a green and brown camouflage pattern with the intakes of both engines painted in bright yellow. The aircraft appeared pristine and intact.

Professor Porcrovicius came forward and gestured to the aircraft as if he was presenting it to them. "It is a training ship. It carries no armament. We use it as a test bed for our engine modifications. There are your engines. Both have been tested and run well."

"Anton!" Djilas shouted.

"Pua!" Crandall called out. "Get Peggy to taxi our bird down here. Then cut the motors, save the gas. Show her where the parking brake is. Go, go! McCabe! Find those engine mounts. Cut the hoses and cables if you need to. Help him, Sam. Nick, go fetch that engine dolly. Step on it. We're gonna purloin us a turbine engine."

As Sam and the crew chief climbed the wing and began searching for the proper panels at the base of the wing pylon, Peggy and Pua entered.

"She already taxied over here," Pua declared.

"What're you doing, fellas?" Peggy asked.

"We're taking that engine," said Crandall, "if these guys can buy us the time."

"This one's no help," said McCabe from astride the engine as he slammed closed a hinged panel.

"No, no. That is for generator access," Professor Porcrovicius corrected in heavily-accented English. "This one here," he patted a panel, "the small one. And then that other small one." He stood on tiptoe and indicated a second panel. "Then another small one on the opposite side."

"Got it, Professor," McCabe said, jumping to his work.

"Why don't we just take the plane?" Peggy asked.

Everyone stopped and turned to look at her. Djilas's eyes flashed from one face to the other. "What did she say? Tell me! What?"

When Professor Porcrovicious translated Peggy's words, Djilas asked, "Can we do that?" as he searched the eyes of the men around him.

"I think we can," said Sam Caloon.

"Button up those panels, Roscoe," Crandall directed his crew chief. "Now, does anybody know how to start this thing?"

The group all turned to the prisoner.

"I believe I am able to accommodate, but I ask a consideration, I beg a consideration."

"What consideration?" Djilas asked darkly. "I'm not disposed to bargain . . ."

"Captain," Porcrovicius said, "if you leave with the engine or the aircraft, it does not matter. They will know I helped you. They will shoot me and perhaps my wife. I ask not for myself, but . . . take my children. Take them to safety. Wherever you are going. Take my children, I beg of you."

Djilas was at a loss for words. "I . . . I don't know if it is possible. I don't know."

Begina recounted the conversation to the American crewmembers.

"Yeah, that figures," said Pua. "The Krauts kill him for helpin' us."

Crandall told Begina, "If we get this rocket ship started there's plenty of room for his kiddies in our bird. Tell your boss. Now let's check out that cockpit."

The two cockpit canopies of the trainer were flipped over and Crandall, Caloon, and Professor Porcrovicius peered in. The professor stood on the wing.

"Fairly standard," said Caloon. "Everything where it ought to be."

Peggy, who stood on the other wing, looked in through the Plexiglas and nodded to herself in assent. Flight instruments on the left, engine instruments to the right. From her side she could see the dual throttles and buttons that most likely controlled flaps and landing gear. Her conclusions were confirmed by the professor's explanation.

As the professor delineated the cockpit workings, a trooper hurried in to speak to Major Djilas. He gestured with his head as he spoke. "We have the pilot of the Yak fighter. She crash-landed on the grass field. We have her by the American airplane. Both arms injured and perhaps a broken nose. But she walked. She refused to be carried."

"I know her," Djilas nodded. "She is being treated?"

The trooper nodded in the affirmative.

"Make her comfortable, hear? Someone stay with her. She is one of us. Understood? And burn the aircraft. One more thing, tell the American we no longer need the metal carriage. Go!" The trooper nodded curtly again and sprinted off.

The professor was in the midst of explaining the turbine's starting procedure when Djilas interrupted with a question.

"Who will fly this aircraft?"

"I will," said Crandall, "of course."

"Whyncha let me fly it?" said Caloon.

"Nah, you fly the Gooney bird," Crandall responded. "I'll do it."

Peggy hopped off the wing. "Both of you are bomber jockeys. I'm the only fighter pilot here. I should fly it."

Crandall and Caloon, affronted, both shook their heads, "No!" In the midst of their declamations, Peggy pressed her point.

"If I fly it and complete our mission, you boys are free to bug out."

Crandall and Caloon adamantly continued shaking their heads in disagreement, when Nick, who had just returned and overheard, put in his two cents.

"Y'know, guys, Sweden is just across the Baltic, less than three hours away. We got plenty of gas. I don't have to tell you: Sweden's neutral, guys."

Peggy added another good point to the now slightly more receptive Captain Crandall. "You could bring your crew home intact. That's something isn't it, Bed?"

"Whoever is piloting this aircraft, do it now. We have no more time," Djilas declared testily.

"So, that is the new turbine airplane," said a feminine Russian voice from the hangar's entrance.

Everyone turned to see that Lilya Litvak, with a gash across the bridge of her nose, a black eye, one arm in a sling and her other wrist splinted and bandaged, had joined their group. She walked forward stiffly, attempting to disguise a pronounced limp.

"Lilya will fly with me," said Peggy. "Come on, Lilya. It's decided! Start us up, professor."

Crandall and Caloon exchanged glances and exhaled in capitulation, grudgingly bowing to the logic of Peggy's course of action.

"Anton, fetch the professor's children. Quickly!" Djilas directed. Begina hurried out of the hangar.

"Remove the screens from the intakes!" the professor ordered, pointing. Pua and McCabe quickly complied.

"Clear the intakes. Away!" waved the professor authoritatively in his heavily accented English. "The exhaust also." He grasped the handle in the nozzle of the engine and pulled on it twice. Each time it yielded a length of cable much like starting an outboard motor. On the third try a small putt-putt gasoline engine sprang to life in the nose of the turbine. "Pilot, to your throttles. I will show you the starting sequence."

Peggy vaulted to the wing and took her seat in the aircraft. "Help Lilya into the back seat, will you, fellas?"

"No!" shouted Slyusalev, as he drew his Tokarev pistol and jammed the muzzle behind Djilas's ear. Djilas slowly raised his hands, staring angrily straight ahead as Slyusalev gingerly removed the submachine gun slung over the major's shoulder, then backed away. "She will remain," indicating the injured woman. "I will accompany 'tovarich Peggy' in the turbine craft." He derisively spoke the name she had been given by her Russian colleagues. "Everyone calm, do you hear me, or I will kill this man. I will kill you all."

"Put down that pistol," Djilas growled, "or I will take it from you and feed it to you."

Slyusalev hurriedly shoved his pistol in his belt and leveled the submachine gun at the angry major and then, the Americans. The group stared helplessly, their eyes fixed on the wavering muzzle of the Russian Tommy gun.

A woman ran into the hangar and shouted, "Zahlman!" Behind her followed Begina and another of Djilas's men. Slyusalev targeted Djilas and barked a command to the men to lay down their firearms and walk to the side of the hangar, then directed the American aviators to do the same. With a quick movement of his weapon he gestured the woman prisoner to stand behind him, between himself and the aircraft where Lilya and the professor stood. Porcrovicius reached out and took his wife's hand.

"Start the aircraft, now! Quickly!" Slyusalev ordered. "The American woman will fly. It will be I who presents to the Soviet Union the turbine aircraft." He puffed out his chest in anticipated glory. "Hurry." His gun's muzzle now directed Peggy to resume her place in the front cockpit.

Slyusalev strode to the wing and attempted to climb up by stepping on a small work stand, bracing his other foot on the side of the engine while keeping his gun leveled at the men. As he stepped up awkwardly, the work stand shifted slightly, causing the muzzle of his weapon to waver. It was this moment that Sofijia Porcrovicius chose to rush forward and, swinging her scarf like an Old Testament slingshot, struck Slyusalev on the back of his head. He was knocked off the wing and onto the ground. When he fell, the men were upon him instantly, tearing the submachine gun from his grasp and wresting the automatic from his belt. When he continued to resist, Sgt. McCabe leaned in and with a short, violent, chopping blow, coldcocked the man.

"Tie him," ordered Djilas, calmly slinging his recovered machine gun. "Tightly."

Sofija Porcrovicius dropped her scarf as the nerves and emotions of the encounter overtook her. Her husband put his arms around his wife and spoke softly into her ear, stroking her hair.

The scarf she had wielded lay on the hangar floor. In its center lay the object that she used to strike Slyusalev. It was a twelve-ounce can of Spam, slightly dented.

"Help her up," said Peggy, indicating Lilya. Caloon, McCabe, and Nick. They boosted the injured woman up into the rear cockpit and strapped her in. Both turbines were now spooling up, uttering a low, mournful roar. A belch of flame emanated from each of the exhaust cones, startling the group.

"It is normal. Do not fear. It is normal," shouted Porcrovicius over the din. The professor stood on the wing beside Peggy, monitoring the instruments, nodding his approval, his fingers in his ears.

"A long take off run, young woman," he shouted. "Do not try to lift the nose until you have attained the ground speed of 180 kilometers per hour. Take all the runway. Then very gradual to climb. Under no circumstance make a fast manipulation of the throttles. *Verrrry* gently advance them."

Peggy acknowledged his instructions with two serious nods.

"The fuel system will stall if throttle movement is abrupt. Gently, very gently. Otherwise flying is like an ordinary aircraft, I'm told."

Peggy's eyes met the professor's and narrowed at this last bit of instruction.

"All right, am I ready?" asked Peggy.

The professor checked the instruments. "Oil and hydraulic are at proper level. There is the nose brake on the left by your knee. You are ready." The professor closed the rear cockpit on Lilya and jumped to the hangar floor. He crouched to remove the chocks and walked forward parallel to the nose. Once in view of the pilot, he gave her the signal to roll.

One of Djilas's soldiers grabbed the ropes that bound Slyusalev and unceremoniously dragged him out of the way of the main gear as Peggy taxied the shark-nosed fighter out of its hangar and turned onto the asphalt ramp.

The Americans saluted Peggy with the aviator's thumbs-up as she taxied past. Nick bolted from the group and sprinted toward the aircraft. He overtook the moving bird from behind, his path taking him through the jet blast, which nearly knocked him down. Regaining his footing, he scrambled up to the wing and stood beside the open canopy of the front seat.

"I . . . I wanted to say . . ." Nick shouted over the turbine roar.

"What?" Peggy shook her head indicating she couldn't hear.

"I wanted you to know . . . ."

The aircraft continued its slow progress down the taxi strip while Peggy was attempting to ascertain what Nick was trying to tell her. After a moment, comprehension. Peggy smiled and reached up out of the cockpit. Pulling him toward her, planted a serious kiss on the surprised mouth of the American navigator.

He straightened, blushing, wide-eyed, a dumb grin forming on his freshly kissed mouth. In the back seat, Lilya grinned impishly at the young man. Nick managed a weak wave before hopping off the wing and scrambling back toward his crewmates, who were whistling and applauding. Even Djilas was grinning.

The turbine craft proceeded down the taxiway that led to the concrete runway. At the turn, Peggy closed her canopy, held the brakes, and set the throttles to the next detent as the professor had instructed.

Nick and the Americans shut the hangar doors, leaving the securely trussed-up Slyusalev behind. They ran to their C-47, now occupying the ramp just past the circus tent. There seemed to be a large crowd of people moving about near the aircraft.

The Americans and the Russian guerillas stood transfixed by the scene of the turbine aircraft moving down the runway. It seemed to be in no hurry at all, rolling down the concrete strip as if it were on a leisurely drive along a country lane.

Inside the cockpit, Peggy applied forty percent flaps as the professor instructed and while keeping the nose pointed straight, kept a constant check on the airspeed indicator. 140kph. 145. The end of the runway, ominously visible ahead, was coming up fast. The 1,500-meter mark had been passed. 155kph. *This was nerve wracking,* Peggy thought, as she eased the throttles forward, bracing them with her right hand. It's going to be close. Inexplicably, the throttles lurched forward under Peggy's hand. It was Lilya, in the back seat, who had not understood the professor's instructions and knew only that this craft required more power if it was to leave the ground. She impulsively shoved the throttles forward with her damaged hand, unaware of the consequences.

The sound of faltering engines conjured up the specter of catastrophe for the onlookers. Peggy instantly backed off the levers and by some miracle the turbines reignited and resumed their revolutions. As the 1,800-meter marker was looming up ahead the airspeed was only 170. 175. 176. Peggy decided that it would have to do. They had run out of concrete. She hauled up the nose with the control stick and the aircraft grudgingly responded. No longer on the runway, the turbine craft lifted from the smoothed dirt beyond the runway's end. But they were airborne. Slowly, agonizingly slowly, the aircraft strained for altitude; air speed grudgingly increased as they flew. Soon, stability graced the aircraft. A reassuring acceleration shoved Peggy back into her seat. She brought up the landing gear, increased throttle, and the turbines settled into a smooth and confident roar.

"This thing is slick," Peggy announced though the wind rush.

On the ground, as the aircraft lifted and charged into the eastern sky, soldiers and airmen cheered. Their mission was a success. Now to escape and live to tell the tale.

27

Adios, Major," Bed Crandall said to Djilas as he shook his hand and gripped his shoulder. "We are bugging out. Good luck to you and your boys."

Begina translated and Djilas remarkably answered in English. "To you, also."

McCabe and Pua were locking down the large cargo portion of the door after discarding the useless engine dolly on the blacktop. Crandall was waiting for them to finish and follow them into the plane when the translator approached him.

"One small matter, Captain," Begina said, halting Crandall's boarding. "My major says that he has given promise to the Lith professor. Would you be agreeable to take his children?"

Crandall looked over at the crowd of prisoners who had all followed when the Porcrovicius children had been sent for. Zahlman Porcrovicius was there standing beside his wife with their two young children in front of them. They appeared subdued but hopeful.

"Sure," said Crandall, waving at them. "Load 'em in. We'll take mom and pop, too. They both helped us out, didn't they?"

Begina waved for the couple to come forward. When husband and wife lifted Petras and little Vanda into the plane they stood on the ramp experiencing an agonizing moment of farewell, not comprehending that they were to be allowed to accompany their children. Djilas gently took the surprised Sofijia Porcrovicius's arm and guided her up the steps and into the aircraft. He then gestured for Zahlman to join her. Zahlman Porcrovicius stared incredulously at the major who smiled and nodded. "Yes, it was true. You are also to be saved." On the blacktop, the other prisoners and their children watched silently and fatalistically.

"Roscoe!" shouted Crandall.

McCabe appeared at the entrance door. "Tell Sam, start 'er up. Then come right back. " He then turned to Nick. "How'd it be if we took the whole flock of them?"

"It'd be great, Skip, but can we handle the weight?"

When McCabe reappeared in the doorway, Crandall asked, "Roscoe, can we take all these people?"

McCabe looked the crowd over, "All of them?" Crandall nodded. "Let's see . . ." He counted heads. "Fifteen adults," he calculated out loud. "Figure one twenty each, with the women. Then the kids . . . seventeen of 'em, they don't weigh much. Then us. Minus that creep, Slyusalev. Uh . . . weight's good, Skip. We can lift off, acey-duecey."

The port engine coughed and sprang to life quickly followed by the whirl of the starboard propeller. With both engines turning and beginning to run smoothly, Crandall leaned toward Begina. "I figure, we take these scientists, it fouls up their aircraft works, right?"

Begina translated. Djilas nodded, affirmatively. Then with a swipe of his arm, gestured for the remaining group of prisoners to board the aircraft. They stood for a long moment motionless in utter disbelief. It had been a long time since any of them could contemplate the luxury of hope. In a trance-like state, parents helped their irrepressibly enthusiastic children clamber into the C-47. Inside, the adults were strapped into jump seats along the sides of the aircraft by Nick and Pua with the small children seated on the deck between them.

Outside, Crandall asked Djilas, "You going to be all right?"

When Begina translated the answer was, "We will disappear in all directions. Into the forest. We have disabled their vehicles and made arrangements to return to Belarus. We will be all right." Djilas punctuated the translation with the word "okay" giving the circle finger sign.

As Crandall saluted Djilas and entered the aircraft, Pua appeared at the door bearing the M-42 machine gun and an ammo box. He exited and with considerable ceremony handed his prize off to Begina, who nodded in dubious thanks. Pua jumped back into the aircraft and swung the door closed. The C-47 began taxiing directly onto the adjacent grass where it turned east and revved up for its takeoff roll. After swerving around the still burning wreckage of Lilya's Yak, the American C-47 lifted off easily from the grass and began a sharp banking turn to the north.

On the ground, the ripping sound of a MG-42 machine gun could be heard shredding the timber and sandbag supports to the entrance of the officer's air raid bunker, forcing the adventurous occupants to reconsider their breakout.

International Pictures
Executive Offices, Culver City, California
July 1943

Milton Aaronson leaned back in his chair, feet up on the ornately carved desk, surrounded by stacks of files and papers. He was determined to read everything concerning studio business in order to bring himself up to speed. In the midst of his inquiries, he strained forward and flipped the lever on the office intercom.

"Marge, could you come in, please?"

"Be right there, sir."

"Thanks, Marge."

The new head of International Pictures had been chosen by the board from the distribution side of the company. Aaronson had nearly doubled the number of theaters in the heartland zone between Pittsburgh and Kansas City. His success was attributed to his affability and his affection for vaudeville. The pragmatic theater owners saw him as one of their own.

International had fielded two short-term presidents in the past six years. One was tragically killed in a domestic dispute. The other, Aaronson's predecessor, resigned after a scandalous incident involving an underage girl. The board hoped Aaronson, a devoted family man, would provide welcome stability.

"Marge," Aaronson said, looking up as his secretary entered with her steno pad.

"Sir."

"This contract," he said, and held up a carbon of the document. "Please sit. We signed this youngster. Screen test, solid. She simply left." He shrugged his shoulders in questioning why.

"I don't think Mr. Zuckerbrod thought she had potential."

"Huh! Well, I've got her file right here, headshots, good test, positive press. Looks to me like she'd be a moneymaker."

"Yes, sir. She was quite attractive."

"Okay, thanks, Marge. I was just wondering."

"Yes, sir." Marge Cummings rose to leave.

"Marge?"

"Yes, sir?" Marge paused, her hand on the door.

"Do you happen to know what happened to her? Just curious."

"As a matter of fact, I do."

Marge Cummings left the office and returned with a folder of newspaper clippings, photos from the *Daily Mirror, Stars and Stripes,* and *The Herald Tribune,* all showing the would-be International Pictures starlet being decorated as a hero of the war.

"Nice publicity," Aaronson acknowledged. "Do you think it would be possible to contact her?"

"I think it would be possible, sir," Marge nodded. "Yes."

29

The jagged Lithuanian coastline lay below. Beyond, the vast green expanse of the Baltic stretched out to the northern horizon. The crew of the American C-47 transport, recently dubbed *Baby II,* breathed a sigh of relief as they left the belligerent continent of Europe behind.

"We're not there yet," reminded Captain Bedford Crandall to anyone on the flight deck who might be considering a premature celebration. "We got a good couple of hours before the Swedish coast. Right, Nick?"

"I make it two hours, ten, twelve minutes," answered the navigator, tapping the chart on his lap. "Plotting a wide berth around the Gotland Island area. I'm guessing lots of air defense installations there."

"Would somebody check on our passengers?" Crandall directed. "You go, Sam. Stretch your legs. Lover boy, you take his seat."

An impish smile formed on Caloon's mouth. Nick was in for a bit of ribbing.

"How 'bout a flying lesson? The gals usually go for the pilots, not the navigators. If you could fly you might actually win the girl."

Nick rolled his eyes. He resigned himself to the consequences of that kiss. On the other hand, when Crandall joked, that meant everything was nicely under control.

As Sam stood, he turned and made the sound of a loud, wet smooch on the back of his hand before entering the passenger cabin, where it seemed that luncheon was being served. Two large bolognas and loaves of bread were being divided up and served to the children of the prisoners. Though the bread was slightly stale, the bologna and bread slices were eagerly devoured by the youngsters. Eventually, the parents shared in the feast. Sofijia Porcrovicius opened her Spam and, with the help of McCabe's pocketknife, divided up the nourishing meat for the adults. When proffered to the children, the kids, being kids, preferred the bologna.

When Caloon returned, he announced to his captain, "Your passengers are fine, Skip. They're havin' a picnic back there."

Crandall nodded. "Fine thing," he griped, "I'm the captain of a finely tuned warcraft and I wind up a bus driver."

Both Sam and Nick looked at their pilot, who didn't appear grouchy at all. He was relaxed, both hands on the Douglas yoke. He was wearing a smile, a wide, contented smile.

30

The speed was exhilarating. *But best to ease up,* Peggy decided. *We've got a long ride.* Even with the throttles in the cruise detent this ship flew smoother than anything Peggy had ever experienced. The handling was surprisingly crisp and adroit. *Our German bird seems happy to be going fast,* Peggy thought, wondering what it would be like to push her to top speed. The fuel issue squelched that impulse. Right now, keeping the air speed indicator under 500 kph seemed the prudent thing to do. At about 275 mph, by Peggy's reckoning, they were making good time toward their destination in the Soviet Union.

Peggy settled in her seat, observing the landscape scroll under her from five kilometers of altitude, low enough to do without oxygen. The turbine aircraft was devouring the kilometers.

As she relaxed, her thoughts meandered back to the kiss. Nick had been standing there mumbling. *If I didn't kiss him, he'd still be on the wing. What else could I do? Still, he's kind of nice. He's funny and smart and sometimes he's shy. Never knew anyone like him. He's swell.*

Peggy's musings were interrupted by a banging on the panel between herself and the rear seat. It was Lilya attempting to get her attention. Peggy loosened her harness and twisted around to ascertain what Lilya was trying to tell her.

With her bandaged hand, Lilya pointed down on the port side of the aircraft to a large lake coming into view. "Novogorod! Novogorod!"

328 • Kurt Willinger

repeated Lilya. A large town was set beside a substantial lake. Peggy nodded. Then, pointing to herself, then pointing down, questioned if they should land at Novogorod.

Nyet. Lilya shook her head. Then, pointed slightly southeast. "Cherepovets," Lilya shouted over the engine rush. She then pointed down and nodded. "Cherepovets."

Peggy acknowledged by saying, "Cherepovets." She faced forward and altered their course to a more southeasterly heading. She turned to Lilya, who confirmed the correction.

The German turbine aircraft and its unlikely crew continued its dash toward the Russian heartland.

Several times along the way Peggy's thoughts returned to the kiss. *It was a good kiss. I liked it. I think he liked it. How could he not like it? Pretty brazen of me, though. But then, it's wartime. And I'll probably never see him again.*

The ominous glint of tracers intruded on her reverie. Two fighter aircraft appeared. One off her wing and the other on her tail. Peggy juked and instinctively grabbed for the throttles thinking, *I can probably out run these jerks. Damn! Why wasn't I paying attention? I let them get the jump on me.*

A second look determined they were Russian Yak 7's. Another burst of machine gun fire cut loose from one of the Yaks, this time closer, the tracers arcing through the air in front of the aircraft, just missing. *They think we're Luftwaffe. Why wouldn't they think we're Luftwaffe?*

Peggy was about to split-S and dive for the deck when the aircraft shuddered and began to lose speed. Are we hit? Then she noticed the landing gear indicator. Lilya had put down the gear. Of course! The universal pilot's signal of surrender. *What was I thinking,* Peggy asked herself, as she throttled back to match the speed of the Yaks.

After an uncomfortable minute or so of flying together in this configuration, one of the Yaks pulled close alongside the German aircraft. Lilya impulsively pulled off her leather and silk flying helmets to reveal her short blonde hair adorned with lots of colored ribbons. She offered the confused Yak pilot a big smile, waved her injured hands and exuberantly blew him a kiss. The grim-faced Russian viewed her incredulously, then slowly responded with a tentative smile. When Lilya offered the "V" for victory sign with the two fingers of her bandaged hand, his face broke into a grin as he returned the "V." The pilot then nodded and pointed straight ahead.

Peggy, who was at a loss as to what to do, turned to observe her passenger's actions. She subsequently removed her own helmet, allowing her honey blonde hair to tumble to her shoulders, and duplicated the "V" sign in support of Lilya's lifesaving flirting. *That Lilya certainly knows her way around the guys,* Peggy thought. When the other Yak moved from his perch on Peggy's six and took his place on the other wing, he, too, received a flurry of airborne kisses from Lilya.

Peggy turned in her seat to face her colleague. The two women exchanged triumphant grins. *What do you know, we did it, and what's more, we are getting a motorcycle escort home.*

Epilogue

The lights were on again in New York City. Hitler's death had been verified by the Russians, who claimed to have his body. Japan was still holding out but everyone knew it was only a matter of time.

The boys began returning home with a few basic objectives on their minds. Having some laughs. Sleeping late. Kissing a girl. Digging in to a thick juicy steak. Living. They had money to burn and people all around to help celebrate their victory, their survival.

"That drink is on me, soldier. My kid brother was at Tarawa."

"What was that blue medal for?"

"Hey, buddy, you get any Germans yourself?"

At bars, restaurants, and movie theaters, a soldier's money was no good. It was either on the house or somebody stepped up and grabbed the tab. The home front considered it was the least they could do for their boys in uniform. The clubs were open again and turning away crowds.

At the Stork Club on East 53rd Street, things were really jumping. On the stage, Marion Montaigne and her all-girl orchestra were slamming out the latest tunes and a few favorite standards. Cece Collins was the featured singer, who at the moment, was rendering "Sentimental Journey." The tiny dance floor, reduced by the addition of so many extra tables, was crowded by couples taking advantage of the slow, torchy tune.

At a table near the dance floor, a couple sat calmly talking, each completely engaged in the other's presence. The girl was dressed in a white gown and long white gloves, her hair pinned up in a sophisticated twist, with dangling, sparkling earrings.

He wore the uniform of an Army Air Corps Captain, silver navigator wings on his left breast pocket and the ribbon of the Distinguished Flying Cross at the top left of his decorations. They leaned into each other, as if their eyes were magnets, involved, happy, their conversation subdued in contrast to the gaiety surrounding them.

A waiter arrived with a silver domed server and placed it between the couple, who were forced to lean back slightly to allow it to pass. When the waiter ceremoniously removed the lid, two hot dogs on buns with brown mustard and sauerkraut were revealed. The young woman smiled delightedly. The young flyer looked pleased. He turned to a spot near the entrance where Sherman Billingsley was standing. Billingsley grinned at the flyer and offered him a wink and a thumbs-up. The soldier nodded his thanks to the Stork Club proprietor and refocused his attention on the blonde girl in the white satin dress.

The End

Afterword

As a child I occupied a seat on the fifty-yard line of the greatest adventure in the history of civilization: World War II. I was glued to the radio as battle after battle, victories, and setbacks were graphically recounted. This war was more exciting than the Lone Ranger, the Green Hornet, Hop Harrigan, and the Shadow put together. America was actively engaging its enemies in the remote corners of the earth and we were making them say "uncle."

Finally, it was over. VE-Day. VJ-Day. The boys came streaming home. I helped welcome these victorious young men, with their pristine uniforms and youthful swagger, back to our Brooklyn neighborhood. Wide-eyed with hero worship, we followed them around, listened to their stories in rapt attention, fetched them Cokes and cigarettes. Worshipped them. Eventually they shed their uniforms and, as civilians, went on to make America the envy of the world.

We never won another war. And most of the young men and young women who won that one are old or have passed on.

Today, America is starved for heroes. The need is so dire that the media will frequently invent them for us. In this fresh new century, there is certainly no shortage of courage. What there is though, is a strangely inward shift from "we" to "me." I am nostalgic for the America of "we."

In my attempt to understand the individuals who were in the

forefront of the valorous WWII era, I have immersed myself in the accounts of the women who ferried aircraft for the Air Corps and the men who flew those aircraft in combat. I have even had the privilege of knowing some of them.

"What was it like flying a combat aircraft?" was my most frequent question. The replies from exceptional men provided some sense of authenticity for this book. Sources included Warren Rogers, B-24 bomber pilot; Gene Gurney, who flew big transports; and Gary Hooker, who is famous for having the afterburner of his F-16 explode and managing to land it safely.

While all the characters in this novel are fictitious, I must admit that the model for the fly girl was borrowed from real life. It is no accident that she looks a heck of a lot like Lauren Bacall, the young actress of the war years who shrugged off the artifice and theatricality of the standard Hollywood "girl in the movie" and gave us a totally new paradigm. She was cool. Up for anything. Nothing fazed her, this prototype for the modern woman. It is her essence that I hopefully have imparted to the fly girl.

Underlying this depiction of skill, determination, daring, and courage, breathes a love story. It occurs to me that a great many of the people alive in America today are here because of a somewhat similar love story.

It was fun to return to this special time. To paraphrase Churchill, "it was our finest hour."

About the Author

Kurt Willinger, former Air Force crew chief and advertising creative director, writes about what he loves: flying. His previous published works include a novel, *The Spy in a Catcher's* Mask, and the non-fiction history *The American Jeep in War and Peace.* He has also written several collections of short stories. He resides in Connecticut, near an airport.

For Willinger, the specific setting of the Second World War holds a special place in his imagination:

"For me there is something unique about WWII. The nation was together, joined to put the bullies in Europe and Asia in their place. Our boys fought shoulder to shoulder. Our girls pitched in every way they could, from flying airplanes to running a rivet gun. Every American contributed from the folks too old to fight, to kids like me who collected scrap and kitchen fat and did without bubble gum. It was the finest team ever assembled in the history of civilization."